SILENTCIDE

THE ART OF UNDETECTED KILLING

An assassin's refusal to kill turns deadly.

WITH 135
ONLINE PHOTOS OF
ACTION SCENES IN
15 CITIES IN
6 COUNTRIES

A SUSPENSE THRILLER BY

RICHARD EBERT

Encircle Books™
The publishing imprint of
Encircle World Photos, LLC
Saint Paul, Minnesota

ISBN: 979-8-9895711-0-9 (Hardcover)
ISBN: 979-8-9895711-1-6 (Paperback)
ISBN: 979-8-9895711-2-3 (E-book)

Library of Congress Control Number: 2023922315

First Encircle Books™ edition: May 2024

Printed in the United States of America

Encircle Books™ is a trademark of Encircle World Photos, LLC

Cover photos: Roman Forum – Richard Ebert; Eyes – Shutterstock/ El Nariz
Cover design: Rafael Andres & Jerry Todd
Author photo: Lisa A. Crayford

Author website: www.RichardEbert.com
Contact author: Author@RichardEbert.com

This book is for Mary Beth ...
My best friend and soulmate for over 54 years

135 Online Photos for Silentcide

135 online photos show *Silentcide* action scenes
in 15 cities in 6 countries.
Each photo annotated by a footnote number in book.
All photos and descriptions by Richard Ebert.

Three Ways to See Photos

Author website: RichardEbert.com. Look for *Silentcide* cover.
Click "135 Silentcide Photos."
Scan QR code at the end of a chapter.
See entire photo gallery:

Scan QR code below

PROLOGUE

His breathing was erratic. Anticipation pounded in his chest. Dopamine and adrenaline flooded George Henniker's brain with a euphoric mix of greed and anxiety.

The six computer monitors encircling the desk were distracting. They displayed pulsating numbers, charts, graphs and tables – normally the lifeblood of a portfolio manager but now irritating. Focus was vital. His steel-gray eyes narrowed as his jaw clenched. He leaned within inches of the screen to fixate on four letters: LFBS.

The bid and ask prices were tumbling on heavy volume, sucked down by a marketwide plummet of the NASDAQ. A nightmare for most investors. A shorting dream for day traders. A fantasy come true for George.

He hesitated. Fleeting doubt gnawed at his confidence before he became emboldened. His trading strategy was flawless, a guaranteed win. Yet he waited. Timing was critical. The best price was essential.

His hand quivered over the mouse. This single trade would restore the limited partners' confidence and salvage Moneyer Capital Management, LLC, his crippled hedge fund. It was an all-or-nothing bet. Failure was not an option. Continued success, accolades and riches were dependent on the next few minutes.

Now!

George's index finger flinched, then clicked Enter, executing the twenty-million-dollar buy order. He hyperventilated while watching the sell confirmations ripple across the screen. $220K, $975K, $3.81 million, $5.24 million, $6.58 million, $7.22 million and $8.967 million.

The price per share was surging. His fists tightened as deep grooves of worry etched his forehead.

$16.43 million, $17.22 million, $17.47 million, $18.21 million … The trade was hitting resistance. $18.33 million, $18.56 million, $18.72 million, $18.96 million …

"Go, damn it!"

The cursor blinked on and off and on and off, waiting for the next seller to bite. The orders trickled in. They were slowing down to chump change. "Take the bait!" he pleaded as his skin dampened from a cold sweat.

The enormous purchase was finally filled. The average execution price was above the target but well within his projected range for maximum profit.

"Spec-tac-u-lar!" he exclaimed.

This stock position in Longfellow BioSciences would easily be worth thirty to forty million dollars within a week, double again by year's end, and become hundreds of millions in the future. George was at the top of his game as the city[1] lay fifty stories below his feet. This was the most fun an Ivy League stud and former investment banking superstar could have with his clothes on.

The cocksure portfolio manager absently twirled a diamond cufflink on his custom-tailored shirt, mentally patted himself on the back, grinned, looked at his Rolex watch, and logged off. The reflection in the mirror portrayed the chiseled good looks of brilliance and cunning.

Today's trades could earn George ten million or more in performance fees in the first year, with larger paychecks to follow. Soon his portfolio growth would qualify as a star performer among Boston's two hundred hedge funds. Then new, ultra-rich investors would stampede into his office with millions bulging in their pockets.

Success was simple and easy ... especially when you knew in advance that a fledgling biotech company had a cure for cancer.

◆◆◆

Blue seemed determined to water every tree along the Charles River Esplanade. The cocker spaniel was named after the school color of Wellesley College, Anna Monteiro's prestigious alma mater. She'd had sole custody of the "only child" since an eight-year marriage was imploded by a cheating husband.

At forty-one, it was hard, if not impossible, to find any man who measured up to the dog's unconditional love and loyalty. The sporadic dates Anna had gone on during the last five years confirmed her commitment to live alone. Cleaning up tumbleweeds of dog hair and piddles on the floor were small irritants compared to the time-consuming drama of a romantic relationship.

Boston in June was filled with tourists, all eager to explore the historic sites along the Freedom Trail. But this Back Bay riverside haven attracted mostly Bostonians. Neighbors of all ages ran, jogged, walked and strolled along this ribbonlike, three-mile path flanked by water. Anna enjoyed speculating about their lives, worries and joys. The pastime provided a temporary distraction from her problem: the quiet battle surrounding the park bench where she sat.

Boston has a rich history of rewarding visionaries but rarely without struggles and casualties along the way. Two hundred Puritans died here in 1630, months after establishing New England's second colony. Up to seventy thousand Patriots died during the Revolutionary War after Paul Revere's midnight ride in 1775.

Today's battle in Boston between visionaries and foes promised a greater impact on human history. Yet there was no gunfire, no parades celebrating victories, and no memorials to the fallen. This war was waged in obscurity.

"Sit, Blue, sit," Anna said while yanking on the leash to prevent the dog from jumping on an elderly couple walking along the esplanade. She and the old woman exchanged smiles in passing, then Anna's thin lips returned to a frown.

Anna took a breath of misery when her dark brown eyes gazed across the river at the shoreline of Cambridge.[2] Inside the inconspicuous buildings was the heart of the largest biotech hub in the world. Within a couple-mile radius of Kendall Square was the MIT campus, twenty big pharmaceutical companies, plus about two hundred fifty biotechnology start-ups. Another eight hundred to one thousand biotechs were officed across the Boston metro. Every one of these entrepreneurs had a dream to enrich human lives or improve the environment.

Encamped behind Anna's shoulders[3] were the redcoats: thousands of hedge funds, venture capital firms, mutual fund companies, analysts, lawyers, accountants and consultants. They all profited from the entrepreneurs' dreams yet barely noticed the collateral damage.

In this battle, only the smartest, best connected and well-funded biotechs survived.

Anna's fingers covered her olive-brown complexion in anguish. By the end of the week, Longfellow BioSciences would be critically wounded and might become the next casualty of this silent war.

A ding from her cell phone interrupted the despondency. She looked down to see who had sent a text. *George! That conceited jackass!*

Why had she ever started dating him a month ago? She deserved better but doubted she'd ever find that someone.

Prologue: Boston, Massachusetts

Photos 1 through 3

ONE

ROME, ITALY
Wednesday

The assassin was enthralled while standing at the Colosseum,[4] the epicenter of Roman killing where four hundred thousand gladiators, slaves and convicts had died in the name of entertainment. He remembered the advice from a childhood trainer. "Rome was born to rule, to become corrupt and to fall. Throughout its ancient history, the transfer of power was facilitated by murder. So study hard, young man, because there is much to learn from the Romans about killing."

Of the seventy-seven Roman emperors from 27 BC until 476 AD, only nineteen died of natural causes, and two retired. The majority died violently. Their reign was typically short-lived.

What interested the assassin were several of the emperors' "natural" deaths that may have been murders but were never proven or suspected. Such homicides required planning, patience, cunning and finesse. That was his specialty: silentcide, the art of undetected killing. He was exceptionally good at his profession.

Benjamin "Sully" Williams raised a Nikon D850 camera, got a few artistic photos of the Colosseum, then took several wide-angle shots showing tourists on the cobblestone walkway named Piazza del Colosseo.

The crowd was an eclectic blend of ages, body shapes and nationalities. The noise was an unintelligible mix of foreign languages. Tour

guides routinely recited their monologues to clusters of people –
some interested, others bored – while roaming vendors hocked
cheap souvenirs, street entertainers performed for handouts, and
pickpockets searched for the vulnerable.

The June sun was intense, the air was thick with humidity, and
pungent odors smelled as old as antiquity.

Sully nonchalantly scratched his head. His scalp was sweating
beneath the bird's nest of stringy black hair dangling across his
forehead and watchful eyes. Perspiration was beading below his
matted beard and mustache. He dared not wipe his face for fear of
smudging the applied Mediterranean skin tone. The disguise for
this persona was effective – he looked like a brash Italian in his late
thirties – but it was as oppressive as wearing a wool ski mask on a
blistering hot afternoon.

After a few more minutes of observation, the assassin rejected the
Colosseum as a manageable kill zone. Movements were too unpredictable. The area was too exposed. Nearly everyone was snapping
random photos on their cell phones, risking being photographed
in the act.

This was day twenty of the current assignment or, as Irene Shaw
called it, the commission. His target was Angelo Moretti. He was
a scumbag, pure and simple.

Moretti's specialty was sex trafficking. He operated under the
radar of the Philadelphia crime family for two reasons: the FBI
had weakened organized crime during the last three decades, and
importing Asian girls for private collectors was not one of the Philly
Mob's specialties.

However, like most career criminals, Moretti was driven by greed.
He wanted to expand his territory into New Jersey and then neigh-
boring states. To solicit financial support, he had met with distant
relatives in Palermo, Sicily, for a week. Now he was spending a few
days in Rome with his family before flying home. The commission
stipulated that Angelo Moretti never return to the States alive.

An absolute rule the assassin had been taught during silentcide training was to never speculate or try learning who commissioned a killing and their motive, but he did anyway.

In the case of Moretti, there were three candidates. One, someone in organized crime wanted this growing problem discreetly and permanently resolved while providing complete deniability. That was hard to do using an internal hitman in the City of Brotherly Love. Two, someone wanted to acquire Moretti's business for free. Three, one of Moretti's high-profile clients wanted to cover his tracks. Who knew? The greatest likelihood was door number two.

The current commission should have been finished by now, but the target was proving to be inaccessible and unpredictable. A safe opportunity had never occurred in Sicily. Since arriving in Rome, Moretti spent almost every waking hour on the phone in the hotel. Yesterday, he had been scheduled for a private tour of the Vatican. His wife and teenage daughter arrived on time, but he was a no-show. What a disappointment!

Three days remained before Moretti would fly home on Saturday. That left today and tomorrow for reconnaissance and Friday for the kill. Time was running out.

The assassin wasn't worried. He was confident Moretti would attend the private tour of the Colosseum and Roman Forum scheduled for Friday based on the marital discord he'd listened to in the target's hotel suite. Okay, it was an all-out screaming match. His wife was livid. She'd demanded he spend at least one day of their trip as a family.

Little did she know, Friday would be the last day the Moretti family would ever spend together.

Chapter One: Rome, Italy

Photo 4

TWO

Wednesday

"Thanks for coming in so early," Liz Walker said with a flat tone. "Please shut the door and have a seat."

Anna Monteiro skipped the normal upbeat or flippant greeting when noticing the exhausted expression of her closest friend since high school. She pulled a guest chair closer to the desk, sat, and placed an iPad on her lap. She waited for Liz to speak.

The chief science officer of Longfellow BioSciences[5] was suspended in troubled thought. Her ultra-white skin was devoid of blush, creating a sickly pallor dotted with freckles. The signature red lipstick had been gnawed away. Liz's curly red hair and bangs encircling her round face looked unwashed and uncharacteristically unprofessional. The normal sparkle in those intelligent green eyes was gone.

Anna got worried. She had to say something to acknowledge the gloom. "Did you get any sleep last night?"

"No," Liz said with a slight shake of the head.

"Judging by the fact that you're wearing yesterday's clothes, I'm guessing you never went home."

"Right." It seemed Liz did not trust herself to utter more than a single-word response.

"Do I dare ask how the meeting of the chiefs went yesterday?" Anna asked in reference to the all-day session among Longfellow's senior management including the CEO, plus the chief medical officer, chief financial officer, chief legal officer, and Liz.

"It was a fucking disaster," she mumbled.

Anna expected a challenging meeting but was shocked by Liz's summary. She rarely swore and, to Anna's knowledge, hadn't used the F-word since receiving a PhD in biomedical science from Johns Hopkins University fifteen years ago.

"What happened? Or would you rather not talk about it?"

Liz leaned forward. "It goes without saying this conversation is just between us besties."

"Of course."

"I shouldn't be talking with anyone about this but, Anna, this is chewing me up. Do you mind if I dump in your ear?"

Anna made an exaggerated motion of pushing her black pixie-cut hair over her ear, then jutted her profile toward Liz. "Dump away. My ear will ding when it's full."

Liz smirked at the attempted levity before the dire expression returned. "The meeting started with a deep dive of the Phase One/ Two clinical trial results we're announcing on Friday. There were many positive cases of tumor shrinkage and controlling the metastasis of invasive ductal carcinoma. Plus, a few trial participants had improvements suggesting lasting remissions. But the numbers were too low to conclude our neoantigen cancer platform was solely responsible for the success. In short, the data falls well below the lofty expectations our CEO promised to the investment community last year."

"So then what happened?" Anna asked with trepidation.

"That started the heated finger-pointing." As Liz listed each criticism, she pointed an additional finger toward herself. "We shouldn't have started with kidney cancer. The trial protocol was designed wrong. The participant group size was too small and the participants' disease progression was too advanced. We rushed the timeline for measuring results." Liz gasped in frustration. "Jesus, the list of faults was endless."

"They weren't blaming you for all that, were they?"

"Sure, without coming right out and saying it," Liz said with a dejected tone. "This cancer platform is my brainchild. I've defended it for five years, since this company started, so I'm used to sharing the credit and shouldering the blame. What's one more contentious meeting, right?"

"So does that mean you turned them around and got their support again?" Anna asked while grasping to hope.

"Under normal circumstances, probably yes. We all have a vested interest in keeping the technology and our company alive. So after the usual blame game stops, we redesign the trials and try again. But we're facing two big roadblocks this time."

With hesitation, Anna asked, "Do I want to know what they are?"

"Probably not, but they're making me miserable, so you might as well be miserable too. That's what good friends are for, right?" Liz said with an apologetic smirk.

"They say misery loves company," Anna said, trying to lighten the mood.

"Then this is going to be a lovefest."

Their shared laugh quickly dissipated.

After taking a breath of despair, Liz continued, "You see, we've only got about six months' of cash. That's barely enough to continue the trials but not to cover overhead."

Anna interrupted. "But Longfellow has stood on that cliff before and always found ways to raise new funding."

"Sure, and each time, we've had to sell more of our soul. But on Monday, we learned a trial participant unexpectedly died. The woman's oncologist says it's unlikely our platform is the cause. But her family is preparing a one-hundred-million-dollar lawsuit. Our legal counsel insists we disclose it immediately as a material risk."

"So fight it in court and win."

"We probably could. But, in the meantime, the FDA will investigate and probably halt the trials until they reach a decision." Liz's face contorted with misery. "I'm telling you, Anna, it's bad. Really bad. No deep pockets are going to bail us out in this situation. Worse yet, institutional investors will dump our stock, and our venture capital partners will try selling us in a garage sale. In short" – Liz seemed to resist delivering the ugly prognosis – "we may be really screwed this time."

"They're not going to just roll over, are they?" Anna asked, refusing to accept a death sentence.

"No, we came up with a plan to stabilize investor support while seeking a cash-rich white knight to acquire us." After a disheartened sigh, Liz added, "But chances are slim. We'll present the plan at an emergency board meeting tomorrow. I expect that'll be another cluster you-know-what."

Anna jumped up, and while pretending to ride backward on a horse, she exclaimed, "This sounds like a job for Dudley Do-Right!" a reference to their favorite cartoon character, the dim-witted Canadian Mountie. "He can rescue the damsel tied to the train tracks."

A huge smile spread across Liz's lips while watching Anna's antics. "Thanks for making me laugh, friend. It's been a while."

Anna returned to the guest chair and asked, "So what can I do to help?"

"You can help my team prepare their board presentations. They're godawful so far. They can use your expertise in wordsmithing."

"Consider it done," Anna said while starting a to-do list on the iPad. "What else do you need?"

There was silence. Anna looked up. Liz was absently twirling her wedding ring while staring blankly at some papers on the desk. After gnawing her lower lip, Liz said in a hushed tone, "I also need your understanding."

"For what?"

"There's no easy way to say this, so I'm just going to blurt it out. On Monday, we're going to downsize by over sixty percent." After another troubling pause, Liz added, "And your name is on the layoff list. That's the real reason I asked you in here. I didn't want you to hear about it first during the company-wide announcement."

Anna was stunned. She had been with Longfellow BioSciences since the fifth month of operations. She was employee number twelve. The bad news foreshadowed the end of her quest to someday prevent cancer from killing millions like her younger brother. The ache in her chest was crushing.

Liz tried consoling her. "I'm sorry, Anna."

"But a reduction that big will be crippling," Anna protested. "How can the company get everything done after that?"

"We'll just have to manage because we don't have a choice."

Anna realized what she must do. "Listen, Liz, I totally understand. I hate it, but I understand. But I'm going to tell you a few things and I want you to listen until I'm done. Promise?"

Liz nodded.

"You recruited me here five years ago with the dream of curing cancer. Through thick and thin, neither of us has ever lost the faith. And I've done everything possible to help you realize that dream. Our dream."

"And you have no idea what your incredible support has meant to me."

Anna pretended to admonish her friend. "You promised to listen, not talk, remember?"

Liz grinned.

"So take me off the payroll after Monday if you must, but I am going to keep working by your side until things turn around. I'm not abandoning you or the vision now."

"That's generous, but I can't ask you to work for free."

"Why not?" Anna asked. "I worked for free the first year I was here."

"Sure, but that was different. You got shares of stock instead. And they'll probably be worthless soon. I can't ask you to do that again."

"You're not asking, I'm telling. This is nonnegotiable." Anna got up and went behind the desk to stand by her friend. "And if the very worst happens, well then, we'll just 'keep going' by driving off the cliff like Thelma and Louise." That was their favorite movie when they were in high school together.

Liz used a pinky finger to dab at both tear ducts, a practiced move designed not to smear her eyeliner and mascara. When she lost the battle against her emotions and began to cry, Anna gave her a hug. Their solidarity was comforting yet offered no protection against the pending doom.

Chapter Two: Cambridge, Massachusetts

Photo 5

THREE

The conditions were optimal for murder. Angelo Moretti had shown up for the private tour of the Colosseum and the Roman Forum, but was not mentally engaged. An iPhone was glued to his ear. His sixteen-year-old daughter, Hannah, plodded along acting bored except when a cute Italian guy walked by or her cell phone dinged. Only Moretti's wife was soaking up the factoids the guide was reciting. She was obviously charmed by his undivided attention, smile and accent. The guide clearly knew how to earn a big tip.

Everyone was distracted by something, and none of the Morettis were paying attention to the others. The assassin would have preferred no family members around, but sometimes it was unavoidable, especially on the drop-dead date for getting the job done.

Another fortuitous factor was the heat. It was barely past one thirty, yet the temperature was nearing record-setting levels for June. Moretti was sweating profusely beneath acrylic shorts and a gaudy Phillies baseball jersey, causing grotesque wet spots to spread across the fabric. His tourist attire exposed plenty of hairy flesh. Not an attractive look – actually repulsive – but it created optimal surface areas to target.

A procession of grade schoolers approached the assassin. They were connected at the waist by a long rope bookended by two female chaperones. One of the kids gave him an inquisitive stare.

The assassin waved and flashed a toothy smile. "Bonjour, mes chéris," he said in French with a shaky feminine voice. "J'espère que vous vous amuserez à explorer Rome aujourd'hui." He couldn't care less if they had fun exploring Rome or not. Preferably they would go away and stop distracting his surveillance.

"Good afternoon, sister," the schoolteacher at the end of the line said, then prompted a couple of stragglers to move along.

Sister Margaret Mary – Marguerite Marie in French – reached inside the billowing sleeve of the black habit, pulled out a wad of tissues and pretended to sneeze. The actual purpose was to scratch an itch below the silicone mask transforming the assassin into an eighty-year-old pious woman. Who could possibly distrust an elderly nun?

Sister Margaret Mary hovered among the crowd circulating in Piazza del Colosseo and stole clandestine glances at the Moretti family. They were being introduced to Arco di Costantino,[6] the massive triumphal arch honoring the victories of Constantine the Great.

Timing was essential. He had to be certain they would be ushered into the kill zone during the next site on their itinerary. Arrive too early and he might become conspicuous while waiting. Arrive too late and he might miss the first planned opportunity. Based on the distance calculations during recon and the walking speed of an ailing nun, he decided to start moving.

Sister Margaret Mary began hobbling over the uneven cobblestones. The bottom of the black habit was wicking up more gray dust and dirt with every step, but the extra length was needed to conceal his size-ten tennis shoes.

It took exactly four minutes to reach a sign reading "Foro Romano – Palatino."[7] The arrow pointed toward Via Sacra. This pedestrian-only street was a perfect entrapment. The narrow walkway was flanked by twelve-foot wrought iron fences, creating a funnel filled with tourists excited to explore the Roman Forum.

Before entering, Sister Margaret Mary pretended to sort through trinkets and trash at a souvenir kiosk while watching Mrs. Moretti take a photo of her husband and daughter in front of the arch. *That'll be a keepsake photo*, he thought. *What a touching memento of Moretti's last afternoon alive.*

The nun fingered a few beads on the two-foot looped rosary dangling from his waist. The oversized crucifix at the end was heavy. The weapon was the assassin's design. It had been used during five previous commissions. He began regulating his breathing in preparation for the sixth time.

After the tour guide made a sweeping gesture directing the Morettis toward Via Sacra, Sister Margaret Mary turned and entered the mouth of the kill zone.

Each step the assassin took was slow and measured. His bent posture was a means to authenticate the disguise while making it harder for people to see the nun's face. The incessant chatter of the passing tourists made it difficult to hear. Yet his ears were attuned like radar, listening for the grating voice of the Morettis' tour guide.

Then he heard them approaching from behind. "So, you've just entered Via Sacra, the Sacred Street of ancient Rome. It was constructed in the fifth century BC …"

Sister Margaret Mary reached down for the cross. The assassin's latex gloves made his fingers look arthritic and his hands discolored by purple-red veins. He touched the trigger button and listened, blocking out every noise except the advancing footsteps.

The guide's shoes appeared in his peripheral vision, followed by the legs of Mrs. Moretti.

He aimed the cross away from his body while maintaining a consistent pace.

The mindless chatter of Moretti and his daughter, Hannah, was six feet away, then five, then four. The assassin lowered his heart rate. Three feet. After picturing Moretti's exposed leg based on the cadence of his walk, the killer made a slight adjustment to the angle of the crucifix. Two feet. He exhaled and held his breath. One foot.

Damn it!

Hannah's body blocked her father's while they walked side by side past him. *Abort the shot.*

Discouraged but not distraught, he lowered the cross and let the long rosary hang at the side of the black tunic. There would be plenty of chances ahead. The next one occurred within a minute.

The tour guide was pointing while the family gawked at ten tall marble columns atop a brick wall.[8] The foursome was clustered together and motionless. This was excellent. Hopefully the tour guide had a long-winded description to deliver.

"You may have heard the phrase 'Nero fiddled while Rome burned.' It refers to the Great Fire of Rome in 64 AD when two-thirds of the city was destroyed."

Keep talking, the assassin thought while trying to catch up.

"The phrase is wrong for two reasons. One, the fiddle wasn't invented until the eleventh century. And two, the Roman emperor was out of the city for most of the nine-day fire."

Sister Margaret Mary lifted the cross again. His eyes focused on Moretti's beefy, right outer thigh. The prey was stationary, vulnerable and unaware of the pending attack. The evil man was seconds from paying the ultimate price for exploiting countless Asian girls, the playthings of disgusting rich clients and the daughters of tormented yet faceless parents. Death was an insufficient punishment for Moretti's sins. It would be an honor to rid the earth of this scum.

The assassin mentally rehearsed the attack as the nun shuffled within five feet of the target. Three feet was the ideal distance for accurate aim and optimal penetration of the projectiles. Only two cautious steps remained.

A ringing iPhone was as startling as a fire alarm. Moretti grabbed the cell phone from his pocket, raised a finger to his agitated wife, signaling he would only be a minute, then dashed away. "Hello ..." he said while walking ahead on Via Sacra. "Yes, I've confirmed your package's arrival for ..."

Moretti's voice was drowned out by the tour guide. "Pretty amazing, isn't it? So let's head toward the entrance of the Roman Forum. We can catch up with your husband there."

The assassin was pissed but maintained a relaxed pulse. Multiple attempts at close-quarter silentcide were common. Patience was essential; anger was a frivolous emotion that blurred the mind and bred mistakes.

The optimal kill site was still ahead … a perfect bottleneck with an adjacent escape route. The nun nonchalantly assessed the scene.

A long line of talking, laughing and perspiring tourists was waiting at the Roman Forum ticket booth. A few feet away was another crowd anxious to pass through the entrance gate. Immediately to the left was an elevated path leading to the site where Saint Sebastian miraculously survived a firing squad of arrows ordered by Emperor Diocletian in 288 AD.[9] Moretti would not be that lucky.

The nun navigated the cobblestones as if each step forward were painful. He watched as Moretti ended his phone call, rejoined his family and got a tongue-lashing from his wife. In response, Moretti barked a string of vile remarks. Perhaps in embarrassment, the tour guide began explaining to Hannah the history of the Roman Forum. All of them were now facing forward with their backsides exposed. This was the moment. The end was about to begin.

The assassin raised the crucifix again during the approach. He focused on Moretti's left thigh. He imagined the muffled puff sound when the tiny gas canister released the projectiles. He pictured the exact point of entry and Moretti's startled response. He planned how the nun would shriek a single exclamation in French while waving her hands across her face and then dashing toward the escape route. He took a deep breath and slowly released it.

"I'm so sorry," a teenage girl said after crashing into the side of the nun.

"Aucun problème, mon cher," he said in a feeble female voice while trying to maintain balance and pull away. As he turned, a selfie stick dangling from the teenager's waist became tangled in the long rosary. The metal chain snapped. Rosary beads scattered. He watched in horror as a passing woman stepped on the cross. To him, the imperceptible crunch of the weapon was deafening.

Almost immediately, all eyes of the crowd turned toward the distraught nun. Several people bent over or got on their knees while collecting beads and placing them in the nun's arthritic hands.

"Merci. Merci. Merci beaucoup," he kept repeating while internally cursing.

When Hannah reached down to pick up two rosary beads near her running shoes, Moretti grabbed his daughter's arm. "Get away from that old hag," he demanded. "It's our turn to go inside the Forum."

The assassin watched as the Moretti family passed beneath the Arch of Titus[10] while he was fenced in by a growing throng of well-intentioned Good Samaritans. Escaping their watchful eyes was essential. A key element of successful silentcide was anonymity. Now at least thirty people could place a flustered old nun at the scene.

This predicament was his fault. He had violated a major lesson of training: never stalk prey like a cat. Felines of all sizes – whether a wild tiger or a domestic house pet – are great hunters but share a common trait of being so focused they become oblivious to their surroundings. They can afford this blind focus because they rarely have natural predators.

Yet anyone could foil an assassin's plot by chance and often did. Had he paid attention to all potential threats, he would have seen the careless teenager and avoided the collision. He hadn't. He had screwed up. Now – after being on the job for almost three weeks – fulfilling this commission was in peril. Time was running out. And at first glance, the crushed crucifix seemed beyond repair.

When the last of the scattered beads were placed in his hand, and he said thank you in French for the final time, he produced a ticket purchased in the morning and walked through the entry gate.

Sister Margaret Mary sought refuge inside Santa Francesca Romana,[11] a tenth-century Catholic church overlooking the Forum.
His face was soaked beneath the mask as he knelt at a pew facing the Chapel of the Crucifixion. The weaponized religious icon
was in three pieces. The latex gloves made finger dexterity difficult
while attempting reassembly. His vision was blurred from sweat.
He dabbed his eyes with a tissue. Then he saw it.

A tiny spring was bent. So small, so insignificant-appearing, yet
so critical to success … or failure. While carefully bending it back
into shape, the thin wire broke. A shard skidded across the marble
floor and disappeared beneath the side-chapel altar.

"Jesus Christ!" he exclaimed below his breath. *That's it. The charade is over. Move!*

The Catholic nun pushed tourists aside while rushing out the
door of the church. While holding up the hem of the black habit,
he hustled down the central pathway through the Roman Forum.[12]
The Morettis and their guide were about fifty yards ahead. There
was still time. Maybe.

The assassin reached the rendezvous point. While staring up
at eight massive Corinthian columns framing the second-century
Temple of Antoninus and Faustina,[13] he dropped to one knee and
made the sign of the cross three times. "Jesus Christ," he said again.

Chapter Three: Rome, Italy

Photos 6–13

FOUR

ROME, ITALY

From atop Capitoline Hill,[14] Doris Mathews had monitored every step the Morettis took through the Colosseum, along the Via Sacra and now in the Roman Forum. Moretti's position appeared as a red dot on the cell phone screen. Sister Margaret Mary's movements were displayed in green. Three times the dots had nearly identical GPS coordinates. Three times she waited in anticipation but never received a confirmation signal. On the third occasion, all she heard was a commotion followed by repeated thank-yous in French.

Her concern was confirmed a few minutes later when "Jesus Christ" echoed in her earbud. If the two words had been spoken in French, it meant a successful shot had been fired. In English, however, it meant something was wrong. But what? Unfortunately, radio protocol during a silentcide commission prevented dialogue except during a physical emergency or imminent threat; you never knew who might accidently intercept a transmission.

Doris flipped aside long black hair dangling below a floppy sun-hat. Then she shifted the inflated bodysuit stuffed inside a size sixteen, ankle-length dress before leaning over a railing. The mask and disguise added twenty years, seventy pounds and six bra sizes. The outfit provided complete anonymity among a group of milling vacationers. She was just another unnoticed American savoring the sights.

The elevated terrace along Via di Monte Tarpeo offered a panoramic view of the Roman Forum below. Using an 80–400mm telephoto lens, she zoomed in on the Moretti family. They showed no signs of alarm. Perhaps boredom, especially the teenage daughter. Heat exhaustion, maybe – Moretti's face was beet red and his clothes were soaked with sweat. But they maintained a slow pace while the animated tour guide kept describing different ancient ruins.

She studied the cell phone again. *What's happening? Move, damn it. Do something!*

Finally, the blinking green dot left Santa Francesca Romana, moved down Velian Hill and headed toward the archeological valley of Foro Romano. He was walking too fast, much too fast for an eighty-year-old nun.

Why's he jeopardizing his disguise?

Through the full magnification of the zoom lens, she watched his hurried pace until he knelt on one knee, made the sign of the cross three times and repeated the code words, "Jesus Christ."

The message was clear. The weapon had malfunctioned. He would remain between the Morettis and the gate at Via della Salara Vecchia in case they exited there. The contingency plan for stalling the family was ready if needed. But other than providing support, he was relinquishing the role of primary assassin. That responsibly was now hers.

She was their last chance for either success or failure. The latter was unacceptable. As a team, they had successfully executed almost every silentcide commission they'd been assigned. Irene Shaw demanded nothing less. The consequences of disappointing Irene were brutal.

Doris tapped her earbud twice, sending two dings over the radio to her brother.

A pending kill was always an adrenaline rush. The surge of anticipation mixed with danger was euphoric. Her eyelids lowered over colored contact lenses. All ambient noise was blocked out. Any distracting thoughts disappeared as her brain focused on the single task ahead. Doris Mathews was ready.

Using the Nikon D850, she saw Sister Margaret Mary plodding along with cautious steps toward the target while the Morettis were gazing at the early-third-century Arch of Septimius Severus.[15] Next they were led toward the Temple of Saturn's[16] eight remaining Ionic columns. Their excursion at the Roman Forum would soon be over.

She had a decision to make. Their itinerary ended with a two-hour tour of the Capitoline Museums behind her. She could intercept them there. The crowded exhibit rooms would provide plenty of opportunities for undetected proximity while administering the kill shot. But Moretti had been unpredictable for almost three weeks. He could easily say screw it and demand a ride back to the hotel after visiting the Forum. That would be a disaster.

She had to risk an open encounter. But which exit would they use? One was north. One was south. Guessing wrong would jeopardize everything. She waited and watched. The travel guide's face filled the camera's viewfinder while she read his lips. Finally, he said, "Let's go out this way." She zoomed out slightly to detect the direction he was pointing.

Time to move. Fast!

While holding the camera against one hip and a purse along the other, she dashed down the sidewalk along Via di Monte Tarpeo, through a short tunnel, followed the elbow in the road, twice jutted into the cobblestone street to avoid strolling tourists, and slowed down when reaching a guard booth. She pretended to be breathless from exertion as she waved at the stationed Roma Capitale policeman and yelled out, "I'm late for my tour bus." If he understood, he didn't care. His bored expression suggested he would not be an issue.

Once out of his eyesight, she peered through a security fence. The Morettis were walking to the exit from below. Double-parked along the street was a black van with the engine running and a driver playing with a cell phone. A door decal read "Migliori Tour di Roma," the agency that had arranged the family's excursion.

She reached into her purse, put on a pair of oversized sunglasses and casually leaned against the fence while intensely surveying the surroundings. She noted every car, every pedestrian and every open window. The area seemed secure.

While mentally timing the arrival of the Morettis, she extracted a package of cigarettes, pushed one between her lips and lit it with a blue Bic lighter. Smoking was disgusting except when used as a prop. After returning the lighter, she palmed another one twice the size and discreetly held it below the purse hanging from her shoulder.

The weapon was similar in design to Sister Margaret Mary's crucifix. Inside were six tiny projectiles of a colorless acidic liquid shaped like barbed stingers using a black synthetic polymer. The active ingredient was apitoxin, more commonly known as honeybee venom. They collectively contained about two-hundred milligrams, equivalent to being stung by two thousand honeybees. According to Moretti's medical files, he was highly allergic to a single sting and had once gone into anaphylactic shock after multiple stings. His prescribed epinephrine injector would be no match for the lethal dose she had concocted.

Doris took a long drag from the cigarette, pretended to inhale, then casually blew smoke rings as if bored. When Moretti's arrogant voice became audible, she began moving along the narrow sidewalk. The walkway was enclosed by a brick wall and parked cars. The room for movement was minimal yet optimal for a kill zone.

The tour guide was the first one through the gate. He graciously directed Mrs. Moretti toward the waiting van. The assassin was ten feet away as the daughter emerged and blindly followed her mother while scrolling on a cell phone. This was ideal. Everyone had their backs turned.

Only five feet to go before reaching the mark.

As the turnstile creaked for the fourth time, Doris counted on Moretti maintaining his rude personality. He did not disappoint. With a self-satisfied grin, he stepped in front of Doris, laughed when she made an abrupt stop to avoid a collision, then turned to walk away. Arrogance has its advantages.

She pushed the trigger on the lighter hidden below her purse. She coughed to cover the sound of compressed gas being released. She watched with satisfaction as his left calf flinched.

"Shit!" he yelled as he reached down and slapped the back of his leg. "What was that?" he asked when noticing her waving a hand in front of her face and jumping back.

"Bees, I think," she offered, then resumed walking.

Moretti pushed her aside while entering the van. As the sliding door closed, she could hear him cursing and his wife expressing concern.

A short distance away, Doris smiled while clicking her earbud four times. The code for success would make her brother smile too.

Chapter Four: Rome, Italy

Photos 14–16

FIVE

ROME, ITALY

After Doris Mathews successfully fired the bee venom projectiles, she watched as the red dot on her cell phone sped toward San Giovanni Hospital. She imagined Moretti's deteriorating condition inside the tourist van – redness spreading up the leg, hives dotting clammy skin, dropping blood pressure, rapid weak pulse, gasping for air, maybe vomiting. She expected full anaphylactic shock would occur before emergency room personnel had the chance to inject epinephrine. The chances of survival were slim to none, but his death still had to be confirmed.

As per protocol, she did not try contacting her brother as he left the Roman Forum dressed as Sister Margaret Mary. Instead, she walked casually to her hotel, stripped off the matronly Doris Mathews disguise, and spent over two hours in a robe, nursing a beer and half-heartedly watching a movie while monitoring the Moretti family hotel room transmitted from the camera in Moretti's laptop. When Mrs. Moretti and daughter Hannah entered, they were clearly distraught. Both were sobbing. The absence of Moretti was promising, yet she waited until the sixteen-year-old wailed, "I can't believe Daddy's dead!" That was it.

Michelle Barton transmitted the four-letter word *Done* into her laptop.

Within the hour, someone from Thanatos – the division named after the winged Greek god of nonviolent death – would receive the message, communicate the news to the client, and arrange for the second half of the fee. The company's collection process was very efficient; there was no such thing as a delinquent payment.

Irene Shaw would notice the confirmation and monitor the transaction until paid, yet never express thanks because perfection was the minimal expectation. The demise of Angelo Moretti was just another successful silentcide, another satisfied client and another hefty bank deposit.

Despite the habitual lack of appreciation from Irene, Michelle was elated. She texted the words "steps one hour," then took a long hot shower. Slowly, the shampoo, conditioner and soap washed away the lingering anxiety and the slight twinge of remorse often felt after a commission was finished.

Michelle wrapped a towel around her tall athletic body and wiped steam from the bathroom mirror before blow-drying and curling her sandy-blond hair. Concealer removed the hint of puffiness that had begun emerging a year ago at thirty-five. Next, foundation hid faint freckles, and mascara plus liner were applied to spotlight deep-blue eyes. Then blush accented high round cheeks and lip gloss with a hint of rose completed the transformation. A bright smile gave her a fresh, wholesome appearance. Michelle was herself again.

She slipped on a sheer camisole below a pale blue sleeveless body-con cocktail dress and added a pair of modest heels to accentuate her long legs. A delicate gold necklace and blue topaz stud earrings completed the ensemble. This was a perfect outfit to celebrate.

◆◆◆

Michelle Barton was the first to arrive at Piazza della Trinità dei Monti. She glanced at the façade of a sixteenth-century church and a tall red granite obelisk[17] patterned after an Egyptian one from the thirteenth century BC. Both landmarks stood atop the famous Spanish Steps,[18] one of Rome's most visited locations. Despite being in the city for almost a week, this was the first time she'd allowed herself to become a tourist. The feeling was marvelous.

The feeling intensified to exhilaration when Chris Davis stepped out of a cab, wearing tailored, dressy-casual attire. He flashed his signature gregarious grin, exposing bright white teeth. His confident blue-green eyes glistened beneath short blond hair and matching eyebrows. Seeing his face without a disguise – oblong with almost genderless features and flawless pale skin – was rare. Although of average height and thin, his muscular build was evident during the heartfelt embrace from the thirty-eight-year-old brother she loved.

"Thanks for coming to my rescue," he whispered. "You were amazing."

"Happy to help a clumsy old nun." She laughed in his ear.

As she pulled back, Michelle knew this quick exchange would be the only time they would mention the events in Rome. They never discussed past commissions. Over two decades ago, they had been taught how to compartmentalize. The faster they suppressed their professional actions, the faster their emotional equilibrium returned to normal.

"I assume you need a new crucifix, dude," she said with a straight face, broke into a giggle, then slid her arm into the crux of his while strolling to a terraced restaurant.

The ambiance was magical. The menu of Mediterranean cuisine looked divine. As dusk crept over the picturesque horizon, lights began illuminating historic domes.[19] They started discussing the sights in Rome they wanted to visit before taking separate flights Monday morning. Although they lived in adjacent cities, they were not allowed to socialize in person at home. This weekend was a coveted opportunity to be together as brother and sister. The waiter had just finished showing Chris the label of an expensive Barolo red wine from the Piedmont region when both of their cell phones chimed.

Michelle cringed. She knew what that sound meant and dreaded it. "Don't look at your phone," she begged Chris.

"You know we have to," he said, hesitated for a second, then pulled the cell phone from his sport coat.

She looked at hers. The three words were simple. "Expedited. Guarded. Antwerp." The message was ominous. They had a new silentcide commission of a heavily guarded target in Antwerp, Belgium, who had to be killed in less than a week. This promised to be a challenging and dangerous assignment.

The mood was shattered. Their celebratory reunion was tainted, probably ruined. Although they stayed long enough to sip some wine and pick at an hors d'oeuvre, barely a word was spoken. Finally, Michelle threw her linen napkin on the table and said, "The hell with it." While pushing back her chair, she added, "I'll see you in Antwerp." Neither said goodbye as she stormed off. Michelle Barton was crestfallen and furious.

Any attempt at a normal life was always aborted by someone with omnipotent authority and control. They had suffered countless abuses since childhood. Each successive trauma was harder to endure but strengthened their bond. They survived together, yet their existence of constant anxiety and subservience was miserable.

Chapter Five: Rome, Italy

Photos 17–19

SIX

When the front door crashed open and slammed shut – rattling the windows in the house – Danny became rigid beneath the covers, paralyzed by routine fear. The dark bedroom was a dungeon of anguish while waiting for the monster to appear. This was not an imaginary beast hiding in a closet or under the bed. Turning on a light would not make the danger disappear into a vague nightmare. This monster was his stepfather. He was returning to his lair in a habitual drunken stupor.

The ten-year-old could trace his stepfather's uneven path through the first floor based on all-too-familiar sounds. Banging off living room furniture accented with vulgar cursing. Clinking liquor bottles followed by ice cubes dropping into a glass. A long silence while chugging his favorite poison, Jack Daniel's. Then the scraping of a chair against linoleum before the vile man sat at the kitchen table. A seizure of coughing and guttural noises ended with a violent spit of phlegm.

Silence meant more drinking. Each gulp was accented by a thud of the glass returning to the table. Then the sound of a Zippo. Danny knew he was safe for the duration of a cigarette. He pictured his stepfather's ruddy face while blowing clouds of nasty smoke. There was no doubt he was either propping his head up with his hands, rubbing his bloodshot eyes, or dragging fingernails through his matted black hair in chronic anger.

Danny listened intensely but heard nothing for several agonizing minutes. He prayed the creep had passed out. Finding him sprawled across the table was a common sight at breakfast. Hearing his wrath in the morning was welcomed compared to being victimized late at night. The fate ahead was uncertain, but there was still hope.

That hope was shattered when the kitchen chair crashed to the floor. Heavy, uneven footsteps approached. Each creak of the stairs was more ominous. Strained breathing grew louder until the monster reached the second floor.

Danny dared to peek through the slit of one eye. The shadow was braced against the banister, swaying while staring into the darkness of the bedroom.

What would happen next? Would he be dragged from his bed and beaten with a belt for some fabricated wrongdoing? Would his eight-year-old sister be molested again? Or would the drunken wrath be aimed at Mom until she submitted to his alcohol-fueled lust? Danny didn't move while struggling to control the panic.

His stepfather stumbled down the hall. This meant he was safe but Sarah was not. Danny wondered if she heard the ominous threat or remained sleeping while the door creaked open. Would she wake with a whimper as he leered over her or not until he pulled back the covers?

"Daddy, no! No!" Sarah screamed before her voice was muffled.

Her cries of torment were gut-wrenching. Hiding beneath a pillow could not shield the images of what was happening to his sister. Danny desperately wanted to rescue her. But he was severely beaten the last time he tried. The failed attempt had only delayed the assault on Sarah.

From the other end of the hall came thundering bare footsteps. His mother's nightgown was a blur as she raced past his doorframe. "Frank, stop!" she kept yelling until silenced by a powerful fist.

When Mom's body hit the floor, Sarah screeched. Danny could hear his sister kicking and scratching in defense until their mother resumed the battle.

Mom was no match for a drunk twice her size. Each blow caused another shriek of pain. His raging obscenities and her cries for mercy intensified during the manic beating.

Danny had to defend them, regardless of the consequences. The price would be cuts and bruises, maybe broken bones, but the agony of doing nothing was worse. He bolted from bed, ran down the hall and entered the chaos. Sarah was cowering beneath a blanket while Mom was thrashing on the floor, shielding herself from repeated kicking.

His stepfather's enraged eyes turned on him, as he threatened to strike with clenched fists. "Get the hell outta here, you freak," he screamed in reference to Danny's alabaster skin and effeminate facial features, "or I'll beat the crap out of you next."

"Save Sarah!" Mom pleaded with blood oozing from swollen lips. "Please save your sister!"

Danny dodged around his stepfather, grabbed Sarah's hand and suffered a blow to the temple while trying to escape. The impact was stunning. A flurry of punches would have followed had Mom not landed a debilitating kick to the groin. While the beast staggered in pain and slurred vulgarities, the siblings raced down the stairs and into the kitchen.

Danny struggled with erratic breathing. "Go next door and call the police," he told his sister.

"Not without you," Sarah sobbed.

"Go! Now!" he demanded, pushing her toward the back door.

She hesitated. Terror consumed her expression as she trembled. "Get outta here! I mean it!"

After Sarah ran out, Danny frantically searched the closet for a baseball bat. With the weapon in hand, he mustered the courage to confront his stepfather. In the past, he had only made feeble and failed attempts at being a defender. Never once was he brave enough to be the aggressor. He wavered until hearing Mom's desperate wailing.

He sprinted up the stairs, bolted down the hall and took aim at the monster strangling his mother on the floor. The next few seconds were a fog of rage. He had no memory of what happened.

Danny regained awareness while begging Mom to wake up. Her ravaged body was lifeless. Fixed eyes stared at the ceiling. A bloodied baseball bat lay a few inches away.

A noise in the doorway was startling. Standing there was Sarah. She was transfixed in horror and clutching a butcher knife. Without a word or emotion, she walked into the bedroom, dropped to her knees and plunged the knife into the heart of their battered and dying stepfather.

They then huddled together in shock.

If the first pair of policemen rang the doorbell or announced their entrance, Danny couldn't remember. All he recalled was lashing out when feeling a hand on his shoulder. Their initial words of comfort were clouded, as were their questions.

When a police officer tried getting them to stand, Sarah refused to let go. She clutched her brother while being escorted down the stairs and positioned on the living room couch.

Soon, the house filled with first responders. Their voices were muted, and the bustle of activity was ignored until a face pressed within inches of the children. "Can you tell me what happened?" a sympathetic policewoman asked.

Danny talked while Sarah whimpered at every detail. When they were done, a man who introduced himself as a homicide detective asked the same questions. Explaining everything the second time made the horror more excruciating. The detective finished by requesting the name of a family member to call. There was no one – only estranged relatives who lived out of state – so Danny offered his stepfather's boss. Afterward, a paramedic treated their superficial wounds yet was helpless to treat their inner pain.

An hour later – maybe it was two – the siblings were ushered into a squad car and driven through the trafficless streets to the police station. When they arrived, they were separated but not until Sarah was forcibly pulled away and dragged down the hall by a woman from Children and Families Services.

Danny was brought to a shower, told to strip, and was watched while scrubbing off the blood. Then he was given a man's T-shirt and pants to replace his bloody pajamas. He had to clutch the trousers to prevent them from falling. Finally, he was sequestered in a dank room containing only a steel table and a few chairs bolted to the floor. The door slammed shut. The sound of the lock was frightening.

Danny was jostled awake by a looming lean figure wearing a black blazer and slacks, with six-inch heels exposing polished toes. The lacy white blouse did nothing to soften the aggressive stance. Her fingers and wrists were covered in expensive jewelry.

"My name is Irene Shaw," she said in a dominating voice, waited a second, then commanded, "For Christ's sake, sit up like a man when I'm talking to you and look at me."

He did. Her jaw was pronounced and rigid. High cheekbones and a strong nose led to a cold stare. The tightly knotted brown hair seemed to stretch her immaculate skin. She was beautiful yet powerful and intimidating. Danny guessed she was in her early forties, but she had the presence of someone a decade older.

"I'm a criminal attorney here to represent you. Your stepfather's employer sent me. So what the hell happened?"

"I … I think I killed my stepfather," he said while lowering his head.

The slap on the face was more surprising than painful. Danny stared in bewilderment as the lawyer corrected him. "No, it was self-defense. Say it."

"Okay, it was self-defense, but I'm really sorry."

The next slap was more painful. "Never, ever feel sorry for killing an evil man. And your stepfather was evil. Do you understand?"

Danny nodded while picking crusted blood from his fingernails.

"I didn't hear you," she taunted him.

"Yuh-huh," he mumbled.

"Yes, Ms. Shaw," she demanded. "You will always address me as Ms. Shaw."

"Yes, Ms. Shaw," he complied.

With an unexpected movement, she sat down and leaned across the table. The proximity was formidable. "Now listen to me. Until I make your problems go away, you will talk to no one without me in the room. I don't care if you have to piss, you will not open your mouth. Got that?"

"Yes, Ms. Shaw."

"And your parents are dead. There is nothing I can do to change that. But if you always do exactly what I tell you – and I mean exactly – I will always take care of you and your sister. Do we have an understanding?"

"Yes, Ms. Shaw."

She slammed her fist on the table. "Goddamn it! Say it like you mean it!"

"Yes, Ms. Shaw, I understand," he said as bravely as he could while fighting the urge to cry. "I will always do exactly what you tell me."

"Good," she said, leaning back and folding her arms across her chest. "We are going to get along just fine."

SEVEN

Anna Monteiro couldn't focus on work at her desk. About two hours earlier, the CEO of Longfellow BioSciences[20] had stormed into the conference room, followed by a rush of senior executives who seemed as anxious as if responding to a medical emergency. Fifteen minutes later, the head of investor relations cautiously entered the fray of contentious voices.

Something very troubling was happening behind the closed door. Anna had assumed this would be a bad day for the company. The vibes were worse than expected.

Even more disconcerting was the clandestine view of Liz Walker sitting inactive in her office chair. The chief science officer was normally a whirlwind of activity. Yet now Liz sat transfixed in front of the computer, either deep in thought, deep in worry, or both.

Anna tentatively tapped on the glass door of the office. Liz flinched, looked up with a startled expression, then slumped her shoulders. Anna pointed to herself, mimicked her fingers walking, and pointed toward Liz. She was waved in.

"Are you okay?" Anna asked while pulling up a guest chair.

"No," Liz said, twirling a curl of red hair. Then, as if catching herself responding to a good friend versus an employee in the office setting, she said, "Yes, I'm okay.... Well, maybe."

Anna smirked. "Now there's a definitive answer if I ever heard one."

"Up yours, smartass," Liz quipped.

"I've always said it's better to be a smartass than a dumbass." After a fleeting laugh, followed by an immediate moment of tension, Anna added, "So are we done talking about the intelligence quotient of my buttocks?"

"Yeah, I guess so."

"Good. So what's going on around here?"

Liz took a sip from her bottomless mug of dark French coffee. With a sigh, she said, "I got a very heated call from the CEO earlier asking if I knew who leaked the results of the clinical trials and the wrongful death lawsuit."

"But I thought the press release was scheduled to go out after the close of markets this afternoon," Anna said.

"Yeah, that was the plan. That way management could do damage control all weekend with big institutional investors before the stock market opens Monday. But apparently, a distorted version of the news broke early, resulting in ugly doomsday rumors. That caused our stock to crash, forcing a halt on trading until we publicly announced the results and lawsuit. That's what all of the scrambling is about."

"Then why aren't you in the conference room with the rest of the chiefs?"

"I suspect for the same reason I was dismissed early from the board meeting yesterday. I was told this is a financial crisis and now, I quote, 'This has nothing to do with your immunology platform, so your opinions won't be required.'"

"That's insulting," Anna scoffed.

"No kidding."

"Was that a girls-are-not-allowed-in-the-boys'-room kind of thing?"

"I don't know anymore, Anna. I really don't. Is it me? Is it my technology? Am I anatomically equipped wrong? Who knows?

Maybe all of the above. But when the ship is sinking, it's no time to quibble over the size of the male iceberg."

"So what's the status?" Anna asked.

"From what I've learned, the release went out about an hour ago. When you knocked, I was watching the computer to see what happens when trading resumes." Liz returned her focus to the screen, then groaned, "Un-be-liev-able!"

"What?"

"Our stock price is down seventy-two percent … seventy-three percent … and still falling. All I see are sell orders and shorts on heavy volume. This is a disaster!" Liz's hand slammed on the desk. "No! No! No! Now trading has been halted again. This is torturous to watch." She flopped back into the desk chair, clenched her teeth and eyes, and rubbed her forehead fiercely below her red bangs. Liz stopped breathing.

Anna felt helpless. She nibbled what was left of a fingernail.

After a loud gasp, followed by a deep sigh, Liz reopened her eyes, seemed ready to say something, but remained stunned.

Anna tentatively asked, "Is there anything you can do this afternoon to fix the situation?"

Liz slowly shook her head. "No, the damage is done."

"Then go home," Anna said with compassion. "You look like you need to get outta here."

"But Todd might be pissed if I leave early."

"Are you kidding me? You tell our omnipotent CEO you assumed your opinions weren't required, that this is a big-boy problem, so go fix it himself."

As expected, Liz ignored the half-hearted advice. Anna knew Liz would never be that insubordinate – both of them were consummate professionals – but she often wished her friend did more to defend herself.

"I just can't go home, Anna."

"Why not?"

"Because if I do, Bill will smother me with sympathy. He is the best husband a woman could have, but as Longfellow's problems have mounted, he's been treating me like someone with a terminal illness. He keeps telling me everything will be okay, or I need to stay positive and keep fighting, or that he'll always love me regardless of what happens. Every single sentence is well intentioned. And I love him for it. But I just can't hear all that right now. I just can't."

"Then come home with me, and I'll call you a dumbass all night."

"You're so considerate."

"I know. It is one of my many endearing qualities," Anna said with a smirk.

"But I thought you had a date tonight," Liz said.

"I do, with that jackass George. And trust me, a jackass is several notches below a dumbass. Hey, wait a minute." Anna pulled out her phone, thumbed a quick text, then returned the phone to her blazer. "See, that's how you fix a problem. My evening just opened up. I booked us at my house for an amazing meal of meatloaf with leftover veggies. How's that sound?"

"Perfectly dreadful."

"Great. Then I'll see you there." Anna stood to leave.

"I need another half hour or so before I can go."

"Thirty minutes tops."

Liz nodded.

"Promise me?" Anna asked with a doubtful raise of the eyebrows.

Liz begrudgingly nodded again.

On nice days, Anna often ran or jogged the three miles from Kendall Square in Cambridge to the Back Bay of Boston. During inclement weather, she took the T, but the subway was too slow. She wanted to get home well before Liz arrived by car. So she grabbed a cab – considered outdated by millennials but often considerably cheaper than Uber.

+++

Anna was just finishing walking Blue when Liz approached the redbrick Victorian brownstone.[21] In excitement, the cocker spaniel piddled on Liz's shoe.

"I'm so sorry," Anna said, "but that's her idea of extending a warm welcome."

"No worries," Liz said while petting the wiggling dog. "Everybody else has been doing that to me, so I'm getting used to it. At least Blue is cute. Aren't you, girl?"

When they entered the sitting room, Liz marveled at the décor. Fluted mahogany pilasters flanked the fireplace, bookshelves and early American art. Panel wainscoting was a backdrop for leather club chairs and an ivory-colored camelback sofa. A handwoven rug with a fleur-de-lis design partially concealed a wide-planked pine floor. The bay window was accented by brass sashes and stained glass. In the center of the coffered tin ceiling was a rotating fan.

"This place never ceases to amaze me," Liz said in admiration. "Any indication your dad plans to evict you soon?"

"Nope, he still wants it available for his occasional overnights in Boston rather than leasing it. But during my five years of house-sitting, I think my parents have only stayed here about twenty times. They'd rather live at the Cape, Naples or Aspen when not exploring the world."

Liz said, "Well, tell your dad I might be out of an income soon if he wants another rent-free tenant."

"Sorry, but that's the line I used when I came back to Boston after my divorce. I think he can only tolerate one deadbeat daughter." Clapping her hands to change the subject, Anna said, "Hey, I have an excellent bottle of Bordeaux I purchased when the clinical trials were going great and I wanted to congratulate you. But the label said something about 'Savor France's finest when times suck.' I think today qualifies in the suckiness department, don't you?"

For the next two hours, the friends drank and laughed and talked about everything except work. The conversation was reminiscent of their senior year in high school: just two naïve girls enjoying each other on a dateless Friday night. But after the meatloaf burned to a crisp and a cheap bottle of rosé was opened, the mood abruptly changed. Liz seemed to melt into the leather chair with gloomy introspection.

Anna felt helpless to provide comfort. Minutes of silence passed. The ambiance remained awkward until she cautiously whispered, "There is no grief like the grief that doesn't speak."

Liz lifted her head, managed a weak smile, then nibbled her lower lip. She clearly recognized the Henry Wadsworth Longfellow quote. The nineteenth-century American poet who had lived in Cambridge was Liz's inspiration for naming the start-up bioscience company.

Liz gulped down the wine, reached over to the coffee table to refill the glass, offered some to Anna, then leaned back and took refuge in numbness. The agonizing quiet returned. Finally, while absently rubbing the glass rim with an index finger, she said, "I have another Longfellow quote for you. 'I am more afraid of deserving criticism than of receiving it.'"

"What's that supposed to mean?" Anna asked.

With a sigh of resignation, Liz began explaining, as if admitting a horrible truth for the first time. "Anna, I've failed. I've failed our employees. I've failed our investors. And you know what, I could live with all that. I really think I could." A pained expression consumed her face. "But I've also failed generations of cancer victims. And I can't forgive myself for that."

Anna debated whether to sound outraged or sympathetic. A middle ground was best. "You know that's not true, right? You've proven personalized, neoantigen-based immunotherapy works. Someday chemo, radiation and all those toxic medications will be as archaic as leeches sucking blood."

"I know. I know," Liz said with growing frustration. "But what good is a revolutionary cure for cancer if it's stillborn?"

It was time to shift tactics toward outrage. "Listen to me, goddamn you! Stop wallowing in self-pity. I'm not going to say everything's going to be all right like your husband. He'd never kick you in the ass. But I have no problem saying when you're full of shit."

Liz giggled.

"What's so damn funny?" Anna asked.

"We sure are stuck on the buttocks theme today, aren't we?"

The tension release felt good. "I did promise to call you a dumbass all night, remember?"

"You're a woman of your word, my friend."

Liz took a long sip, as if building up courage, then said, "Anna, just hear me out. I've not told this to anyone. In fact, I've been denying the truth. But I've come to realize this really is all my fault."

"I don't believe that for a minute."

"Believe what you want, but it's true. You see, I compromised the clinical trials by accepting too many stage-three and -four patients because they were easy to recruit. Hell, at that point in the disease progression, people grasp at any Hail Mary to stay alive. But our platform works best on earlier stages, before conventional treatments ravish their immune systems. But no one wants to forgo standard oncology procedures in favor of an unproven treatment. So I caved to the pressure of management when they demanded we expedite the trials before the money ran out. Now we are in the worst of all possible positions. Our technology is unproven, the money is almost gone, and as of today, we've lost everyone's confidence. And when you lose investor trust, it's game over."

The confession hung suspended. Liz seemed on the verge of giving up. Maybe she already had. Maybe the sense of hopelessness was justified. The reality sank into Anna. Longfellow BioSciences was on its deathbed. The life expectancy was probably measured in months, six at best. The dream was dying.

The unsettling quiet was shattered by the doorbell ringing. Blue jumped up, ran over to the door and began barking.

"Who's that?" Anna wondered out loud. Her head swooned while standing. Obviously too much drinking on an empty stomach. She hushed the dog while going to the door, then recognized George Henniker's unstable stance beneath the stoop lamp. She placed a hand on the crystal doorknob to let him in, but reconsidered. The owner of Moneyer Capital Management was red-faced and seemed angry. His hair, necktie and expensive suit were askew.

"I'm sorry, George, but I canceled dinner tonight," Anna said through the windowpane. "Didn't you get my text?"

"Yeah, I got your damn text. You were afraid to face me after what you did, right?"

"It was just a date, George. No big deal."

"It was a gigantic fucking deal!" he screamed, misstepped and grabbed onto the wrought iron banister for support. "You lied to me."

"I have no idea what you're talking about," Anna said. Apprehension crept across her chest.

"Then let me in and I'll explain." The comment sounded like a threat.

"I can't. I have company."

George pressed his face into the glass and saw Liz also standing in the foyer. He went berserk. "That bitch! You've ruined me. You both did. Open the goddamn door!"

"George, please go home and sleep it off. If you want, I'll call you a cab. Then let's talk next week when you've settled down. Sound good?"

"No! We'll talk now! Right now! Open this door!"

When he started pounding, the dog started barking. Both were out of control.

"George, please leave or I'm going to call the police."

"You do that, bitch, and you'll regret it."

There was no reasoning with him. The two women retreated to the kitchen. Liz clutched a butcher knife while Anna made the call.

The 911 operator kept asking questions and providing reassurance as the sounds of cursing, banging and barking intensified. The wait was interminable.

The police arrived in about six minutes. Liz heard a heated confrontation outside, then a few seconds of quiet before the bell rang and a policeman announced his presence. "Are you all right, ma'am?" he asked.

"Yes," she answered, although she was nervous and anxious.

"Do you know that man?" Anna saw George standing in a huff next to the squad car with another policeman. She couldn't tell if he was handcuffed.

"Yes, his name is George Henniker. He runs a hedge fund in the city."

"How do you know each other?"

"We've been on a few dates, nothing serious. We were supposed to have dinner tonight, but I canceled at the last minute."

"Was he threatening you?"

"Well, I guess so. I mean, no, not really. I think he just had too much to drink or maybe had a bad day in the markets."

"Do you want to press charges?"

Anna considered her answer. "No, that won't be necessary. Could you just help him get home to sleep it off? He's basically a good guy."

The policeman glared at Anna, obviously sizing up her and the severity of the situation. Then, with a tip of the hat, he said, "We'll take care of your friend. Now relax and enjoy the rest of your evening."

Anna walked back into the living room, still trembling. "God, that was scary, huh?" She expected a similar reaction from Liz.

Instead, Liz stared with a defensive stance. Her expression was cold. "What was that really all about, Anna?"

"He was drunk. Other than that, I have no idea."

"Sure you do, so tell me."

Liz knew she was hiding something. They could always read each other. Waves of guilt washed over Anna. She had never lied to her friend and wouldn't start now.

"Well, on our last date," Anna began, "George was too interested in my job at Longfellow. I couldn't be sure, but I suspected he was trolling for inside information for a hedge fund investment. So, when he asked me for a dinner date tonight, I said it would be perfect because I'd have something exciting to celebrate."

"That's it?"

"Yes, it was a test to see if he was trying to exploit me. If he was, he'd know the clinical trial results would be announced today, he'd assume they were positive, and he'd place a bet, which is obviously what happened."

Liz looked betrayed. "So you used Longfellow for an ethics litmus test?"

"No, it was nothing like that," Anna protested.

"Yes, it was exactly like that." Liz seethed.

Anna hurried to say in her defense, "It's not like I shared any confidential information, Liz. You know I'd never do that, right?"

"Good night, Anna."

"Please don't go until we've talked this out."

"We have, and I've heard enough."

"Can I at least call you a cab?"

"No. Suddenly I've gotten very sober."

As the front door slammed shut, a torrent of remorse assaulted Anna for betraying her best friend.

Chapter Seven: Cambridge, Massachusetts

Photos 20–21

EIGHT

Most of Saturday was consumed by flying from Rome to Antwerp. Chris didn't know Michelle's flight schedule and accommodations in advance. He and his sister never had the same itineraries during a silentcide commission. But it was certain Thanatos had booked him in the same hotel as the next target: Johannes Umar.

According to the US passport copied by the front desk, Chris posed as Theodore Robert Collins from Madison, Wisconsin. A partial face mask consisted of oversized ears, sideburns, and a well-trimmed beard above an emerging turkey neck. Tinted thick glasses helped to obscure brown contacts and stenciled crow's feet. The brown wig was short and impeccably groomed, consistent with a businessman in his early fifties. An off-the-rack suit suggested respectability but not significant success.

After flopping his luggage on the bed, Chris returned to the lobby still dressed as Ted Collins. He assumed anyone with a bodyguard would also have the ego and wallet to stay in the best room. According to the hotel's website, their two luxury suites were on the first floor. Signs on their doors made them easy to identify.

In his room, Chris used a burner phone with a Belgian SIM card to call the hotel and asked to be connected to the first suite. A woman answered. Wrong number. The second attempt was successful. "Yes," a gruff voice said, "this is Mr. Umar. Who's this?"

"Mr. Umar, this is hotel management calling to see if we can do anything to make your stay more enjoyable."

"Everything's fine," he barked before hanging up.

That was easy.

Chris opened his Dell XPS. The laptop allowed for two operating systems. One was Microsoft Windows. The other, Parrot OS, was bootable for clandestine activities and hacking. He clicked on an inconspicuous icon in the corner of the screen, waited for the retina recognition camera to unlock a direct link to Thanatos, and typed in Johannes Umar's name in the Commission Search Bar.

Six file folders appeared: Description, Health, Business, Industry, Schedule, and Hate. These standard Thanatos-produced folders were called phantoms because they didn't really exist on his laptop, nor could they be copied or saved. The highly encrypted images and text also bounced around random worldwide servers and IP addresses before appearing on the screen as long as retina contact was maintained. His eyes were the code to unlock and read the information.

Chris sighed. He was reluctant to open the first file. As soon as he did, the commission was real and wouldn't end until someone died. *Enough procrastination. Do this!*

He left-clicked on the cursor, pointing to the Description file. An image of Johannes Umar appeared: egg-shaped face with a bald head, ruddy complexion, and white stubble above fat lips and encircling three chins. Oversized horn-rimmed glasses straddled a broad nose and magnified small eyes glaring with malice. The tailored silk suit failed to camouflage the rotund physique of the middle-aged man.

Umar's residence was listed as Cape Town, South Africa. The official occupation listed in the Business file was an independent wholesaler of precious metals. The next line described Umar's real specialty: a black marketeer of blood diamonds. *Another scumbag!*

Pages of information described his frequent business associates and rumored notorious transactions, plus his less-than-stellar standing with police in five countries and INTERPOL. Often accused, never convicted. Umar was dirty but careful.

Chris scrolled down to the current status section. The details were sketchy, but the assumption was Umar was in Antwerp to auction conflict diamonds from a rich vein in a remote northern section of the Democratic Republic of Congo. Six months prior, an artisanal miner who made the discovery visited several storefront dealers before selling a couple of nearly two-carat gems for four hundred dollars. The transaction attracted attention. The man was tracked to the mine and slaughtered by rebel forces, as were all independent miners and their families within a one-mile radius. Under new, heavily armed supervision, the site then began producing high-quality diamonds. A disproportionate number averaged from a half to almost three carats.

Greed bypassed the normal distribution process of middlemen. None of the jewels would have a legitimate Kimberley Process certificate designed to prevent blood diamonds from being internationally traded. Umar's business trip allegedly had a simple mission: sell uncut and untraceable diamonds direct from a war-torn mine to the highest bidder among unscrupulous dealers in Antwerp, the diamond capital of the world.[22]

Chris leaned back in disgust, ran his long fingers through his short blond hair and across his boyish face. Umar was repugnant. Heinous. Chris wanted to see the bastard. Hopefully, Umar's phone and laptop were connected to the Wi-Fi.

Chris snapped upright, put his fingers on the keyboard, and began following the Thanatos procedure. He identified the hotel's wireless access point, ran a Common Vulnerabilities and Exposures review to identify how to exploit the WAP weaknesses, and used a SQL injection tool to gain admin privileges. Within sixty seconds, he had access to Umar's computer screen, giving him audio and visual surveillance of the man's suite. The room was a pigsty. Unfortunately, the swine had left the pen.

Disappointed but determined, Chris spent fifteen minutes creating a DNS hijacking attack that would later trick Umar's PC and phone into thinking they were using the hotel's domain name server. When successful, this man-in-the-middle hack would allow Chris to take over both devices without being detected.

Then the real work would begin. Chris dreaded the hours required to harvest Umar's laptop and cell phone for valuable information. A facilitator from Thanatos would do the same, as well as open encrypted files, conduct downstream research on contact names, emails and texts, plus attempt to open relevant password-protected accounts, including health and financial records. By morning, summaries of findings would be available for Chris and Michelle to review in the phantom files.

But diligence had been instilled in Chris from an early age. He always did his own homework. The rigorous analysis brought him closer to a mark. The more you knew about a life, the easier to end it.

His cursor was positioned over the word *Hate*. Inside would typically be a video montage portraying the atrocities associated with a target's business, in this case blood diamonds. No doubt Chris would see heinous examples of genocide, torture, village burning, rape, female genital mutilation, child labor and starvation, beatings and bloody executions. The file would also contain statistics about each hideous inhumanity.

A Hate file was mandatory viewing designed to loathe the target and desensitize the act of killing. Irene Shaw had devised the concept of hate channeling. Lionel Jørgensen, who Chris and Michelle called Preceptor, had reinforced the training every month for ten years while living on a remote Amish farm in Pennsylvania. The brainwashing had the desired effect. Chris often pictured the lives he was saving prior to a killing. By doing so, the act of murder seemed as justified as when he'd raised a baseball bat over the head of his stepfather.

Chapter Eight: Antwerp, Belgium

Photo 22

NINE

Twenty-Six Years Ago

D anny woke in a startled daze when a pillow was thrown at his head. As he sat up, he heard the boisterous laughter of Kevin, his roommate over the last two years.

"Get up, you lazy slob," Kevin said with a cheesy smile. "Breakfast is getting cold and Momma is getting hot." The smell of bacon drifting from the kitchen was ample reason to get out of bed.

Kevin was already living in the foster home when Children and Families Services assigned the Millers to also care for Danny and his sister, Sarah. They'd moved in after being cleared of wrongdoing for killing their father. The juvenile court judge had declared, "This is the most obvious case of self-defense and justifiable manslaughter I've seen in my thirty years on the bench. My heart goes out to you two traumatized children for the years of abuse you suffered and for the loss of your mother. Case dismissed."

Kevin was awesome. As Danny watched his best friend put on yesterday's underwear, he marveled at the physical changes that had occurred over the summer. Kevin now had sideburns, chin stubble, tufts of hair on his chest and between his legs, plus muscles and a deeper voice. Danny had none of them. In fact, bullies called him the Albino.

Despite their two-year difference in age – Kevin was starting high school in a couple of weeks – they had bonded together as brothers from day one. Kevin also treated Sarah with the same respect and affection. They called themselves the Three Amigos. Kevin had once said, "Us orphans have to stick together. We're the only family we got." And he meant it.

Danny left the bed unmade, put on shorts and a T-shirt, did a lousy job of aiming at the toilet bowl, ran his fingers through his shaggy pale-blond hair and skipped brushing his teeth; the gunky scum wasn't that bad. Then he plodded barefoot down the hall and into the kitchen.

Mrs. Miller always made a special brunch on Saturdays. It was the best meal of the week. On the table were platters heaped with scrambled eggs, hash browns with grated cheese and onions, crispy hash, waffles and plenty of glorious bacon. The cost for this banquet was doing chores around the house until late afternoon, but that was a small price to pay.

"Sit down, donkey breath," his ten-year-old sister razzed him, with a broad smile and mischievous blue eyes framed by long blond hair. Sarah hadn't smiled and barely spoke during the first year after the death of their parents. During the second year, she had slowly become vivacious and spunky, and now considered herself one of the boys.

"Shall we say grace?" Mrs. Miller asked rhetorically as they bowed their heads. After the prayer, she made the sound of a trumpet, then exclaimed, "Let the feast begin!"

The decibels of chatter rose as a flurry of hands rotated the platters while scraping food onto their plates. Every morsel was delicious. Mrs. Miller was an excellent cook, yet a better surrogate mother. Of course, no one could replace Mom. Danny missed her almost every day. But Mrs. Miller balanced strict discipline with fun, encouragement, and love.

Her husband was rarely home. Most weeks he traveled internationally and often was gone for a month at a time. Danny was never really sure why. He had been told Mr. Miller was a distributor rep for a global manufacturer of industrial tools, yet the details were sketchy. Danny sometimes wondered if something else was going on with the way his wife said before every trip, "Please be careful, John. Please." Her eyes often got misty during their long goodbyes.

"Oh my gosh," Mrs. Miller said while standing and absently wiping her hands on the apron. "I forgot the orange juice. I knew we were missing something."

Danny didn't pay attention as she shuffled to the refrigerator. The kids were playing rock paper scissors for the right to claim the last piece of bacon. He won. While he made an exaggerated motion of savoring every nibble to taunt the losers, Mrs. Miller filled the children's juice glasses.

The chatter slowed as he shoveled the last of the eggs and hash into his mouth, then swallowed them down with a gulp of OJ. Next, he slathered a waffle with red raspberry preserves and, without bothering to cut it, took several large bites.

While asking Sarah to pass the platter of remaining hash browns, he noticed she looked pale and sickly. "You okay?" he asked with concern.

"I feel weird," was all she could muster while leaning over the table and burying her face in her hands.

"You seeing this?" he asked Kevin before realizing his friend was acting the same way. The teenager cautiously placed the juice glass on the table and pushed out the chair before his head flopped backward. He appeared unconscious, maybe dead.

A large crash startled him. Turning, he saw his little sister had fallen face first into a plate of food.

"Momma!" Danny shrieked.

Mrs. Miller was stoic. She seemed oblivious to the fate of Kevin and Sarah. There was no emotion, none, as if she didn't care. Her only reaction was two arms tightening across her chest as blank eyes stared forward.

A weird cloud of confusion began swirling in Danny's brain. The capacity for fear was shutting down. Tingles consumed his muscles as they softened and lost control. The room was becoming gray. He heard himself fall to the floor, but it was dreamlike. He felt nothing. The last thing he saw was Mr. Miller entering the kitchen. That was odd. He was supposed to be in France.

✦✦✦

When Danny regained consciousness, he was woozy, disoriented and scared. As the fog lifted, pain rushed in. His fingers instinctively pushed aside a flimsy nightgown to cup the source of agony between his legs. The feel of a bulging diaper was alarming.

He tried sitting up, felt dizzy and flopped down again into the pillow. While rubbing his head to ease the pounding, he realized his shaggy blond curls were gone. His hair had been shaved off.

He finally dared to open his eyes. The strange bedroom was tiny. There was a whitewashed wooden ceiling, lime-green walls devoid of decorations, and a worn linoleum floor with a braided rug. At the end of the bed was an antique dresser. Inside the base of the matching nightstand was a propane tank. It seemed to be powering a very bright and glowing lamp. He could feel the heat on his face.

"Hello," he shouted, sounding surprisingly weak. "Anybody here?"

"You're awake," said a plain-looking, middle-aged woman as she opened the door and hustled into the room. Heavy black glasses were suspended by round cheeks. Brown hair was tightly parted in the middle before disappearing below a white bonnet. Her gray dress was nearly shapeless from the hooked collar down to her exposed ankles, black socks and worn shoes. "How are you feeling, boy?"

"What happened?" he blurted out. "And where am I?"

"Oh, I see you have lots of questions. That's totally understandable," she said while placing a hand on his forehead.

Whether she was checking for a temperature or trying to be comforting, Danny wasn't sure. Either way, the gesture felt disturbing. "Just tell me what's going on," he pleaded.

"Oh dear, I'm not the one to give you answers. But there is someone here who can," she said, then began leaving the room. "I'll send her right in to talk with you."

Beyond the doorframe, Danny could see a modest, outdated kitchen. There was a wood-burning stove with an elbowed pipe extended to the wall. A glowing lantern was suspended over a small table with bench seating and a worn plastic tablecloth. A single wooden cabinet had jars of spices arranged on a yellowed doily. Most curious was a red cast-iron well pump extending over the sink.

The tailored blue suit, coiffed hair and sparkling diamond necklace of Irene Shaw was a frightening contrast. The tall high heels sounded like a snare drum as she strutted into the bedroom. Her expression was tense, cold and intimidating. She had only made about three or four unscheduled visits annually to the foster home during the last two years. None lasted more than thirty minutes. Each time, the residual trauma lasted for days. The woman was the devil.

As she approached the bed – towering over him – Danny sank deeper below the quilt. But he had learned never to lose eye contact. He never did.

"I hear you have lots of questions," she said with a belittling sneer. "Of course you do. Feel free to ask whatever is on your mind and I'll answer what I can." A threatening hand went on her hip. "But mind your manners. Please ask only one question at a time."

He hesitated. She was being too nice. Was this a trap? He didn't care. "What happened to me?" he dared to ask.

"Well, according to the police, it seems you, Sarah and Kevin decided to go for a swim yesterday afternoon. Your clothes, shoes and backpacks were found along the shoreline at Boathouse Row.[23] You must have drowned in the undercurrents of the Schuylkill River, then were dragged over the Fairmount Dam. Body parts were discovered near the old water works below the Museum of Art[24] and as far away as New Jersey along the Delaware River."

Danny was dumbfounded. None of this made sense. "That's all a lie!" he screamed.

A terrible long pause followed the accusation. There was no reaction on her face. In a slow, controlled motion, she encroached within inches and asked in a voice seething with anger, "Are you calling me a liar?"

He dared not cross that line. "No," he mumbled.

"No what?"

"No, I'm not calling you a liar, Ms. Shaw."

"That's better. I thought I misheard you." She resumed an erect posture, yet her shadow still loomed over him. "So let me tell you what this means. As of today, Daniel Ritchie is dead and Chris Davis was born. Over time, you will learn a lot about Chris. I know you will like him."

With trepidation, he asked, "What happened to Sarah?"

"Do you mean Michelle Barton? She's sleeping peacefully upstairs."

Relieved his little sister was in the house and safe, despite the confusing name change, he asked, "And Kevin?"

Ms. Shaw shook her head while saying with fake sorrow, "I'm afraid your friend is gone. And as soon as the Millers emotionally recover from this terrible, terrible tragedy, they will be gone too. You'll never see any of them again."

He wondered if the word *gone* meant dead but was afraid to know, so he asked, "How did I get injured?"

"Oh my, does it hurt," she said rather than asked with a phony sympathetic smile. "I'd imagine it does. Let's save the answer to that one until the end, shall we?"

Almost on cue, the woman returned carrying two Dixie cups. She stood in the doorframe, waiting to be invited in.

"Excellent timing," Ms. Shaw said. "Are those Chris's pain meds?"

"Yes, along with the sedatives you ordered."

"Perfect." Ms. Shaw made a hand gesture indicating the woman should enter and deliver the medications.

After he washed the pills down with water – he really had no choice – Ms. Shaw put an arm around the woman's shoulder. He thought he saw her flinch at the touch. "This is your new foster mother. You will call her Mamm, which means mom in Amish."

"Welcome, Chris. I look forward to having you and Michelle living with us." He remained quiet and Mamm seemed to have nothing else to say to him. "Ms. Shaw, I will be in the next room if you need me." After a slight curtsey, she exited.

Chris's next tentative question was, "So where am I?"

Ms. Shaw leaned against the dresser and crossed her long legs at the ankles. "You're in a quaint, very isolated farmhouse in Lancaster County, Pennsylvania. Life is simple here. There's no electricity, no heat or air conditioning, no phones and no running water. Over time, you'll learn to accept simplicity devoid of frivolous material things and personal gratification. In fact, you'll learn many things during your stay here. Which reminds me." Turning toward the open door, she shouted, "Samuel!"

In walked a bear of a man. Beneath a straw hat was a weathered face with bushy eyebrows, two deep scowl lines leading to an over-sized nose, barely open eyes with puffy bags of skin beneath them, and a scraggly black beard. Gray strands of hair in the beard looked like tinsel. He wore a long sleeved, blue-denim shirt and suspenders holding up dirty black pants. His stance was like a wrestler.

Almost with pride, Ms. Shaw said, "This is Samuel Lehman."

The man smiled – actually more of a twitch of the lips – but said nothing.

Ms. Shaw chastised Chris. "Where are your manners, young man? Please say hello."

"Hello," Chris managed to say.

"That's better. Now then, I'd also like to introduce you to Lionel Jørgensen."

When she nodded toward the man she'd introduced before as Samuel, he took off his straw hat and black wig, revealing a blond crewcut. Then he peeled off his beard, his brows, the bubbles of skin beneath his eyes, popped out dark contact lenses and opened his eyes wide. Next, he pulled a red bandanna from his back pocket. Ms. Shaw handed him the Dixie cup with water. After soaking the handkerchief, he rubbed away the weather-beaten coloring and most of the wrinkles from his face. Finally, he pulled off the cracked, dirty skin of a farmer from around his hands. After the transformation, he lost twenty-five years and became a handsome, fair-skinned Scandinavian with a cleft chin, chiseled features and fierce blue eyes.

Chris was shocked, scared and speechless. Ms. Shaw seemed to relish his petrified reaction for a moment before talking again. "Now, the Samuel you saw a minute ago will be called Daed, meaning dad in Amish. And Lionel here will be your mentor. You will call him Preceptor. The word means teacher or instructor. Do you understand how you will address these two men going forward?"

Chris was afraid to admit his confusion, so murmured, "Yes, Ms. Shaw."

"Excellent. So perhaps I should answer a question you're probably thinking but may be hesitant to ask. Can you escape from here? In a word, no. You see, we've installed a tracker so we'll always know where you are. If you run, it will be very easy to find you. And the punishment will be severe. So severe, in fact, you'll consider your stepfather's beatings gentle love taps in comparison. Allow me to demonstrate." She again nodded to Preceptor.

The man used his thumbs to lower the suspenders over both shoulders. With massive hands, he pulled open his shirt without first unlatching the hooks, yanked the denim from the waist, threw the garment on the bed, and struck a pose. His chest and muscles were incredible. They reminded Chris of the bodybuilders on the covers of *Men's Health* magazine from the grocery store checkout line.

Ms. Shaw leisurely rubbed her long, polished fingers across the man's six-pack abs while licking her lips. Her leer was beyond creepy.

"I think Chris gets the message," she said while tracing his pecs. "Thanks for your help, Lionel. You may go."

"Yes, Ms. Shaw," was all he said before grabbing his shirt.

She ogled the man's bare back until he left the bedroom. In an instant, her scary professionalism returned. She faced off against Chris. "Wow, it's been a busy day, huh? I'll bet you're getting tired from all of this excitement. I should let you get some sleep. The sedatives should be kicking in soon. But before I leave, I promised to explain how you got injured. Do you still want to know?"

After everything that had happened, Chris was petrified to learn the answer. Mustering what little courage remained, he mumbled, "Yes, Ms. Shaw."

"Well, the minor medical procedure consisted of snipping your cavernous and pudendal nerves."

"What does that mean?"

"Basically, it means you'll never have sex."

"What!" he shrieked in overwhelming terror while grabbing the front of the diaper and beginning to sob. "Why?"

"Because being horny plus having sex, relationships and, heaven forbid, children, are so distracting for a man. We want you focused at all times. Plus, your androgenous face is a rare blend of muted male and female characteristics. It will be a perfect canvas for disguises like you saw a moment ago. And here's the good news. With the proper blend of hormonal supplements and physical training, someday your body will look exactly like Preceptor's. Won't that be wonderful?"

"I hate you!" he screamed. "I hate you, I hate you, I hate you!"

"That's good," Ms. Shaw said with self-satisfaction. "You just learned your first lesson today. Over time, you'll see how hate is a powerful and motivating emotion when properly channeled."

She turned to leave, then spun back around. "You know what, come to think of it, that wasn't your first lesson today. You also learned never to trust anyone, regardless of how well you think you know them. You will never forget the betrayal of your loving foster mother Mrs. Miller, will you?"

Ms. Shaw gave a half-hearted wave goodbye. "Sleep well, Chris. See you again soon. And welcome home."

Chapter Nine: Philadelphia and Lancaster County, Pennsylvania

Photos 23–24

TEN

Present Day – Sunday

The sun was shining, the sky was a perfect blue, and the Sunday morning air was crisp as Chris Davis sat in a funk in front of the Cathedral of Our Lady,[25] the sixteenth-century centerpiece of old town Antwerp. The overpriced triple-shot espresso seemed powerless to chase away the exhaustion. He had fallen asleep around one a.m. while studying in the hotel room, then rallied at the five-thirty wakeup call.

"Good morning," Michelle Barton said from inside the matronly Doris Mathews disguise she had worn at the Roman Forum. She joined him on the bench.

"Not much good about it," Chris answered, then gave an apologetic smirk above his Ted Collins half-mask. He increasingly resented having to be cloaked in secrecy whenever meeting his sister in public during a commission. This was supposed to be a rare vacation day spent together in Rome. Instead, their morbid conversation would focus on the demise of Johannes Umar. *What a waste.* He handed Michelle an iced white chocolate mocha, her favorite.

"Thanks, this is delicious," she said after taking a sip. A pause was followed by the gentle probing question, "So what's wrong?"

"While I was waiting for you, I've been staring at that tympanum."[26] He pointed toward the ornate archway above the cathedral's main entrance. "The reliefs in the middle represent the

Last Judgment. On the left are people destined for Heaven. On the right are those banished to Hell. Will we always be with the dammed souls on the right?"

"Oh, wow, now there's a simple philosophical question." She hesitated before continuing. "Perhaps we should get drunk before trying to answer that one."

"Then drink your coffee." He added with a playful grin, "I had the coffee shop add a triple shot of tequila to yours."

"No wonder it tastes great. Cheers."

After clinking their cups, Michelle placed her hand lightly on his shoulder. The simple gesture spoke volumes. Chris knew she heard his doubts, empathized with him, and would always be there to support him. But now was not the time for a heartening talk between siblings. It was time to resume being assassins, a profession they loathed with zero chance of liberation or redemption.

Chris asked, "So what did you learn about the charming Umar?" He wanted her assessment of health issues that could be exploited.

Michelle was an expert. Her five concurrent years of medical and pharmacy study would have qualified for degrees at any accredited university. But the excellent caliber of homeschooling in Lancaster County – supervised by Mamm and provided by subject-matter experts – didn't issue framed certificates at graduation.

"Fortunately for us," Michelle began her report, "Umar is as ugly on the inside as he is on the outside. His list of medical maladies is long, including the perennial favorites among old fat guys, such as high blood pressure, high cholesterol and coronary artery disease. But the area of focus is his heart."

"Does he have one?" Chris asked in jest.

"Not a good one, and I'm referring to the muscle and not his victimization of people in the Congo. Three years ago, Umar had a sudden cardiac arrest from a blood clot during an international flight. Then he developed an irregular heartbeat called atrial fibrillation. Treatments include antiplatelet, beta blocker and statin medications, plus the surgical placement of two stents and an implantable cardioverter defibrillator, or ICD for short. So I think our objective should be to arrange another heart attack, but make this one fatal."

Chris loved how animated his sister became during the early stages of planning. Her hands were waving, her eyes twinkled, and he sensed her excited expressions below the mask. He asked, "So how can you induce a fatal heart attack?"

"I have a few witch's brews in mind," Michelle said, "but I'm going to have to visit a sanctioned pharmacist. And the closest one is in Amsterdam. So after we're done here, I'm going to make the two-hour drive. I'll be back sometime late Monday after I get what I need."

"Can't you find someone locally?"

"Too risky."

"But that means we'll lose two days."

"I know, I know!" Michelle exclaimed with irritation. "I really wish Thanatos would send me a target's medical files before reaching the designated city. I could've easily flown to Amsterdam first and saved a lot of time."

"Do you anticipate any special requirements that I need to design?"

"Yes, focus on the defibrillator."

"What does that mean?" Chris asked.

"In a worst-case scenario, we induce a heart attack and the damn defibrillator brings him back to life. In a best-case scenario, we control it to produce high-energy shocks that cause asystole. His chance of surviving from that type of heart failure is less than two percent."

"Sounds tricky, but I'll see what I can do."

"Are we done?" she asked, seemingly eager to start driving.

Chris became animated. "No, it's time to play the Name that Client game. Michelle Barton, you're the next contestant. Come on down!"

"Okay," she said with a smile. "Tell me who you think sponsored this commission. But make it quick."

Despite the flippant name, this was not a game. Chris always tried speculating on the motive for murder. The thought process helped him better understand and villainize the target, plus identify vulnerabilities and risks.

"There are four top candidates," Chris began explaining while she sipped her coffee and listened. "One, a rival rebel force in the DRC wants control over the black-market distribution chain. Two, the DRC. The country is the third-largest producer of African diamonds yet has a disproportionately small revenue in exports. Stopping blood diamond smuggling is economically rewarding for the government's coffers. Three, one of the legitimate mining companies in Africa wants a larger share of Congolese diamonds. And finally, the four diamond exchanges in Antwerp collectively control two-thirds of the world's rough diamond sales. Guys like Umar who peddle conflict diamonds in their town are bad for business."

"That sounds about right. Any guesses yet?"

"No, and that worries me. The assignment came too fast and the timeframe is too short. That means the stakes are high, probably very high. Worse yet, someone knows the killing is going to happen this week in Antwerp. So I wouldn't be surprised if that someone has someone else watching with the goal to identify us so they can monitor our actions. They might also be tasked with eliminating loose ends when we're done."

"That sounds ominous," she said, tightening her grip on the coffee cup.

Chapter Ten: Antwerp, Belgium

Photos 25–26

ELEVEN

Anna Monteiro spent the weekend dredging up Friday's horrendous events: the collapsed stock price, the company's potential demise, Liz's raw self-condemnation of failure, and George's belligerent threats. Equally bad, she had betrayed Liz's trust. She hadn't meant to. But she had unintentionally crippled, and maybe destroyed, a twenty-seven-year friendship. That was unforgivable.

She had called Liz several times and left apologetic messages. They were followed up with a couple of remorseful texts, plus an email. There was no response. The silence spoke volumes.

On Monday morning, for the first time in a challenging yet mentally rewarding career at Longfellow BioSciences,[27] Anna dreaded walking into the office for fear of more catastrophic company news. The apprehension was similar to entering a funeral home. Intellectually, you know you've lost someone special. Yet emotionally, you are in denial until you see the open casket. Then the reality is crushing.

Anna nodded hello to the somber receptionist – a young woman who normally bubbled with enthusiasm – and trudged down the hallway lined with framed cover stories and feature articles about Longfellow and Liz's breakthrough technology.

As senior VP of marketing and public relations, Anna had toiled for five years to promote the company and her friend in medical and oncology journals, financial publications, business and women's magazines, local periodicals, and on the internet. Some of the headlines read: "The Next Frontier in Medicine," "Imagine a World without Cancer," "Cancer's Holy Grail Discovered," "The Next Apple, Amazon or Google Stock." Now they were all a mockery.

Adjacent to executive row was the open floor plan for staff functions. The atmosphere always buzzed with activity. Today was different, very different. Anna assumed a majority had read, heard or manufactured rumors all weekend.

Clusters of people huddled in corners or cubicles in hushed conversations. Watchful eyes darted over the tops of office dividers. Some had their heads down, facing their computers or papers on the desk, but they obviously were not being productive. None of the chiefs were sitting in their chairs. The conference room door was closed. Everyone sensed their fate was being decided and the verdict would be delivered soon. The ambiance was thick with dread.

Anna wrung her hands while the computer booted up. Reflected in the monitor was her oval face, small nose and lips, deep brown eyes accented with thick brows, and delicate ears peeking below a black pixie haircut. *Cute* was the word many people had used to describe her since childhood. Devastated and drained was all she saw. She looked and felt miserable.

For the next two hours, Anna struggled with the unfinished conference presentation she'd started Friday. The PowerPoint deck was crap from the beginning and getting worse by the second. All attempts to concentrate were blurred by emotions. She was rarely, if ever, distracted like this but couldn't control it. The loss of discipline made matters worse.

Suddenly, an interoffice communication box popped up on the screen. At the same instant, her cell phone dinged, as did all of the cell phones in the office. The message was succinct: "Mandatory all-company meeting at 10:30." The implication was clear.

The decibel level mushroomed. Most people began chattering, some cried, others swore, and several stood in stunned silence. The moment dreaded since Friday was thirty minutes away.

Anna jumped up and began addressing questions and concerns of her two direct reports. She also tried consoling many others. It was difficult to know what to say, but saying something was better than being quiet.

Soon, the death march began. As employees plodded through the lobby to reach the auditorium, they passed below a red ticker for LFBS. The real-time sign had been a great motivator when the stock price reached a peak of $132.25 about two years ago. Now it read $0.98, the equivalent of a heart monitor nearing the flatline.

Over sixty people anxiously waited for the meeting to start. Muffled gasps, coughs and shushes were heard when the chiefs – the five most senior executives – took the stage. Todd Milken, the CEO, stepped behind the microphone while the others stood behind him with grim expressions and hands folded.

His remarks were distressing. They sounded like a eulogy, made more unsettling by his ever-present saccharine smile. Everyone knew he was the money man, hired because of his contacts with capital markets and institutional investors. Todd could parrot the right words to describe the business and the cancer technology but never really understood them. So his words of praise for Longfellow and for all of the accomplishments of hard-working, dedicated employees rang hollow.

If only Liz could have spoken. Nearly everyone respected her as the visionary, as the cancer platform's creator, and as the company's driving force. Instead, they watched as she winced and grimaced during the insufferable speech. Her ashen face telegraphed the severity and perhaps hopelessness of the situation.

"So, because of all the negative and unfortunate factors I've just described," Todd said, obviously preparing to drop the bombshell, "it is with great sadness that I must announce our regretful decision to rightsize our workforce by sixty percent, effective immediately. The list of affected personnel will be forwarded to your email following the meeting, along with a document describing your two-week severance package and healthcare options. Furthermore, in order to share the burden, the senior officers have agreed to a fifty-percent salary cut until further notice."

An irate voice from the audience shouted, "That's your fucking idea of sharing the burden? That's easy for you after selling ten million in stock two years ago. Why not give that money back so we can all have a job!"

"Well, yes," Todd stammered, "I did sell a block of stock after the IPO restriction period ended, but I have two kids in college."

"Seriously? Ten million is a hell of a lot of tuition. What are we supposed to tell our families when they want to eat?"

Todd tried unsuccessfully to regain control, but the clamor of discontent kept growing. With a weak, "Thank you all for coming," he left the stage. After a moment of hesitation, the other executives followed.

Similar to everyone else, Anna clicked the email icon and waited for the layoff memo to appear. Surprisingly, she was not on the list. But there was an uproar in the auditorium as people discovered their names. Emotions ranged from anger to tears, both among the fired and the survivors.

Anna spent the next several hours consoling people, helping them pack and saying goodbyes. The gloomy situation worsened when the departing realized their computers and keycards had been deactivated. Senior management's lack of trust was the last ugly slap in the face. In disgust, several people not on the list quit in protest. She tried talking a few of them out of their impulsive decision, but failed and totally understood why. Jumping the sinking ship seemed preferable to drowning in misplaced loyalty.

As Anna was carrying a box to someone's car, she saw Liz across the street engaged in a tearful farewell to a long-term colleague, a woman who was start-up employee number nine. Liz mouthed the words, "My office."

Anna nodded in response.

Walking back into the building, up the elevator and down the hall lasted an eternity. Anna's mind raced with options of what to say and how to say it. Any words would fail to describe the eddy of torment. She mentally kicked herself for this pitiful opening line. "You wanted to see me?"

"Yes, come on in and close the door."

While sitting down, the dam of emotions burst. "Goddamn it, Liz, that was the cruelest thing I've ever seen in my career. All of those people who gave everything to this company were cast aside like garbage. Most of them were our friends, with families, and just like that" – she snapped her fingers – "they're jobless. I understand why it had to be done, but couldn't there have been a more humane way?"

"Yes," Liz responded solemnly, "and I advocated for a better approach, but lost."

"Then why aren't you as pissed off as I am?"

Following a deep sigh, Liz said, "Because I spent the whole weekend crying, cursing, shouting, and moaning until there was nothing left inside. I also promised to keep myself together today, regardless of what happened, because if people saw me give up hope, there might not be anything left. But trust me, I'm just barely hanging on by a thread."

"I'm sorry, Liz, I didn't mean to imply …"

"Stop it. I know exactly what you meant, and I agree. Regarding our people, I've arranged for a search firm to contact everyone within a couple of days. I'm confident most will be employed in a few weeks or a month in this town filled with biotech companies."

"That's good for them, but bad for Longfellow."

"I know. I doubt we can ever assemble a talented team like that again."

"You can and you will," Anna said, but internally agreed with her friend's assessment. She cautiously added, "I was surprised my name was not on the list."

"I thought you said you wanted to stay."

"I did. I do. But after Friday night, I doubted you'd ever want to talk with me again, let alone keep me here." Anna leaned forward with elbows halfway across the desk and fingernails digging into her forehead. "What I did was so incredibly stupid. I can't believe I did that. And worst of all, I betrayed your trust."

"Yes, you did," Liz said with a pained look while crossing her arms. "I can't tell you how much that hurt."

"I am so sorry."

"You know, I spent a lot of the weekend thinking about it, and what I don't understand is why you bothered testing George. I mean, if you didn't trust the guy, just stop dating him."

"Because I wasn't sure. It was only an inkling. And it's almost impossible to find a decent, employed, unmarried guy our age who's not divorced with kids or has lots of other baggage."

"That's your excuse?"

"That's my reason, but it's a shitty excuse," Anna said in self-admonishment.

"I totally agree."

"I hope you can forgive me."

Liz stared, as if contemplating an answer. The pause was excruciating. Then, with all seriousness, Liz said, "I will ... eventually." After another pause, she added with a smirk, "But right now, I consider you a giant pain in my ass."

They both laughed, which led to misty eyes. Their friendship was wounded, would take time to heal, but would remain intact. At least one good thing had come from this crappy day.

"Listen, Anna, I have to make this quick. The chiefs are meeting again in about ten minutes. When I told them you graciously offered to keep working without pay, most of them readily agreed. But I said that wasn't fair. So I advocated for a fifty percent pay cut like the rest of us. After a little bit of arm wrestling, they accepted. Is that okay with you?"

"Yes, of course. Thanks for going to bat for me. And again, I am so, so sorry."

"Now you're just being redundant. Get outta here." As Anna stood to leave, Liz asked, "By the way, did anything else happen with George?"

"Yes. I got an angry and threatening text from him Saturday saying he spent the night in the drunk tank."

With a sardonic tone, Liz said, "Couldn't happen to a nicer guy."

"Absolutely. So I blocked his number and, hopefully, that's the end of it. I'll see you tomorrow." Anna was almost out the door when she added, "One more trivial question. Should I cancel my upcoming cruise?"

"When is that again?"

"About two weeks out."

"Are you still planning on going with your friend from San Francisco?" Liz asked.

"Yes, Jessica and I haven't seen each other since I moved back to Boston five years ago. But I can cancel and stay here if you want."

"No, go. You deserve to have a little fun, sun and relaxation. I wish I were going with you."

"So what can I do in the meantime for you and the company?"

Liz thought for a couple of seconds. "Well, because we fired most of the HR staff, I really need your help to deal with people's grief over this whole mess, then motivate everyone to rethink their roles and work processes and get this ship sailing again. I'm going to focus on the revised clinical trials before the money runs out. And let's pray to God that Todd's inane smile can secure more funding or find a white knight buyer. With any luck, we can avoid the death penalty. Would you do that for me?"

"Absolutely! And thanks again, Liz. For everything."

The office had cleared out long before normal closing. Most likely Longfellow's surviving and ex-employees had taken refuge in local bars. Anna changed clothes in the locker room of the company gym, stuffed them into a backpack, and laced up pink Asics. Then she ran hard on the Broad Canal Walk.[28] The wind blowing in her face and the gorgeous skyline provided some solace while crossing the Longfellow Bridge.[29] Yet passing an Art Deco band shell[30] rekindled unpleasant memories of a date with George. The free outdoor concert had been great. George had been a big-headed bore. She accelerated along the Charles River Esplanade[31] at full speed as sweat began rolling off her brow and stinging her eyes.

Her chest pounded. She gasped deeply. Calf muscles ached and twitched. Each high-kick step reverberated through her body. A three-mile sprint might not be sufficient to clear her mind – a marathon would be needed to erase all troubled thoughts – but the intense workout was a welcome distraction.

When reaching her block of Back Bay brownstones,[32] Anna bent over with hands on her thighs until all vitals were regulated. After sipping water from a plastic bottle in her backpack, she walked toward home and up the stairs.

BITCH! The black letters were spray-painted across the door. A bullet had penetrated the bay window. She dared to look inside. Lying on the rug of the sitting room was Blue. The dog was in a pool of blood.

Anna screamed, looked for immediate threats, then ran and didn't stop until reaching a park bench along a lagoon[33] parallel to the esplanade. Every muscle shook with fear. Hyperventilation and a pounding heartbeat were suffocating. Fainting seemed imminent. She grieved over what happened to her loyal companion. It was impossible to believe Blue was dead.

When two patrolmen responded to her 911 call, she was slumped over the bench and still clutching the cell phone. They gave her a ride home, and while she sat in the back of the squad car, they entered with guns drawn. After declaring it safe, they waited until a detective arrived.

The investigator was obviously a seasoned veteran. The stocky woman – Sergeant O'Neill – seemed capable of wrestling down any criminal yet had a reassuring voice and affable mannerisms. Her first concern was Anna's emotional well-being followed by a genuine sympathy for the death of Blue.

Sergeant O'Neill then launched into a series of questions. Each one was asked with patience and eye contact along with copious notes. She wanted to hear Anna's account of the incident, inquired about the events of Friday night, asked about witnesses who could corroborate the story, promised to review Friday's police report, wanted to see Saturday's text message, and explored Anna's relationship with George. When she asked if there was any concrete evidence that George was the assailant, Anna remembered her neighbor had a Ring security system. The wide-angle camera had captured George walking toward the house, the gunfire and him running away.

"Well, it all seems pretty obvious to me," Sergeant O'Neill concluded while stuffing the notebook into a back pocket. "I'll make arrangements to arrest Mr. Henniker and bring him in for questioning."

"Do you think he'll be charged?"

"I won't make promises I can't keep, but I'm betting at the least we can get him for aggravated cruelty of a domestic animal, and maybe aggravated assault for discharging a weapon at the house. They're both serious felonies."

"Does that mean if convicted he'll never work in the financial industry again?"

"You're getting ahead of yourself, Ms. Monteiro. However, at the risk of bedazzling you with law enforcement and legal jargon, let's just say your buddy George is in a big pile of shit." The detective's smile was mischievous. "Any other questions before I go?"

"Yes, one. Am I safe staying in the house?"

"That's for you to decide. But if it were me, I'd stay with a friend or in a hotel until he's arrested. I'll call you with an update when that's done. Then understand he'll probably get out on bail. And it's impossible to know for sure what he'll do then. Most of the time after people are arrested, they suddenly go on their best behavior. But you never know for sure."

Chapter Eleven: Cambridge, Massachusetts

Photos 27–33

TWELVE

ANTWERP, BELGIUM
Tuesday

Their rendezvous point on Tuesday morning was at Grote Markt. The historic town square was surrounded by sixteenth-century guildhalls[34] and eighty-seven colorful flags decorating Antwerp City Hall. Chris wore the Sully Williams disguise. He saw his sister sitting transfixed on a bench dressed as Doris Mathews. The way Michelle's eyes darted, she seemed to be watching a little girl and boy playing tag around a fountain featuring a bronze statue of Silvius Brabo,[35] a legendary hero of Antwerp.

While approaching her, Chris ventured to ask, "Do they remind you of anyone?"

She said sadly, "If you mean us, then no. We were never that carefree and happy. And I'm jealous of their innocence."

What could he say to that? Yes, their childhood was consumed by fear and control. Their adult lives were worse. But there was no way out.

Michelle abruptly sat upright and looked at her brother. The melancholy moment was over. "What did you learn about Umar's defibrillator?"

"It's not good news."

"Of course it isn't," she said with a frown. "Tell me."

"It's doubtful we can control his ICD like you hoped. Although they are often connected to the internet by Wi-Fi or Bluetooth, we'd need to know the make, model and unique unit number or PIN. Our facilitator at Thanatos is clueless. We considered hacking into Umar's cardiologist in Cape Town, but decided the doctor's office probably can only monitor the ICD remotely, not control it. I also looked into ways to shut it off. Problem with that is a malfunction triggers an alarm."

"So you're telling me if we induce a heart attack, the ICD might save him?"

"Maybe."

"What's that mean?"

"An ICD can be deactivated at a cardiologist's office using a programming device, or when a medical-grade magnet is held directly on the chest. Because neither of those are an option, I've designed an electromagnetic mechanism using an N52 neodymium magnet."

"What's that?"

"Suffice it to say a 52 mega gauss oersteds magnet is one of the most powerful ones made. It should be strong enough to be disruptive at a distance yet will fit inside a hollowed-out camera. I hope to have it assembled later today. But I don't know how close I have to be for effectiveness or how long it has to be used before he dies."

"That's a lot of unknowns," she said with disappointment.

"I said it wasn't good news."

"And you were right."

"So what did you come up with?" Chris asked.

"This was a tricky one, but the pharmacist and I finally created a tasteless liquid that should neutralize the anticoagulants he's taking, along with a very heavy dose of antifibrinolytic drugs that promote blood clotting. Given Umar's medical history, we expect the combination will create a massive blood clot. When it breaks off in about four to six hours, he'll either have a debilitating stroke or sudden myocardial infarction. And the ICD will probably be defenseless against a blood-clot-induced heart attack."

Chris asked tentatively, "Does your concoction need to be ingested?"

"Of course," she answered curtly.

"Then that may be a problem."

"Why?" Michelle snapped with a cold stare.

"Umar is clearly paranoid about something – or should I say someone? – because his brutish bodyguard hangs over him like a shadow. The creep takes excessive precautions over Umar, as if protecting a head of state."

Her eyes narrowed. "But surely you've found some way to get discreet proximity, right?"

"No, not really," Chris had to admit. "The only people who get close are perspective clients and a regular hooker. I doubt we can leverage them."

"What about eating habits?"

"The man eats like a pig at the finest restaurants, but the bodyguard monitors everything. I even saw him swap entrées. I'm telling you, Michelle, there is no way to get close enough for your ingestible liquid."

"Goddamn it, Chris!" she yelled, then lowered her voice in seething anger while clenching her fists. "You had two days to figure this out. What the hell is the matter with you?" She turned away from her brother in disgust.

Chris said nothing to her uncharacteristic outburst. Long ago, he'd learned the best response was no response at all. Silence typically defused her agitation, especially when the anger was situational frustration.

After a long pause and a deep sigh, she faced Chris. "I'm sorry for snapping at you. I'm just tired. No, I take that back, I'm exhausted."

"No need to apologize," he said with compassionate reassurance. "I feel the same way." They were both chronically tired. Their two-month pace of nonstop silentcide commissions was unsustainable. In this profession, burnout could lead to fatal mistakes. Chris sensed they were both reaching that breaking point. They needed extended time to relax soon. Until then, they had to persevere.

In a calm voice, Michelle said, "Okay, so let me state the goal another way. We need something that's predictable, clandestine and happens within twenty-four hours. We're running out of time."

Chris gave the request considerable thought, was coming up with nothing, then offered weakly, "Well, there's only one thing I've found that sort of matches that description, but it doesn't involve eating or drinking."

"What?"

"This morning before breakfast, Umar stuffed dress shirts into a laundry bag, dropped them off at the front desk, and was assured they'd be returned tomorrow."

Michelle became animated. "That's it! Oh, this is so devious. It's brilliant!"

Chapter Twelve: Antwerp, Belgium

Photos 34–35

THIRTEEN

Antwerp, Belgium

Michelle's second plan to kill Johannes Umar was brilliant but challenging. There were plenty of risks and countless things that could go wrong. In short, this was no different than most attempts at undetected killing. The siblings created a to-do list, then left the bench at Grote Markt and walked in separate directions.

Chris returned to his hotel, filled a laundry bag with shirts, brought it to the front desk and asked if a same-day service was available. He was delighted to hear there wasn't. Then he asked when the dry cleaning would be returned the next day. The answer was two o'clock. To learn the exact procedures, Chris planted microcameras in the lobby, loading dock and service elevator.

His next focus was on the device to deactivate Umar's defibrillator. He revisited the basement workshop of an electromagnetic engineer who'd retired early to serve a ten-year prison sentence for burglary. Thanatos had found and vetted the outsider resource. The price to create the unit to Chris's specifications was exorbitant, but the workmanship seemed excellent and there were no questions asked. Chris returned to his hotel room and practiced how to handle the electromagnetic device inside a retrofitted camera. He was satisfied after mastering all of the operations blindfolded except one: turning it on. The engineer had warned him the unit would generate excessive heat and may burn out after one or two uses.

Michelle was equally busy. She began by forging prescriptions for three aliases, then filled them at several local pharmacies. Although this was against protocol, there wasn't time to return to Amsterdam. After acquiring a mix of class III antiarrhythmic drugs, she tested how to liquify them.

The goal was to cause drug-induced arrhythmias. She calculated how much exposure to the drug compound was required in order to exacerbate Umar's preexisting arrhythmia and trigger erratic heartbeats. When the ventricular fibrillation became severe enough, it should cause a sudden cardiac arrest. The operative word was *should*. The downside was Umar's implanted defibrillator might stop the V-fib and restore normal heart rhythm. It was essential to deactivate the ICD while he was having the heart attack.

Michelle's genius was the simplicity of the delivery mechanism: skin contact. Just as several drugs are dispensed by transdermal patches – nicotine, hormones, contraceptives – this concoction added to Umar's shirt collars would be steadily released by body heat and perspiration. The tighter the collar, the faster he would die.

Shortly before noon, Chris met Michelle in her hotel room,[36] a risk rarely taken but sometimes essential. She was monitoring a four-way split screen on the laptop. Three views were from the concealed microcameras in Umar's hotel. The fourth tracked Umar's movements around Antwerp. As Chris stripped off his disguise, he asked, "Do you mind if Sully is not invited to this powwow? He and I are sick of each other."

After nearly two hours, the siblings agreed to a plan. Chris would first moisten his fingertips with the liquified drugs using a travel-sized rollerball applicator. Then he would transfer the lethal concoction to Umar's shirt collars. To avoid personal exposure, he would wear Sister Margaret Mary's latex gloves after painting flesh tone over the purple-red veins so the hands didn't look so old.

Chris was pacing the room when Michelle pointed at the laptop. "Hey, look what Santa is delivering!"

"Ho, ho, ho," Chris said while looking at his watch – it was 1:46 – and then leaned over her shoulder.

The view from the hidden camera showed a doorman pushing a luggage cart with dry cleaning into the lobby of Umar's hotel. The bad news was each order was held together by a twist tie. That would restrict access to the shirts. The cart was staged in an isolated corner. Another fourteen minutes elapsed before a hotel employee pushed the cart toward the elevator, presumably to bring the dry cleaning to guest rooms.

"This is great," Chris said while slapping his hands. "We now know the procedure and general timeline, but we can't count on those fourteen minutes."

After repeatedly rehearsing every step while identifying potential problems and developing contingencies, they finally felt prepared but not confident. Confidence lowered awareness and bred mistakes.

Chapter Thirteen: Antwerp, Belgium

Photo 36

FOURTEEN

The next day, Chris – disguised as Ted Collins – had lunch in the hotel restaurant. Afterward, he had coffee delivered to the lobby, where he sat on an oversized couch facing the front door and pretended to work on his laptop. At one thirty, Michelle would be in position down the street. Her role was to alert him when the dry-cleaning truck arrived outside the hotel.

Each passing minute on the laptop's clock seemed like an eternity. The longer the wait, the more the brain conjured up risks. That triggered doubt, which led to anxiety, which impacted the pulse, breathing and nerves, which, if not controlled, would guarantee failure. He struggled to enter a mindset of serenity. He had just succeeded when there were two dings in his earbud.

It's game time!

Chris initiated a pretend call on his cell phone so he could nonchalantly survey the hotel lobby. Within three minutes, the doorman began pushing a luggage cart lined with dry cleaning into the foyer, then hustled back to hold the door open for Michelle. Her oversized sunglasses, long auburn wig and flamboyant makeup camouflaged her recognizable facial features. The ankle-length lavender dress was formfitting.

Clearly the doorman was infatuated, because instead of staging the cart in the remote area used yesterday, he followed behind

Michelle until she sat at the concierge's desk. He left the cart there. The location was a showstopper.

Unable to proceed, Chris stroked his Ted Collins beard in frustration. He assumed Michelle noticed the problem and would do something to run interference. Flipping her hair and pouring on the charm with the concierge were insufficient distractions. Time was ticking.

Two more long minutes passed before the concierge flashed Michelle a big grin and retreated through a door behind the desk. As Chris gripped the travel-sized bottle, the latex gloves made it difficult to loosen the tight cap. A rising pulse echoed in his ears. He coated his right fingers with the liquified drugs, glanced around the lobby, took two calming breaths, and approached the cart.

There were more dry-cleaning orders than the previous day. They were not logically arranged. Chris tried reading the attached handwritten receipts while quickly flipping through the clothes. He was vulnerable with his back to the lobby. Angst trickled through his bloodstream.

Finally, he found Umar's order. There were five shirts. He squeezed his fingers past the twist tie and moistened the first collar, then the second, then the third …

"May I help you, sir?" a male voice asked from behind.

Without flinching, Chris turned around and gave a disarming smile. The man was the same employee who removed the cart the day before. Chris calmly said, "I was just looking for my dry cleaning."

"Sir, that will be delivered to your room shortly," the lanky older man declared in an authoritarian tone as if the guardian of all of the hotel's procedures.

"Is there a problem here?" another voice asked from Chris's flank. The concierge had a scowl and a defensive stance, with arms across his chest and papers in one hand.

"No problem," Chris said, hoping to defuse the standoff. "I was just explaining to" – Chris glanced at the name tag – "to Lucas here that I was looking for my clothes."

Michelle tried intervening by telling the concierge she was in a hurry and wanted to finish soon. With a charismatic accent, she said, "Monsieur, je suis un peu pressé. Pourrions-nous terminer ici?"

"Oui, mademoiselle," he responded in French, then turned to confront Chris in rigid English. "Sir, I'm sure you understand why we are protective of our guests' belongings."

"Yes, that's an excellent policy," Chris said while thinking of how to make a graceful exit. "Would it help if I showed you my laundry receipt?"

The concierge said yes and then was distracted by Michelle's request. "Puis-je voir ces pages que vous avez photocopiées?" He sat down at his desk, flashed his best customer-service smile, and began explaining the photocopied material to her.

The lanky employee obviously disapproved of the policy exception. He eagle-eyed Chris searching through his wallet. Hopefully, he did not detect the latex gloves. Chris showed the receipt to the concierge, who then said to the employee, "It's okay, Lucas. Help Mr. Collins find his clothes." He wished Chris a good day before turning his attention back to Michelle. While Chris tipped Lucas five euros, he winked to his sister indicating the task was complete and she did not need to act as backup.

Step one of the plan was successful … sort of. Poisoning three out of five shirts wasn't bad, but it wasn't ideal. There was nothing to do now but wait and hope Umar wore the drugged shirts and had a heart attack in the next forty-eight hours.

From the laptop in his hotel room, Chris monitored Umar's movements in Antwerp's diamond district. The afternoon vigilance was boring until the end of the workday. Umar returned to his suite, showered, and put on different clothes for dinner. The frustration was that the closet was off-camera from the position of Umar's laptop, so Chris couldn't see if he unbundled his dry cleaning. They were all identical white dress shirts. Umar totally lacked a fashion sense.

Chris needed to immediately begin tracking Umar closely while carrying the electromagnetic camera device. So, while Umar pigged out on Kobe steak and an expensive wine, Chris ate Pringles with bottled water outside the restaurant.

The late-night shift began when Umar was ushered through the lobby by his bodyguard and then passed out on his bed fully clothed. The conscientious thing to do was to monitor Umar all night. At any sign of physical distress, Chris planned to run outside and aim the electromagnetic camera at the window of Umar's first-floor suite. But Chris was tired. He needed sleep. The compromise was to set the cell phone alarm every hour. The intermittent vigil was exhausting.

FIFTEEN

ANTWERP, BELGIUM

Thursday–Friday

arly the following morning, Sully Williams and Doris Mathews met at Het Steen,[37] an early thirteenth-century castle along Scheldt River. Chris was staring blankly at a bronze statue when his sister approached. He was too cranky to be cheerful. "Did you see Irene's love letter to us?" he asked with disgust.

Michelle's shoulders tensed as she cringed. "No."

"It said, and I quote, 'Get this damn thing done now, right now, or else! Then get back to the States. A potential new commission in Boston may start soon.'"

"Oh shit," she gasped.

"Yeah, that was my reaction too." After a pause of mutual irritation, Chris added, "Listen, I'm getting worried here. I can't see Umar's closet to know if he's wearing the tainted shirts. So I feel like we're playing pin the tail on the donkey. And even if he is, how do you know your drug concoction will produce a fatal V-fib?"

She lowered her head as if weighing Chris's concerns. "I'm confident my potion will do the trick, but it may need another twenty-four to thirty-six hours."

"That's assuming he's wearing the right shirts."

"Of course."

"I don't like the odds here, Michelle. Not at all. Tomorrow is Umar's last full day in Antwerp and the commission drop-dead date. We need a backup plan."

"Okay, I agree. If everything remains status quo tomorrow, let's consider spiking his food or drink during dinner. I know that's risky. And I'm also worried a blood clot from my first drug mixture might cause a crippling stroke, not a deadly heart attack. So the current plan is better."

"If it works," Chris said with lingering doubt.

◆◆◆

By the end of the day, the plan hadn't worked. Nor did Umar show signs of medical ailments during the night. Early Friday morning, Chris listened to Umar rant to hotel management that two of his shirts had brown stains on the collars. "No, goddamn it!" Umar shouted into the phone. "Taking the cost of dry cleaning off my bill is not enough. These are custom-made, Egyptian cotton shirts you people ruined. They cost four hundred euros each. I demand full replacement credit and nothing less."

The good news was Umar had worn two of the tainted shirts. The bad news was he might steer clear of the third one. Equally troubling, there was now potential evidence the shirts had been tampered with. This was a crappy way to start a morning.

The situation got worse as Chris watched his laptop's split screen. On the left was the man's repugnant yet giddy face and his obese body, naked from the waist up. On the right was Umar's email as he typed it.

The short message to his business associates in the Democratic Republic of the Congo was the diamond auction price far exceeded their expectations and the deal would close midday. Chris assumed whoever sponsored the commission wanted Umar dead before that happened. Too bad. Let Thanatos deal with any client dissatisfaction. Their task was to kill the man by the end of the day. That left sixteen hours.

Then some great news for a change. As Umar left his hotel suite, he received an alert from his cardiologist as a simultaneous email on his phone and PC, plus a text. The message read:

> The patient's ICD has detected an abnormal heart rhythm with a ventricular rate of above 120 beats (tachyarrhythmias). However, the ventricular tachycardia (VT) was normalized by antitachy-cardia pacing. It is doubtful the patient experienced symptoms of either event. However, out of an abundance of caution, the patient should come to the office soon or be examined by an equally qualified cardiac physician.

For the first time in days, Chris beamed as he deleted the alerts from Umar's email box and Google Messages. He then sent a note to Michelle from the encrypted laptop.

> Medical alert received and deleted. Plan working. Concurrent cat-and-mouse today. Acknowledge.

Fifteen seconds later, an animated yellow smiley face filled the screen. Chris hated that insipid emoji. This one made him laugh.

Simultaneous surveillance of a subject was always tricky. The technique required moving in divergent paths so they would never be seen together or by the target. The task was complicated without radio communications. But after years of practice, they had developed a sixth sense for each other's patterns. And monitoring the ever-changing dots on the GPS maps on their cell phones was essential.

But this morning was perplexing. After a leisurely breakfast, Umar's actions were unpredictable for the first time all week. He wasn't rushing from one scheduled meeting to the next. Instead, he was acting like a tourist. Umar and his bodyguard strolled along Meir,[38] the city's premier pedestrian shopping street in the heart of the fashion district. They ogled the façade of Opera Antwerpen,[39] the performance arts center. They explored Antwerpen-Centraal,[40] the "Railway Cathedral," considered to be among the world's most ornate train stations. Even more bizarre, they bought tickets to the adjacent Zoo Antwerpen.[41] What the hell was he doing?

After a gluttonous lunch, Umar entered a building in the Diamond Quarter for his one meeting of the day. More waiting. More impatience. Chris was getting annoyed and the Sully Williams disguise was getting hot.

Two hours later, Umar emerged. He was ecstatic. He vigorously shook the bodyguard's hand, followed by a dramatic fist pump. Obviously, the deal had been consummated and his brain was orgasming with dopamine.

Suddenly, Umar blanched. His celebratory smile turned ashen. He clutched his chest, staggered, grabbed a bicycle stand for support, and collapsed. The sickening thud was heard from across the street.

While the rotund body spasmed on the ground, Chris cautiously moved in. His senses were on high alert while calmly holding the camera down along his leg. He watched the bodyguard's frantic yet futile attempts to help his boss.

Bystanders started noticing the unconscious man. Some hurried away. Chris mingled among those who gathered to watch. His finger slid up to the shutter-release button while feigning a horrified expression. He inched forward. Two teens began filming the incident on their cell phones while the bodyguard dialed 1-1-2 for emergency assistance. Chris was within a few feet when he started the electromagnetic device.

The damn thing started humming.

"Help!" Chris shouted to cover the noise while continuing to press the trigger and discreetly aiming the telephoto lens toward Umar. "We need help over here. Medical emergency! Get some help! This man needs a doctor. Someone help! Please help!"

Unexpectantly, the teens stared at their phones in confusion. The bodyguard cursed at his. It took Chris a second to realize the electromagnetic device had shorted out their phones. *Shit!* He pretended not to notice while continuing to yell for help and pushing the button.

"I'm a nurse," Michelle said breathlessly as she ran up wearing the Doris Mathews disguise. "How can I help?"

What the hell is she doing? Then it dawned on him. Maybe he was in trouble. She probably couldn't warn him because his earbud may have also blown out. One look into her eyes confirmed a danger. But where was it?

As Michelle dropped to her knees and began administering chest compressions, Chris spotted a tiny epidural needle extending from his sister's sleeve. Everyone watched her heroics except one suspicious brute. He was tall, muscular, had a bulge under his suitcoat, and was staring at Chris. The feeling was ominous. Chris released the trigger and stepped back.

About a block or two away, a high-pitched oscillating sound was moving closer, no doubt the police or an ambulance driving toward the scene. Prudence suggested disappearing before they arrived, but he couldn't abandon Michelle. He took a few pretend photos to try legitimizing the camera, then waited, watched and felt the potential adversary's unyielding glare.

After another minute, Michelle checked Umar's carotid artery, looked dejected, stood up and sadly said to the bodyguard, "I'm afraid your friend is dead."

That was the confirmation. The commission was a success. Now they had to find their own way to escape.

Chris shook his head as if saddened by the tragedy, lingered for another second, then moved away. From behind, he heard the assailant gruffly push past onlookers and begin following. Survival instinct surged.

Chris decided running would confirm his guilt while walking might suggest his innocence and prevent an attack. He calculated the likelihood of being shot along a busy street. He looked for exits, contemplated hijacking a car, and considered charging the man. He weaved among pedestrians, trying to always keep someone between him and the thug. He turned a corner, then another. The distance between them remained constant, step by step. The sinister man was unrelenting yet cautious in his pursuit. A lethal inflection point was imminent. *Do something or die!*

Up ahead was the mouth of an alley. Chris weighed the odds of sprinting down it. That risked being shot in the back. Better to dodge around the building and ambush the assailant. Every muscle tightened. His breathing slowed. His pulse lowered. He rehearsed a flurry of deadly moves.

When Chris reached the alley, there was movement in his peripheral vision. He aborted his plan and kept walking.

Three seconds. Five seconds. Seven seconds.

The sound of exploding bone was brutal. A muffled scream preceded the crash of a large body dropping to the sidewalk. Chris turned. Michelle was gripping a long bloody pipe, prepared to strike again. Another blow wasn't needed. Hollow eyes stared from a crushed skull.

"There's another guy looking for us," Michelle warned as she dropped the pipe. While hustling toward a dumpster in the alley, she removed the Doris Mathews facemask as Chris pulled at his Sully beard, mustache and wig. She stepped out of the oversized dress and unfastened prosthetic breasts beneath a bra. Chris discarded his shirt, untucked a T-shirt above his shorts and helped her out of the inflated bodysuit, revealing a summer blouse and cutoff jeans. The disguises and camera were hidden behind trash bags when footsteps approached the other end of the alley.

Michelle slapped Chris across the face. "I can't believe you screwed my sister!" she screamed. "You're a bastard!"

"And you're a bitch!" Chris yelled back as a man holding a gun stopped to watch the argument and chuckled before walking away.

They maintained their loud altercation for another thirty seconds, then ended the charade with a smile.

"Did you have to slap me that hard?" Chris asked. "That kinda hurt."

The siblings clung to each other with relief. Michelle was trembling.

Chapter Fifteen: Antwerp, Belgium

Photos 37–41

SIXTEEN

Anna Monteiro closed the hotel room door, kicked off her heels, threw the black-and-white houndstooth blazer over the bed, and sank into the couch. The week had been hellish.

Since the layoffs on Monday, the atmosphere at Longfellow Bio-Sciences was dismal. Some surviving employees were silent sufferers, others chronic complainers. Lack of motivation and abundant stress seemed universal. There was also growing evidence that organizational changes were being sabotaged.

Anna had spent most of the last four days listening to employees' worries and offering encouragement without sounding saccharine, Pollyannaish, or overpromising. The balancing act was challenging. She often chastised herself for falling short. In the interim, little meaningful work was getting accomplished. The company was crippled.

Anna's personal life was equally tumultuous. Contrary to what Sergeant O'Neill implied on Monday evening, George Henniker was not arrested until yesterday morning. By midafternoon, he was released on his own recognizance without bail. She was able to secure an ex parte temporary restraining order, but only after answering the judge's embarrassing questions about her relationship and intimacy with George. The judge then told her the restriction expired in five days. Totally worthless. A hearing date to consider a longer period was set for twenty-five days out. That left twenty days without a legal safeguard, and then she would have to confront George and his highfalutin attorney in court. The system seemed designed to protect the abuser, not the victim, especially a female victim. Where the hell was justice?

Why had she ever started dating him in the first place, let alone slept with him once? Her gut had told her George was wrong from the start. But loneliness had overridden logic. Idiot! *Look at the damn mess that happened by ignoring your instincts. You deserve better than George — much better. Lesson learned: having no one is vastly superior to being with the wrong man. Don't keep making the same mistake.*

Anna surveyed the overpriced, austere hotel room. The carpet was grungy, the wallpaper faded, dust covered too many surfaces, and God only knew what had happened on the stained bedspread. Anxiety mixed with claustrophobia. She could not spend the weekend here. Home might not be safe from George, but it had to be better than hiding in this hotel.

An hour later, she dragged a suitcase up the steps of the Back Bay brownstone, hesitated at the sight of the bullet hole in the window, then entered. A faint odor of decay assaulted her nose. The bloodstain on the sitting room rug was an ugly shade of brown. Memories of boxing up Blue's remains and bringing her to the vet for cremation were gloomy. Anguish consumed her senses and offered no hope for release anytime soon. Anna wanted to cry.

She dropped the luggage, retreated to the bedroom and pulled the curtains before turning on the lights. Hiding beneath a gold-and-blue comforter on the canopy bed initially seemed appealing, but it was way too early to sleep. It was doubtful she could sleep anyway. A hot shower helped. Yet the longer the water cascaded, the more her mind drifted toward unsolvable thoughts. The bathroom mirror wasn't foggy enough to hide the forlorn expression, nor could makeup conceal the feelings. Her favorite Lululemon blue leggings and loose-fitting white tee were comfortable but not comforting. Nothing offered the needed solace.

Get a grip on yourself. Stop wallowing in self-pity. Do something.

Anna dialed Jessica on the cell phone, hoping her friend in San Francisco would just be getting off work. Hearing her bubbly voice always brightened any mood. Soon, they would be laughing about Jessica's endless antics, or the mischief her four-year-old son had caused, or the ridiculous things common acquaintances had done in the bank's marketing department where they had previously worked together. Best of all, they could jabber and gush about the fun they would have during the upcoming cruise.

"Hi, this is Jessica Daly. Please leave a message."

After Anna tapped the red stop button, she considered calling her ex. They met at the University of Pennsylvania while she was getting her master's from Annenberg School for Communication and Paul was studying at Wharton for an MBA; he never finished. His graduation present to her was an engagement ring. After a grand wedding at the Cathedral of the Holy Cross in Boston, she'd moved to San Francisco. Their marriage was initially great, then slowly deteriorated for eight years until he cheated with the neighbor's husband. One of Paul's best qualities was listening when she needed an empathetic ear. He didn't always have realistic suggestions, but he would patiently let her vent without judgment and provide emotional support. She could use that right now. *No, it's unfair to impose.*

"It's me," Anna said when her mother answered the phone.

"Hi, honey," Donna said with a delightful lilt. "It's great hearing your voice. What's up?"

"Nothing special, just wanted to say hi. Where are you and Dad now?"

"We're on a ferry headed to Martha's Vineyard. We're spending the weekend at the Johnsons' cottage. It's actually a gorgeous generational estate. You remember Betty and Ron?"

"Oh, sure," Anna said without having a clue. "Say hello to them for me."

"Will do. How's work going?"

"Going great," Anna said, trying to sound upbeat, "and getting closer to ending cancer every day."

"I'm so proud of you, honey," her mom said with genuine sincerity. Then, with a hint of concern, Donna probed, "But your dad said your company's having some troubles lately."

"Yes, normal young biotech kind of challenges, but we're managing."

"That's good," Donna said, sounding relieved. "I'm sure you and your friend can handle anything." That subject was done in her mom's mind. "Have you talked to your brothers lately?"

"No, been too busy."

"Well, I'm sure they'd both enjoy talking with you. Give them a call. Say, listen, honey, the ferry is nearing the Vineyard. I'm sure your dad is waiting for me in the car. Gotta run. It was great hearing from you."

Despite the brevity of the conversation, Anna felt better. Her mom was typically optimistic, complimentary and supportive with one major flaw: she shared everything with Dad. He had always been a quick-thinking, fast-acting and logical top executive, whether as president of a life insurance company or a father dealing with family matters. To him, wealth was his personal scorecard for tracking success and equated to family security. It too often seemed money was his proxy for fatherly love. He hadn't changed in retirement. If Dad knew Anna's problems, he would remind her of his advice against working for a start-up – "the odds of success are minuscule" – and her questionable taste in men – "find someone who wants to love a woman and not another man." Anna stopped being Daddy's little girl at puberty. Instead, she was treated like a third child who wasn't a male.

Anna cautiously pulled back the bedroom curtain. She would love to go for a run on the Charles River Esplanade. But she feared a confrontation with George. There was no telling what he might do next, despite the court order.

SEVENTEEN

Sunday

N icollet Island Inn[42] was a late-Victorian-era boutique hotel encircled by the Mississippi River within view of downtown Minneapolis. The outdoor patio beneath a flawless summer sky was the perfect setting to forget two months of European silentcide commissions and spend the first morning home since returning from Antwerp. Michelle was savoring every moment of the charming tranquility as she sipped a cappuccino and nibbled on a French pastry – the first of five courses served during a leisurely Sunday brunch.

As she read a mindless novel, a light breeze tousled her sandy-brown hair and rippled across a colorful Bohemian blouse. It felt wonderful to be herself. Only light makeup instead of heavy disguises. An empty schedule instead of incessant planning and monitoring. Relaxed instead of tense. Alive not dead. This was nirvana.

She did not glance at the waiter while he placed a glass of orange juice on the wrought iron table. "Thank you," she said absently.

"You're welcome, donkey breath."

Startled by the expression, she looked up. The man was about forty with a six-foot, solid build. His engaging facial features were accented by short, wavy black hair and a week-old mustache and beard. What Michelle recognized immediately were the deep-set sparkling eyes and mischievous grin.

"Kevin?" she exclaimed.

"You're the last person to ever call me that, but yes."

"Oh my god!" she blurted, then jumped up and threw her arms around the former roommate from foster care in Philadelphia. "I thought you were dead," she whispered in his ear as emotions of joy made her misty-eyed.

"I thought you were, too," he said while extending the incredible reunion hug. "It's great to see you, Sarah."

"The name is Michelle now. Michelle Barton."

"I know, but you'll always be Sarah to me," he said affectionately. "But you've changed a little bit since I saw you last."

She didn't detect suggestive overtones, only a genuine delight to be together after twenty-six years. Rather than declare how a scrawny teenager had transformed into a very attractive man, she asked, "You don't work here, do you?"

"No, I bribed the waiter so I could deliver your orange juice and surprise you."

"Is it safe to drink?" She giggled.

"If you mean is it spiked, the answer is yes ... with lots of vodka. So, if you drink too many, you might pass out," he said with a wink.

"God, I missed you," she said. "How did you find me?"

"The same way you and Danny – or should I say Chris? – were trained."

Michelle stood inert. His single sentence spoke volumes. He was probably an assassin, too. He nodded subtly as if reading her thoughts.

"We've gotta go," she said in a hurry while picking up the book and sunglasses.

"What's wrong?" he asked.

"Nothing. But there is so much to talk about and we can't do it here."

"Don't be silly. I'll join you for brunch and then we can really talk later."

"What safe topics can we discuss with all these people around? The weather? No, let's go," she said, then summoned the waiter, apologized for having to leave, and gave him fifty dollars. After explaining there was nothing wrong with the service, the waiter returned with the change and two red Solo cups: one empty and the other filled with a large screwdriver.

They began a leisurely walk across a late-nineteenth-century truss bridge[43] spanning the Mississippi toward the picturesque path along historic Main Street Park. Whenever a jogger, biker or pedestrian neared, they talked in hushed voices.

There were so many questions that it was difficult to know where to start. Michelle started at the beginning. "I assume you also have a different identity?"

"Yes, my name is Ansel Meehan, which means honorable and divine protection. Ironic, huh? I live in downtown Baltimore because many of my assignments are along the East Coast."

"Do you like it there?"

"Not in the least, but that's where they sent me. They never asked my opinion."

"So what happened to you after that fateful breakfast?"

"I was shipped off to an Amish farm, with two other orphans my age, for a decade of training courtesy of Irene Shaw."

"In Lancaster County? That's where Chris and I were."

"No, in York County."

"We probably lived only a few miles apart," Michelle said. "So close, yet so far away. Say, did you ever run across a guy named Lionel Jørgensen?"

"You mean Preceptor? Yeah, he was evil incarnate. Despite all I learned from that guy, I've taken him off my Christmas card list."

"We stayed at his farm," Michelle said. "I'll bet we shared a lot of the same instructors over the years."

"And learned similar skills," Ansel added.

"So you're part of Thanatos?" It was more of a statement than a question.

"No, what's that?"

Michelle hesitated. Maybe she shouldn't disclose too much. But this conversation would go nowhere unless they were totally open, so she risked explaining, "We specialize in silentcide commissions, which are undetected killings."

"Interesting," Ansel said, as if thinking about what silentcide techniques entailed. "No, our group is called Phonoi. It's named after the Greek god of violent death. Our killing missions are designed to send a strong message or warning to others."

"That sounds ominous." Michelle cringed at the thought of her older foster brother – the guy she revered as an eight-year-old – had become a violent assassin. Then she considered the irony of her reaction. They had been equally brainwashed to do similar jobs. Neither of them ever had a choice. She asked, "How many people and divisions do you think Irene controls?"

"I have no idea, but it's scary to think about, right? Regardless, that she-devil has an iron fist over every minute detail, despite being in her early seventies. She'll never retire."

For about fifteen minutes, they shared Irene Shaw stories. Most of the encounters were traumatizing. The topic could have stretched on for hours. The conclusion was they were both still terrified by her with no hope of escaping her authoritative rule.

Michelle switched topics by asking about their foster parents. "What ever happened to the Millers?"

"Good question," Ansel said. "I tried tracking them down once, but they disappeared. Maybe dead, but probably moved to a different city under different names. Regardless, they clearly worked for Irene."

"I've often wondered if my stepfather worked for her too. But he was a thug, not a professional."

"Maybe he did," Ansel surmised. "I'm guessing Irene's recruiting techniques got more sophisticated over time. You know, like abducting and training young orphans. Or maybe she inherited the business and improved it. Whatever, she clearly has an efficient organization now. And I suspect it generates a fortune."

Michelle often thought about the money Irene earned while they took all the risks. She resented it; obviously Ansel concurred. But why complain about something you couldn't change?

"You said you grew up with a couple of other guys," she said. "Do you work with them now?"

"Sometimes. But one of them specializes in international jobs. The other one – a woman – washed out. She couldn't handle the stress, so they made her a facilitator. In fact, she's the one who electronically tracked you down as a favor to me."

"Please thank her for me."

"I will. And from what I gathered from the limited files I read, you and Chris are exceptional at what you do." His inflection suggested he was proud of his foster siblings.

Ansel's statement sparked a long conversation about the type of work each of them did, the close calls they had experienced, plus several funny things that had happened. They never disclosed target names. Toward the end, Michelle snuck a peek at Ansel's biceps and forearms. They were ripped, yet his grip on the bridge railing seemed gentle.

"This is absolutely gorgeous," he said while admiring the panoramic view.

"That's why I love coming here," Michelle said. "We're standing on the Stone Arch Bridge,[44] built for the railroad in the late nineteenth century. Over there are the upper dam and locks of Saint Anthony Falls,[45] the only natural waterfall on the Mississippi."

"Look how the sunshine glistens off the water," Ansel said, paused, then asked a totally unexpected question. "So are you happy, Michelle?"

"What?"

"You heard me," he said while making eye contact.

"I am right now, yes. This is the first time I've been able to talk with anyone other than Chris and just be myself."

He thought about her answer, then asked, "Do you know who that is anymore?"

Michelle was taken aback. "Oh wow. Wow! That's a really deep question." She tried deflecting the sudden seriousness with humor. "Have you come to be my prince charming and sweep me off my feet?"

"That's hardly appropriate for my little foster sister. Besides, I make it a policy to never date someone who could kill me in my sleep and have no regrets." There was that boyish grin again. How she missed his smile.

They continued walking as Ansel asked probing questions about her mindset. She had contemplated many of the same questions in the past but always suppressed the honest answers. Now she readily expressed her feelings. Maybe it was the vodka talking. Although she didn't always like hearing the truth bubbling from her heart-shaped lips, each statement added to an inner calm. And Ansel was a tremendous listener.

"You missed your true calling," Michelle said.

"How so?"

"You should have been a psychologist."

"I'll add that to my LinkedIn qualifications."

Michelle studied his expression to see if he was kidding. A quick laugh confirmed he was.

A block ahead was her high-rise condo[46] building at the edge of downtown Minneapolis. Perhaps she had subconsciously led Ansel toward it this entire time. The last couple of hours had been amazing. Emotions were swirling, but she couldn't decipher them. Did she suddenly want a friend, another brother, a companion, or a romantic partner? Michelle had not dated a man in over two years and had never talked with one so openly. Long ago, she had dismissed having a serious male relationship as a whimsical folly. Amorous emotions were impractical in this business and an occupational hazard. But maybe not now.

"Over there is where I live," Michelle said, pointing. "Would you like to come up and I'll make us something to eat? You must be starving."

"Thanks for the invite," Ansel said, "but I'm going to have to pass."

"Are you sure? You'll love the view." She wondered if that statement could be misinterpreted.

"Sorry, but I really need to get back to my hotel." His regret seemed sincere. "I'm, ah …" He hesitated. "I'm working this week and have homework to do."

"You're working in my backyard?"

"Yes, but it's not your kinda job."

His words reminded her again that Ansel was an assassin, not the boy she had shared a home with. This time together had been nothing more than a fleeting oasis. But she wanted more. "Will I see you again?" she asked, sounding a bit vulnerable.

Ansel held her outstretched hands. Her fingers were dwarfed in his comforting palms. "I'd like that," he said with a melancholy expression, "but I'm not sure when … or if we can."

That wasn't the answer she wanted to hear. "Are you going to see Chris while you're in town?" she asked. "He'd love to see you. Better yet, let's get the Three Amigos back together. How's that sound?"

"That would be great, really great," he said, then his enthusiasm disappeared. "But I can't. I've already taken a huge risk seeing you. Imagine how Irene would react if she knew we were together comparing notes. We'd both be in danger. So please, maybe it's for the best if you didn't mention today to Chris."

Michelle had rarely kept a secret from her brother, especially one like this. Their lives were an open book. She began wondering if these hours of happiness had been worth knowing Ansel was alive yet potentially never seeing him again.

"Come here," he said while extending his arms.

She clung to Ansel's shoulders and did not want to let go.

Chapter Seventeen: Minneapolis, Minnesota

Photos 42–46

EIGHTEEN

SAINT PAUL, MINNESOTA

Sunday–Monday

S unday was bliss. After sleeping in late, Chris Davis dawdled at the grocery store, did laundry, cooked a fat juicy burger on the charcoal grill while sipping a Summit Extra Pale Ale, and dirtied his fingernails by puttering in the garden. Then he mowed the small front lawn even though a neighbor kid had done a reasonably good job of maintaining it during his European travels. The smell of fresh grass clippings on a summer afternoon was calming. The mindless activities were beginning to camouflage months of tension.

Chris lived in a modest Highland Park neighborhood of Saint Paul.[47] When the near-identical, two-bedroom ramblers were built in the early 1950s, newly married parents gave birth to future baby boomers. Today, the houses were still great starters for young couples or places to downsize for retirees, but they also attracted some late-Gen X and early millennial singles like himself. The setting provided safe, unpretentious, and discreet cover.

Chris had just turned off the lawn mower when a door opened across the street. A yellow Lab came bounding out. Rascal's ears were flapping and his tail was wagging while racing toward Chris's open arms. After skidding to a stop, the dog bathed his face with affection. "Good boy," Chris said, causing Rascal to wiggle more. "I missed you too. Such a good dog. Okay, okay, that's enough."

Rascal began sniffing the pockets of Chris's shorts, nudged the one containing two dog biscuits, then spun with excitement. *If only all of life were this simple*, Chris thought as he pulled out the dog treats.

Rascal was mesmerized.

"Sit," he commanded. "Stay." The dog was panting with his eyes crossed as Chris placed a biscuit on the moist black nose. "Get it!" In a well-practiced move, the Lab snapped back his head, caught the biscuit midair, snarfed it down, then repeated the routine. "That's all I've got, buddy," he said. "How about a game of fetch?"

Chris had thrown a tennis ball for the second time when approached by Nicole, a smart yet shy software programmer who had moved in a decade ago, shortly after he did. Nicole had never married and, from what he could tell, rarely dated. She had hinted at her availability a few times. They usually talked in the yard, had shared several summertime beers, and Chris had taken her out for a fortieth birthday dinner. Otherwise, they maintained a friendly neighbor relationship and shared a mutual affection for her dog.

"Hey there, stranger," Nicole said with a pleasant smile framed by shoulder-length black hair. "I thought you had skipped town for good." She seemed a bit pale for midsummer – probably too much time in front of a computer screen – yet she always had a fresh, wholesome expression behind oversized eyeglasses. He probably would try dating her if life were different, but knew he could never have a relationship with anyone while in this business.

"Nope, just a long trip this time," he said while tossing the tennis ball again. "I really hate being gone during part of a fleeting Minnesota summer."

Nicole wanted full details of his recent destinations. Years ago, she claimed to have never traveled out of state, so she lived vicariously through his globetrotting. He described several famous European cities, none of which he had visited in years. Lying came easy. He had mastered the skill during years of training. Most important was to remember every lie.

After a pleasant half-hour conversation, Chris went inside, popped open another beer, watched a film on Netflix, and laughed at the action scenes of an assassin being chased by endless black-ops guys who couldn't shoot straight and conveniently died in seconds. Reality would make a boring movie.

♦♦♦

In the morning, Chris had a stiff neck when he woke up on the couch. The TV was still on. He took a long shower, didn't bother shaving, put on relaxed shorts and a Minnesota Twins T-shirt, and ate a simple breakfast of fruit over bran cereal. Then he reluctantly sat down at his desk in the study. His blood pressure rose as the laptop booted. After the retina camera recognized his irises, he hesitated, then clicked on the Thanatos icon. There were two phantom messages.

The first was a detailed assessment of the demise of Johannes Umar. The list of criticisms was long, including breaches of protocol, using unsanctioned pharmacists, their habit of waiting until the waning hours of a drop-dead date to complete a commission, and carelessly leaving a dead body with a crushed skull on an Antwerp street. These actions were not commensurate with silentcide principles. As a result, their pay was cut twenty percent, along with a stern warning of larger reductions if performance did not return to expected standards. Finally, because their electromagnetic device had destroyed their cell phones, the replacement costs would be subtracted from their compensation.

Chris was furious! No doubt Irene Shaw had written every word of this insulting memo. He visualized her self-righteous face, grating tone and conceited superiority. He also felt her iron-fisted control. Over twenty-five years ago, he had concluded the only way to escape Irene Shaw was by dying. Some days, that seemed like a viable and maybe even attractive option. But if he ever chose that path, Michelle would suffer the same fate. Chris would never let that happen to his sister.

After two hours in the basement exercise room, he returned to the desk and dared to read the second memo. They had a new, three-week commission starting immediately. Travel and hotel details would be forwarded by midmorning. Michelle had already confirmed receipt of the instructions and suggested a rendezvous place and time after arrival in Boston.

Chapter Eighteen: Saint Paul, Minnesota

Photo 47

NINETEEN

After Chris checked into a Back Bay hotel wearing the Ted Collins disguise, he dutifully spent an hour reviewing the preliminary files of their next target: Anna Monteiro. The details were unusually sparse. Half-Brazilian, half-Italian, the forty-one-year-old woman had an exceptional education at exceptional universities before getting married, spending eight years at Wells Fargo in San Francisco, then moving back to Boston after an uncontested divorce and no children. Her social media accounts were rarely used.

She was the only daughter of Mr. and Mrs. Upper One Percent. Her retired father was a generous philanthropist. Her mother was active in charitable nonprofits. The oldest brother was a partner at Boston Consulting, the middle son a vice president at Bank of America, and both had lovely wives with adorable kids. Such a squeaky-clean family was an anomaly in Chris's business.

He skipped over Anna's Health file – that was Michelle's domain – and studied the Business and Industry files. That's when he saw the potential red flag. Longfellow BioSciences had just experienced a catastrophic drop in stock value followed by a massive layoff. Numerous analysts predicted the company's collapse within the year. This seemed to be an ample motive for a silentcide commission. But why would the head of marketing be the target?

Still dressed as Ted Collins, Chris hustled to Boston Public Garden,[48] a twenty-four-acre greenspace in the heart of the city, adjacent to the larger Boston Common park, and a couple of blocks from the Charles River Esplanade.

Michelle was waiting for him at the Swan Boats dock. The sightseeing pontoon rides had closed hours earlier. She had on a bland version of her tourist disguise: a floppy hat over an auburn wig, large sunglasses and a long loose-fitting dress ending above worn sandals. Few people would notice her and no one would remember. It was eight o'clock and the sun was setting as they walked around a four-acre pond.

"Welcome to Beantown," Michelle said with refreshed energy. "How was your weekend?"

"Wonderful," Chris answered, "and then Irene's memo ruined everything. Do you believe the audacity of that woman?"

"Let it go," Michelle advised with a comforting hand on his shoulder.

He kept venting. "I wasn't expecting gratitude, or even thoughtless platitudes, but Irene's endless rant followed by a dock in pay was outrageous!"

"Irene is just being Irene. What else do you expect?" It was a rhetorical question. "Okay, if you're done now …" She waited a second until he begrudgingly nodded. "Then give me your impressions of this target."

"I'm totally confused," Chris said, still sounding irritated about the incendiary memo. "Rather than our typical sleazeball, Anna Monteiro seems more like a rich Pollyanna, pun intended. The only flare I saw was the financial collapse of the company where she works, but I don't see the connection with her. And did you notice there was no Hate file this time?" A missing hate file had only occurred twice during their career. "I suspect it's difficult to paint an ugly picture of people dedicated to curing cancer." He let that observation sink in, then asked, "Did you learn anything from her Medical file?"

"So far, nothing. It was empty."

"That's great," Chris said in frustration. "Either our Thanatos facilitator has totally dropped the ball this time, or there is something very clandestine going on."

"Does a bullet hole qualify?"

"What's that mean?"

"Before coming here," Michelle said, "I placed a microcamera outside of her house and saw a bullet hole in the front window."

"That's interesting," Chris said. "Maybe someone tried a DIY murder before hiring a professional. We've got a lot to learn. I've asked the facilitator to get a trojan horse into Longfellow's computer system so we can read this woman's office files. We also need to find a way into her phone and laptop. The faster the better. Let's get this one done soon so we can go home."

For an hour, they planned a dual cat-and-mouse surveillance for the next day. As their meeting ended, Chris suggested they grab a beer at the original Cheers bar[49] across the street.

"I'm not sure Irene would approve," Michelle said cautiously.

"And I'm not sure I care," he said, then flashed a whimsical smile while quoting Norm Peterson. "It's a dog-eat-dog world, Michelle, and I'm wearing Milk-Bone underwear."

•••

Early the next morning, Michelle was positioned near Anna Monteiro's house while Chris was stationed at Kendall Square within view of Longfellow BioSciences. He tracked his sister's movements on the phone GPS during her surveillance from the Back Bay to Cambridge. His first sighting of Monteiro was favorable. She was small – maybe five foot three – with a determined stride. She was wearing a black blazer and matching slacks with white sneakers. No doubt her dress shoes were in the backpack. She looked professional, yet also kinda cute. Her intelligent brown eyes accented her olive complexion. This was an accomplished person.

When Monteiro passed her office building, Chris hoped she was going to the coffee shop behind him. He rushed inside, sat at a table and used a Wi-Fi Pineapple device concealed in a backpack to execute a man-in-the-middle hack. As Monteiro waited in line, her phone auto-connected to an evil twin access point that mimicked the coffee shop's Wi-Fi hotspot. Then he quickly devised and sent a thirty-percent-off coupon for the next coffee purchase in appreciation for being a loyal customer. When she clicked it, the coupon "malfunctioned" while successfully installing a rootkit. The electronic ruse gave him access to her sensitive information without leaving a trace.

Moments later, Chris and Michelle briefly shared a bench at a small park across the street and agreed to retreat to their respective hotels. With any luck, the facilitator would soon harvest and analyze Monteiro's phone data and maybe also gain mirror control over her other devices. They planned another rendezvous in four hours.

In the afternoon, the siblings met in front of the impressive, late eighteenth-century Massachusetts State House[50] and admired the golden dome glistening in the sun. Then they meandered through the tree-lined paths in Boston Common.[51]

Michelle delivered her report first. "Okay, so unfortunately, this Monteiro woman does not have any medical maladies to exploit except an occasional bad back, which is treated bi-weekly by a chiropractor. Her only prescription is for oral contraceptives. She drank plenty of bottled water during her walk this morning, so that's one possible delivery point. The coffee shop is another, assuming that's a daily routine. But it has to happen by Friday because she flies to Miami Saturday morning for a five-day cruise."

"No problem," Chris said with confidence.

"An absolute problem," Michelle protested. "Working that fast causes mistakes."

"Not if we join her on the cruise."

Michelle stared at her brother. "What?"

"Sure, I've already booked our flights and two cabins. You should've gotten a confirmation email."

"That's ridiculous," she said while looking at her phone.

"Not really. We said in Rome we needed a vacation, so this is it. We can justify it to Thanatos because the cruise is a large chunk of the commission timetable and it gives us plenty of access to her. Besides, deaths in foreign countries and aboard ships are poorly investigated. And hell, I don't care if they reimburse us for the expense. We deserve a few days of sightseeing and pampering. I'll pay for everything if needed."

A crease spread across Michelle's forehead. "But it looks like the reservations are in our real names. Why would you do that?"

"Because I'm tired of slinking around every day in a disguise. I just want to relax for a change. Besides, killing this Goody-Two-shoes should be easy compared to our normal targets."

"Irene definitely won't approve of this."

With a defiant stance, Chris said, "I really don't care. Irene already yells at us when we do everything right, so what difference will it make? Look, if you want to vacation in a persona, be my guest. Just change your reservation."

Michelle's apprehension slowly melted into excitement. She asked all about the itinerary and ports of call. After ten minutes, she switched gears to her professional excitement. "Okay, this is great. Since this morning, I've been monitoring her phone activity and watched as she placed a pickup order at a local pharmacy. Among other things, she stocked up on travel-size supplies."

"Like what?" Chris asked.

"The items I could possibly taint include suntan lotion, Tylenol, Midol and tampons."

"I can imagine how you might drug the first three, but tampons?"

"Yes, I could lightly coat them with Staphylococcus aureus bacteria that causes deadly toxic shock syndrome. That assumes I can get to them and she has her period for three to four days. Listen, I have an appointment with a sanctioned pharmacist in one hour. Let me work on the details and I'll get back to you. What did you learn?"

"I've been trying to figure out who wants Monteiro dead. My initial guess was it was a disgruntled major stockholder or venture capital investor. But why would they blame her for the problems at Longfellow? With lots of digging, my main candidate for the Name that Client honors goes to Elizabeth Walker."

"Who's that?" Michelle asked.

"She's the company's chief science officer and the brains behind the cancer treatment technology. Anyway, for a couple of days after the company stock plummeted over seventy percent, Monteiro wrote several texts and emails apologizing to Walker and asking for her forgiveness. She kept saying how sorry she was. It's not clear what Monteiro did, but it must have been a major screwup because Walker never responded. Instead, on that Friday and the following Monday, a guy named George Henniker attacked Monteiro's house, was later arrested, and now has a restraining order against him while awaiting trial. According to Monteiro's correspondence with police, he's the guy who created the bullet hole. I'm guessing Walker hired him to kill Monteiro, which seems a bit odd because the guy runs a moderate-size hedge fund. But maybe he was also pissed over a financial loss. So they could be partners in all of this. Or maybe after his failed attempts, Walker got tired of amateur hour and decided to hire discreet professionals."

"Then why does Monteiro still work there after a major layoff?" Michelle asked.

"I have no idea. Maybe it's the old adage, 'keep your friends close and your enemies closer.' What better way to avoid suspicion than keeping her employed? Listen, let's spend the next three days tracking and digging through files. We'll probably learn more. But also take some time to shop for cruise attire, courtesy of your big brother."

Chapter Nineteen: Boston, Massachusetts

Photos 48–51

TWENTY

LANCASTER COUNTY, PENNSYLVANIA, AND
PORTOVENERE, ITALY

Twenty Years Ago

The rhythmic clip-clop of the hooves and the squeaking steel wheels were hypnotic as the three of them rode back in silence in a horse-drawn buggy.[52] Daed was aloof behind the reins. When they arrived at the Amish farm,[53] he led the horse to a water trough, patted the animal affectionately on the head, and commanded, "Get back here."

Chris and Michelle did an immediate about-face and returned to their surrogate father. There was no telling what he might say when using that tone of voice, but it was normally a preamble to a long list of chores. This time was different, remarkably different.

A rare smile formed above his scraggly pepper-gray beard. With hands casually in his pockets versus his normal authoritarian stance, Daed said, "How would you two like to go to the Italian Riviera?"

"Where's that?" Michelle asked, sounding puzzled but also excited.

"Along the northwestern coast of Italy," Daed said.

"Really?" Michelle beamed. "Oh, wow."

During the six years the siblings had lived in Lancaster County, Pennsylvania, they had rarely traveled beyond a ten-mile radius. Italy seemed to be in another universe. And the thought of a first airplane ride was appealing. But among the many lessons Chris had learned so far was skepticism. Never believe anything good comes without a cost.

He was right. As soon as they entered the house and Daed removed the weathered farmer disguise, he transformed into Preceptor ... both physically and in personality. Their main teacher was always intense and dictatorial. He pointed to the kitchen table, swept aside the plastic tablecloth, and ordered them to sit. Chris and Michelle shared a bench. Preceptor sat across from them and, as if on cue, was joined by Mamm. Their foster mother adjusted her white bonnet as if nervous. Her expression was unusually stoic.

"We believe the time has come for your first silentcide commission," he declared calmly, yet his Nordic blue eyes were ablaze.

Chris struggled to remain passive despite the instant anxiety. His sister clutched his hand and squeezed. They had been extensively trained for this moment over years of classes taught by different instructors. They had also hunted countless wild animals to desensitize them to death. Twice they had watched Preceptor silently poison men. Yet, up to this point, they had always assumed their adult role would happen sometime in the distant future. Now it was a reality, far sooner than expected.

Preceptor opened a file folder and pushed an eight-by-ten photo across the table. The teenage girl in the portrait had long dark-blond hair, a natural tan and beautiful complexion, rose-colored pouty lips, plus riveting hazel eyes. "Meet Gianna Lombardi," Preceptor said. "Don't be fooled by her innocent expression. She's seventeen going on twenty-seven and a real vixen."

Michelle seemed baffled while looking around for an explanation. His sister was only a year younger than this Gianna yet naïve by comparison.

Chris whispered to her, "Vixen means she is sexually promiscuous."

"Oh," Michelle said sheepishly.

"That's right," Preceptor confirmed. "And now meet her number one beau." He tossed over another photo. The man had dark curly hair, a dark complexion, dark brown eyes and a charming smile. A tuft of chest hair was visible from an unbuttoned white shirt and open leather jacket. "This is Lorenzo Bianchi. He's twenty-five, entitled, cocky, a relentless partier and an irresponsible playboy. These two met last summer at a seaside resort town called Porto-venere. Apparently, they became secretly involved and have planned another two-week rendezvous."

"What's wrong with them dating?" Michelle asked with a hint of defiance.

Chris cringed at her question. She was too inquisitive. He wished she would just shut up and listen.

Preceptor also seemed irritated by the interruption. "Number one, as your brother just told you, this is much more than dating. Number two, their parents are from rival crime families in southern Italy. They're bad people. Number three, the charming Mr. Bianchi has already impregnated two other teenage girls. Number four, someone disapproves and wants Bianchi to quietly go away … for good. And number five, your job is not to ask why. Your job is to silently kill this man, soon."

Michelle was stunned. Her eyes watered, then her shoulders quivered as emotions began taking control. Although equally scared, Chris tried comforting her. Mamm rushed over to add her reassurance.

"Stop!" Preceptor yelled. "Immediately!"

They all froze.

"Listen to me, Michelle," he demanded. "Would you want to be pregnant right now?"

"No, sir." She sniffled with a bowed head and lowered eyes.

"Would you want the father to be some jerk who uses your body and then runs away, leaving you to be a teenage single mother?"

"No, sir," she said without conviction.

"Look at me, damn it! Imagine being all alone, without a job, and having to raise a child all by yourself for the next twenty years because some guy had sex with you for a few minutes. How would you feel?"

"Not good," she managed to say.

Preceptor slammed a massive fist on the table. "A lot more than not good, I assure you. It would be a living hell. And that's what this man has already done twice and plans to do again with a girl your age. That girl," he said while tapping the photo. "She could easily be you. And trust me, he doesn't care. You shouldn't care either when you stop him. So I want you to concentrate on all of the young girls whose lives you're saving when you take his. Understand me?"

"Yes, sir," Michelle said in a firm voice while sweeping away a tear trickling down her face. She seemed to be entering the zone of acceptance and compliance, as she had been taught.

"And, Chris, believe in your soul that this guy would screw your younger sister multiple times and never remember her name. You've killed your father to protect Michelle. Now find that inner rage and do it again to this man."

The next couple of days were busy planning, reviewing maps, memorizing false identities and creating disguises, practicing Italian, and learning about the endless atrocities of the two crime families. This left no time for the siblings to think about what they were preparing for until they tried to sleep.

♦♦♦

Nineteen hours of flying on three planes from Philadelphia to Genoa, Italy, were followed by a nearly two-hour drive along the Italian Riviera formed by the Ligurian Sea and the Apennine Mountains. The scenery was gorgeous, but each kilometer brought them closer to their first commissioned kill.

Chris nudged his sister awake as Preceptor drove into Portovenere.[54] The medieval maritime village was stunning. Fairy-tale pastel buildings huddled together overlooking the Gulf of Poets.

Colorful wooden fishing boats bobbed in the turquoise water. Perched above them were the early twelfth-century San Lorenzo Church domes and the equally old Andrea Doria Castle.

Chris waited in the car while Preceptor checked Michelle into the five-star hotel where Gianna Lombardi and her mother were staying. Then they backtracked to Le Grazie,[55] an adjacent seaside town that was pleasant but without the charm. Their accommodations were rated three stars, and that was being generous, but this was Lorenzo Bianchi's hotel for the next two weeks.

The game plan for the following day was simple. Michelle would track the movements of Lombardi and her mother while Chris followed Bianchi.

Preceptor bounced between them every three hours for an update. At midnight, they met on a rocky point at the end of Portovenere in front of Chiesa di San Pietro,[56] a small Catholic church with a history dating back to the fifth century.

Michelle was the first to summarize her findings. "Well, they had a continental breakfast at the hotel, shopped along the waterfront boutiques, took a private boat to the island of Palmaria for a fancy lunch, did some sightseeing in the afternoon, and then had Ligurian cuisine for dinner back at the hotel. The mother talks nonstop. Gianna looked bored out of her mind all day. Then, at about nine o'clock, Gianna snuck out of the hotel, hurried to the edge of town, and spent a couple of hours in a small bed-and-breakfast before returning. That's it."

"Did you see who she met at the B and B?" Preceptor asked.

"No, but I'm assuming it was Bianchi."

"Okay, Chris, what did you learn?"

"This guy is everything you said he would be. He woke up late, had breakfast, and spent the whole day in a swimsuit at the beach partying with friends. He drank a lot of beer, flirted with every girl he saw, spent a few hours on a sailboat, had a rowdy dinner with a bunch of guys his age, then left on a motorcycle about eight thirty.

You were there when he returned to Le Grazie at eleven fifteen and went into a bar."

"Now for the important question," Preceptor said. "Where is Bianchi vulnerable?"

Chris thought for a second, then said, "He's young, seems heathy and is very fit. The guy has amazing muscles. So I doubt there's a medical condition to exploit. Perhaps he could have a drowning accident on the sailboat, if that becomes a routine, but I'm not sure how that would work. We could spike his food, but that might be hit or miss unless he always goes to the same places. The only consistent thing so far is he drinks lots of beer. That might be our best angle."

Michelle piped in, "I could get to know him at the beach, or at a party, and slip something into his beer."

"No way," Chris said, sounding overprotective of his sister.

Preceptor agreed but for a different reason. "Michelle, never, ever socialize with a target if you can avoid it. You'll be easily remembered. Besides, it's harder to kill someone you know. Remember your lessons about how it's always easier for a soldier to kill a faceless target from a distance. Do you hear me?"

"Yes, sir," Michelle said timidly.

"Good." Changing subjects, Preceptor asked Chris, "Does Bianchi take drugs?"

"Not that I saw, but I can watch for it. Although he did bum a few cigarettes during the day because he doesn't carry his own."

"Good observations. Chris, tomorrow I want you to break into his hotel room and learn every product he uses, including toothpaste, shaving cream, even hair gel. The guy obviously uses lots of that. Otherwise, we'll keep following them for a couple of days and see what else we learn."

+++

The fourth night was hot and starless. Excess humidity and anxiety dampened their clothes as Chris and Michelle huddled in brush and tall grass on a cliff behind a guardrail. Swollen welts from sandfly bites itched incessantly. Their bare legs were scratched with a criss-cross of coagulated blood from a patch of thistles.

Chris fiddled with the antenna on the walkie-talkie while staring at the large steel eyebolt attached to a boulder. Preceptor had been furious when he saw Chris had purchased a lifting ring versus a swivel ring. The former wasn't designed for angular loads. The consequences might be dire. Chris worried what that meant.

Neither of the siblings had said much during their three-hour wait alongside the winding road between Portovenere and Le Grazie. They had been taught idle chitchat breaks concentration and readiness. But the silence was a breeding ground for angst. The battle between calm and dread seemed unrelenting.

Chris flinched when he heard loud static from the walkie-talkie, followed by Preceptor's booming command, "Now!" Chris looked at Michelle. She seemed transfixed. "Go, go, go," he yelled.

She grabbed one end of the galvanized steel cable, tripped while feeding it below the guardrail, and got halfway across the road before stopping in a frenzy. The coiled section of the cable was tangled in a bush. While she kept yanking, Chris struggled in the dark to unravel the problem. The rumble of a motorcycle could be heard in the distance.

Michelle got wide-eyed. Chris scratched and clawed. The motorcycle backfired and sputtered while navigating sharp turns. The cable worked loose. With a violent tug, she ran into shrubs and beneath a tree. A shaky headlight began lighting up the road. Chris pictured her attaching the snap hook. He waited. Bianchi's motorcycle was visible and traveling fast. Chris waited.

"Got it," she screamed into the walkie-talkie.

Chris tightened the cable as the engine of the BMW K1 roared in his ear.

When the front tire hit the cable, the bike lurched up, flipped over, and tumbled amongst a shower of sparks and screeches of crushing steel and aluminum. The clamp snapped, causing the cable to whip wildly until the end jammed into the back tire, sending the bike ricocheting backward. Bianchi went airborne. His flailing body slammed into the asphalt, skidded, then crashed into the guardrail.

The violence became a sickening quiet. The only sound was Bianchi's moans. He might be dying, but he wasn't dead.

"Michelle!" Chris screamed as he ran down the road. "Get the cable! Get the cable out of the motorcycle!"

Bianchi was hardly recognizable. Limbs were in contorted positions. Road rash had peeled away much of his skin. Bloody abrasions disfigured his face and head.

Chris acted on instinct. He tried lifting the body over the guardrail. The man was heavy. Slick blood made it hard to get a firm grip. Headlights brightened the scene. Chris numbed. He was petrified.

Preceptor raced toward him as a giant black shadow. He grabbed Bianchi by the belt. Together, they raised the target over the guardrail and let go. The body tumbled down the cliff, ricocheted off boulders, then splashed into the bay.

"Move!" Preceptor screamed while sprinting back to his car.

"Help!" Michelle screamed while still struggling to loosen the cable from the motorcycle.

Preceptor tried freeing the cable. Chris reached down to stabilize the bike and grabbed the crumpled hot engine. "Shit!" he yelled while burning his hand.

The cable would not work loose. It was hopelessly tangled. Preceptor started jumping on the tire to break it free. A distant car was approaching. Michelle was hysterical. Chris banged on the twisted tire with a boulder. Preceptor pushed him aside and pounced on the motorcycle with his full weight. Again. The car was closer. Again. On the fourth try, the tire snapped off. Chris grabbed it and the snarled cable before jumping into the back seat with his sister. They were both hyperventilating. A moment later, bright headlights shone through their windshield as they passed the other car. They heard the car's screeching brakes when it arrived at the accident scene.

Their ride back to Portovenere was morbid. None of them said a word. Chris mindlessly wrung his hands covered in blood. Michelle seemed comatose.

Preceptor parked in a near-empty lot overlooking the town. He got out and opened the back door. "Get out!" he yelled at Michelle.

She complied but seemed in shock.

"Brush yourself off. You're a mess."

She did.

"Come here," he said in a gentle voice.

She collapsed into his consoling arms.

"Chris, you too."

Preceptor's uncharacteristic compassion was comforting.

Chapter Twenty: Lancaster County, Pennsylvania, and Portovenere, Italy

Photos 52–56

TWENTY-ONE

Day One of Cruise
Saturday

A nna Monteiro got excited as the cab traveled across Port Boulevard Bridge in Miami. She caught a first glimpse of the cruise ships lined up along Dodge Island. They were enormous. Each one promised fun, pampering and an escape from reality. Sailing away from her problems at Longfellow and with George – however temporary – was exactly what she needed.

Anna had initially been opposed to a midsummer Caribbean cruise. But when her friend from San Francisco had continuously stressed what a great bargain they were getting, Anna had realized this was probably the only five-day cruise Jessica Daly could afford. So what difference did it make? The ports of call were far less important than the chance to be together for the first time in five years.

When the taxi arrived at the cruise terminal, Jessica was leaning against a traffic barrier. Her slumped shoulders seemed to rob a few inches from her tall, slender figure. Long blond hair parted in the middle – it had been shoulder-length and brunette years ago – and little makeup drained her face of color. Her dull eyes and slightly parted lips depicted exhaustion, uncharacteristic of her normal gregarious personality. Probably the long flight from the West Coast the night before was to blame. Anna hoped her friend wasn't sick.

"Jessica!" Anna yelled as she got out of the cab.

The change in Jessica was immediate. Her eyes lit up, a row of perfect white teeth formed a thrilled smile, and her features became animated while running with outstretched arms. "Oh my gosh!" Jessica exclaimed. "You're here. I'm here. We're finally together. Can you believe it? And we're going on a cruise. This is going to be so awesome!" That was the singsong cadence Anna remembered about her friend.

When they entered their cabin, Jessica dropped the hand luggage on the bed, squealed with delight, rushed out to the balcony and, at the railing, assumed Rose's "I'm flying" pose from the movie *Titanic*. Anna grabbed a bottle of champagne from an ice bucket and two flute glasses. "Ta-da!" she announced while stepping onto the balcony.

"Where did you get that?" Jessica asked with excitement.

"My travel agent arranged to have this delivered to our room," Anna answered while removing the foil and wire from the top of the bottle. "What better way to christen our cruise?"

They both jumped back as the cork unexpectantly popped and flew overboard. Jessica giggled while trying to catch the spray in the glasses.

"To us," Anna toasted. "This is going to be a spectacular vacation together."

♦♦♦

The friends rushed to the bon voyage party. Jessica was eager to try the endless drinks package they had purchased. While each of them ordered a rum punch – a smile to the bartender earned her friend an extra pineapple wedge – Jessica used plastic straws to mimic the beat of the steel drums, then gyrated toward the calypso band playing, "Hot! Hot! Hot!" Surrounding the pool were festive people, predominately in their twenties and thirties. Beer and tropical cocktails plus loud talking and laughing were plentiful. Most were already in bathing suits or colorful summer attire. Several were dancing in frenzied circles while singing, "Ole ole, ole ole! Ole ole, ole ole!" The fun vibe was infectious. The ship was already living up to its party reputation, even before setting sail.

Suddenly, the music stopped – literally. The announcement of a mandatory lifeboat drill sparked grumbles from the crowd. Anna and Jessica returned to their cabin, put on bulky orange lifejackets, then managed to find Muster Station D. Anna felt a tad light-headed from the alcohol while having her room key swiped by a crew member. They were directed to form a new row in front of a line of people already facing the port terminal.

While the friends shuffled into position, Anna noticed a strangely alluring man. The fair complexion of his oblong face, together with short blond hair and almost white eyebrows, accented the intensity of gorgeous aquamarine eyes. Full, well-defined lips and a small nose were almost feminine. He wasn't tall – maybe six inches taller than her – nor big, yet his lean body seemed muscular without the pretentiousness of a gym rat. There was a quiet confidence about his expression, making him seem older than his youthful face im-plied. His smile was quick, warm and charming as Anna stopped, returned a shy grin, then stood in front of him.

Passengers continued arriving at the muster station. Every few minutes, a crew member asked the rows of people to move closer to the wall. Each time, Anna used this as an excuse to turn around and apologize for encroaching while stealing another glance at him. His proximity was oddly titillating. She closed her eyes to con-trol the nervousness yet kept picturing him during the lifejacket demonstration.

"Do you think the Great Pumpkin will arrive?" came a whisper almost directly in her ear.

"Excuse me?" Anna said in surprise while turning around.

His face was inches away. With a playful grin, he said, "I feel like Linus waiting in the pumpkin patch."

Anna's spontaneous laugh drew the attention of others. A crew member gave her a disapproving glare. She covered her mouth to suppress the giggling while nodding in agreement. When the lifeboat drill ended, Jessica grabbed her arm in the hopes of making a fast exit. Anna turned to talk with the man, but he was gone.

"Did you see that guy?" Anna asked her friend.

"You mean the ship officer with the tablet? Yeah, he was cute. I loved his white uniform and accent."

Anna decided against describing the man she meant.

After watching the cruise ship[57] push away from the dock, they returned to their room. The luggage had arrived. Jessica had three overstuffed bags. From experience, Anna knew it was easier to have one person unpack at a time in a cramped cruise cabin. She poured them another glass of champagne, then sat on the balcony to wait. The view was serene as the skyline of Miami[58] drifted into the horizon. The waves were hypnotic. Her thoughts kept drifting back to the man from the lifeboat drill.

After finishing the glass, Anna stepped back inside. Fancy dresses, shoes, purses, hats, and beachwear were scattered everywhere. Many of the expensive clothes had price tags. Anna wondered how her friend could afford the shopping spree, then chastised herself for speculating that Jessica might return the items after the cruise.

Anna unpacked while Jessica was in the bathroom. When her friend emerged thirty minutes later, her face was completely transformed into a runway model. Radiant skin, a touch of blush defining high cheekbones, mauve lips, and dark mascara and liner that drew attention to glowing eyes. The tousled blond hair was expertly coiffed. Her formfitting scarlet cocktail dress had exposed shoulders, a daring neckline, and a dramatic slit from one knee up to her inner thigh. Suede lace-up heels elongated slender legs. Jessica was radiant. In comparison, Anna felt middle-aged in a conservative floral dress.

"How do I look?" Jessica asked while twirling in front of a mirror.

"Spectacular, but then you'd look good in a gunnysack," Anna said and meant it.

The next few hours were great. They ate a scrumptious, five-course meal with plenty of red wine at a table of eight. The other people were a mix of married and dating couples, about their ages with lots of interesting things to say. After dinner, the friends had two shots of Don Julio – Jessica claimed with a chuckle that post-meal shots of tequila were good for digestion – then enjoyed a toe-tapping medley of Broadway show tunes in the theater. They each lost twenty dollars at the penny slots and checked out the boutique shops before finding the nightclub.

The music was pounding. Lights were flashing. People had come to party hearty. The dance floor was packed. It was challenging to reach the bar and get a bartender's attention. Anna asked for a Captain and Coke. Jessica ordered an old-fashioned and, with a flirting tilt of her head, asked for an extra shot of rye plus lots of maraschino cherries. She proceeded to demonstrate to an adjacent guy her talent of tying a cherry stem with her tongue. Not surprisingly, he was all grins while leading her to the dance floor.

Anna sat next to the empty stool, sipped her cocktail, watched Jessica's moves, and twice declined the advance of men. They seemed nice enough, and normally she would have talked with either of them, but she was suddenly exhausted. It had been a very long day since arriving at Boston Logan Airport at five thirty that morning.

That was when she noticed the man from the lifeboat drill sitting in a darkened corner by himself. Adrenaline lifted her spirits. She hoped he would make eye contact. He didn't. As she built the courage to approach him, she was distracted by another guy. By the time she politely conveyed the message she wasn't interested – it was impossible to hear without shouting – the mystery man was gone. She visually scoured the room without luck.

Her exhaustion returned. She told Jessica she was going back to the room for the night and to have fun. The last part seemed superfluous; Jessica was obviously having a blast.

+++

Anna was startled awake when the cabin door flung open, flooding the room with light, then got dark again when the door slammed. Jessica sounded tipsy while trying to walk. The digital clock on the nightstand read 3:18 a.m.

Anna asked, "Have fun?"

"Lots," Jessica slurred. A single-word response was a rarity for her friend.

"Want me to turn on a light?"

"Nope," Jessica said while tossing off her heels. She struggled to get out of her dress before throwing it on a chair.

Anna expected to hear her friend put on pajamas, then brush her teeth. She did neither. Anna felt the covers pull back – the room steward hadn't separated the beds like she had asked. The mattress depressed, a pillow fluffed, and after a rustle to get comfortable, Jessica passed out within seconds.

Anna listened to her rhythmic breathing. She sensed body heat between the sheets. The nocturnal aura was comforting. She tried remembering the last time she'd slept with a male partner she loved. More than five years since the divorce, so probably six or seven years ago. She missed the companionship. Would she ever have it again?

Chapter Twenty-One: Miami, Florida

Photos 57–58

TWENTY-TWO

ATLANTIC OCEAN

Day Two of Cruise

Sunday

A t six a.m., there was a knock on Michelle Barton's cabin door. In walked Chris wearing black jogging shorts, a blue T-shirt, and a cheesy smile. "Good morning, sunshine," he said with enthusiasm. Her brother was often too cheerful in the morning, an annoying trait to a confirmed night owl like herself. "You look ravishing at this hour," he added sarcastically.

"And you look like your normal dorky self," she quipped back. There was a twinge of envy that Chris wasn't wearing a disguise. She should've had the courage to be herself on this cruise, but it was too late now.

Michelle had just spent two hours readying her goth girl persona. The nylon wig cap was already starting to itch. The layers of white foundation covering her face felt thick and unnatural. She had blended the makeup down her neck until matching her body's sun-starved skin tone. There was never time for something as frivolous as tanning.

After tightening the belt of the ship-issued bathrobe, Michelle plodded farther into the room in the ship-issued slippers and pointed to a tray delivered earlier by room service. "You might want to look under that plate cover," she said. "I left you something."

With exaggerated delight, Chris squealed, "Bacon! Lots of bacon! You do love me."

"No, I love my arteries, but to heck with yours. Enjoy."

He did. She watched as he savored every morsel. Eating bacon was one of the many times Chris acted like a kid. His antics were refreshing respites from their professional tension, especially on days when executing a silentcide commission. This was one of those days.

"So what did you need so early?" Chris asked.

"I need your help finishing my disguise," she said while opening the robe, throwing it on the couch, and revealing a black bikini.

"Whoa!" Chris exclaimed. "That's a bit revealing, don't you think?"

"No, I think you're a prude. For crying out loud, Chris, it's a swimsuit. That's what people wear around the pool when it's ungodly hot."

With a sigh of resignation, he said, "But I like your new tats."

She did a little curtsey while he focused on the mermaid on her arm, a rose on her thigh, and a vibrant monarch butterfly encircling her navel.

"Don't get used to them," Michelle said. "They'll fade away by the end of the week. Okay, so now I need your help with that one for my back." After pointing to the semi-permanent tattoo package, she lay face down on the bed and undid the string of the bikini top.

Chris reviewed the instructions. He had done this several times but didn't want to screw it up. He rubbed an alcohol patch across her back, then began peeling off the first decal. "Hold still," he said.

"I am."

"No, your shoulder muscles are tense. Just relax."

"I am relaxed," Michelle protested. "Just do this already, and get it straight this time."

He methodically positioned both stencils in place and applied blue ink over each design. They needed time to cure.

While waiting, Chris sat on the cabin balcony as a giant orange fireball lifted slowly above the horizon, painting puffy white clouds with pinkish-red hues. The sound of crashing waves drifting through the open sliding glass door was serene. Michelle fell asleep.

"Hey, sleepyhead," Chris said a couple of hours later. "Time for the big unveiling."

"How do they look?" she asked.

"Absolutely heavenly," he declared in reference to the angel wings stretching from her shoulder blades to her lower back.

For the next half hour, they reviewed the plan and every contingency. "So are we ready?" Chris finally asked.

"Yes, I think so," Michelle answered, feeling the first twinge of apprehension.

"You'll do great," he assured her. "And don't worry. As always, I'll have your back, or should I say wings," he said with a snicker.

She could tell he was equally nervous.

"See you later," he said while walking out the door and entering his gameday readiness.

◆◆◆

Michelle positioned herself in an isolated chair on the deck overlooking the pool.[59] Oversized sunglasses shielded her flamboyant black-and-purple eye makeup while allowing her to observe the movements of early risers during the first day at sea. Every few minutes, she flipped the page of the book she wasn't reading.

An hour slipped by. Michelle was wondering if their plan was a bust when she saw Anna Monteiro. Their target grabbed two ship towels from a bin, looked around as if judging where to sit, approached two empty poolside loungers, and claimed them by stretching out the towels and putting a book and canvas tote on the chairs. As Chris had predicted, Monteiro's roommate was absent and would presumably sleep in very late after a long night of partying.

From the corner of her eye, Michelle saw Chris starting to jog on the upper-deck track parallel to the pool. Thankfully, Monteiro saw him too and responded as they had hoped. She climbed up the stairs, tightened both shoelaces, and began running. So far, the fox-and-the-hound ploy seemed to be working.

Michelle bowed her head. Under the cover of a floppy hat, she discreetly put on black lipstick and a nose ring, then waited until Chris and Monteiro finished another lap. The target remained about seventy-five feet behind her brother. No way would Chris let her get closer.

Time to go. Michelle removed the sunglasses, bathing coverup, and hat, put them into a beach bag, then used her black fingernails to comb out the bangs on a long black wig. With a deep breath for courage, she was ready.

After walking down the stairs, Michelle claimed the empty pool lounger next to Monteiro's, lay down, and surveyed the crowd. She waited until a few guys got tired of staring at her. Fortunately, they seemed too lethargic to try any creepy pickup lines. She cautiously lowered Monteiro's tote between the chairs and began rifling through the contents without looking down. Feeling a bottle of suntan lotion, she lifted it up. It matched the brand she had tainted and hidden in her beach bag, but Monteiro's bottle felt half-full. Obviously, a swap would be easily detected. The first scheme had failed.

She replaced Monteiro's tote, leaned back, and crossed her legs. Chris would read the signal. Feigning sleep, Michelle watched through slit eyes until Monteiro completed the next lap. As expected, Chris had disappeared. When the target paused, caught her breath, and began walking down the stairs to the pool level, Michelle lowered the back of the lounger and flipped onto her stomach.

Michelle heard Anna Monteiro sit down, take off the tennis shoes, shove shorts and a top into the bag, and walk to the pool. The target emitted a small squeal when jumping into the water, then began swimming laps. Michelle snuck a peek. Monteiro was an excellent swimmer. This woman probably excelled at several physical activities.

Michelle pretended to be asleep again when Monteiro exited the pool, came over, and began drying off. Michelle sensed she was being stared at. Lifting her head, she said, "Hi."

"Hi," Monteiro said with an engaging smile. "I was just admiring your wings tattoo. It's gorgeous."

"Thanks," Michelle said while sitting up.

"Oh my, you have lots more. They're beautiful, too, especially the butterfly. I've often thought about getting a tattoo, but never found the courage."

Michelle quipped, "The first time, it helps if you're drunk."

Anna Monteiro laughed. "I guess that's true for a lot of things we know we shouldn't do."

This was perfect. A connection had been made. The target was relaxed and engaged. They spent a few minutes in idle chitchat before the conversation naturally drifted to an end.

Michelle leaned back as if enjoying the sunshine. The warm rays and tropical breeze would have felt great if she weren't contemplating the next steps. About fifteen minutes later, she shifted uncomfortably, arched her back and, while holding her stomach, emitted a barely audible gasp. There was no response. After a short delay, Michelle repeated the ruse.

"Are you okay?" Monteiro asked.

"Cramps!" she declared. "Can you believe the audacity of Aunt Flo to visit on a cruise?"

"Unfortunately, I'm also expecting my period soon," Monteiro said. "And my cramps are hellacious for the first couple of days. Are you taking anything for them?"

"No, like an idiot I didn't pack anything," Michelle said. "If they get worse, I'll buy something from the giftshop when it opens."

"I think that's a few hours from now," Monteiro said with concern while sitting on the edge of the chair. "You might be really miserable by then. Listen, I can go grab something from my cabin if you wish."

"No, I don't want to bother you."

"It's no bother at all. Really. My cabin is just down the hall. I'll be right back."

"That would be so awesome. Thank you."

Michelle waited thirty seconds, then put on her floppy hat, a signal to Chris that scheme number two was in progress. She reached into her beach bag, opened a small tin, and extracted two white caplets prepared by the sanctioned pharmacist in Boston. One was Tylenol Extra Strength and the second Midol Complete. They looked identical to the over-the-counter drugs Anna Monteiro had purchased before the cruise, yet these were radically different.

The primary ingredient was MDMA, a pure crystalline powder with mood-enhancing and hallucinogenic properties. The common street name: ecstasy. The dose was not sufficient to be dangerous but would test positive in a postmortem blood test. A euphoric buzz would normally last two to four hours, but not in this case.

Each time-release tablet was formulated to reach the second ingredient within thirty minutes. The synthetic opioid – predominately used to immobilize large animals – was ten thousand times more potent than morphine, four thousand times more than heroin, and one hundred times more than fentanyl. The twenty-five micrograms of carfentanil – less than a grain of salt – would be fatal within minutes. Any attempt by a first responder to administer the antidote naloxone for a drug overdose would be hopeless.

As Anna Monteiro returned, Michelle controlled the nervousness while appearing calm. The two tablets were in her left palm.

"Here you go," Monteiro said while holding out a box of Midol.

Damn it! Of course the damn thing hasn't been opened. "Thank you so much," Michelle said with a smile. "You're really awesome."

Michelle sensed being watched while shifting the tablets behind her lower three fingers in order to open the box with both hands. Her pulse rose while struggling with the childproof cap. *Hope to God a fingernail doesn't snap off.* Of course there was a foil seal on the bottle. As she picked away at the edges, her palm got sweaty. She worried the painted brand names on the tabs might smear. *This is a disaster.* In frustration, she looked up at Monteiro. "Opening this thing is a bigger pain than my cramps," she kidded.

"Tell me about it." Monteiro laughed.

For a further distraction, Michelle glanced out over the pool. Instinctively, Monteiro did also, then seemed to lock on to Chris standing bare-chested on the upper deck with a towel around his neck while eating a pastry. *Perfect timing, brother.*

With a fingernail, Michelle punched a hole in the seal, peeled it back, poured several caplets into her left hand, dropped the Tylenol on the lounger, pinched out two real Midols, then poured the rest back into the bottle including the lethal Midol. Her heart was racing when Monteiro resumed eye contact.

"Thanks again," Michelle said while returning the bottle to the box and handing it back. "You're a lifesaver."

"No problem. Happy I could help. Do you have any water to get those down?"

Stop being so damn nice. "Yes, I have a bottle in my beach bag. Thanks anyway."

After taking the two Midol caplets, Michelle leaned back and closed her eyes as a wave of guilt and remorse washed over her. She had just sealed the fate of a gracious and maybe innocent target.

Chapter Twenty-Two: Atlantic Ocean

Photo 59

TWENTY-THREE

SANTO DOMINGO, DOMINICAN REPUBLIC
Day Three of Cruise
Monday

"Just let me sleep," Jessica groaned while pulling the covers over her head to block out the early morning sunshine on day three of their cruise.

"Come on. Get up, grumpy," Anna said with light encouragement. "We don't have much time to catch the tour bus. Let's go."

"I'm not going," her roommate mumbled into the pillow. "I promised people at the club I'd go with them to a beach on Catalina Island."

"But I've already paid for excursion tickets to Santo Domingo," Anna said with growing frustration. "They're nonrefundable."

With equal annoyance, Jessica declared, "Nope, not interested."

Anna gave up. It wasn't worth an argument. "All right, I'll meet you back on the ship. And if you need something for that hangover, I have medicine in the bathroom."

Anna hustled down the gangway and climbed aboard the tour bus. She was thrilled to see the guy from the lifeboat drill sitting alone but disappointed he was napping. Thinking it was rude to disturb him, she sat a few rows behind, watched him for a while, then fell asleep during the two-hour ride to Santo Domingo.

About twenty people exited the bus at Parque Colón in the Colonial Zone. They were immediately given headsets, foiling Anna's attempt to talk with the mystery man. A middle-aged Hispanic gentleman with short gray hair, a caterpillar mustache, an affable demeanor and a heavy accent introduced himself as José. He pointed out the Christopher Columbus Monument[60] and explained the explorer's arrival in 1492. Then he walked the crowd toward the oldest cathedral[61] in the Americas, dating back to 1504.

The Ozama Fortress[62] was next. Because the Spanish fort was closed on Mondays, people were only allowed to wander around the medieval ruins after a brief description. The entire time, the lifeboat guy darted in every direction, taking photos with a fancy camera.

The group was then led along Calle Las Damas, the first cobblestone street in the New World. The historic sites along the way were interesting, especially the National Pantheon.[63] Most fascinating was the fifty-five-room former mansion of Diego Colón,[64] the son of Christopher Columbus. Yet catching up to the lifeboat guy was like chasing a cat. When José announced they were stopping for a one-hour lunch at Plaza de España,[65] the crowd approved. Mystery man said something to José in Spanish, then walked off.

Emboldened, Anna followed him. "Excuse me," she called out. "Hi, my name is Anna. I'm with the tour group. Can I ask where you're going?"

Those aquamarine eyes were intense. His jaw was tight. His face was expressionless. His stance was guarded. Unexpectantly, he flashed a boyish smile. "I'm going to find the Great Pumpkin."

After a second of surprise, Anna laughed. "Do you mind if I follow you to the pumpkin patch?"

He seemed to contemplate the question before answering. "Sure, why not. I'm Chris. Nice to meet you, Anna." They shook hands. "I'm going to run around taking photos of nearby sights not on the tour. So, if you don't mind missing lunch, you're welcome to tag along."

Chris was a fast walker. She should have assumed that after trailing behind his runner's stride the previous morning aboard the ship. He brought them to Plaza Reloj de Sol[66] and explained how the sundial was the oldest Spanish timepiece in the New World.

From the top of the defensive wall, he described the Ozama River[67] below. Then he pointed to a tiny, inconspicuous building[68] on the opposite riverbank. "That's where Bartholomew Columbus founded La Nueva Isabela in 1496. Six years later, the colonists moved here, renamed it Santo Domingo, and it became Spain's de facto New World capital."

Anna was fascinated by his knowledge. She kept asking questions about the city's history as they walked down to San Diego Gate.[69] Then they stared at the San Diego Low Battery[70] and a bastion called Invincible Fort as they moved toward the Ozama River.

"How do you know so much about Santo Domingo?" she asked.

Chris answered, "I always research the history of a foreign city before visiting. I also map all of the sights I want to photograph."

"Do you travel a lot?" she asked.

"Almost constantly."

Anna wanted to learn more, much more. "What do you do for a living?"

"I'm a cybersecurity consultant for international corporate clients. And you?"

"I'm in marketing and PR for a biotech company in Cambridge."

"That's impressive," he said. "Are you traveling alone?"

"No, I'm with a dear friend who was a former co-worker in San Francisco. She's at the beach today. How 'bout you?"

"Well, I was supposed to have a good buddy along, but he had to cancel at the last minute. So I'm constantly sending him photos so he sees what he's missing."

"That's mean," she said with a smirk.

"I know. It's devilish," he said with that charming grin again.

Anna felt disappointed. Chris was smarter, nicer, and more interesting than she expected. But the way he described his buddy led her to believe Chris might be gay.

Nothing wrong with that. Just eliminates him as a potential romantic interest. Then she chastised herself. *Do you really want a whirlwind romance? No. Just be glad you got the chance to meet him. Try arranging another time to talk.*

After lunch, the tour group was loaded back into the bus. Fortunately, Anna finagled to sit next to Chris. The rest of the city highlights were drive-bys. Chris kept hanging out the window with his fancy camera. At one point, in frustration, he shook his head and mumbled, "This is ridiculous. I knew I should've booked a private tour."

As the bus left the city, Anna anticipated a two-hour conversation during the ride back to the ship. Unfortunately, Chris quickly leaned back and closed his eyes. Perhaps he was just tired. More likely, he was signaling a lack of interest in her. That seemed confirmed while walking up the gangway. "It was great meeting you, Anna," he said flatly. "Enjoy the rest of your cruise."

When Anna entered their cabin, Jessica was half-dressed, half-drunk, and mostly sunburned. Beachwear and towels were scattered on the floor. A party dress and heels were on the bed. She was frantically fluffing her hair in the mirror.

Anna asked, "How was your day?"

Without making eye contact, Jessica said, "Awesome! I spent the whole time with a guy I met at the club last night. He's so hot. And I'm running late to meet him at the bar."

"That's great." Anna meant to imply she was happy for Jessica, but it came out sounding disappointed. "So I guess I'll see you at dinner?"

"No, I'm having dinner with him at the steakhouse tonight. I hope you don't mind."

"No problem at all," Anna said but didn't mean it. She opened the sliding glass door, stepped onto the balcony, and watched the last stragglers boarding the ship while contemplating spending more time by herself. So disheartening.

About ten minutes later, Jessica came out. She was stunning despite her uneasy footing. "Well, I'm off," she announced.

"Have fun," Anna said, trying to sound supportive.

"What are you going to do?" Jessica asked.

"Not sure. I originally thought we were spending the evening together."

"Me too. But you always poop out too early."

"What's that supposed to mean?" Anna asked, perhaps too harshly.

With hands on her hips, Jessica said, "It means you always go to bed just when the party is getting started."

"I'm sorry, but I get tired."

"Don't talk to me about getting tired," Jessica snapped back. "You have no idea what tired is until you're raising a toddler by yourself." Her voice got louder during the rant. "And don't go getting all judgmental on me for spending time with a cute guy. This is the first time I've been really free in about five years. And I'm going to make the most out of every single minute. If you disapprove, that's too damn bad."

"Jessica, I never said I disapprove," Anna said softly.

"You didn't have to. It's written all over your face."

"You're blowing this all out of proportion." Anna was trying to mitigate the situation but failing. "You're not acting like yourself."

"Well, maybe I'm no longer who you remember," Jessica screamed. "So get over it!" She stormed off. The cabin door slammed shut.

Anna rubbed her eyes and ran fingers through her short black hair. *What was that all about?* She felt bad about coming across as judgmental. It wasn't intentional. Of course, being a single mom at thirty-six must be hell. So naturally, Jessica wanted to have a good time. But they were supposed to have a good time together. This cruise was now becoming a disaster, a disaster to be endured alone.

As a hoped-for diversion, Anna made the mistake of grabbing her cell phone, then reading and responding to emails and texts from work. The situation and mood at Longfellow were increasingly worse. The notification of the court appearance date with George was equally depressing.

During dinner, Anna hardly spoke to the other couples except about her tour while eating a cobb salad. She felt bloated, so skipped the big entrée. After wandering the ship with hopes of bumping into Chris, she went to the show. Later, listening to a talented violinist, harpist and pianist trio for a couple of hours was soothing. But the soft, relaxing music gave her too much time to brood. She considered going to the club and trying to make amends with Jessica. But why be accused of spoiling her party again? The only way to end this day was by going to sleep.

There was a Do Not Disturb sign on the cabin door when Anna approached. She must have forgotten to take it off after dressing for dinner. That meant the room steward would not have exchanged all the bathroom towels Jessica left on the floor. *That's just great. Dirty towels until tomorrow.*

When Anna opened the door, Jessica screamed. Her friend was riding some guy.

"Goddamn it, Jessica!" she yelled. "You're having sex in my bed?"

Chapter Twenty-Three: Santo Domingo, Dominican Republic

Photos 60–70

TWENTY-FOUR

GRAND TURK, TURKS AND CAICOS ISLANDS
Day Four of Cruise
Tuesday

W hen Michelle let Chris into her cabin at eight a.m., he was surprised to see his sister appearing as herself. Her free-flowing, sandy-brown hair encircled her glowing skin with hints of new freckles, bright eyes and a cheerful smile. She seemed refreshed and happy … a rare combination.

"Wow, you look great," Chris said.

"I feel great," Michelle said as she flopped down on the couch. "It's amazing what nearly two days of vacation can do for a girl's spirits. Thanks for giving me the time off."

"You're welcome. I thought you could use a little R & R. But you've ditched the goth girl?"

"Yup, just following my big brother's lead," she said with a charismatic twinkle. "Besides, I figured it would be easier to ride along with Monteiro today if she didn't recognize me from the pool."

"Makes sense. From what I can tell, Monteiro's still booked on the island excursion this morning. And I suspect she'll be alone again."

"How do you know? I didn't see Daly partying at the club late last night."

"No, she was entertaining a guy in her room until Monteiro walked in on them. I couldn't hear their hallway conversation because the microcamera doesn't have sound, but their body language was, well, let's call it less than amicable."

"That's awkward."

"Very. Monteiro stewed in the hall for a few minutes until Daly and her boyfriend left in a walk of shame. Then Monteiro went to sleep for the night."

The siblings proceeded to discuss the details of the day's cat-and-mouse surveillance. Michelle was responsible for tracking the target until the ship left the Cruise Center[71] at the southwestern tip of Grand Turk. Chris had the evening shift.

After a leisurely breakfast and a quick daily report to Thanatos, Chris hired a cab driver to give him a private tour of the seven-square-mile island, the capital of the Turks and Caicos archipelago. They visited several pristine beaches.[72] He enjoyed the unhurried freedom to photograph the charming Cockburn Town.[73] Plus they made a fifteen-minute stop at a historic lighthouse.[74] It was easy to steer clear of Monteiro's tour bus by tracking his sister's GPS location on his cell phone.

When he returned to the Cruise Center, Chris wanted to treat himself to a couple hours of serene sunshine for the first time during the cruise. He went to a large public pool[75] adjacent to the Grand Turk Margaritaville but immediately saw Jessica Daly partying with her friends. Judging from their demeanor, they had already sampled most of the bar's fifty-two types of margaritas.

Chris couldn't risk Monteiro showing up to meet her friend, so he walked a short distance to the shoreline facing the ship. On the right was about four hundred feet of gorgeous sand[76] and gaggles of not-so-gorgeous sunworshippers. *Too crowded.* On the left was a sliver of sand with loungers[77] beneath palm trees. *Perfect.*

He savored the rhythmic swish of ocean waves. Drifting across the deep blue sky were alabaster clouds and an occasional seabird. His toes and fingers absently played in the soft, warm sand. His mind drifted toward a rare relaxation … until the moment was shattered.

"Hi, Chris," Monteiro said with a radiant smile while coming close to him.

Un-friggen-believable! "Hi," he said in a polite tone, purposely not using her name so she'd think he forgot it.

She sat down in the adjacent beach chair. "Did you see the island today?"

"Yes, I hired a great cab driver. I wasn't going to make the same mistake as yesterday," he said with a reserved grin while looking at his watch, hoping to come across as standoffish. "Did you and your friend go on a tour?"

"I did and loved it. This is a beautiful island."

Chris was surprised she glossed over Jessica Daly's absence. After being abandoned yesterday and again this morning, plus the confrontation last night, a normal person would complain. Was Monteiro that loyal to her friend? Or just didn't want to talk about her? "It sure is beautiful," he said while studying her face for the first time.

"I'll bet you got some great photos," she said.

"I did actually."

"Can I see some of them?" she asked eagerly. "I know they're better than mine."

Chris instinctively grabbed his camera. He rarely got the chance to show off his photographic talent. As he began displaying photos through the window in the back of his camera, Anna leaned closer. Her compliments were gratifying. She often looked up with wide-open brown eyes to ask questions. Chris was oddly becoming transfixed by her pretty tomboyish enthusiasm.

Then a voice in the back of his brain – either Preceptor's or Irene's or both – screamed, *What the hell are you doing? Stop now! This is the goddamn target, remember?*

"Hey listen," Chris said abruptly. "I should be getting back to the ship." He sensed her watching while he put on his shirt.

"Me too." She stood and brushed sand from the back of her shorts.

He chastised himself for ogling her innocent move. *Stop looking, you idiot.* As a diversion, he asked, "Did you buy that conch shell on the beach?"

"Yes, it's a gift for a good friend and co-worker back in Cambridge. I promised to buy her something during the cruise."

Chris was surprised Anna was mentioning another friend. From what he had observed previously, she seemed to be an introvert and loner. But he was beginning to believe his initial impressions were wrong. Anna might be a bit insecure socially, but she was warm and engaging when given the chance.

As soon as Chris returned to the cabin, his cell phone dinged. The text from Michelle was simple: "My room. Now." Using phones for messages, especially on unsecure networks like the ship's, was against protocol. This had to be serious.

After entering her room, his sister immediately confronted him. She was pissed. "Have you lost your mind?"

"What are you talking about?" he asked, genuinely confused.

"I just watched you snuggling up to the target for a half hour. You know very well Preceptor warned us repeatedly to never, ever socialize with a target."

"We were hardly snuggling," Chris said defensively. "I was just showing her my photos of the island, for god's sake. And besides, Anna approached me."

"Oh, so now you're calling her Anna and not Monteiro?"

Chris was surprised by the observation. It was true. He had inadvertently personalized the target, a major infraction. Yet he resented his sister's condescending tone. "Are you questioning my professionalism?"

"Never. But in this case, I'm warning you to stop talking with her."

"So now you're warning me, huh?" He was becoming equally confrontational.

"Yes, Chris, I am. Don't get too close to her. Wear your Sully disguise tonight while tracking her so she doesn't approach you again."

"You want me to wear that hot clown costume while you have

PDAs in the club again tonight? Doesn't that sound like a double standard?"

"No, it's not," she said, trying to control her frustration, yet her complexion was turning red. "Stop being so snarly. I can't remember the last time I danced, drank and had some fun. Besides, we're not assigned to kill the guy I was dancing with last night."

Chris curtailed a biting retort. She was right, but he wasn't going to give her the satisfaction of saying it. "Fine. You go have your fun again tonight with Mr. Gym Junkie while I work. I'll let you know if Monteiro – get that? Monteiro – takes the Midol. Otherwise, I'll talk to you in the morning." He turned to leave.

"Speaking of which," Michelle said, "I'm thinking we should try switching her suntan lotion again tomorrow at the pool while at sea. Tomorrow's the last full day. We're running out of time."

"Whatever," he said with a backward wave of the hand while leaving the room.

Chris was in a funk. He deftly monitored Anna's movements when the ship left Grand Turk, at the buffet, the show, and then at a trio of musicians catering to a handful of sedate seniors. On several occasions, Anna talked to nearby people, but the conversations were always cursory. She seemed miserable. The audacity of Jessica Daly to abandon her. Friends don't treat friends like this on a cruise.

Why would anyone want to have this woman killed? He needed to find out before it was too late. This was more than Name that Client curiosity. This was becoming personal. Having an obvious and compelling reason to kill someone typically lessened his twinges of guilt. Preceptor's inner voice started yelling, "Your job is not to ask why. Your job is to silently kill this woman, soon." *Screw you, old man.*

Chris returned to his cabin and removed the Sully Williams disguise. Following the smart-casual dress code for the night, he put on white chino pants, a navy shirt, a light-blue blazer and boat shoes. At a high-end bar, he paid an extravagant amount for a bottle of Cakebread cabernet sauvignon with two wine goblets before returning to the salon music room. The musicians were on break. Anna was head down, scrolling aimlessly on a cell phone.

"Hi, Anna," he said.

When she looked up, she was beaming. "Hi, Chris."

"Do you like red wine?" he asked.

Her head tilted at the curiosity of the question. "Yes," she said simply.

"Do you like this trio?"

"Yes," she said again.

"So if you had to choose one, which would you pick?"

She glanced at the bottle and goblets. "The wine."

"Excellent choice. Follow me."

Chapter Twenty-Four: Grand Turk, Turks and Caicos Islands

Photos 71–77

TWENTY-FIVE

"Where're we going?" Anna asked while matching Chris stride for stride through the ship corridor.

"Just wait," he responded. The hot evening air greeted them beyond the sliding glass door near the pool. He led her to a quiet corner of an upper balcony shielded from the wind and isolated from strolling passengers. A nearly full moon provided most of the illumination. "How's this?" he asked, pointing to two deck chairs.

"Looks wonderful," she said with an air of anticipation.

He handed Anna the wine cork. She inspected it while he poured a sample of the cab into her goblet. She gave the glass a swirl, watched the legs forming on the sides, placed her pug nose over the rim, and savored the aroma. She took a sip. "Wow, that's good," she said with delight.

While pouring more into her glass, he asked. "How'd you become a wine connoisseur?"

"I'm hardly a connoisseur," she was quick to say. "But my dad always made a big deal of wines at family occasions, followed by an elaborate toast. But I'll keep mine simple." She raised her glass. "Chris, thanks for this very special treat."

"My pleasure." As they clinked, he observed her genuine appreciation. She seemed cheerful for the first time since day one of the cruise. Twisting his chair so they were face-to-face, Chris said, "So tell me all about Anna Monteiro."

She hesitated with a curious glance. He suddenly realized she had never disclosed her last name. To cover the faux pas, he quipped, "I assume you were born as a small child."

With a nervous chuckle, she said, "You're very insightful."

"Then what happened?"

Thankfully, Anna started opening up. "Well, let's see. I grew up in a northern suburb of Boston with two older brothers, went to neighborhood girls' schools for high school and college, and then Philadelphia for postgraduate."

Chris was surprised by her modesty. Anna failed to mention her neighborhood was one of the wealthiest in the United States, her schools were all prestigious, and she graduated with honors from an Ivy League university with two master's degrees. "So answer this critical question," Chris said in mock seriousness, "Pat's or Geno's?"

"Are we talking Philly cheesesteaks now? How do you know about them?"

"Just answer my question," he said sternly.

"Well, the only right answer of course is Pat's."

"Correct." Chris flashed a corny smile. "Now I know you're a true connoisseur of excellent wines and greasy cheesesteaks. You're a woman of refinement and culture."

Her face brightened with a laugh. "So how do you know about cheesesteaks?" she asked.

"Because I grew up in South Philly," he said, prepared to begin reciting the Chris Davis persona created for him at the farm in Lancaster County, Pennsylvania, before joining Thanatos.

"Do you still live there?"

"No, I'm in the Twin Cities now."

"Still have family in Philly?"

"No, my parents were killed in a car accident when I was ten."

"I'm sorry to hear that." Her sentiment seemed sincere.

"Thanks. So then my sister and I bounced around foster homes until we were both over eighteen. Then we were on our own."

"Does she also live in Minnesota?"

"No, San Diego. We have different lifestyles, so we've been estranged for about ten years."

A crease crossed her forehead. While sipping wine, she seemed to contemplate the next question. To her credit, she didn't pry into his relationship with his sister. "So where did you go to college?" she asked.

Chris feigned embarrassment. "I didn't."

"But didn't you tell me yesterday you're a cybersecurity consultant for international companies?"

"That's right."

"So if you don't mind my asking, how did that happen without a degree?"

"Well, the short version is I stole some computer equipment shortly after foster care and developed a lucrative hacking business until I was ratted out by a friend. When I was convicted, I was given the choice of eight years in prison or five years as a white hat hacker for the City of Philadelphia. That was an easy decision. After that gig, my record was expunged, and I was hired by the company I work for now."

Anna said with admiration, "That's impressive that you turned a tragic childhood into a great career."

If only that were true, he thought. "I was lucky," he said instead.

"Can I assume you're also lucky by traveling internationally for work?"

"Business travel isn't very glamorous," Chris said, "but it has allowed me to see a lot of the world."

His comment launched a ninety-minute conversation about their favorite foreign countries and cities. Anna had vacationed extensively with her family while growing up, plus had studied abroad for a couple of summers, yet had a long bucket list of places to visit. She seemed fascinated by his descriptions and recommendations.

After a discussion of Spain, she said, "I noticed yesterday in Santo Domingo that you speak fluent Spanish. Any other languages?"

"French, Italian, and a bit of Dothraki," he said with a smirk.

"Dothraki? What's that?"

"From *Game of Thrones*," he answered, then added, "Alikh sewafikh, tih khaleesi?"

"What did you just say?"

"More wine, my queen?"

With a charming giggle, Anna inched closer and held out the near-empty goblet for a third refill. Her hand seemed unsteady while he poured. The moonlight revealed dilated brown eyes and a glowing complexion. Her inhibitions were fading.

A ding from Chris's cell phone shattered the mood. It was no doubt an angry text from Michelle asking what the hell he was doing with the target. He didn't need to tolerate another inquisition. "Sorry about that," he said while muting the phone and stuffing it back into his pocket. "Now, let's see, somehow we got distracted from your life story. What happened after graduating in the City of Brotherly Love?"

"Well, I got married and moved to San Francisco." As if hesitant to divulge more, Anna looked away and took a long sip of wine.

He verbally nudged her along. "And what did you do there?"

"Well, I worked in a bank's marketing department," she said, again being humble by not explaining she had become a senior manager at Wells Fargo within eight years.

He asked, "Is that where you met the friend you're cruising with?"

"Yes. Jessica and I started as co-workers and just naturally clicked. We got even closer when our marriages began fizzling out." Anna sighed.

Chris gave a nod of understanding yet remained silent, hoping she'd fill the void.

"You see, Jessica's great at making you forget life's troubles. Always fun. So anyway, we started partying on weekends until I caught my husband with the guy next door. Even weirder, Paul announced he was moving in with the guy and his wife. So we agreed to get divorced and I moved back to Boston."

Sounds like the ex-husband is a jerk but has no motive to kill her.

Anna's shoulders slumped. Chris considered consoling her, but didn't. *Just let her keep talking.*

"Jessica's separation was slower and more painful. Just before her husband left her, she got pregnant. I was gone by then, so couldn't emotionally support her. I always felt bad about that. Now she's a single mom with a four-year-old. And this cruise is her first escape from reality, so I'm happy for her." Anna shivered.

Chris stood up and put his blazer around her shoulders. She clutched the lapels and drew them close.

In a weak voice, she said, "Chris, I'm sorry for going down that rabbit hole. You didn't need to hear all that."

"That's okay," he reassured her, feeling genuinely empathetic. "It sounded like you needed to talk about it."

"But that's not fair to you. We hardly know each other." Anna ran her fingers through her hair as if struggling to recover. "Let's talk about something else, can we?"

They did. The more they talked about safe topics, the more comfortable Anna seemed. She regularly mimicked his motions: sipping wine, crossing legs, leaning forward, unblinking eye contact, and an occasional flirt.

Chris struggled against growing infatuation. *Slow down on the wine, man. This isn't a date. You're working. Find out who wants this woman dead.* He asked, "So tell me about this biotech you work for."

Anna sat up. Her expression became animated. "It's called Longfellow BioSciences. I joined them as a start-up five years ago. They specialize in personalized cancer treatments."

"What's that mean?" Chris asked, genuinely interested.

"Well, most cancer patients are treated with some combination of drugs and radiation. They're formulated to kill cancer cells, but they're so toxic they often ruin people's quality of life before too many of them die anyway."

Anna's hands were gesturing with excitement as she continued the explanation. "In contrast, our patented immunotherapy technology analyzes the neoantigens of each person's cancer and measures their natural immune responses. Then we determine how to accelerate the positive immune responses, block the body's tendency to dampen those responses, and create a personalized treatment to optimize a person's natural ability to fight and cure the cancer."

"If I'm following you," Chris said, "instead of a scorch-the-earth approach, you're treating each person's cancer and immune system as if they're as unique as fingerprints."

"Exactly!" Anna said with unbridled excitement.

"Tell me how it works."

Anna explained the scientific details of the technology, the process steps, and the encouraging results from the clinical trials. Chris was enthralled, both by the vision and her unbridled passion. They were equally incredible. "So you're telling me your group has found a cure for cancer?"

"Not yet," she said with her characteristic humility. "We know the technology works, but still have years of testing ahead of us." Then she deflated like air seeping from a balloon. "But we might not have that chance."

"Why not?" Chris asked.

She paused before saying, "We're almost out of funding."

Trying to lighten Anna's sudden melancholy, Chris asked, "I suppose a GoFundMe page wouldn't work, huh?"

The joke brought a pained smirk to her lips. "Hardly."

"But if your technology is so promising, why can't you find more money?"

"Because we recently lost investor confidence."

"How'd that happen?"

"We fell short of the unrealistic clinical trial results our CEO promised."

Chris considered how to frame the next critical question. "Was there anything you could have done differently to change the outcome?" He studied her expression.

"No, nothing," she said with a wince. "Absolutely nothing. And that's what's so frustrating."

He surmised Anna had no part in the company's problems. To the contrary, she was a dedicated champion. *So why would Liz Walker and George Henniker want her killed?* This friendly interrogation hadn't uncovered any new answers. "What happens next?"

"Well, unless some big company buys us out, Longfellow could be dead soon."

"That would be tragic," Chris said with empathy.

"No, the really tragic part is not saving millions of lives like Jamie's."

"Who's Jamie?"

Anna recoiled, squeezed her eyes, wrung her hands and began explaining with a shaky voice. "He was my younger brother, ten years younger in fact. A whoops baby, and according to Mom, the best mistake she ever made." Anna managed a slight smile. "Anyway, he was smart, cute and full of life until age five when he started getting headaches and falling a lot." She grimaced as if hesitant to repeat the diagnosis. "It was an inoperable brain tumor."

"Oh, god," was all Chris could say.

"Yeah, well anyway, my older brothers were away at school, and my dad was traveling a lot, so Mom and I were his caregivers for two years. Countless treatments were tried, even experimental ones, but nothing worked. Toward the end, he was skeletal, blind, and attached to endless machines. One night after singing to him, I knew it was time." Anna choked up. "I told him I loved him and held him tight. After two horrific gasps for breath, he was gone."

"I'm so sorry for you, Anna." The standard response seemed so hollow.

"Thank you," she said while struggling to regain control.

"Is Jamie the reason you're so passionate about Longfellow?"

"Absolutely. No one should have to die like that, especially at his age. But they will because our company has failed."

Her ominous conclusion loomed between them. She was despondent. Her eyes were misty. Chris felt horrible. He was beginning to understand her pain, what drove her, and the emotional impact of Longfellow's pending demise. But there was no way to help.

He was also envious of Anna's mission. She was dedicated to saving lives. He had been taught to justify killing scumbags by picturing the lives he was saving. That was a crock of shit. He took lives and doubted there was a way to stop.

She glanced at her watch. "Oh my gosh. Do you believe it's one thirty? I've got to go to bed." She stood up slightly off balance, returned his blazer, and placed a hand on his arm. "Thanks for a wonderful evening. Sorry it had to end on such a downer."

"Not a problem. I enjoyed every minute of it." As they walked together, he added, "Maybe we can talk again tomorrow."

"I'd like that," she said while entering the corridor toward their rooms. "I know – how about a run around the deck in the morning? Say nine o'clock?"

"Sounds great," he said when stopping at his cabin door.

Chris hoped their separation wouldn't be awkward. He wasn't sure how he would handle it if she expected a kiss. Thankfully, their goodbye was cordial and fleeting.

He hadn't been in his cabin for more than a minute when there was a knock. "Did you forget something?" he asked.

"This is so embarrassing," Anna said apologetically. "Jessica has the Do Not Disturb sign on the door, meaning she's sleeping in our room with her new boyfriend. I don't have the energy to confront her again. Mind if I crash on your couch?"

Chris hesitated while contemplating her request. This was a severe rule violation of getting too close to a target.

Anna quickly added, "I assure you this is just about sleeping, nothing else. And that assumes you're not an axe murderer or something."

Meant as a joke, her statement hit too close to home. Then he rationalized if they were together all night, she couldn't take the

Midol in her cabin and, with luck, he might find it in her purse while she slept. Hopefully, he could also prevent her from using the tainted suntan lotion in the morning. She seemed worth saving, a rebellious decision he had never contemplated before. He wasn't sure it warranted the potential repercussions, but he could manage this. "Sure," he said. "You're more than welcome."

Once inside, he offered her the bed and said he would take the couch.

"No way. I'm taking the couch."

"If you insist." He handed her an extra blanket and pillow from the closet, said good night, and took another blanket with him toward the balcony.

"Where're you going?" she asked.

"To sleep on the deck so you can either use the bed or the couch. Your choice."

Anna followed him outside with her blanket, lay down on the adjacent lounger and got comfortable. "Sleeping under the stars sounds better," she said with a sweet smile.

A minute passed in silence except for the sound of waves crashing against the ship. She quietly asked, "Chris, what's your last name?"

"Davis," he answered.

"And how did you know mine?" Anna had obviously been wondering about his blunder all night.

"José, our tour guide from yesterday, told me when I asked."

"Why did you ask?"

"Because I thought you seemed interesting."

"Oh," she said simply. "Good night, Chris Davis."

"Good night, Anna Monteiro."

TWENTY-SIX

ATLANTIC OCEAN

Day Five of Cruise

Wednesday

Anna woke up to the sound of Chris putting a cup of coffee on a table between the balcony loungers. While squinting in the bright sunshine, she could see he had changed into blue running shorts and a Ralph Lauren polo shirt. "Good morning," she said while shuffling beneath the blanket.

"Good morning," Chris said with his cute smile. "I'm not sure if you like coffee, but it always gets me going after a night of drinking wine."

"Thank you. But the first order of business is this cottonmouth," she said with slight embarrassment, then pretended to brush her teeth with a finger. "Do you mind if I use some of your toothpaste?"

"Be my guest."

While standing, she noticed her wrinkled dress. She worried her face was equally ghastly. One look in the bathroom mirror confirmed it. With limited makeup in her purse, she tried salvaging her appearance, brushed some kinks from her hair, then shrugged. *Screw it. What you see is what you get.*

When she returned to the balcony, Chris was arranging covered plates on the table. "What's all this?" she asked.

"Have a seat and you'll find out." He placed a cloth napkin on her lap, draped another on his arm like a waiter in a fancy restaurant, and simultaneously lifted two silver plate warmers. "For your dining pleasure, madam," he said with charisma.

Parsley sprinkles were the garnish atop hollandaise sauce smothering poached eggs, ham slices and English muffins. On the other plate were cheese wedges, plus a mix of fresh fruit. Chris's breakfast was almost identical.

With an exaggerated pouty face, Anna asked, "How come I didn't get any bacon?"

"Because I stole yours," Chris said with a deadpan voice. "If we're going to get along, you have to realize I'll always steal your bacon. So like it or lump it." While laughing, he snapped one strip in half, pretended to give it to her, pulled it back, and ate it himself.

The food was delicious but the company was better. They engaged in playful banter while talking about nothing important. Anna had never felt this at ease with a man. Everything was natural. He was smart and successful without being pretentious. A gentleman, never pushy. Innately sexy. An interesting conversationalist. He was insatiably curious about her, a great listener, and was never judgmental about the problems she shouldn't have disclosed. Chris made her feel great, a feeling that had been absent a long time. She watched as he bit into a watermelon wedge, then wiped dripping pink juice from his long fingers.

Anna folded the napkin, placed it on the empty plate, and said, "That was an incredible breakfast. Thank you. The only thing better was last night. Everything about it was wonderful."

"No need to thank me," he said with those aquamarine eyes. "I thoroughly enjoyed it." The way he stammered over the last word made her think he was going to say "I thoroughly enjoyed you."

Anna said while placing a hand on his leg, "I've never met anyone like you before."

With a shy grin, he asked, "Is that a good thing?"

"Yes, you're amazing." She leaned forward for a kiss.

Unexpectantly, Chris recoiled and removed her hand.

"I'm so sorry," Anna said, surprised she had misread his signals. "I shouldn't have done that."

"No problem," he said with trepidation.

"Are you gay?"

"Hardly," he answered.

"Then not interested in me?"

"Very interested."

"Then what's wrong?"

Chris gazed at the ocean. "This is embarrassing to explain," he started, stopped, sighed, and resumed eye contact. "When I was twelve, I had the mumps which led to viral orchitis."

"What's that?"

"Severe inflammation of the testicles. Normally, it's very treatable. In very rare cases, like mine, the infection spreads and causes permanent ED."

"The little blue pill doesn't …"

"Nope, believe me, I've tried everything."

"I'm so sorry for you."

"Don't be," he said with conviction, then added with a wry grin. "But listen, if you lower your expectations, there are plenty of things we can do … if you're still interested."

As they rushed into the room, Chris asked with a glimmer in his eyes, "So do you want the couch or the bed this time?"

Anna pushed him onto the bed and joined him.

The next three hours were nothing like Anna had experienced or imagined possible. The pace was slow. Each touch was sensual. Every embrace was joyous. Exploring each other was natural. The waves of affection and passion and warmth were endless and divine. Their bond was incredible and rare. This time would always be cherished.

"Oh my god," Anna sighed while they cuddled beneath a sheet and stared at the ceiling. "You realize what you've just done, right?"

"No," he said with a touch of apprehension.

"You've forced me into a convent."

Sitting up with a curious look, he asked, "Was it that bad?"

She laughed. "To the contrary, it'll never be that good again, so I might as well become a nun."

After a few more minutes of closeness, Chris shifted the mood. "So are you ready for that run?"

"You've got to be kidding," Anna said. "One, you've drained every ounce of energy from me. And two, it must be a sauna out there."

"Then how about a swim?"

"In my dress?"

"No, I was thinking we'd go skinny-dipping."

Anna decided to go to her room to get a swimsuit and clean clothes for the day. When she saw the Do Not Disturb sign still hanging on the knob, she almost turned around, then got angry. "Jessica!" she screamed while pounding.

When her friend opened the door, Anna barged in and turned on all the lights. A guy quickly covered himself with a sheet.

Wearing only a towel, Jessica protested, "What are you doing? A little privacy would be nice."

"Sleeping in my own bed would be nice too, but you haven't given me that option."

Jessica's weak excuse – without an apology – was, "I didn't mean for him to spend the night. We just fell asleep."

"How romantic," Anna said sarcastically while rifling through the closet. "I've just come for some clothes, then you can have your precious privacy back. Just disinfect the place afterwards."

"You seem pissed," Jessica said.

"Of course I'm pissed! You ditched me for days, you locked me out of our room, and you've been nothing but selfish during most of this cruise."

"It hasn't been that bad."

"Yes, Jessica, it has been. Obviously not for you, but for me. This is no way to treat an old friend who hoped to have fun together. So let me get my stuff, then you can go back to having fun with your new friend."

"Anna, I didn't mean to …"

Cutting her off, Anna said, "I don't want to hear about it. Just give me a minute and I'll be gone."

Anna was devastated. Within the space of ten minutes, she had plummeted from an emotional high to an emotional low. After returning to Chris's room, she simmered in hurt anger. He didn't probe, offer sympathy, or give advice. He just held her. His perfect response was comforting and soothing. She gave him a long kiss for his understanding.

As expected, the pool area was crowded for the last day at sea. The band, alcohol and tropical sunshine created a festive atmosphere. People seemed in jubilant denial that the cruise would end tomorrow.

Chris and Anna did a few laps in the pool, sipped mimosas at the bar, and were lucky enough to snatch two loungers from a departing couple. When he lathered her back with suntan lotion, it was as relaxing as a massage. Later, while standing at the snack buffet, Anna pointed to the amazing wing tattoo on the woman she met on Sunday. Chris was equally impressed with the design.

When they returned to his room in the late afternoon, she told Chris she worried she had gotten sunburned. After a cursory glance, he said she seemed fine. Anna insisted he look closer. It took him a few seconds, but he finally got the memo.

✦✦✦

A couple of hours later, they dressed for dinner. It wasn't a formal night, but she had selected an elegant dress. Chris was handsome and debonair in a coat and tie. The maître d' accommodated their request for a table for two, then surprised them with an intimate corner near a window. The moonlight was glistening along the ocean waves.

"Excuse me for interrupting," Jessica said as she approached their table. With a nod of acknowledgment toward Chris, she said to him, "This will only take a minute." Then back to Anna. "I want to apologize for everything. You're right. I've acted terribly. I should've never been that selfish and rude." She took a deep breath to calm the visible trembling. The pause was long and excruciating. "Well, I guess that's all I want to say. Enjoy your meal."

As Jessica left, Anna felt like her good friend was walking away forever. She leapt up and ran after her. Without a word, they hugged. A few crappy days on a ship were not worth sacrificing years of supportive companionship. After making amends, Jessica explained she had dumped her new boyfriend. His true character had come out when he badmouthed Anna after leaving their cabin.

Anna was indecisive. The right thing to do was invite Jessica to dine with them, otherwise, she would also be guilty of abandoning her friend. But she wanted to spend the remaining hours alone with Chris. They might never see each other again.

As the women returned to the table, Chris immediately understood. He grabbed a vacant adjacent chair, signaled the waiter for an extra place setting and graciously welcomed Jessica. The meal was delicious and the conversation enjoyable. After eating, Jessica provided a gastrology lesson by suggesting they each have a couple shots of tequila.

Later, while exiting the theater after a cabaret show, Jessica pulled Anna aside. "Listen, I really like Chris and I can see why you do too. He's a keeper. So I'm going to disappear to the club so you two can be alone. Have a great time. You deserve it."

"Thanks, my friend," Anna said, getting a bit misty-eyed.

"Stop that," Jessica admonished her, "or your mascara will run." She handed Anna a tissue from her purse and used another one herself. "Are we good?"

"Yes," Anna said. "We'll always be good."

Chris and Anna held hands on the way back to his room. Before entering, he reminded her everyone needed to have their luggage outside of their cabin by ten o'clock. He was even gracious enough to help her pack. She declined, saying she could probably do it faster alone. He insisted, saying he was an expert after fifteen years of almost weekly travel experience. And he was right. The job was done in half the time. Packing his luggage was even faster.

After placing his bags outside the room, he held up the Do Not Disturb sign with that charming smile. He asked, "Do you think it's appropriate to put this on the door handle?"

"Absolutely!"

TWENTY-SEVEN

Miami, Florida

Disembark Cruise Ship

Thursday

M ichelle Barton fumed while watching her brother from afar in the US Customs section of Miami's cruise terminal. After collecting his luggage, Chris wheeled a cart toward Monteiro, added her bags, then her friend's. As the three of them waited in line for an available customs agent, Chris had the audacity to chatter in Monteiro's ear. His charming grin was beaming. The target was blushing like a lovesick teenager.

Has he lost his mind? He must know I'm watching.

While the women's luggage was loaded onto an airport shuttle by a porter, Chris and Monteiro engaged in a passionate kiss. He then shook hands with Jessica Daly and waved goodbye as the bus pulled away from the curb.

Michelle stood in disbelief among the hustle of departing cruise passengers. *What'll he do next? Keep avoiding me? Or come over?* Chris looked guilty as he approached Michelle. Her stance broadcast anger as she seethed in silence wearing the goth girl persona.

"Hi," was Chris's lame opening statement.

"Hi?" Michelle said in mockery of his salutation. "That's the best you've got? Hi?"

Chris lowered his eyes. "What do you want me to say?"

"What I want you to say is why you've been off the grid since the other night. And with the target, for god's sake."

He remained quiet while staring at his feet.

"Chris, look at me." He did. "Tell me you didn't sleep with Monteiro. And before you answer, realize I've seen your GPS coordinates on top of each other for the last thirty-six hours."

His evasive answer was, "That was never my intention."

"That's not what I asked. I want to know what happened and why."

Chris paused as if debating how truthful he would be – his jaw tightened with indecision – then he got emboldened. "Yes, I did. So what?"

Michelle became incredulous. "So what? It's totally unprofessional, that's what. What the hell's the matter with you? You've never been this reckless with a target before."

"Maybe that's because guys like Moretti and Umar weren't as cute." His sophomoric smile was infuriating.

"Knock it off, Chris. I'm in no mood for your asinine jokes. Just tell me how you let this happen."

Defensively, Chris said, "Because I wanted to know who wants Anna killed and why."

"Your damn Name that Client game again?" Michelle bristled. "How many times were you told to never try learning the name of a client and their motives?"

In frustration, he asked, "Are you going to keep yelling at me? Or do you want me to tell you what happened?"

Checking the impulse to keep lashing out, she let him explain.

"I inadvertently started to get to know Anna during the Santo Domingo tour and again on the beach in Grand Turk. My initial impressions were favorable."

"You mean you thought she was hot."

"No," Chris said forcefully. "I thought she was smart and intriguing. And the fact that there was no Hate file from Thanatos on her bothered me. I had to find out why. So I invited her to talk on Tuesday night."

"That's when you seduced her?"

"No, and I resent your implication. We just talked. And the more we did, the more I learned how intelligent, humble and passionate she is about finding a cure for cancer. Michelle, there is nothing to hate about Anna. Just the opposite."

"That's why you slept with her?"

"No, that part was an accident."

"How the hell do you sleep with someone by accident?"

Her question got a disapproving stare from a passing old couple.

The siblings moved to an isolated corner for privacy. Chris explained how Anna was locked out of her cabin, how they slept on the balcony, had breakfast the next morning, then got carried away by mutual desire. He ended with the admission, "I know it was wrong."

"You mean stupid," Michelle said.

"But it happened. Listen, Irene may have taken away my ability to have sex, but she didn't surgically remove my emotions."

"Instead, she surgically removed your brains," Michelle continued her hushed rant. "Chris, what you did was selfish. You know Monteiro has no future. And even if she did, do you expect her to fall in love with … with someone in our business?" Neither of the siblings had ever dared to have a love interest. Relationships were strictly forbidden.

"No," he said with a pained expression.

"And imagine what Irene would think about you sleeping with a target."

Chris got angry. "I'm tired of worrying about what that old hag thinks."

Michelle made another quick scan for eavesdroppers before asking, "Are you also tired of living? We both know if we don't kill

Monteiro, Irene will assign someone who will. Then she'll retaliate against us."

"Now you're being melodramatic. There is no way Irene would kill us for one unfulfilled commission. She has too much invested in us."

"And you're being delusional," Michelle countered. "She'd snuff us out in a heartbeat."

Chris's shoulders slumped, his eyes closed, and his face was pinched with distress. The silence was excruciatingly long. While shaking his head, he said in a whisper of denial and uncertainty, "I'm not sure I can kill Anna."

"We have to," Michelle said firmly. "There's no other option."

He seemed debilitated with indecision.

Michelle's next appeal was slow and measured. "Chris, if you had to choose between Monteiro's life or mine, which would you pick?"

His expression softened. "You know the answer to that, right?" He stared at his sister as if imagining her dead, then reached out with a reassuring touch. "Nothing's ever going to happen to you," he said emphatically. "Never."

After a shared moment of tenderness between siblings, Michelle pushed back and asked, "Does this mean you're back in the game?"

"Yes," he said in a noncommittal tone.

"Are you sure?" she asked again.

"I said yes." This time, his answer had more conviction.

"Okay, so what do we do next?"

"Well, I helped Anna pack last night and didn't find her bottle of Midol. Maybe she lost it by the pool after you did the exchange. So I told her I had business in Boston on Monday."

"Why would you do that?"

"Because I knew she'd invite me to her house, which is exactly what she did. I'm supposed to see her on Saturday."

"See her or stay with her?"

He said sheepishly, "Probably the latter."

Michelle shook her head in continued disbelief. "So you're going to fly home now and then go back in two days?"

"No, I rebooked my flight back to Boston tonight."

"To do what?"

"Photograph the city until Saturday night, I suppose. It's better than all that flying and expense."

"What about me?"

"You're still scheduled to fly to Minneapolis today. Then, if you want, join me again on Monday."

Michelle became incredulous. "Now you're doing this solo?"

"No, I thought you'd want to get home and enjoy a summer weekend."

She studied him for a hint of deceit. None was evident, but they were both trained liars. He often gave her short time-offs to decompress from stress. But she suspected his real reason was to spend a weekend with Monteiro out of her watchful eye. But he'd never admit it.

As if reading her mind, Chris said, "Seriously, I was only thinking of you."

She had to accept the explanation at face value. Further accusations and arguments would go nowhere. Then Michelle cringed at the thought of how Chris would know the answer to her next question. "Is she having her period yet?"

Chris involuntarily smirked. "Not that I saw." Her brother could be such a jerk sometimes.

Michelle unzipped a travel bag, considered giving him the tin box with the poisoned Tylenol tablet, then reconsidered. Instead, she grabbed a handful of tainted tampons. "The drug overdose scenario is too risky now. You could be implicated if it happened while you're with her. So replace these with her other tampons. Nobody will blame you if she dies of toxic shock syndrome. Can you do that?"

"Yes," he said while putting them into his luggage.

"If you succeed with the exchange, send me an encrypted note on Sunday. Then we'll decide if it's worth my trip back to Boston. Sound like a game plan?"

"Yup."

There was lingering reason to doubt him, but Michelle was convinced her brother would do the right thing. He always had before.

TWENTY-EIGHT

BOSTON, MASSACHUSETTS
Thursday

During the shuttle ride to Miami's airport, Anna basked in the afterglow of the magical time with Chris. But the warm memories turned to flickering embers and then white ash when entering her brownstone in Boston's Back Bay. The bullet hole was still in the window. Blue's faded bloodstain loomed on the rug. Soon the washing machine would remove the lingering sand and smells of the Caribbean.

The real world was back.

Anna's problems multiplied in the study. Although the speed of the internet was a joy compared to the ship's, it delivered bad news faster. George's attorney wanted to schedule a deposition. Longfellow's stock had dropped another fifty percent. Employee emails sounded panicky, hopeless, or in denial of the company's short-term prognosis. Turning off the computer did nothing to stop the swirling anxiety.

Her thoughts returned to Chris. They would be reunited within forty-eight hours. *Will the passion continue? Or will it fade away over the weekend? Could a long-distance romance work? They rarely do, especially if he's traveling all the time. Stop overthinking this. Don't have expectations. Enjoy the euphoria while it lasts. You deserve it.* Anna spent the rest of the evening cleaning the house in anticipation of his arrival.

He was the only promise of happiness on the horizon.

TWENTY-NINE

Miami, Florida & Boston, Massachusetts
Thursday

Chris declined Michelle's suggestion to share a ride from the cruise terminal to Miami International Airport. He claimed he was going to photograph local sights before his late flight back to Boston. The real reason was he didn't want to risk another confrontation with his sister or, worse yet, suffer through more of her judgmental stares.

Yet Michelle was right. They both knew it. He had screwed up. But he was still unwilling to accept the inevitable. There had to be a better solution than to kill Anna.

Chris took a taxi to the nearest big-box electronics store. Despite the cabbie's ticking meter, he spent over an hour selecting a new laptop and cell phone. These disposables would allow covert activities out of the watchful eye of Thanatos. He paid for them using the credit card of an off-the-books persona he had created years ago to hide similar clandestine actions.

Chris was dropped off at Villa Casa Casuarina[78] in South Beach. After dragging his luggage toward the front door of the elite hotel, he stopped to admire the statue of the Kneeling Aphrodite – the Greek goddess of love – and the spot where fashion designer Versace was assassinated in 1997. He had hoped the symbolic contrast would provide inspiration. The opposite occurred. A forbidding shadow of the future created greater dread.

Chris barely tasted the extravagant lunch of carpaccio and wild salmon with a glass of pinot grigio. Instead, he contemplated multiple scenarios. Each one ended in disaster. The only difference among the options was how many people died.

As a diversion, he sipped after-lunch coffee while configuring the new electronics. He downloaded apps, modified settings and created a new email account to communicate with Anna.

The return flight to Boston was uneventful. Surprisingly, he slept most of the way. In a Logan Airport bathroom, he donned his Ted Collins disguise before checking into the Back Bay hotel where he had stayed the week before. The receptionist remembered him and graciously provided the same room overlooking the Charles River.[79]

Upon entering, he pulled out the Nikon camera and used the zoom lens to zero in on Anna's brownstone. The lights were on. Anna was somewhere beyond that brick façade. He pictured her in his mind.

His smile was consumed by a bolt of worry. What if he had overlooked the Midol in her cruise cabin while helping her pack? What if she took the poisoned pill? She could be dead already.

On an impulse, he wrote her an email using the new laptop. The message was succinct. "Hope you arrived home safely. Thinking about you. Looking forward to Saturday." He pushed Send before common sense could object. He was relieved when Anna responded in ten minutes.

The last task was dreadful but obligatory. He opened the company-issued laptop, waited for the iris scan to recognize him, then ignored two days of unanswered messages from Thanatos and Michelle.

His daily report was unusually brief. It summarized his false tracking activities during the last day of the cruise and explained Monteiro had not yet taken the Midol. He also wrote he was now back in Boston and would develop alternatives. He remained confident the commission would be implemented by the deadline in one week.

That commitment was a bald-faced lie. He would not let Anna die.

Before going to sleep, Chris used the camera again to stare at Anna's home.

Chapter Twenty-Nine: Miami, Florida & Boston, Massachusetts

Photos 78–79

THIRTY

The following morning, Anna stopped at the coffee shop before entering the lobby of Longfellow BioSciences. Mercifully, someone had removed the real-time stock ticker above the receptionist, plus the framed articles of praise along the hallway. If still there, they would have been a mockery of the current morass. But their absence seemed symbolic of impending ruin.

Anna tapped lightly on the glass office door of Liz Walker.

A bright smile spread across the Irish face of her friend while waving her in. Liz asked, "What are you doing here?"

"Hopefully I still work here."

"Thanks," the chief science officer said in acknowledgment of the coffee. "What I meant is I didn't expect you until Monday."

"I just came by to pick up some stuff. I won't be staying long."

"Yeah, right," Liz said as if knowing Anna would probably stay all day. With a tilt of her red hair and a stare, Liz added, "The vacation seems to have been good for you. You're glowing."

"I did get some time in the sun."

"I wasn't talking about your tan." Liz leaned forward. With a beaming chuckle reminiscent of their high school days, she proclaimed, "You met a guy, didn't you?"

"Is it that obvious?"

"Yes, it's obvious." Liz's eyes began to gleam. "Tell me, was it a hot-and-heavy fling?"

Anna felt her neck blush. She giggled. "Yes."

"Attagirl," Liz said with joy while clapping her hands. "You needed that. And did you abandon the boy's broken heart, or are you going to see him again?"

"Tomorrow night actually."

"You mean he lives nearby?" Liz was excited.

"No, in the Twin Cities."

"Yet he's flying here so soon?" Liz laughed. "Sounds like serious lust to me."

"Okay, that's enough."

"Baloney! You're talking to an old married woman here. I've got to live vicariously through your wanton ways."

"How about a consolation prize?" Anna dug into her backpack and produced the conch shell from Grand Turk.

"That's lovely. Thanks," Liz said while examining the gift. "But I'd still rather have a decadent tryst in the Caribbean."

"Me too," Anna said with a giddy grin.

The enjoyable moment between best friends disappeared when Liz looked at her watch. Her professional demeanor returned while saying, "Listen, I want to hear everything about this guy and your trip – I really do – but I've got a meeting in a few minutes."

"I understand," Anna said while standing. "Just give me a quick update on things here."

Deep lines spread across Liz's pained expression. She gnawed her lower lip. Her eyes squeezed with tension. After leaning back and emitting a sigh, she said, "Not good. Todd assures us he's doing everything he can," she said, referring to Todd Milken, Longfellow's CEO. "But current investors are bailing out by the day. And finding new money is harder than he thought. You know it must be bad for Mr. Omnipotent to admit that."

Anna hesitated to ask, "What does that mean?"

"It means we're in the ninth inning, but not out. Todd claims he's pushing hard on a potential white knight. I can't tell you who it is. All I can say is it's a big pharma with deep pockets."

"That's encouraging," Anna said, trying to sound hopeful.

"Sort of," Liz said. "It seems their president is on the fence about the deal."

"Is there a strategy to make him commit?"

"Well, that's where I come in. Todd has arranged for me to make a personal appeal to the guy on Tuesday while he's in Chicago. But it's got to be hush-hush. We can't be seen together or we might spark acquisition rumors."

"That's great. I know you'll win him over."

"Let's hope so," Liz said, lacking her normal confidence.

"Is there anything I can do to help you get ready?"

"No, but thanks. Just wish me luck. On second thought, yes, there is something you can do." A fleeting smile crossed Liz's lips. "Create lots of juicy stories this weekend so I can hear all about them."

THIRTY-ONE

Friday

The alarm on Chris's cell phone went off at six thirty. As he lumbered to the bathroom, he glanced out the hotel window at Anna's brownstone thirty-three stories below. The memory of waking up with her twenty-four hours earlier was wonderful.

Instinctively, he pulled out the company cell phone and clicked on the app to track her movements on GPS. The red dot was moving away from her house, headed toward the river. Presumably she was walking to work. Chris debated. He could transform into Ted Collins, take a cab to Kendall Square, and maybe catch a glimpse of her entering Longfellow.

The juvenile impulse was rejected. Only focused professionalism, not indulgent romanticism, would save Anna. There was plenty of work to do. The homework could take all day.

He considered several possible scenarios while trying to be objective. He concluded only two outcomes were viable. Either Anna died within a week. Or the person who initiated the commission had to die. Surely Thanatos would cancel the silentcide contract if they knew they weren't going to be fully paid. Yes, this was the best option. Frankly, the only option.

The unanswered question was who did Chris need to kill? Liz Walker? George Henniker? Or both? Once the kill list was determined, he could focus on the how.

The first task was an in-depth introduction to George Henniker. Chris had identified him on day one of the commission through Anna's correspondence with the police. Back then, Henniker was a potential client. Now he was a potential target.

Chris started with a visit to the Moneyer Capital Management website. The homepage was all dazzle and fluff: mission statement, company profile, unprecedented hedge fund track record, deep commitment to clients, lover of stray animals, blah, blah, blah.

A click on "Our Team" featured a prominent photo of Henniker. Mid-forties. Slicked back hair. Oval face with cleft chin. Deep-set eyes. Strained smile. Power black suit with crisp white shirt, red silk tie, diamond cufflinks and a showy Rolex watch. In the background was a colorful array of computer monitors. All that was missing was a banner above his head declaring: "I'm a conceited ass."

A quick scan of his social media confirmed his self-importance. An extravagant house, a fast car and a network of socialite friends. Public records revealed a nasty divorce, several liens, a few lawsuits and his current legal troubles with Anna.

Step two was to gain electronic access to Henniker's files without using any of the tools or facilitator support provided by Thanatos. He began by downloading a VPN. The virtual private network's encryption would provide a modicum of online anonymity. Then he added a Tor browser using a secure node. The onion routing allowed untraceable access to the dark web.

The next step was identifying an appropriate hacking software suite. The options seemed endless, ranging in price from free to over ten thousand dollars. Chris sought advice in hacker forums on the dark web. That was a creepy and convoluted trip down an internet back alley. Everyone was an expert. Nobody could be trusted. Most seemed illiterate. Greed was rampant. Chris assumed most of the chatters were eighteen-year-old hacker wannabes who were hyped up on Red Bull and testosterone.

Chris finally found BlackHatWorld.com. He spent several hours on the platform's marketplace uncovering and cross-validating what he hoped were reliable and experienced sources. The best choice seemed to be OdinOne, named after the Norse god of wisdom. The "computer security consultant," aka a professional hacker, answered every question, provided numerous tutorials with schematics and screenshots, and made a final recommendation based on Chris's requirements. Seven thousand dollars consummated the purchase of the sophisticated hacking toolbox.

Next on the to-do list was to lure Henniker into the scheme. Chris developed an elaborate portfolio spreadsheet of current investments and embedded the malware into Excel macros. Then he wrote an email explaining he was seeking a hedge fund portfolio manager who could generate a high return for his seven million dollars of fun money. That should make Henniker salivate.

Chris chuckled while hitting Send. Chances were high that Henniker's greed would compel him to open the attached Excel file. Once he did, Chris hoped to win the Golden Ticket by acquiring administrative access to the company's multiple servers, after which he'd be able to observe all user activities and control any device from his laptop. Achieving this ultimate goal of complete vertical privileged escalation would require a healthy combination of work and luck. Chris felt lucky.

The hook was in the water. Chris had to wait for Henniker to take the bait.

Chris turned his attention to Elizabeth "Liz" Walker. His research revealed the chief science officer had flowing red hair, a field of freckles and energetic green eyes. She had been married for fourteen years to an optometrist. They had a ten-year-old son, a budding soccer player. Liz's education in biomedical engineering was impressive: bachelor's degree from the University of Pennsylvania, an MBA from Massachusetts Institute of Technology, and an MD from Johns Hopkins University. She had worked for bio-science companies for several years before co-founding Longfellow BioSciences. Numerous online articles called her a cancer visionary.

Scrolling through her computer files and emails produced little of value until Chris chanced on communications from the company's CEO, Todd Milken. The man had brutal assessments of Liz, essentially blaming her for every corporate shortcoming and the biotech's dire situation. Even if partially true, the man's tone and arrogance were atrocious.

Chris diverted his attention to Milken's computer. It seemed the CEO treated most senior managers with contempt. Worse yet, from Milken's presentations to the board, the company's potential lifespan was shorter than Anna thought: two months at best.

Milken's outreach to current investors was conciliatory yet failing. His appeals to new investors were dismal, except one. There was a flicker of hope with Fármaco, the second-largest pharmaceutical company in oncology revenue. They were discussing a two-hundred-fifty-million-dollar buyout. Terms and conditions were being negotiated. Lawyers and financial officers were haggling over details. Nothing seemed assured, but Milken had painted a rosy picture to his board. The next meeting had been arranged with Fármaco's president and Liz Walker for Tuesday afternoon in Chicago.

Chris smiled. Perhaps Anna's dream and passion for curing cancer had a future. Now he had to make sure she had a future without betraying Michelle or incurring Irene's wrath.

His thoughts drifted toward Anna. He checked her GPS location on the phone. She was home. He looked at his watch and realized he had been working for nearly twelve hours. He stood to stretch and drifted toward the window to glance at Anna's brownstone. He had promised Michelle he would remain disciplined, but he wanted to hear Anna's voice. *To hell with it.* He called using one of his burner phones. Anna answered. They chatted for an hour.

Talking with her was natural and engaging. They discussed the cruise, their time together and made weekend plans. When she promised to make him a special dinner for Saturday night, he laughed when she asked for his favorite food besides bacon.

He was so enthralled in the conversation that the sound of an advancing police siren barely registered. If she heard the same siren outside her window, his ruse of being in the Twin Cities would be exposed. He raced into the bathroom, closed the door and abruptly said goodbye.

He chastised himself. His feelings for Anna were making him careless. If his plans to identify and kill the Thanatos client were to be successful, he must be controlled, diligent and cunning. Anything less could be disastrous.

When Chris returned to his desk, he saw Henniker had responded to his email. Excellent! There would be a long night ahead trolling through the Moneyer Capital Management computers plus Henniker's files and emails. Then, on Saturday morning, Chris could start tracking Henniker in order to learn his activity patterns.

For the moment, George Henniker seemed despicable but might not be culpable. Liz Walker seemed less likely to be Thanatos's client, but good people often do strange things under extreme pressure. In short, the jury was still out on who had to die.

THIRTY-TWO

WESTON AND BOSTON, MASSACHUSETTS
Saturday

While wearing his Sully Williams disguise – stringy black wig, matted beard and mustache, plus aviator sunglasses – Chris surveyed the golf course clubhouse[80] from the parking lot. After seeing an unattended bag of clubs, he nonchalantly walked up, grabbed a five-iron, then returned to his rental car. This would make the ideal prop.

He drove a few blocks until reaching the dead end of a service road. Then he strolled along the wooded edge of a fairway[81] as if searching for an errant golf ball. Three minutes later, he reached the perimeter of George Henniker's two-acre property in Weston, one of New England's wealthiest neighborhoods, located about fifteen miles from downtown Boston.

The isolated American colonial mansion had a refined brick exterior. Yet, according to Zillow, the seven and a half thousand square feet of ego had a value of about four million dollars.

Chris chuckled. Based on the Moneyer Capital Management files he had scoured the previous night, there was no doubt Henniker would soon be selling the over-mortgaged estate. His hedge fund was a disaster and sinking fast. Year-to-date, the firm's investments had declined twenty-seven percent in a thriving bull market. Assets under management were down thirty-nine percent because clients were leaving in droves. And Henniker had not yet reported the nineteen-million-dollar bloodbath in Longfellow BioSciences.

Investors were also unaware of his legal problems. According to email exchanges with his attorney, Henniker was facing potential prison time for assaulting Anna's home.

In short, George Henniker was professionally and personally screwed.

Unfortunately, Chris hadn't uncovered any correspondence confirming Henniker was the client responsible for the kill order on Anna. Perhaps Henniker used steganography to encrypt and hide the files inside inconsequential ones on the hedge fund's system. Or more likely, the damning evidence was on a computer outside the network or on a detachable drive.

With reluctance, Chris vowed to remain patient and to learn more before taking action. Jumping to a conclusion was unprofessional. A man's arrogance and incompetence did not justify being killed … at least not yet.

Chris looked at the screen of the cell phone he purchased in Miami. The yellow GPS dot indicated Henniker was downtown. But his property no doubt had security cameras. Chris remained hidden in the surrounding trees while placing three microcameras aimed at the front and back of the mansion, plus the four-door garage.

After returning to his hotel in the Back Bay, Chris began a shopping spree. He didn't dare wear his cruise attire during the weekend with Anna. He also needed to find the right woman to help establish an alibi.

Chris first searched nearby Newbury Street.[82] The mile of nineteenth-century brownstones contained an array of expensive boutique shops, galleries and restaurants. His next hunting ground was among the premier retailers at Prudential Center[83] and Copley Place. Both produced the clothes he wanted. Neither uncovered a desirable accomplice.

His criteria was simple yet hard to find. The right woman had to be mature but not old, reliable yet gullible, trustworthy with a bendable moral compass, and financially motivated without the risk of becoming greedy or calling the police. Although both high-end retail venues were crowded with women, none seemed to fit the bill.

On a lark, Chris entered the McKim Building, Boston's central library since the late nineteenth century. The lobby's marble floors and vaulted ceilings with mosaic tiles were striking. More magnificent was the Grand Staircase[84] with ivory steps, yellow marble walls and paintings by a famous French muralist. The fifty-foot-high vaulted ceiling in the Bates Hall[85] reading room resembled a European cathedral.

Sitting humbly among the grandeur was a potential candidate: an average-looking woman – maybe late twenties – with badly cut brown hair and red highlights, drooping oversized glasses, a dimpled chin and pockmarked complexion. She was wearing a baggy sweatshirt while hunched over an old book. Beside her on the reading table was a worn Gucci bag.

She's perfect.

Chris's opening line was, "What are you doing in a stuffy library on a glorious Saturday afternoon?"

At first startled, the woman looked up with a glare. Then her academic expression melted into a shy smile as she said awkwardly, "Rewriting history."

"How so?" Chris asked with charisma.

Still acting cautious, she answered, "I'm working on my dissertation."

"Can I ask the topic?"

With a hint of pride and excitement, she said, "How the thirteen colonies would've evolved into New Britain had the English won the Revolution."

"That's a fascinating hypothesis," he said – and meant it – then paused as if considering the topic. "Is that for a master's degree?"

Sounding insulted, she said, "No, a PhD." Then quickly added, "From Harvard."

"That's impressive," he said while sitting down across from her and placing the shopping bags on the floor. He locked eyes on his potential accomplice.

Initially she flinched. But, to her credit, she didn't look away. He decided to make the proposition fast and direct. "I'd imagine you have a pile of student debt, right?"

Her defensive wall rose. She said cautiously, "I've gotten lots of scholarships but, sure, what doctorate candidate isn't swimming in debt?"

"How'd you like to earn five hundred dollars a day for the next week?"

"How'd you like to fuck off?" came the angry retort.

"No problem," Chris said while standing. "Good luck with your dissertation."

He took three steps before she called out, "Hey, wait a minute. What would I have to do?"

As he returned, he lowered the bags again, removed the Thanatos cell phone from his pocket, and placed it on the table. "If I said all you have to do is walk my dog for a week, would you do it for thirty-five hundred dollars?"

"Maybe," she said cautiously.

"Then consider this my dog," he said, pointing at the phone.

"What's that supposed to mean?"

Chris scrolled to the GPS map. "See that red dot. If it moves, follow along at least two blocks away. If it goes into the house where it is now, retreat to your hotel room."

"What hotel room?"

"An executive suite where you'll be staying. Drink anything from the mini-fridge. Order all the room service you want. All expenses paid. Plus enjoy the solitude to work on your dissertation."

"I'm guessing that's your room, right?" she asked with disdain.

"Nope. The next time you'll see me is when I retrieve the phone."

She shook her head with disapproval. "Whatever this is, it sounds illegal."

"I assure you, what you'll be doing is perfectly legal and safe. I just need you to distract the people who are tracking my movements on that phone."

"So you can do something illegal?"

"If I tell you that, you might become implicated. It's better you remain uninformed."

She leaned back and said with conviction, "Nope, this all sounds too shady."

He placed two bulging envelopes with hundred-dollar bills next to her purse. "That's five thousand dollars," he said, "for a week's work plus expenses."

She hesitated. He waited. She pushed her glasses up while staring at the wad of money. He waited. She peeked inside one of the envelopes. He waited longer, then grabbed the money and declared, "Okay, never mind. Nice meeting you."

Chris left the reading room and was about to go down the staircase when he heard hurried footsteps.

Breathless and scared, yet greedy for a windfall, she asked, "If I said yes, when would I start?"

"As soon as I can get your phone number."

After a moment of reluctance, she complied. Chris called the number using his Miami-purchased burner phone. After her personal phone rang, he had her install the Find My iPhone app, asked for her Apple ID, and ran a quick test. Then he handed her the money and the Thanatos phone. She stuffed both into her purse while looking around nervously. With hesitation she asked, "How do you know I won't run away with your money?"

"Because I can track your movements. See, you're now the dot at the library. And if you ditch the phones, it'll be easy to find a history grad student at Harvard."

They spent a few minutes discussing the details. As Chris left, he realized having his sister as a trusted partner during clandestine activities was so much easier and less risky than recruiting a novice.

If only he could convince Michelle what he was doing was the right course of action. In time, he was confident she would understand … at least he hoped so.

During the walk back to the hotel, Chris purposely took a weaving path around Copley Square[86] until he found a sleeping derelict. For a hundred dollars, he purchased the man's hoodie.

After entering his hotel room, Chris packed for the weekend with Anna but didn't check out. The room was booked for a week to store his extra clothes, disguises and Thanatos equipment.

On the drive to Logan Airport, he encountered hideous traffic. He returned the rental car, called Anna from baggage claim and said he had just arrived. The airport announcements added credibility.

Hearing the excitement in her voice was exhilarating.

While waiting in line for a cab, he happened to glance at his luggage. The airline tag read MIA to BOS.

Goddamn it, he cursed to himself while ripping off the tag. *Stop being so sloppy. A single error could get you killed.*

Chapter Thirty-Two: Weston and Boston, Massachusetts

Photos 80–86

THIRTY-THREE

BOSTON, MASSACHUSETTS

Anna felt like a swooning teenager but couldn't help it. After Chris called from the airport, she kept returning to the front window until a cab arrived forty minutes later. She debated running out to greet him. She didn't want to appear overanxious. But heck, she was overanxious. Their first kiss was spectacular.

Once inside the brownstone, Chris began with accolades similar to most people's reaction during their first visit. "This place is amazing," he said while scanning the sitting room. "It has an aura of – what should I call it? – an elite Victorian social club."

Anna laughed. "That's the best description I've ever heard."

"No offense," Chris said with hesitation, "but I didn't picture this as your style."

"Rest assured, this is my father's taste," Anna explained. "I've just been house sitting for the last five years. Now, if you want to see a completely different style, follow me."

The French country kitchen was elegant. The color scheme on the cathedral-style cabinetry was off-white and sky blue surrounded by intricate crown and corbel moldings, copper pans, plus a chandelier above an oversized island topped by Carrara marble.

"This is my mother's taste," Anna explained. "And as you'll see later, her influence permeates the rest of the house. So now you know who wears the designer pants in the family."

Chris looked around as if impressed by the lavish ambiance. Yet to Anna, the décor was excessive and embarrassing.

He asked, "You know what the best part of this kitchen is?"

"What?"

"The aroma. Something smells fantastic. What are you cooking?"

"Beef stroganoff. In fact, my special recipe. Would you like to try it?" she asked while lifting the cover off a pan.

Chris beamed when dipping in a spoon. "Is that what I think it is?"

"Sure is," she said. "There's a pound of bacon floating around in there. That way I'm sure you won't hog it all ... pun intended."

He gave her an impromptu kiss, then asked, "Doesn't it seem like we've known each other more than a few days?"

"I'm offended," Anna said in jest. "Today's our one-week anniversary when we met at the lifeboat drill."

"God bless the Great Pumpkin!" he loudly declared.

They kissed again. This one was long and tender.

"And to celebrate," Anna announced with excitement, "I got us a bottle of Cakebread."

"Now you're really spoiling me."

"Just returning the favor."

After toasting, Anna said, "Hey, grab your glass and luggage and I'll show you the rest of the place."

The next floor was dominated by an enormous master bedroom. The walls were baby blue. The intricate crown and floor molding were stark white. A gorgeous and soothing color contrast. At one end was a Victorian cast-iron fireplace. At the other was a king-size canopy bed with four tall spiral posters. All of the early American furniture was handcrafted in cherry wood.

"Lovely," Chris said in a low voice.

"It is a wonderful room," Anna agreed.

As they made eye contact, he said, "I wasn't referring to the room."

An amorous pause followed. The mutual attraction was tangible. Excitement and anticipation fluttered in her chest. She unconsciously licked her lips. Unsure if she could trust her voice, Anna asked, "Is it childish to make out right away?"

"Probably," Chris said with an impish grin.

"Wanna be childish?"

An hour later, while wrapped warmly within a comforter, Chris gently ran his fingers through her short black hair. Her toes absently played with his. Their closeness was affectionate and caring. This was a cherished moment of serenity with a man Anna never expected to find and never wanted to let go. She emitted a soft sigh of joy.

"You look happy," Chris whispered.

"I am," she said while lightly touching his lips. "I could spend the whole weekend here."

"Me too," he said with tenderness, then added with a smirk, "Only one problem."

"What's that?"

"Our wineglasses are empty."

Anna gave him a playful slug on the shoulder yet was enamored by his charm. "I suppose you're also thinking about all that bacon, right?"

"It had crossed my mind."

When they returned to the kitchen and refilled their wineglasses, Anna asked if he was ready for dinner. Or first they could nibble on cheese and crackers in the sitting room. He chose the latter after sampling more of the stroganoff.

While they cuddled on a camelback sofa lined with overstuffed pillows, Chris surveyed the room again as if savoring every intricate detail. His eyes stopped abruptly at the bullet hole in the bay window.

"What happened there?" he asked as a rare wrinkle swept across his brow.

Tentatively, she answered, "Someone shot at the house."

"I can see that. Do you know who did it?"

Anna tensed. Her eyes squeezed in anguish. The trauma of George was shattering her rare happiness. The memories felt like a repeat assault.

Chris shuffled his position. She felt his concerned stare. "Anna, what's wrong?"

"Nothing," she mumbled.

He cupped her hands, leaned closer and said with compassion, "Please tell me what happened."

The details came spilling out. She told him about George Henniker, how they dated a few times, how he threatened her at the door, spent a night in the drunk tank, and shot at the house a few days later. She also explained about the restraining order and pending criminal trial. "The worst part," she said as her lips quivered, "was what George did to Blue."

"What's Blue?"

"He was my cocker spaniel. I loved that dog." She struggled to contain the sorrow. "See the rectangular outline on the floor where the wood looks darker. A Persian rug used to be there. That's where Blue was shot and bled to death."

Chris said nothing. He didn't have to. His hug was consoling as she succumbed to grieving. She began to cry.

When the tears slowed and another minute passed, he asked, "Feeling better now?"

Anna nodded with a sniffle. In embarrassment, she said, "I'm sorry about the waterworks. I rarely cry. Really. But this is, what, the second time I've done it in front of you."

"Don't apologize. They've been totally justified," Chris said. "But what I still don't understand is why this Henniker guy did this to you."

"It's all my fault really," Anna admitted.

"I doubt that."

"Yeah, in a way it was."

"What could you've possibly done to justify his violence?" Chris asked with concern.

"See, during a date, George was asking a bunch of questions about Longfellow. As a hedge fund manager, I suspected he was fishing for insider information. So when he asked me out for the following Friday, I said that'd be great because I'd have something exciting to celebrate." She internally chastised herself for such a stupid lack of judgment.

Chris looked perplexed. "That's it? I don't get it."

"Well, the results of our clinical trials were going to be announced that day. If George was following the company, he'd know that, assume the announcement was good news, and make a bet the stock price would soar."

"Is that what happened?" Chris asked.

"No, just the opposite. It dropped about seventy-five percent and has fallen ever since."

"And that's when his attacks began?"

"Yup. That night George came pounding on the door in a drunken rage while Liz and I were sitting right here."

"Who's Liz?"

"Liz Walker. She's been my best friend since high school and is also my boss at Longfellow. In fact, she's the brains behind the cancer technology. What made that night even worse was, after the police hauled George away, Liz blamed me for the whole thing."

"That seems unfair."

"No, she was right," Anna countered with increasing guilt. "I should've never used the company for an ethics test on George. As Liz said, I should've just dumped the guy if I didn't trust him."

"So she's mad at you?"

"Yeah, initially she was pissed, but I think it was more hurt than anything."

"But she still holds a grudge?" Chris asked.

"No way, not Liz. Our friendship is stronger than one mistake. Besides, she's too focused on saving the company right now."

"Any news on that front since you've gotten home?"

"No, not much has changed." Anna stopped herself. "Chris, I really shouldn't talk about the company's problems. I don't want to make the same mistake again with Liz."

"I totally understand."

With a sigh and an attempted smile, Anna said, "Hey, all of this unnecessary moaning and complaining has worked up an appetite. How about we start dinner?"

Chris gave her a kiss on the forehead before they moved into the kitchen. While she turned on the flames under pans for the egg noodles and green beans, Chris poured more wine and asked how he could help.

Before she could answer him, her cell phone rang. Anna reached over to push Cancel, then reconsidered when the unknown number on caller ID had a San Francisco 415 prefix. She asked Chris, "Is it okay if I grab this real quick?"

"Sure, go ahead."

"Hello," she said with curiosity.

"Jessica's dead!" came an angry male voice.

"What?" A burst of dread was all-consuming. "Who is this?"

"Jeff," Jessica's ex-husband spat. "She died of a drug overdose this morning."

"Oh my god, no." Anna clutched onto Chris for support and stared with wild-eyed disbelief. "How'd that happen?"

Chris cocked his head in worried bewilderment. While placing a finger on her lips, she turned on the phone's speaker.

Jeff continued his rage. "That's why I'm calling you. To find out what happened."

"How should I know?"

"Because Jessica's done a lot of wild stuff in her years, but she never took drugs. She must've gotten them with you on the cruise."

"If you're accusing me, you're terribly mistaken. Besides, I barely saw her on the cruise."

"How could you not see her during a five-day cruise?" His tone was accusatory.

"Because she spent a lot of time partying with people on the ship and a guy she met."

"What's his name?" Jeff demanded.

"I have no idea."

"Goddamn it. How could you not know? What kind of friend are you?"

Anna cringed at the rhetorical question. Obviously, she had been a shitty friend. She cautiously asked in reference to Jessica's four-year-old son, "Does Billy know yet?"

"Oh yeah," Jeff said with angry exaggeration. "He's the one who found her naked on the bathroom floor. She was twisted like a rag doll, with blue lips, covered in vomit."

"My god, the poor little guy must be traumatized."

Jeff said with disgust, "Right, so now I guess I'll have to raise a screwed-up kid."

"You guess?" Anna asked in disbelief of the apathetic and selfish statement. "He's your son."

Jeff's arrogant response was, "You never even met the kid, so why do you care?" He disconnected.

Anna stood in silent shock. She had always been too busy to visit Jessica and her son. Instead, she had abandoned her friend when she needed her most, then barely talked with her during their only time together in five years. Now Jessica was dead.

THIRTY-FOUR

T he hours after the phone call were gut-wrenching. While huddled together on the couch, Chris tried comforting Anna's waves of denial, grief and guilt. Nothing eased the pain. She reminisced, shivered and sobbed until exhaustion drew her into a restless sleep. Chris held her for most of the night while feeling his own remorse. Jessica's horrific death was consistent with digesting carfentanil in the missing Midol.

When she awoke, Anna declared the need to do something. She booked a flight to San Francisco, packed her bags and called a cab. He offered to travel with her. She was appreciative, said maybe later in the week, but right now she had to face this alone. After that, few words were spoken. When the cab dropped Chris off at his hotel, she remained transfixed in the back seat. Her eyes were dull and bloodshot. Her spirit was shattered. A kiss goodbye was barely acknowledged.

Now bent over – with head down and elbows on the desk of his hotel room – Chris stared at the cheap wood veneer. Jessica was dead. Anna was devastated. The depth of his contrition was surprising. Ten years of training and sixteen of killing had made him callous, or so he thought. Yet he had never murdered an unintended target. He had never robbed a small child of his mother. He hadn't felt this despondent since his own mom died. He had become as heinous as his drunken father.

Chris cringed. The past couldn't be changed. *Stop wallowing in regret.*

With renewed conviction, he deepened his resolution to shape the future and to save Anna. *Start doing something proactive.*

After a sigh of determination, he sat up, grabbed the Miami-purchased phone and saw the white dot was positioned at the hotel across the street. He called the grad student from Boston Library.

"Hello," she answered tentatively.

Chris said, "This is the guy whose dog you're walking."

"Yeah, I recognized your number."

"Okay, let's get to the point. You may've noticed the red dot is driving toward Logan Airport."

"Yeah, I wasn't sure if I should try following it." She sounded increasingly nervous.

"Don't bother," Chris said. "In about nine hours, it'll be in San Francisco."

"Does this mean my job is done?" she asked with concern.

"No, it just got easier. Until further notice, I want you to randomly walk the phone around downtown for at least a couple of hours a day, then return to your hotel room."

"That's it?"

"Yup, couldn't be simpler. I'll call you again when I need the phone."

Chris next considered calling Michelle's burner. He wanted to explain everything, to make her understand, to convince her his plan was justified, and to get her advice regarding next steps. He missed her collaboration. Most of all, he regretted his growing lies and deceit.

Then he reconsidered. Keeping his sister in the dark was the best way to keep her safe from Irene's potential wrath. It would be selfish, careless and unloving to put Michelle in harm's way for his rogue actions. Deniability was essential. He owed her that.

The wise approach was to comply with Michelle's request in Miami to send an encrypted status report today. The message would certainly be read by a Thanatos facilitator and forwarded to Irene, so maintaining a professional, factual and confident tone was essential.

He opened the company laptop, waited for the iris recognition and began typing.

Michelle –

I gained access to Monteiro's home Saturday night. Successfully exchanged tainted tampons as planned. I assume the onset of fatal toxic shock syndrome will occur two to three days after target's menstrual cycle begins. I've subsequently learned Jessica Daly, her friend from the cruise, died yesterday of a drug overdose in San Francisco, presumably from the Midol tablet. Monteiro is flying there now. I'll remain in Boston until midweek, then monitor target's condition in SF and pursue alternative tactics if warranted to ensure the commission's Friday deadline. I'll advise you of travel plans soon.

Chris

He reread the letter several times, worried Michelle would detect the sham, rationalized he was being paranoid, then clicked Send. He spent another half hour writing an official daily report. It was longer, yet essentially said the same thing. Together, the memos should provide the needed cover for his covert activities in Boston during the next few days.

Chris's thoughts shifted to Liz Walker. After listening to Anna's glowing admiration of her friend and boss the night before, it seemed increasingly unlikely Walker was complicit in ordering the commission against Anna. However, in case there was a hidden motive, he would still try to verify her innocence.

But there was no doubt George Henniker was culpable. The sleazeball had to die. Soon. The question was how?

Chris opened his new laptop with the intention of learning Henniker's medical history. This was always Michelle's first step for a new silentcide commission. After searching through Henniker's files for an hour, Chris stopped, leaned back and reassessed.

If Henniker died from a medical condition, Chris would be safe from a cursory police investigation. However, a sudden death from apparent natural causes would be a huge red flag to Irene. There was no question she would recognize his signature tactics.

Chris debated the pros and cons of a silentcide approach versus a random violent shooting. The latter was the better choice. To avoid being caught, careful planning, detailed scouting and dispassionate implementation were critical.

The first possible kill zone was Henniker's house. Chris reviewed the videos from the previous twenty-four hours. The only activity had been Henniker driving a flashy red Porsche 911 Carrera S into the garage, and an equally flashy woman who visited for exactly two hours. There was no question about the nature of that social call. Dirtball.

The satellite view on Google Maps of Henniker's elite neighborhood revealed two blocks of tree cover encircling the house. Ideal conditions for an unseen approach and exit. Chris contemplated possible murder scenarios. A house robbery gone bad. A revenge killing. A hate crime against the wealthy. Each one had merit, but all would spark extensive media coverage and an intense police investigation. It might also point a finger back at Anna. Too risky.

Another possibility was targeting Henniker at work. It was eliminated after cursory research because the security at John Hancock Tower[87] – New England's tallest skyscraper since 1976 – was easy to penetrate yet impossible to escape undetected.

When Chris pulled up Henniker's calendar, he smiled. There was a dinner reservation for Monday night at an Italian restaurant in the

North End. Little Italy – the city's oldest residential community – had a mishmash of streets, narrow alleys, tree-lined parks and close access to the wharf. This kill zone had potential.

Chris donned the Ted Collins disguise but, instead of the traditional suit, opted for shorts, a summer shirt and Red Sox cap. The dangling Nikon camera completed the middle-aged tourist appearance. No one would notice him on a Sunday afternoon nonchalantly photographing exit routes, streetlights, security cameras and potential evidence dump sites along the way. The surveillance would require hours. Then, at nightfall, he would practice and time the planned escape as well as two contingency directions. Nothing would be left to chance.

Chris hailed a cab outside the hotel and directed the driver to take him to the city's oldest residence: the home of Paul Revere.[88] The 1680 landmark was at the epicenter of Henniker's pending demise.

Chapter Thirty-Four: Boston, Massachusetts

Photos 87–88

THIRTY-FIVE

C hris had hoped to talk with Anna last night. She didn't answer. However, a text indicated she had arrived safely in San Francisco. It was too early to call now. He wished he were there to support her, but what he was doing in Boston was infinitely more important.

The first item on the day's to-do list was to further investigate Liz Walker to either confirm or vindicate her role in plotting against Anna. The best place to start was by rummaging through Liz's email account at Longfellow again.

The most recent email exchange was between Liz and Anna. Her boss seemed genuinely saddened by Jessica's death and was fully supportive of Anna's absence from work. Liz's last words were, "Take all the time you need, my friend. You're in my thoughts and prayers." That sentiment hardly sounded adversarial.

Chris then found two informative emails sent to Liz over the weekend. The first was from Todd Milken. The CEO of Longfellow BioSciences said he had tried every negotiation tactic with Robert Nole – the president of Fármaco – including lowering the buyout price, but the big pharma president was still noncommittal. The arrogant son of a bitch then stressed to Liz how the potential acquisition was Longfellow's last chance. Its success or failure depended on her meeting with Nole in Chicago. Milken closed by writing, "Do whatever – and I mean whatever – it takes to get Nole's commitment. Close the deal and save our company! If you fuck it up, we lose everything!!!"

Chris flashed the finger at the laptop screen.

Opened next was an email exchange between Robert Nole and Liz. The pharma president said he was looking forward to their noon appointment Tuesday, and to ensure absolute secrecy, he suggested they have lunch in his presidential hotel suite. Liz confirmed the time and place. She also promised to send Nole a PowerPoint presentation by noon Monday.

Chris scratched his forehead. Obviously, this meeting was critical to Longfellow's survival. If he could watch, it was also an opportunity to judge Liz's character. Chances were good Chris could hack into Nole's laptop and activate the camera. The long shot was whether the president would leave his laptop open during the meeting. It was worth a try.

On OdinOne's hacker program, Chris selected the appropriate virus application and familiarized himself with the tool designed to encode the malware into PowerPoint, normally a time-intensive task. Then he had to wait.

After minimizing the Sent Items screen of Liz's email account into the upper left corner of his desktop, he used Google Maps to again study the layout of Little Italy, while also committing to memory his photos of streetlamps and security cameras. A laborious yet essential task.

Two hours later, Liz emailed her presentation to Robert Nole. Chris intercepted it, downloaded the PowerPoint, added the malware, then resent the email. The trap was set. Hopefully, the mouse would take the cheese.

The next task had associated risks, but going to the wrong person or place was riskier. Chris opened the Thanatos laptop, clicked on Local Resources, typed in Boston, then scrolled down to Sanctioned Arms Dealers. Only one was listed.

Chris begrudgingly suited up in the Ted Collins disguise, took a taxi for the half-hour drive, and was dropped off four blocks away from the gun shop. Unlike most retailers, Second Amendment was discreetly housed in a one-story office building with minimal signage. No doubt the dealer catered to discerning customers.

After a knock on the door, a buzzer sounded and Chris walked into what looked like a military arsenal. In the center were rows of shotguns and rifles. Displayed on two walls were automatic and semiautomatic assault weapons with a tiny sign reading: "Some models only available for law enforcement purchase." Along the third wall were antique firearms below deer mounts. The customer service area was encircled by showcases of pistols and revolvers.

The man behind the counter wore tattered jeans and a bulging black T-shirt revealing colorful sleeve tattoos of lion heads, roses, barbed wire, mythical women and skulls. Beneath the NRA cap was a ruddy face. "Welcome," he said with a toothy smile. "How can I help?"

Chris said, "I'm looking for a Glock 19 ghost gun."

The man's expression soured. "Sorry, but Glocks and ghost guns are prohibited for sale by Massachusetts law."

Pretending not to have heard the answer, Chris continued, "I also need a silencer."

"They're banned too," the man said with a hint of irritation. "But if you show me a state ID and have a license to carry, I can run a quick NICS check, then find you a suitable handgun you can have today."

"That's disappointing," Chris said while making direct eye contact. "I was led to believe you accommodate special requests."

The man's stance became defensive. "Who told you that?"

"Ben Franklin told me that thousands of times, and time is money."

The mutual glare was intense. The distrust was tangible. The protracted silence reflected the man's inner debate between greed and caution. Chris refused to blink.

The gun dealer asked, "Are you with any federal or state law enforcement agency?"

"That's a ridiculous question," Chris taunted him. "Even if I were a cop, you know I could legally deny it to your face."

"Then you won't mind if I frisk you for a weapon, badge or wire."

With a sly smirk, Chris said, "Only if you promise to remain a gentleman."

While being led to the back room, Chris thought how much easier this would be if he could simply recite a Thanatos approval code. The transaction would be finished within minutes.

After a thorough pat down, the gun dealer seemed to relax. He opened a gun cabinet, pulled out a locked box, twisted the combination, then held up a 9mm handgun shaped like a Glock 19 with a black plastic body plus a metal slide and barrel.

The dealer said, "A local gunsmith made this beauty on his 3-D printer. That's eighteen hours of loving craftsmanship you're looking at. It's guaranteed not to jam. It also has threads to accommodate a silencer." While lifting a loaded magazine, he continued, "It has the standard fifteen plus one round, which also exceeds state law, but you clearly don't give a rat's ass about that, do you?" He shoved the mag into the grip and, in a nanosecond, released the slide and aimed the gun at Chris's head. "But I do give a rat's ass, so I'm calling the cops."

The man may have had decades of experience selling guns, but he was incompetent at covert ops. When he inadvertently looked down to retrieve a cell phone from his pants pocket, Chris simultaneously grabbed his wrist and pistol, twisted until a bone snapped, forced the screaming man to his knees, and pushed the muzzle into his ear.

"Stop blubbering," Chris demanded. "You have two options here. One, I can test the gun right now to see if it works. Or two, I'll give you five thousand in cash. That's double the worth of the Glock and silencer, plus some extra for your urgent care visit, your store's security tape, and amnesia. Do you have a preference?"

The man made the logical choice.

THIRTY-SIX

SAN FRANCISCO, CALIFORNIA
Monday

Anna was reaching for the doorknob of the hotel room in downtown San Francisco when her cell phone rang. She looked at the caller ID, then her watch, and hesitated before swiping Accept. With rising apprehension, she said, "Hello, Mrs. Daly. Thanks for returning my call. I just wanted to extend my deepest sympathy and see how you're all doing."

"We're in shock," Jessica's mother said with a quivering voice as if controlling tears. She had probably been crying nonstop since her daughter's overdose two days before. "Absolute shock."

"I can only imagine," Anna said, then chastised herself for the trite phrase. There was no way she could understand a mother's pain. With a sigh, she cautiously asked, "Is Billy doing okay?"

"No, not in the least," came the despondent reply. "He's withdrawn one minute, then throwing violent tantrums the next. He won't eat and can't sleep. And when he does, he wets the bed during horrible nightmares. It's awful. Just god-awful."

Anna was flooded with heartache. Discovering his mom dead on the floor could traumatize the four-year-old forever, especially if raised by his self-centered father. Anna struggled to say something meaningful. "Is there anything I can do to help?"

"That's sweet of you but no, we just need privacy now. Unless ..." She paused. "Do you know if Jessica's death is somehow connected to your cruise?"

Before Anna could respond, there was a commotion in the background. A male voice barked, "Is that her?"

"Yes," Mrs. Daly said with hesitation.

"Then give me the phone."

"Howard, let me handle this."

"Mary, I'm not going to tell you again. Give me the goddamn phone. Right now!" After a shuffle, Mr. Daly's outrage burst into Anna's ear. "Where did Jessica get the drugs?" was his opening salvo.

Rattled and intimidated, Anna said, "I have no idea."

"That's bullshit! She clearly OD'd from some damn party drug she got while vacationing with you. So you're obviously holding something back."

"Sir, I honestly don't know. Really. And I'm just as upset as you are."

"I highly doubt that, dearie. Jessica was our daughter, for Christ's sake, and you were just a fair-weather friend."

Being called that triggered a torrent of guilt. She had deserted Jessica when she was divorced and pregnant, then again on the cruise. And now she was dead. Anna was barely able to say, "I'm not sure what I can tell you."

"Why not start by telling us the whole truth." He paused.

Anna was frozen by his seething anger and accusations.

Mr. Daly shattered the silence. "Just as I suspected. You're hiding something." He concluded with an implied threat. "Okay fine, we'll just let the police get the honest answers out of you." Then he disconnected.

Anna could barely breathe. Her heart beat erratically until a ding from her phone announcing a scheduled appointment interrupted her paralysis. She was going to be late for the meeting.

Anxiety followed her down the elevator, across the street and through the double glass doors. After checking in at the security desk and getting a visitor's badge, Anna paced the lobby. Despite having worked at Wells Fargo's corporate office for eight years, she had rarely paid attention to the bank's small history museum.[89]

While staring at several exhibits, she was oblivious to what she saw. Was this reunion with her co-workers from five years ago a mistake in the dark shadow of Jessica's death?

Cammy Hanley stepped out of the elevator. Beneath the tailored black suit, it was obvious the executive was still thin as a rail because of her tireless hustle during a stellar thirty-five-year career. The woman was a grueling taskmaster with almost impossible high standards, yet also a terrific mentor, motivator and champion of her direct reports. Anna had always looked up to Cammy as a role model. It was great seeing her again. The feeling was clearly mutual.

While riding up to the marketing department floor, they engaged in mindless pleasantries to avoid acknowledging what had happened. Their denial worked until passing Jessica's cluttered desk. It appeared as if she had just walked away and would return any minute. Prominent on a shelf was a picture of Billy. Several of his drawings were thumbtacked to the cubicle walls. Cammy grabbed Anna's hand, squeezed, and choked out the utterance, "I still can't believe she's gone. I just can't."

When they entered a conference room adjacent to Anna's old office, six people were sitting around a table. She recognized half the faces. A flurry of joyful greetings and tearful embraces was followed by introductions to the others Anna had never met. Their names and titles were a blur.

After Cammy announced they would wait for one last person to arrive, a barrage of questions was aimed toward Anna. The accusatory ones came from Brenda, the office gossip. "I heard you guys were on a real party boat, right?"

"I guess you could call it that," Anna begrudgingly admitted.

"Do you know what kind of drug she took?"

"I have no idea."

Brenda was unrelenting in her pursuit of dirty details. "Was she taking anything during the cruise?"

In a feeble attempt to deflect the interrogation and lighten the mood, Anna said, "Only getting her money's worth from the drink package." With a nervous laugh, she added, "We both were."

"But you must know something, right?"

Cammy finally came to Anna's rescue. "Let's get started, shall we? When I reached out to Jessica's sister and asked how we could help, she said the first priority is raising money for Jessica's son."

Jessica's sister had never returned Anna's calls. Clearly the whole family must think she was somehow complicit in Jessica's death. She also sensed some of the marketing staff besides Brenda were suspicious too. The mistrust was distressing and hurtful.

Anna remained passive while the group brainstormed for ideas until her cell phone rang. The conversation abruptly stopped. All eyes stared at her again. She had violated one of Cammy's major rules to keep phones off during a meeting. Anna frantically dug through her purse while the damn thing kept ringing. She gasped when she saw the caller ID: San Fran Police Dept.

Chapter Thirty-Six: San Francisco, California

Photo 89

THIRTY-SEVEN

G ame plan. Game day. Game time. Those were the expressions Michelle used to describe an imminent silentcide. Chris hated those terms. Getting ready to kill someone was hardly a game. Murder was always savage, regardless of how despicable the target might be.

Now, while sitting against a dumpster in a Little Italy alley, he was questioning everything. That was a consistent problem while waiting for a target to appear. There was too much time to think. The mind wandered into distracting thoughts. But diversions were dangerous. He must stay sharp and engaged.

Chris picked up a stained paper bag from the grimy asphalt, unscrewed the bottle top and took a swig of the unsweetened green tea. Then he wiped away some backsplash on his Sully Williams beard with his latex-covered hand while staring across Hanover Street at the Italian restaurant.[90]

Henniker had already given Chris two opportunities, but they were poor ones. The first was when Henniker arrived at eight o'clock, stepped out of an Uber, and hustled into the restaurant while buttoning his suitcoat. The entire exposure time was maybe seven seconds.

About an hour later – thirty minutes after sunset – Henniker unexpectedly came outside for a smoke break. When he began pacing back and forth while talking on a cell phone, Chris verified the silencer was tightly screwed onto the barrel of the ghost gun, pulled the hoodie over his wig, and drew the drawstring tightly around his disguised face. He was perched, ready to pounce. But there were too many passing cars or too many walking couples or both. The perfect moment never came. When Henniker stepped back inside, Chris's rush of anticipation faded.

Since then, Chris had spent the time mentally rehearsing. He imagined Henniker alone on the sidewalk. After a quick search for potential witnesses, Chris would stand, conceal the weapon behind his back, casually cross the street, stagger a bit while approaching the target, grab the man by the lapel or collar, and jam the muzzle into his temple. Then he would demand Henniker step into an alley. Once concealed, death would come quickly. One 9mm bullet to the head. In .00037 seconds, the hollow-point would pierce the skull and mushroom while shredding lobes, veins, arteries and the brain stem. Life would cease before the bang of the pistol was heard.

Chris would grab Henniker's wallet and unclasp his Rolex. While running away, he would remove the money and credit cards and discard the wallet where it could easily be found, creating an obvious motive of robbery. Two blocks away at the wharf, Chris would throw the gun and Rolex into the water, bury the credit cards, remove the disguise, then casually walk to the cab stand at Faneuil Hall Marketplace, a popular site among tourists.

That was the optimal scenario. But things rarely went according to plan. So Chris kept imagining worst-case scenarios and picturing alternative escape routes in the urban maze of the North End.

At 9:46, Henniker emerged from the restaurant with his client.

Chris peered around the edge of the alley in search of anyone on the sidewalk.

The two men talked and laughed loudly, obviously drunk.

With the pistol at his back, Chris stood in the shadows.

A black, late-model Chevy pulled up to the curb with an Uber decal on the front passenger windshield. The driver shouted out, "Steve White?"

Chris stepped into the street while the client entered the car. As it drove off, Chris staggered toward Henniker who turned, saw him, gave him a look of disdain, and turned away.

Chris began smoothly raising the weapon. But the well-practiced motion stopped. The fourteen-inch Glock and silencer assembly was snagged on the back of the hoodie. He struggled to loosen it while maintaining his pace. Once freed, he snapped the pistol upward.

The restaurant door opened. Two women appeared. One screamed. The other ran back inside. Chris had no choice. The gun fired as Henniker spun around. The sound echoed off the brick walls. The muzzle flash was blinding. Henniker grabbed his shoulder and took one step to run. The next bullet pierced his back. Blood splattered on Chris's face. Henniker staggered, fell and twitched before lying silent.

As Chris bent down to find Henniker's wallet, flashing blue lights brightened the darkness. The siren was piercing. The police cruiser sped up and then slammed to a stop.

Chris dashed down Hanover before zigzagging through a labyrinth of cars on Prince Street while trying to remove the cash and credit cards from the wallet. The blood on the latex gloves was slippery. It was impossible to run, hold the gun and wallet, and also extract the valuables. He threw the wallet behind a trash can, pocketed the silencer, and jammed the pistol into the back of his jeans before cautiously nearing a park.

A distant police siren was coming fast, yet he had to walk slowly along a basketball court where teens were playing hoops. Running in a hoodie would be noticed.

He was in a disastrous position. The next several blocks were a minefield of streetlights and security cameras. So run. The faster he could go, the less likely he could be photographed and later identified.

He raced past a darkened community center, sprinted left for a half block, right through a parking lot, left for a quarter block, then right again until reaching a niche between buildings at the north end of Paul Revere Mall. He pressed against a vine-covered wall while gasping. The hyperventilation was caused more by anxiety than exertion. Beads of distress dampened his brow.

Is now the time to transform? No. His hands and face were speckled with blood. Cleaning off the evidence was the first priority. Fifty feet away was a water fountain[91] encircled by a large granite base. He skimmed along dark recesses, watched for intruders, then dashed to the fountain in the elongated park.

As he began washing, a patrol car's takedown light illuminated the mall. He cowered out of sight. The brilliant beam swept back and forth. The potential exposure lasted an eternity. When the danger drove away, seconds passed before regaining his night vision.

They're closing in. Gotta keep moving. Gotta transform.

Chris struggled to remember the layout of the North End until picturing the only logical escape route. His plan was almost immediately thwarted. The entrance gate to the Old North Church[92] was padlocked. He draped the hoodie atop wrought-iron spears, jumped over the fence and bolted into a remote corner.

The persona change was fast and efficient. He stripped off the gloves, plus the Sully wig, beard and mustache. Beneath his blue jeans were summer shorts. In the pouch of the hoodie was a plastic trash bag with the Ted Collins disguise and a Red Sox cap.

He stuffed everything, including the pistol and silencer, into the bag and was about to hide it before reconsidering. Too many tourists visited the historic church where Paul Revere's first warning was signaled. Someone could easily discover this treasure trove of incriminating evidence. A more permanent disposal was essential.

After leaping over another fence marking the start of the Freedom Trail, Chris walked casually for a block until hearing a helicopter overhead. A sweeping search light was a block away.

He climbed a brick wall and took refuge in an old burying ground.[93] As the police helicopter thundered overhead, he pressed against a 1696 tombstone. The winged skull carving at the top was an ominous premonition. The graveyard became bright as day. Ghostly shadows swept across the dead.

When blackness returned, he saw a row of blue flashing lights blocking access to the wharf. The city's entire police department seemed to be converging on the third-of-a-mile North End neighborhood. Becoming trapped at the end of Shawmut Peninsula appeared inevitable.

Shitty planning! Shitty kill zone! Shitty execution! This type of catastrophe had never happened during a silentcide. But he was a damn rookie at violent murder. Now his arrogance would suffer the consequences.

Stop bitching. Keep moving.

He left the cemetery and began inching along the outer wall of a parking garage when a burst of radio static rang out. The subsequent words were muffled, yet the danger was clear. Two patrolmen were nearby with their flashlights illuminating the sidewalks, street and buildings.

Chris was cornered. Running in either direction would leave him exposed for over a block. Acting casual risked being searched. He cowered in a dark corner beneath the parking lot's up ramp, but the cover was temporary. He'd be discovered when they walked by.

The sound of footsteps intensified.

Reaching into the plastic bag, Chris screwed the silencer onto the ghost gun. He grasped the Glock with two hands and aimed where the policemen would appear. Killing cops was abhorrent, something he had never done and vowed never to do. He only had two other choices: surrender, or fire rapid shots into their bullet-resistant vests. The impact would drop them to the ground, giving him time to escape.

This evasion plan, however, was loaded with risks. The kinetic energy of the stopped bullets could cause severe injury or death. Their bodycams might capture his image. And the noises and flashes might broadcast his location to nearby police, causing a deadly shootout. Shit!

Chris lowered his heartbeat. His breathing slowed. Adrenaline was suppressed as his finger tightened on the trigger.

The voice of a police radio dispatcher shattered the tension. "Possible suspect wanted for Hanover Street shooting reported running west on Commercial near Charter Street."

One of the policemen said, "Copy. 449 responding," as they turned and hustled away.

"10-4," the dispatcher said.

Flames of angst consumed Chris while lowering his weapon. A toxic mix of sweat and chills was rampant. Staccato breaths tried taming an erratic pulse. He struggled to regain control until the acute stress lessened and his survival skills kicked in.

Chris leaped over a fence and snuck along the parking lot exterior canopied by trees. Crowd noises were ahead. Lines of people were moving in one direction along Causeway Street. He mentally pictured Google Maps. The TD Garden was nearby. The arena must be emptying out after a concert or event.

He rolled the bag tightly under his arm and, with confidence, stepped into the crowd. He chatted with a woman as they walked past the watchful eye of a policeman directing traffic. After crossing the street, he ducked behind an indoor skating rink leading to a promenade along the wharf, filled the bag with rocks, and stood along the guard rail as if mesmerized by the mouth of the Charles River. Along the opposite shoreline were the three masts of *Old Ironsides*,[94] the world's oldest warship still afloat.

Chris looked left and right before throwing the bag into the water. Bubbles popped on the surface as it sank. With luck, this was the eternal grave of Benjamin "Sully" Williams. He felt remorse, as if killing an old friend.

To cover his action from anyone who may have seen or heard the splash, he tossed three large rocks into the harbor.

After a sigh of relief, he tried calling Anna. She didn't answer. He texted: Thinking of you.

Chapter Thirty-Seven: Boston, Massachusetts

Photos 90–94

THIRTY-EIGHT

C hris woke in his hotel room at four fifteen so the coffee could brew before the start of Newscenter 5 EyeOpener. The early-morning TV news program wasted no time in sensationalizing the events of the night before. With a video of a police helicopter flying in the night sky, the female co-anchor said, "Last night, the North End experienced one of the largest manhunts in the city's recent history after a man was shot multiple times during an attempted robbery on Hanover Street. An unidentified witness had this to say."

A tearful woman filled the screen with yellow police tape fluttering behind her. "Well, I was coming out of a restaurant when … oh my god. It was just, you know, the scariest thing ever … just like a scene from a violent black ops movie. This guy comes running up with one of those, you know, those big assault gun thingies and starts shooting bullets everywhere. It was horrible. Like really terrifying. I was sure I was gonna, you know, die right there."

Toward the end of the lead story, a solemn police spokesperson stood behind a podium while saying, "The gunshot victim is an unidentified male in his mid-forties. He was rushed to Massachusetts General Hospital where he was stabilized yet remains in a coma and is listed in critical condition. Here is a photo of the alleged assailant. He is described as having dark skin with a beard and mustache, less than six feet tall, wearing a gray hoodie and blue jeans. He is considered armed and dangerous. Anyone with information is asked to call your local police precinct or, to remain anonymous, use the CrimeStoppers Tip Line or Text-A-Tip listed at the bottom of your TV screen."

For a couple of hours, Chris flipped among channels and read online articles. All of the reports were big on drama yet thin on facts. The only consistent fact was the victim was alive. Thankfully, the description of the assailant was sketchy and the photo was so blurry and black it seemed impossible to identify facial features.

Chris berated himself and questioned everything. He had been sloppy. The kill zone should've been Henniker's house. What if Henniker doesn't die and provides a full description? He should've put a bullet in Henniker's head before running. What if a security camera captured a better photo or, worse yet, revealed the transformation from the Sully to the Ted disguise? Could the police trace Ted's movements to the evidence in the harbor? What if Ted was recorded returning to the hotel? The concerns were endless.

His only conclusion was it was easy to walk up and shoot a guy, yet the aftermath had the potential to become excruciating. This never happened with a silentcide. The time spent researching and planning for an undetected killing were minimal compared to the days, weeks, maybe months ahead of worry about getting caught. *What a careless dumbshit!*

Chris sighed with self-disgust. He couldn't risk attacking Henniker again. There was only one thing to do: get out of Boston, but not too fast in case the airport was being monitored. With the unsettling feeling of the hotel room's door being breached at any minute, he began searching for flights to San Francisco.

Then he sent an encrypted message to his sister saying he would arrive in San Francisco Wednesday night, would monitor Monteiro through Friday's deadline, and would provide confirmation of death when appropriate. He knew the brevity of the message might raise suspicions, that Michelle could assume he was going rogue again, and the lack of an invitation to join him was against protocol. But going dark was a worse option, and the message was hopefully sufficient to give the appearance to Thanatos that he was still pursuing the silentcide commission. How long could he maintain the ruse?

He next opened the malware program and was disappointed to learn Robert Nole, the president of Fármaco, had not yet opened Liz Walker's email. There was still time to hack into his laptop before their meeting at noon Central Time, but the chances of success were growing dimmer by the hour.

Chris turned on his burner phone and pulled up the GPS map. The white dot was moving along the northern edge of Harvard Yard, the historic greenspace in the epicenter of Harvard University. He dialed the number of the grad student.

She answered by saying, "Your dog is doing fine."

"That's great," Chris said, "but it's time to bring him home."

"What? Really?" Her voice crackled with nerves. "I thought you said this gig lasted until Friday. Did I do something wrong?"

"No, nothing's wrong, just a change of plans."

Sounding disappointed, she said, "I was really counting on that money."

"No problem. Keep it. I may need your services again next week."

"Thank you so much."

"But that's assuming I can get my phone back now."

With hesitation she said, "Well, that's kind of a problem because I'm in Cambridge at the moment."

Chris said, "I know. I can see you walking in front of the Harvard Memorial Church."[95]

"You realize that's creepy, right?"

He didn't respond.

"So, uh, anyway," she rambled to fill the awkward silence, "I'll be at Harvard Library for a couple hours. But I could meet you this afternoon at the Boston Library if that works."

Chris was about to suggest a time for a handoff when he realized
he'd been wearing the Sully disguise when they first met, and Sully
was at the bottom of the harbor. "I'm busy this afternoon," he said.
"Put the phone in a sealed envelope, write the word *Sam* on it, then
leave it at your hotel's reception desk by three o'clock this afternoon.
Can you do that?"

"Sure, no problem."

"Good." He disconnected before giving her the chance to reply.

Then a fleeting flash of uneasiness swept over him. If the grad
student saw the grainy photo of the assailant on the news, would she
suspect him and call the police? He sighed while rubbing his tired
eyes. Would every little uncertainty soon mushroom into raging
paranoia? *Get a grip on yourself, man.*

Chris stood to rid the cobwebs of worry. From his hotel room
window, he saw Anna's brownstone[96] in the distance. Despite knowing she was in California, he used the zoom lens to get closer to her.
He looked at his watch, did the math, and assumed eight o'clock
Pacific Time was not too early to call. His anticipation and excitement grew as the phone rang.

Anna didn't answer.

He wrote a text:

Flying to SF tomorrow night. Text your hotel info. I'll send plane
schedule later.

Within five minutes, Anna replied:

Sorry missed call. Waiting for fundraiser meeting for Jessica's
son to start. U don't have to come, but love if do. Celebration of
life at 6 tomorrow. Funeral Thursday morning. Talk later if can.

Chris longed to escape his cesspool of problems and be with
Anna again. If only he were the man she thought he was versus a
pile of endless lies.

Chapter Thirty-Eight: Boston, Massachusetts

Photos 95–96

THIRTY-NINE

C hris was in an unsettled daze. He was monitoring the malware program on his Miami-purchased laptop with last-ditch hopes the pharma president would open Liz's PowerPoint. Time was running out.

The gambit to monitor the meeting in Chicago seemed to have failed until green words flashed across the screen. "Trojan Horse has entered the city of Troy." OdinOne, the hacker who had written the malware program, had a historic sense of humor. The president of Fármaco had finally taken the bait. Ten minutes remained before Liz was scheduled to arrive at Robert Nole's hotel room. There was little doubt she would be punctual.

Chris left-clicked his mouse to access Nole's laptop. The results were almost immediate. He had a clear view of the Longfellow BioSciences presentation the pharma president was reading. He also had access to the executive's files and emails. But there was no visual or audio of the room. The malware was not controlling Nole's camera and microphone as expected.

Chris scrambled for a solution. He scanned the tutorial about the malware. He tried several proposed solutions. Nothing worked. In desperation, he clicked the Need Help? button, hoping OdinOne would answer.

A chat box opened, asking "How can we help?" Chris explained the issue, then waited. One minute passed. No response. Two minutes. Three. *Come on, goddamn it!* Finally, dancing dots indicated someone was typing.

whats up

Again, Chris typed in a description of the problem. The response was disheartening.

cam/mike r likely disabled firmwre level

Can fix it?

tomorrow. busy now

Need help now. Right now!

you rude

OK please.

cost 1000 extra

The greedy bastard.

Fine.

2 secs 2 bill card

Good lord, man. You really have to process my credit card first? Just help me. Ninety irritating seconds ticked off before the hacker returned.

card good I be back

Then another four minutes passed before OdinOne's next message.

> fixed. must reboot
> target PC

He notice?

> maybe. malware could
> break 2

Chris worried Nole might get spooked if his laptop unexpectedly shut down. He also knew if the malware was disabled during a reboot, there was no way to reestablish the connection in time to monitor the meeting. He had no choice.

Do it

Nole's desktop screen should've gone black as the reboot started. Instead, a message appeared on a blue background. "Installing update. Do not turn off your computer." The countdown started at one percent as dots began spinning in a circle.

"No, no," Chris screamed. He typed into the chat box:

Can you abort update?

> nope - micrsoft update
> not me

Chris pounded the desk. For seven torturous minutes, the percentage counter inched forward. Several times it was stuck on a number and paused forever before jumping ahead and resuming the painfully slow rise. At forty-two percent, the screen went black. *Shit! No!* Chris's worst fear seemed to be a reality.

what happen? Lost access!

> maybe update reboot.

what do?

> nothing wait ☹

An emoji? Seriously? Be a professional, you damn idiot.

Chris paced the room in tight, angry circles. He went to the bathroom. The screen was still black. He stared blankly out the window with an occasional glance toward the desk. No change. Fury pulsed in his neck for another twelve agonizing minutes. He gnawed a cuticle until raw and bleeding. The situation seemed hopeless. The malware must've died. Failure.

While Chris gasped in defeat, he reached toward the mouse to abort the hack. The laptop screen flickered. A wide-angle view of an ostentatious hotel suite appeared. Chris was in. But there was no audio. *Where the hell's the sound?* He clicked the speaker icon on his laptop, taking it off mute. He pushed Record. Everything seemed functional. "Yes!" he exclaimed with a victorious fist pump.

The hacker typed:

> U welcom/ happy
> snooping

                                        Thx.

Now go the hell away!

In the background was a butler in a tux cleaning off china plates from a long dining room table. From the looks of the scraps, the lunch had been braised rack of lamb with cubed potatoes and steamed asparagus … a significant contrast to Chris's soggy grilled-cheese sandwich from room service.

Sitting at one end was Robert Nole. He was a late-fifties executive with a long face, flawless white hair and brows, deep scowl lines, and penetrating eyes with an intimidating expression despite his obvious attempt to seem cordial and casual.

At the other end was Liz Walker. Her long curly hair, lips, and cheeks were varying shades of red. The contrasting hues drew attention to her intelligent green eyes, which made only fleeting contact with Nole's. She seemed nervous while struggling to remain confident like a brainiac scientist thrust into an alien powerplay environment.

To Chris, the pair seemed like a lion stalking prey.

After dropping a linen napkin on the table, Nole said to the butler, "We have a business meeting now. So perhaps you could clean this up later."

"Yes, sir."

"But before you go, please pour more wine into fresh glasses and place them on the living room table."

"As you wish," the butler said.

Nole stood and, with an outstretched hand, directed Liz toward the center of Chris's laptop screen. She buttoned her blazer and hesitated, as if trying to decide which leather sofa to sit on. With a dramatic flair, Nole removed his pinstripe suitcoat, draped it over a high-back chair and sat next to her. Chris could tell Liz was uncomfortable with the proximity.

"Lovely lunch, wasn't it?" he asked.

"Yes, everything was delicious. Thank you."

While leaning back yet remaining formidable, Nole said, "I always break bread first with a potential partner. You'd be surprised by how much insight I gather about someone while sharing a meal."

Chris detected something perverse about the president's body language.

The butler interrupted by delivering the glasses, pouring the last of the wine, and then presenting an uncorked new bottle in a silver wine bucket before exiting the presidential suite. Nole raised a crystal glass. Liz did the same.

Nole said, "Here's to potential partners."

After taking a sip, his forced smile disappeared as he said, "Okay, before we start, I must ask if you have a cell phone with you."

"Yes," she said while producing it from her blazer pocket.

"Would you turn it off please?"

Looking perplexed but compliant, Liz pressed the off button and placed the phone face up on the mahogany table.

He watched the screen turn black, then said, "You know, this all seems too formal for me." He started loosening his striped silk tie. "How about if you stop calling me Mr. Nole. The name's Bob. And instead of calling you Dr. Walker, may I call you Liz?"

"That sounds good, Bob," she said with a weak grin. "So perhaps you'd like to see the presentation I've prepared for you."

"If that's the PowerPoint you sent, I've already reviewed it. No, I'd rather you answer several questions."

"Sure, I'd be happy to."

"Why should I invest anything in Longfellow?" he asked.

Liz's face was radiant while describing the company and technology, the encouraging clinical trials, and the dream of an industry-changing and patient-saving personalized approach to curing cancer.

Nole sipped wine while patiently listening to Liz's passionate speech. Then he asked with savage frankness, "If even a smidgen of that's true, then why the hell is your stock price in the shitter?"

Liz was flustered by the brutal question, then struggled to recover. "Probably for similar reasons why Menexonal was a disaster when you endorsed it fifteen years ago. Remember that? You were the laughingstock of the medical and scientific communities. Fármaco stock went down, what, thirty percent? But you personally championed it and now it's, what, the fifth-largest oncology drug worldwide?"

Chris cheered and clapped at the laptop screen. Liz was amazing.

At first, the pharma president was stunned. Then he emitted the first genuine sign of being human: he laughed hysterically. "That's one of the best damn comebacks I've ever heard," he said. "You've got spunk."

Emboldened, Liz said, "Listen, Bob, would you tell one of your male senior executives they've got spunk? I don't think so. Let's keep this professional, shall we?"

"Okay," he said while symbolically rolling up his sleeves. "The way I see it is your institutional investors are leaving in droves, you're struggling to raise new capital, you've got a damaging lawsuit hanging over your heads, and your cash will dry up in a couple of months. Sound about right?"

Liz quickly countered. "And the way I see it is Fármaco's new drug pipeline is running dry, it takes over ten years and up to two billion to bring a new drug to market, and Longfellow has already done most of the work and it will only cost you a rounding error of your revenue. So we sound perfect together, don't you think?"

Nole smirked. "I was wrong about you earlier. You've got balls. And yes, I would say that to any senior executive I respect."

Liz seemed to relax as if finally on equal footing. Her comfort didn't last long.

Nole leaned toward her with elbows on his knees and hands tightly clasped. "Todd tells me there are a couple of other potential offers by white knight investors. Is that true?"

Liz's hesitation betrayed the truth, so she seemed resigned to answer honestly. "Not that I'm aware of."

"So, if Fármaco backs out of this deal, then Longfellow dies. That means the patents will get hopelessly tied up in bankruptcy court. And if the trustee assumes your noncompete contract because you're the technology's brainchild, you could be prevented from working with another biotech for five years. Understand me? Your career is gone and your dream is finished."

Liz hung her head. She suddenly seemed defeated.

"Look at me," Nole said with what sounded like compassion. "Todd told me you were willing to do anything to make this deal happen, is that right?"

"Those were his words, not mine, but sure, what's it going to take?"

With a lecherous smirk, he blatantly suggested, "How about if we become personal partners first?"

Liz got wide-eyed and outraged. "Are you fucking kidding me? You're an asshole, Bob, you know that?"

"You're right. So what's your answer?"

Liz threw wine in his face. She grabbed her phone, briefcase and purse, then headed toward the door.

Nole called out, "The second you walk out is the second Longfellow dies. It's your choice."

Liz stopped. After a ten second pause, she dropped her things and disappeared into a bedroom. Nole quickly followed.

Chris screamed, "Noooo!" at his laptop screen yet was helpless to intervene.

FORTY

While aimlessly searching the web for updates on the Little Italy shooting, the other open window on Chris's laptop was a live video feed of the Chicago hotel suite. He couldn't see or hear anything in the darkened bedroom, but there was no doubt what was happening.

Over an hour elapsed. With each passing minute, Chris felt worse about what Liz was enduring. Nobody should be forced to make a degrading personal sacrifice in order to keep a company and a dream alive, especially at the hands of a rich, powerful and despicable executive. He admired Liz. He hated Nole.

Chris almost missed seeing Liz finally rush out of the bedroom, gather her things and make a fast exit. A few minutes later, the big pharma president emerged wearing a plush cotton bathrobe and a cocky grin of satisfaction. He poured himself a glass of wine, sauntered toward his laptop, sat down, stared into the screen as if charmed by his reflection, pushed a strand of white hair into place, and began working as if nothing had happened. *Liz was right: he's an asshole.*

Chris turned off the video feed, played back a few minutes to make sure the meeting had been recorded, and saved the file. Then he noticed the time: 3:10. Certainly, the library girl had dropped off his phone by now.

He debated wearing the Ted Collins disguise. If the police had traced his escape from the North End to Copley Square, they'd be looking for a middle-aged man with brown hair, a beard and glasses. It was safer to appear as himself. Nobody would suspect a late-thirties guy with short blond hair and androgynous facial features partially concealed behind aviator sunglasses.

Chris bought a cup of coffee and a *Boston Herald* at the gift shop. On the cover of the daily tabloid was a dramatic photo of two 9mm shell casings marked with yellow plastic police evidence stands. The headline was in big black letters: BANG! BANG! IN LITTLE ITALY. Then he walked next door to the adjacent hotel.

Chris selected a comfortable chair near the hotel's main entrance, took a sip and pretended to read while cautiously surveying the elegant lobby of the Fairmont Copley Plaza.[97] Most of the bustle in and out during the next fifteen minutes were typical tourists and businesspeople.

Yet in a far corner was an athletic guy who seemed uncomfortable in a coat and tie. He spent a disproportionate amount of time looking around with a cell phone pressed to his ear. The cadence of his conversation seemed unnatural.

At the concierge desk, two additional men were hunched over a map of Boston. They were randomly pointing to different sites yet not fully engaged. Then a glance at the front desk revealed a man standing behind the reception staff with his arms folded. He could be a manager, but his eyes kept sweeping the lobby.

Was this a police ambush? Or raging paranoia? Chris couldn't be certain. But when you're guilty, everyone looks like a cop. He decided against claiming his phone at the front desk. Too risky.

He downed the rest of the coffee before going out the sliding glass doors with the newspaper tucked under his arm. He circled back to his hotel and, when no one else seemed poised to pounce, he walked in and took the elevator to his room.

Chris flopped on the bed and stared at the ceiling. Was he being overly suspicious and unreasonably cautious? Maybe. But the Preceptor had always stressed the importance of trusting your instincts. He used to say, "If you sense something is wrong, then it probably is. Never, ever allow logic to rationalize away a valid gut feeling. It could get you captured or killed."

He jumped up and grabbed the burner phone. For the first time since Saturday afternoon, there was no white dot on the GPS map. He called the grad student. Her recorded message said, "Can't answer the phone. You know the drill."

That confirmed it. His dog walker had ratted him out to the police. Disappointed but not surprised, Chris sprang into action to cover his tracks. He opened the Thanatos laptop, scrolled down to the Communications section and clicked on the Phone app.

A click of the cursor permanently deleted everything in the encrypted section of the company-issued cell phone that was probably sitting in an envelope at the front desk. If a digital forensics team analyzed the phone, they'd find nothing incriminating because the abort feature also auto-populated the phone with useless information.

While using the bathroom, a new worry surfaced. What if the phone's GPS map still showed Anna's red dot in San Francisco? A resourceful detective might link him and Anna with George Henniker. He rushed back to the computer and deleted the map.

Then he saw the burner phone on the desk. He had used it several times to call the library girl and Anna. Could a digital analyst also make that connection? *Jesus, all this smart technology is the nemesis of criminal minds.* He extracted the SIM card, snapped it in half, wrapped it in a tissue and flushed it down the toilet. He would buy a new SIM later in the afternoon.

Chris shut his eyes and racked his brain for anything he had overlooked. This process of identifying then destroying incriminating evidence was taxing. With a sigh of relief, he declared himself safe … at least for the moment.

Robert Nole. It was time to investigate the lecher posing as a white knight.

Chris spent two hours trying to hack into Fármaco's corporate server. But a seven-thousand-dollar malware program was no match for a cybersecurity system that probably cost millions. He would have to focus on the president's laptop.

Two emails had been sent since Liz Walker left the hotel suite. The first was addressed to Todd Milken, the CEO of Longfellow BioSciences.

Todd –

I just had an excellent meeting with Dr. Walker. She was everything you said she was and more. She's a brilliant scientist, an amazing visionary, a superb negotiator, and a passionate champion for Longfellow BioSciences. As a result, I'm happy to announce I'm on board with the acquisition. I will inform my team to proceed with the details in earnest. Of course, as always, I anticipate the typical minor points of contention. But I'm confident they will be resolved to our mutual satisfaction.

I look forward to Longfellow joining the Fármaco family of life-saving products soon.

Robert Nole

Chris smiled. The guy was still a sleazeball, but it appeared Liz's sacrifice wasn't in vain. Longfellow would be saved.

He opened the next email with the subject head: Longfellow Acquisition Team.

Longfellow Team –

I just had a meeting with Liz Walker, the chief science officer of Longfellow. As we suspected, their situation remains dire and there are no other investors on the horizon. By email, I've informed Todd Milken of my willingness to proceed with the acquisition subject to the resolution of "minor points of contention." So keep stretching out the negotiation process. Within a couple of months, maybe less, their stock price should approach zero, their cash will dry up, and they will be forced into bankruptcy. Then we can make the purchase for a penny or two on the dollar for just their equipment. But remain vigilant. If another investor emerges, we'll need to act quickly to prevent a competitor's buyout. I'm counting on all of you to implement this strategy flawlessly.

Robert Nole

Chris was violently cursing at Nole when he heard a distinct ding from the Thanatos laptop. That sound meant he had just received a rare message directly from Irene Shaw. With trepidation, he stared at the iris recognition camera and clicked on the encrypted email.

Chris & Michelle –

Your attendance is required for a meeting at the Lancaster farm on Saturday morning at 10:00 Eastern. This is mandatory. No excuses will be tolerated.

Ms. Shaw

"Oh, shit!"

Chapter Forty: Boston, Massachusetts

Photo 97

FORTY-ONE

Michelle was oblivious to the outdoor art as she ambled around the Minneapolis Sculpture Garden[98] on the outskirts of downtown. Her enraged thoughts were consumed by Chris.

She kept replaying their altercation in Miami after the cruise. His cavalier admission of sleeping with a target. His initial unwillingness to kill Monteiro. His total disregard for Irene's wrath if the commission failed because of his blatant disobedience. Yes, he had begrudgingly agreed to exchange Anna's tampons. But his true actions in Boston had been suspicious since sending Michelle back to the Twin Cities.

Her unquestioned faith in Chris had been rattled that day, yet she had assumed he would ultimately do the right thing. Now, after five days of radio silence – except for a vague message on Sunday and another ambiguous one this morning – trust was being stretched if not shattered, especially now that he was ignoring her increasingly desperate emails, texts and phone calls.

What the hell's he doing? Has he gone completely rogue? Why'd he cut me off? What will happen when Irene notices? How can he ignore the fact that he's putting both our lives in jeopardy? Can't he see that?

As Michelle's dread spiked, she fought the urge to scream. The mix of anger, fear and abandonment was toxic. And the guilt over accidently killing a single mom was still gut-wrenching. No young child deserved to grow up motherless. She knew all too well the emotional pain that would cause for a lifetime.

"Hi there," came a feeble voice from behind.

Michelle turned to see a frail man with bent posture beneath a checkered shirt and suspenders holding up black dress pants well above the waist. His bald head, wrinkled skin and thick-rimmed glasses still telegraphed intelligence. The toothy smile was warm and welcoming. His small eyes radiated excitement.

"Dr. Yasin!" Michelle exclaimed as she rushed toward him.

His thin arms lightly returned the affection. Then he pushed back to study her. "My, my, my," he said with a paternal tone, "I can't remember the last time I saw that wonderful face."

Although they had met professionally countless times, protocol prohibited Michelle from meeting a sanctioned resource without wearing a disguise. Appearing as herself was a serious breach of one of Irene's endless and iron-fisted rules.

"You look great too," Michelle said.

With a chuckle, he retorted, "And you were always a shameless flatterer. But thanks anyway. Here, let's have a seat." He cautiously lowered himself onto a park bench. Michelle sat close to him. "So what's the urgency all about?" he asked.

"Nothing urgent. I just wanted to give you something," she said while handing Dr. Yasin a small jewelry box.

After tilting his head with a perplexed look, he studied the golden caduceus. At the top of the hand-crafted pharmaceutical symbol – two snakes intertwined on the winged staff of Mercury – was a one carat diamond.

"Do you like it?" Michelle said with anticipation. "I bought it in Antwerp."

"It's lovely." With a curious tone, he asked, "But what's the occasion?"

"For your seventy-fifth birthday, of course."

Dr. Yasin laughed. "I appreciate the gift – I really do – but you missed that milestone three years ago."

"Oh my gosh. I'm sorry."

"Don't be." He paused. With a penetrating stare, he said, "Okay, so now why don't you tell me what's really on your mind."

Dr. Yasin had been able to read Michelle's thoughts since he'd been her instructor for two years at the Amish farm before becoming the sanctioned pharmacist in Minneapolis. When she was transferred to the Twin Cities, he had been her advisor for devising drug combinations for challenging commissions until he retired five years ago.

With hesitation, Michelle asked, "Can this conversation be strictly confidential?"

His brow furrowed as if slightly offended. "Of course. I'm always happy to help my best protégé. What's up?"

"Well, I was thinking about getting out of my current role."

His expression became cautionary. "That seems like an unlikely goal."

"No, I mean finding a different job that would be acceptable to Irene."

"What did you have in mind?" he asked.

"I don't know, like maybe becoming the sanctioned pharmacist here."

"I think my son might be offended if you took his job."

"Then maybe in another city."

He slowly shook his head. "Michelle, you have the best pharmaceutical mind I know. I really mean that. But your training on the farm won't qualify. You'd need four years of college, plus another four at pharmacy school, plus a residency to get your certified doctorate degree. Plus you'd be bored most of the time. And after racking up enormous debt, you'd make a fraction of what you do now. Is that worth it?"

"Then how about if I became a resource to others to come up with drug concoctions?"

"I doubt that would be a full-time job."

"Then maybe I could also be a trainer at Irene's farms."

"As far as I know," Dr. Yasin said, "Irene already has a stable of qualified medical and pharmaceutical teachers."

In desperation, Michelle said, "There's got to be something."

The doctor lowered his head as if deep in thought. When he raised his eyes, they did not look encouraging. "I promise to give it more thought, but my initial conclusion is your greatest value to Irene is what you do right now. It's highly doubtful she'd ever let you give that up. But that's just my opinion. What does Chris think about it?"

In a low voice, she admitted, "I haven't asked him."

"Oh my, I hope there's no trouble between my favorite siblings."

She was quick to respond, "No nothing like that. Everything's fine." The words sounded hollow to her. No doubt Dr. Yasin wasn't fooled but thankfully didn't pry.

Her Thanatos cell phone dinged. The unique sound was rare yet unmistakable. The instant distress was paralyzing.

The doctor said with trepidation, "I'm assuming that's from Irene?"

Michelle barely nodded. She stared at the screen while waiting for the retina recognition, then read the message. Her greatest fear was happening. Irene had summoned her and Chris to the farm. Her intentions were ominous. Saturday morning could be – no, probably would be – their final day of reckoning.

Chapter Forty-One: Minneapolis, Minnesota

Photo 98

FORTY-TWO

Chicago, Illinois

Wednesday

Chris admired downtown Chicago[99] as the jet approached O'Hare Airport. After the plane landed, he walked down the concourse wearing the Ted Collins disguise with a suit and tie. There was almost a two-hour layover before the connecting flight to San Francisco. Plenty of time. He glanced at the departing flights monitor, then ambled toward the gate while rolling his carry-on luggage.

There was an open seat among a sparse yet growing crowd of waiting passengers. He sat down and gave a cursory smile to the adjacent businessman. The man barely acknowledged him with a nod before returning to the laptop on his knees.

In an attempt to engage in a friendly conversation, Chris asked, "Are you flying out or flying home?"

Obviously annoyed by the distraction, the man answered without looking up, "Flying home."

Chris waited a few seconds, then said, "Everybody thinks business travel is so glamorous. But we both know how time-intensive and exhausting it can be, right?"

"Uh-huh."

After another pause, Chris leaned over and stared at the laptop screen. "You know, in order to ensure your privacy, you really should keep your camera lens covered with masking tape or a Post-it® Note."

Robert Nole looked up in exasperation. "What are you rambling about?"

Chris pointed. "That little hole right there. Keep it covered. You have no idea how easy it is to hack into a laptop camera and see everything you're doing."

"That's an urban myth."

"No, not really. Let me demonstrate." Chris raised his cell phone, clicked on a video clip, and showed a brief conversation between Nole and Liz. "Todd told me you were willing to do anything to make this deal happen, is that right?" "Those were his words, not mine, but sure, what's it going to take?" "How about if we become personal partners first?"

The pharma president was stunned. His face was turning a sickly gray.

Chris said, "By the way, I agree with Liz's assessment. You're an asshole, Bob."

"What the hell do you want?"

"Perhaps we should find a private place to discuss this."

Beginning to regain his executive prowess, Nole threatened, "Or perhaps I should yell for the police and have you arrested."

Unfazed, Chris said, "Sure, you could do that. But in one hour, unless I abort it, emails will be sent to two dozen media outlets. On the highlight reel is everything from the meeting on the couch until you emerge from the bedroom wearing a robe and a shit-eating grin. Everyone's going to love that part. Heck, I'm sure the video will go viral."

Nole was furious while struggling to remain contained. His eyes bored into his adversary with a mix of alarm and hatred. Perspiration beaded on his furrowed brow. A burst of violence or an anxiety attack seemed imminent.

To ridicule him, Chris said, "I see you're worried about missing your flight. Don't be. I promise to get you back in plenty of time to board, but you might miss the call for first class."

Without a word, Nole capitulated. He shoved the laptop into his briefcase.

With smug satisfaction, Chris led his target to an empty waiting area of a gate. "This seems quiet and cozy, don't you think? Too bad your butler isn't here to serve us wine." The flippant remark was ignored.

When they sat down, the standoff began.

Nole seemed tense, guarded, yet controlled, as if accustomed to high-stakes negotiations and accustomed to winning them. With a penetrating glare, he said, "Stop the bullshit. Tell me what you want."

"It's simple really. I want Fármaco to purchase Longfellow BioSciences."

"That's what we're in the process of doing."

"Tsk, tsk, tsk," Chris said sarcastically. "See, if our potential partnership is going to work, we've got to be totally honest with each other."

"But that is the truth," the president said with defiance. "We're negotiating a deal right now."

"Sure you are, subject to the resolution of a few minor points of contention which will require – what? – about two months of talks until Longfellow is bankrupt. Isn't that the strategy you want implemented flawlessly?"

With venomous malice, Nole hissed, "Fuck you."

"You sure have an overinflated opinion of your sexual attractiveness, don't you?"

Nole didn't respond to the insult.

"What's the matter, Bob? Am I being too spunky for you?"

Nole leaned back with a cold stare. No doubt he was sizing up his situation and opponent. He knew he had been caught red-handed, that he was screwed, and the only outstanding question was how to minimize the damage. Slowly, his look of contempt transformed into determination. He leaned toward Chris with his elbows on his knees and his chin resting on clenched fists. With a sideways glance, he said quietly, "I'm listening."

"Excellent! So here's your new strategy. When you get back to Boston this afternoon, you will personally expedite the purchase of Longfellow."

With hesitation, Nole said, "That may be difficult."

"Why's that?"

"Because, as you apparently know, it directly contradicts the email I sent yesterday to the acquisition team."

"No problem. Just tell them you got a call from Todd Milken that a new investor has surfaced. Now it's going to be an auction to the highest bidder. That'll get your team jumping into action."

Nole's nod was almost imperceptible, as if the suggestion was a plausible scenario.

Chris continued, "Good. Now let's talk price. Last I saw, the buyout number was two hundred fifty million. That seems fair to me."

Nole sat upright. "That won't work."

"Why not?"

"Because their market cap has plummeted considerably since then. And now they have a hundred-million-dollar lawsuit hanging over their head. Our board would never approve a two fifty price tag."

"Even if a major competitor was in hot pursuit?" Chris asked.

"Nope. Any company with an iota of acquisition moxie would never pay that much."

"Okay, assuming you're right, what number would you propose?"

Nole paused, as if crunching numbers. "Probably one hundred million at best."

"You can do better than that, can't you?"

After further thought, the president proposed, "Maybe one twenty-five."

Chris shook his head. "Bob, you're thinking about this all wrong. See, we're not just talking about the worth of Longfellow here. You should also factor in the worth of your reputation and the impact on Fármaco's public image and stock. Also consider what happens if the company can't acquire promising young drug companies to fill your pathetic new product pipeline."

Nole folded his arms with a groan of defeat. After a long deliberation, he said, "Tell you what. I think I could sell the board on one eighty."

"You think or you know?"

"Yeah, that's doable," Nole said with confidence. "But anything higher would be a showstopper."

"And so would anything lower. Understand? Plus, I want the deal finished by the end of this week."

"Now that's impossible," the pharma company president said definitively.

"Why? From what I've seen, the paperwork is ready to go."

Gripping his forehead while deep in thought, Nole said, "Give me one week."

"Okay, I'm a reasonable guy. Announce your letter of intent by the end of business Monday. You won't mind putting in a few extra hours over the weekend, will you?"

"Fine." Nole looked at his watch. "Are we done here?"

"Not yet. There's one more thing to sweeten our deal."

"You're a greedy son of a bitch, aren't you?"

"Yup, I'm a greedy son of a bitch and you're an asshole. We sound like perfect bedmates."

Nole flinched.

"Jeez, I'm sorry," Chris said in mock apology. "Maybe that's too personal for you. But it leads me to the next condition."

"Let's hear it."

"Fármaco will create a foundation dedicated to stopping sexual harassment in America's workplace. You'll fund it with at least fifty million annually."

"Is that payback for Liz?" Nole asked.

"In the future, you will refer to her as Dr. Walker. And yes, that's payback for her and all of the other women you've coerced. But instead of me exposing your lechery, you have the chance to champion a noble cause, be perceived as a concerned business hero, and hopefully prevent other women from being raped by powerful and disgusting bastards like you."

After a moment of consideration, the president said, "That's doable. So are you done with your demands yet?"

"Yes."

"Then let me ask a few questions. What do you get out of all this?"

"Nothing." *The bastard doesn't deserve to know the real reason.*

"Stop bullshitting me."

"Seriously, I'm just being a Good Samaritan here."

"Says the guy who just extorted me for two hundred thirty million dollars."

"Extortion is such an ugly word," Chris taunted him. "Let's call me a financial advisor who's nudged you into making the right decisions."

"Nudged, huh? By holding a sex tape over my head? How do I know if I meet your demands that you won't release the tape anyway?"

"Frankly, you don't. But you have my word on it."

"That's not very reassuring."

"Okay, then let me up the ante. If you don't do the deal, I'll definitely release the tape, shaming you and the company. Then, when the firestorm is almost over …" Chris moved within inches of the man's face. "I'll kill you."

Nole jolted back in disbelief.

While maintaining a threatening pose and expression, Chris added, "And you also have my word on that. Any other questions?"

The president's Adam's apple twitched. His jowls tightened, but to his credit, he didn't resist. He knew he had been defeated. He stood up, buttoned his suitcoat, gave Chris a final look of disdain, and walked away.

Chris watched as Robert Nole moved past two airport gates. He suddenly stopped, calmly reached into his briefcase, extracted the laptop, and smashed the device repeatedly against a wall. After pieces scattered in every direction, he shoved the computer into a trash bin and proceeded to his departure gate.

Chapter Forty-Two: Chicago, Illinois

Photo 99

FORTY-THREE

Wednesday

Anna remembered her excitement while waiting for Chris to arrive at her brownstone in Boston. There had been a tingling anticipation of romance and passion. Then, for one hour on Saturday, she couldn't have been happier. That happiness was shattered during the phone call about Jessica's death.

Four days later, she stared at the bathroom mirror while waiting for Chris to arrive at her hotel room in San Francisco. The baby-blue blouse paired with white skinny jeans were a mockery of her crippled spirit. Her brown eyes were dull and puffy despite repeated eye drops and makeup. Previously unnoticed lines were forming along her cheeks and mouth. The dreams of youth were fading, if not gone. She had entered middle age alone and with waning self-confidence. The despair was disheartening.

Chris had barely entered the room before his arms encircled her waist with strength and reassurance. While standing on her toes, she buried her face in his neck and held on, fighting the urge to cry. She wanted his emotional support while cursing her weakness.

He leaned back and gave a precious smile followed by a gentle kiss. The action spoke volumes. Chris was there for her and was willing to help without reservations or judgment. His compassion was incredible.

"Hi," he said softly. "How are you doing?"

Anna winced. "As you can probably tell, not great. I'm really glad you're here."

After pouring cocktails from the mini-fridge, they sat on the couch facing each other. An awkward pause ensued before he opened the inevitable topic. "I'm sorry I missed Jessica's celebration of life. How was it?"

"Beautiful and miserable," she said with a grimace. "I just got back about an hour ago."

"Do you want to talk about it? Or should we change the subject?"

Anna considered keeping everything bottled up – that was her normal way of handling hard situations. But his expression telegraphed a genuine interest to understand and perhaps soothe her hollowness. She decided to risk sharing her unfiltered feelings.

"You know," Anna began, "after the initial shock of Saturday's call, I intellectually knew Jessica was dead. But it wasn't real until I walked in and saw her lying in an open casket. Then I saw she was wearing a new dress from the cruise. I was devastated."

Chris held her hand and nodded while listening.

"I was so upset, in fact," she continued, "I didn't have the decency to kneel down and say a prayer beside her. Instead, I rushed back into the crowd. What a wuss." Anna squeezed her eyes while reliving the sadness and remorse.

Chris offered, "That's a normal reaction to losing someone you care about."

"Maybe, but I came to realize I knew very little about her. The tributes were wonderful, filled with tears and bittersweet laughter. But I didn't know the people who gave the speeches. I'd never heard any of their stories. And I learned more about Jessica after she was dead."

"Did that bring you closer to her?"

"No, just the opposite. It made me realize we were just mutual support for a short time when our marriages were falling apart. Maybe not true friends at all. And that feeling was reinforced while

I was looking at the photo collages. Her sister did a beautiful job of chronicling Jessica's life. There had to be over two hundred photos. But I wasn't in a single one, and justifiably so. Worse yet, the last photo was a group selfie of Jessica at the pool at Grand Turk. I avoided her that day because I was pissed off. How damn petty, right?"

"You're being too hard on yourself."

While shaking her head, she said, "No, if I had been a real friend, I would've prevented her from partying with those druggies. But I abandoned her. Now she's dead."

"Anna, stop it." His admonishment was caring, not harsh. "You're not responsible for Jessica's death."

"Some people think I am, especially her dad and her ex. Jeff came running up to me while I was at the photo collage and demanded to know, in his words, 'which guy was screwing Jessica?' When I pointed him out in the Grand Turk photo, he ripped it off the board, said he was giving it to the police, and he hoped they nailed me to the wall for withholding the truth."

"That's just a baseless threat from a guy you already described as heartless," Chris said.

"I'm not so sure. In fact, the police also implied I was hiding information."

His forehead tightened. "You talked to the police?"

"Yes, they interrogated me for about ninety minutes yesterday. They kept asking me over and over again what I knew about the drugs and the guy Jessica was seeing."

"Did they accuse you of something? I mean, do you need a lawyer?"

"No, I don't think so. But they did ask me to remain available for follow-up questions. Oh, and they might also be calling you."

"Why?"

"Because I told them I didn't see Jessica much because I was with you. So the police may call you to verify my story. I'm sure it's nothing to worry about."

FORTY-FOUR

Thursday

C hris felt despicable. As the morning sunlight entered their hotel room windows – along with an occasional blaring horn and the clatter of a passing streetcar – he focused on Anna's uneven breathing while she clutched a pillow in the fetal position.

He had caused her pain and guilt. He had killed her friend and subjected a toddler to an uncertain life without a mother. And why? So an arrogant fund manager could get revenge for his own incompetence? No, Henniker's motive was the initial impetus. Chris was responsible for the consequences. How many other lives had he devastated throughout his career?

From a few inches away, he looked fondly at Anna. She appeared distraught, even while sleeping. Furrowed brow. Pursed lips. Tight jaw. Eyes darting below pinched lids.

He wanted to hold her, to shield her from reality, and to eliminate her grief and self-doubt. Given different circumstances, he might love her. Yet everything he had done was the opposite of love. Worse yet, she respected him, unaware she was sleeping with the devil.

Quietly, so as to not wake her, he slipped out of bed, grabbed his laptop and locked the bathroom door. Jessica's GoFundMe page had generated eleven thousand dollars so far. Anna and her former co-workers hoped to raise another eight or nine thousand at tomorrow's event. Plus, he had been told the bank provided a thirty-thousand-dollar death benefit. That was fifty thousand at best … the paltry value of a life. How far would that go raising a son?

Chris made an anonymous donation of ten thousand. Hopefully, the guilt money would do some good. He felt worthless.

He also worried the San Francisco police had his name. It seemed unlikely they could trace him back to the drugging of Jessica, but they would surely make a connection if Anna also died soon.

In an attempt to distract his thoughts, he logged onto the Thanatos site. There was an unread message from Michelle. It was atypically succinct yet spoke volumes.

Chris –

Not sure what's happening and why you've locked me out. I presume you will be at the farm at 10:00 Saturday. See you there.

Michelle

His sister was justifiably pissed. He also expected Irene's full wrath when Anna was still alive after tomorrow's deadline. As wretched as the last few days had been, the future promised to be worse. He felt helpless to change fate. He deserved whatever happened. Anna and Michelle did not.

Anna was quiet and introspective when she awoke. They went through the motions of getting dressed, having breakfast, and walking a block to Old St. Mary's Cathedral,[100] a historic landmark dating back to 1854 in the core of downtown. Few words were spoken. None seemed appropriate.

On the front steps, Anna introduced him to her ex-husband Paul and the couple he lived with. Everyone was cordial, yet the moment was strained. Chris sensed the threesome was sizing him up while he was doing the same.

Chris couldn't imagine Anna being married to Paul. The man was disheveled, pallid, edgy and avoided eye contact. He was nothing like the confident professional Anna had described.

After handshakes and brief exchanges of disbelief over Jessica's death, an awkward pause led to meaningless versions of, "Nice to meet you." Anna managed a smile, turned, tucked her arm into Chris's and led him inside. He hadn't been in a church since his mother died.

For most of the Mass, Chris remained stoic, mimicked the motions of others, and occasionally held Anna's hand when she struggled with emotions. He was oblivious to the music and the words of the priest. Instead, he stared at the casket topped with flowers and a photo of Jessica.

During the sermon, Jessica's four-year-old son bolted from a pew and raced down the center aisle. Jeff followed in hot pursuit. All eyes watched the chase. When the father caught the toddler, he slapped Billy across the head, then lifted the screaming child over his shoulder and carried him out.

Chris was alarmed by what he saw. Standing in the back of the church was an athletic guy wearing a coat and tie. They made fleeting eye contact before the man turned away. He seemed vaguely familiar. Without the mustache, glasses and curly brown hair, he resembled the guy in the lobby of the Boston hotel when Chris went to reclaim his cell phone.

It seemed unlikely – no, improbable – that an undercover Boston policeman had followed him to San Francisco. The man had to be associated with Thanatos. Had Irene sent him to track Chris's movements? Or was he an assassin? If the latter, was his target Anna, or Chris himself, or both?

When the crowd faced forward again, and the sermon resumed, Chris's mind flooded with scenarios, options and doubt. Was he being paranoid? Or was he in peril? The heightened alert and the inability to act consumed his thoughts during the balance of the service.

After the final blessing, the casket was ushered down the center of the nave, followed by the solemn family. Jessica's mother was overcome with tears while led out by her ashen husband. Her sister was grief-stricken while holding the tiny hands of two children. Billy squirmed in the tight grip of his father. The other man had vanished.

When their turn came to exit the pew, Chris let Anna go first so he could scan the remaining mourners. At the top of the outside steps, he continued searching the faces assembled along the sidewalk. There he was again. Unlike most people, the man was neither walking away nor talking with someone else. He stood stationary, sideways, as if trying to blend in.

Chris recognized the technique. He had used it himself for decades. This would be an ideal kill zone for a silentcide. People were compacted and distracted. The close quarters would conceal a fatal move and provide cover for an escape. He might be mistaken, but a bigger mistake would be to ignore his instincts. He had to get them to safety.

Chris suggested to Anna, "Hey listen, you told me the interment is private, so let's also skip the funeral luncheon."

"But why? It's only about a block away at a charming Italian restaurant," she countered. "Jessica and I went there often. Their food is great."

"No doubt. But haven't you been through enough already? Why torture yourself for another hour?"

"You sure?"

"Yeah, let's go," he said while stepping into California Street before she could object. He hailed a cab. The sudden evasion attracted the man's attention, or so Chris thought.

Anna asked, "Where're we going?"

"You tell me. This was once your city."

She thought for a second, then leaned over the seat to talk with the driver. Chris glanced through the rear window. The man was gone. It seemed probable he would try again.

Chapter Forty-Four: San Francisco, California

Photo 100

FORTY-FIVE

SAN FRANCISCO, CALIFORNIA

T he taxi dropped them off at a welcome pavilion near the northern tip of Presidio, a fifteen-hundred-acre national park. Anna led Chris down a concrete path. He gasped at the sight of an icon that had been on his bucket list for decades: the Golden Gate Bridge.[101]

"Isn't that magnificent?" Anna asked.

"Incredible," he said while watching sailboats float beneath the nine-thousand-foot span between the Pacific Ocean and the entrance to San Francisco Bay. "Better than I ever imagined."

"I used to come here all the time," she explained, "especially when I was feeling down. Its beauty and strength always lifted my spirits."

"I can see why," Chris said, then looked over his shoulder to see if they had been followed.

After admiring the view in silence, Anna said, "Another great thing is this spot begins one of my favorite places to run."

"You're planning on running in that dress and heels?"

She chuckled. "Hardly. But if you're game, we could walk. It's about a three-mile path along the waterfront."

At a leisurely pace, they watched water lapping along the shore, saw families picnicking and playing in the park, occasionally nodded at strollers, casually read historic markers, and savored the warm sunshine. Chris also kept searching for danger.

Totally unexpectedly, Anna said, "I've been thinking. For all the time we've spent together, I don't know much about you."

He hoped she didn't notice his flinch. "What do you want to know?"

"Everything."

"That narrows it down," he joked, trying to conceal his trepidation. What could he say that was truthful without revealing the truth? He began by describing his job as a cybersecurity consultant. That was a well-rehearsed fabrication. The answers to her subsequent questions were more difficult. She asked about his family and foster parents, then if he and his sister might ever reconcile their differences. The lies kept multiplying. He was thankful when they reached the Palace of Fine Arts.[102]

"This is your next stop on Anna Monteiro's city tour. This gorgeous Beaux-Arts rotunda was built in 1915 for the Panama–Pacific International Exposition."

Chris snickered.

"What's so funny?" she asked.

"I just pictured you in twenty years as a tour guide who looks like José in Santo Domingo."

Anna slugged him on the shoulder, then said with tenderness, "I remember wanting to talk to you that day, but you were so standoffish. I almost had you pegged as a conceited jerk until we started walking around together. Then, within thirty minutes, you had me hooked."

Within an equal amount of time, Chris had become infatuated with her. He had tried resisting but instead had selfishly put them in a hopeless situation. So, instead of expressing his true emotions – speaking the truth would be a welcome change – he chose to be noncommittal. Without looking into her waiting brown eyes, he said, "It's strange how fate can bring two people together." He gave her a kiss on the cheek. To him, it felt like a Judas kiss.

They sat along the edge of a lagoon and watched birds swimming in the reflective blue water. Chris said, "I can see why you love this place. It's gorgeous."

"It really is. When I first moved to San Francisco, I'd come here to dream about my future. You know, a satisfying career, a wonderful marriage, having two kids and a dog." With a woeful smirk, she added, "All I got was the dog. Later, this was my haven when things were falling apart with Paul. In fact, it was right over there I decided to get a divorce, go back to Boston and accept Liz's invitation to join Longfellow. So it's probably apropos I'm here again."

"What do you mean?"

"I guess I'm …" She hesitated. "I'm, uh, at another crossroad. I want to personally accomplish something, but all I've done is ride Liz's coattails. And despite that, I'll probably be out of a job soon. I also want to get out of that brownstone. I'm just soaking off my parents. I'm forty-one, for god's sake. And, as Jessica proved, life can be unpredictably short. So it's about time I do something by myself that I'm proud of … like you have."

God, if she only knew. "Like what?" he asked, trying not to betray his inner disgust.

"That's the problem. For the last five years, I was proud to be helping to cure cancer. I really saw the impossible happening. But now that the dream is shattered, I'm clueless about what to do next that's equally important." After a sigh of resignation, she added, "I wish I could just run."

"Run away or run toward something?"

"Both."

They resumed walking, but their conversation was superficial. He sensed Anna was contemplating her future. He hoped she had one. He also worried about his own while remaining vigilant for a concealed observer or an imminent attack.

Minutes later, Chris said, "Hey, I could use a bathroom. Do you know if there's one around here?"

"Yeah, see that big Hyde Street Pier[103] sign?" she asked while pointing. "I think there's a public restroom just before that."

"Thanks. I'll be right back." When he returned, Anna was slouched over her cell phone looking distraught. He asked, "Everything okay?"

"No, not really. I just got an email from Sergeant O'Neill, the Boston policewoman who's handling the George Henniker investigation. He's the guy who shot at my window, remember?"

"Of course I remember. What's up?"

"He was shot during an attempted robbery on Monday."

Acting concerned, Chris said, "Wow. Is he going to be okay?"

Anna looked up and said, "Not according to this," then looked down at the phone again. "Apparently, he's in intensive care and a medically induced coma. Seems a bullet severed a thoracic spinal vertebra. If he survives, he'll probably be a paraplegic."

Chris finally had an answer about Henniker's condition but again admonished his sloppiness. "That's tragic," he said as sincerely as possible.

"Yeah, I guess so," Anna said softly.

"What does that mean?"

"Well, it means I no longer have to worry about him attacking me or the house." With a perplexed expression, she asked, "Does looking at it like that make me a terrible person?"

"No, not at all. He scared the hell out of you. And now he's no longer a threat."

"Maybe, but I still feel bad it happened like this. Anyway, Sergeant O'Neill wants to meet with me."

"What do you think she wants?"

"I'm not sure, but I'm guessing she wants to discuss what to do about the pending criminal case."

Chris asked, "Would you consider dropping the charges?"

"If that's possible, sure, why not? He's already sentenced to a fate worse than prison."

That's better than being dead.

The next few blocks along Jefferson Street[104] were increasingly filled with tourists and shops catering to tourists' wallets. Anna was doing a yeoman's job trying to sound upbeat. While distracting him by pointing out a fishing boat she and Paul had chartered years ago, a concealed man leaped from behind a shrub and pressed into Chris's face.

"Oh shit," Chris yelled while flexing into a martial arts stance.

Anna laughed hysterically. "He got you!" Her eyes sparkled. Her expression was priceless.

Realizing he was the brunt of a practical joke, Chris asked, "Who's he?"

"That's David Johnson, aka the Bushman.[105] He's a local legend. He's been scaring the crap out of people like that since 1980."

Chris started to relax, chuckled at himself, then wondered how someone sitting on a milk crate behind handheld branches could get the jump on someone with decades of defensive training. He reached out to Anna. "Here, give me your cell phone and I'll take a picture of you with the Bushman." Her smile was adorable. Before getting a five-dollar tip from his wallet, Chris pocketed her phone.

"Next on the itinerary is lunch," Anna announced while pointing. "That window serves the world's best sourdough bread bowls filled with clam chowder."

"What kind?"

"Boston clam chowder, of course," she said with a grin.

"Excellent. Should I get one or two?"

"One's plenty. You want to save room for the Dungeness crab or shrimp cups[106] served next door."

While waiting in line, she peered around the corner and said, "Oh, this is perfect. A place to sit under the famous Fisherman's Wharf sign[107] just opened up. I'll go grab the spot and meet you there."

As soon as she left, Chris pulled out her phone, removed the back cover, and bent a tiny lead near the SIM card. She'd later discover the phone would turn on but hopelessly malfunction. This was the only way he could think of to prevent Thanatos from tracking her.

The wait for lunch was excessive. After finally being served, he proudly carried the soup bowl toward her with a big smile. She seemed transfixed while sitting on a concrete bench, as if deep in thought.

Just as he was saying, "Your lunch, madam," a seagull swooped down and attacked the food. The bread bowl tumbled to the ground. The soup splattered everywhere. "This is a dangerous place," he said while laughing, expecting her to do the same.

"That's okay," she said instead with a somber tone.

"What's wrong?" he asked, assuming she was thinking about Jessica's funeral.

"We've got to talk."

"Isn't that what we've been doing?" he asked while stepping over the mess, shooing away a growing flock of hungry birds and sitting down beside her.

Ignoring the question, she said, "Remember I said earlier that I didn't really know you."

"Yeah."

"Well, I just realized you only know two sides of me. One is a giddy girl who wanted a whirlwind romance. The other is a drama queen who's always whining and complaining and looking for a prince to save her."

"That's not true at all," he protested.

"Yes, it is. So please let me finish before I chicken out, will you?" She took a deep breath, as if mustering courage. "I'm neither of those extremes, Chris, and I'm ashamed that's all you've seen. As I said before, I also don't know what I want to become. But I do know this. I have to solve my problems by myself. Then maybe when I get my act together, we can pick things back up."

"What are you saying?"

"I guess I'm, uh ..." She paused a moment to control her emotions before blurting out, "I'm saying it's over, Chris. I have too many issues. It's not fair to keep burdening you with them. So, as much as I appreciate everything you've done — and believe me, you've been wonderful — let's go our separate ways."

Chris felt helpless. It was the right decision. Frankly, the only answer. He couldn't expect a future with her. That was a delusional fantasy. He couldn't warn her or tell the truth. That would lead to a life in prison. He couldn't protect her forever. If Thanatos wanted her dead, they'd eventually find a way, and he didn't want to be anywhere near her when that happened. All he could do was mumble, "I understand."

"Good. I hoped you would. Thank you."

After they stood up, she gave him a quick kiss, then looked at him with sadness.

The next morning, as he flew to Philadelphia, Chris doubted he would ever see her again. The realization was devastating.

Chapter Forty-Five: San Francisco, California

Photos 101–107

FORTY-SIX

S weltering heat with oppressive humidity had already engulfed the City of Brotherly Love, and Michelle's Friday morning had barely started. She hadn't been back to Philadelphia in twenty-six years. It was too soon. Hibernating traumas of her wretched childhood were awakening. Dark emotions were ambushing her with a vengeance. Sitting in downtown's LOVE Park, next to the giant red LOVE sculpture,[108] was a cruel mockery.

Too much of Michelle's life had been shrouded by control and hate. Wickedness had molded her. She resented who she had become, despised what she had done, and felt trapped by destiny. There seemed no way to escape the scared emptiness and judgmental self-criticism. She was alone with despair.

Michelle resumed walking from the hotel to the rental car office a few blocks away to pick up a car for the drive to Lancaster County on Saturday morning. Previous biannual meetings with Irene Shaw had been scheduled well in advance and held in different cities. They were unpleasant but tolerable.

In contrast, the impromptu meeting at the farm felt as ominous as a death row inmate awaiting an appointment with the executioner. A reprieve seemed possible yet slim. There was no doubt Chris was in bigger jeopardy.

As Michelle observed the sun glistening off the intricate façade of City Hall,[109] she wondered if Chris would have the courage to attend the meeting. Since becoming enamored with that woman ten days ago, he had stopped communicating and, when he did, he stopped being honest. He was no longer acting like the brother she knew. It seemed he had chosen Anna Monteiro and was abandoning his sister. The betrayal ached.

In search of breakfast, Michelle entered Reading Terminal Market,[110] an enormous old train station filled with about seventy-five food vendors. The aisles were crowded. Half the people were locals who moved with hurried determination. The other half were tourists who meandered and gawked. Michelle's decision was easy when spotting an Amish diner. The customers were shoulder-to-shoulder sitting on tall silver stools while shoveling down the homemade Dutch Country foods.

The blueberry shortstack with a dollop of melting butter was delicious, but not as good as Mamm's. Her second foster mother's cooking was one of the few good things during the decade on the farm. Michelle remembered eating her pancakes with fingers stained from berry picking and wrists sore from churning butter. Their taste was divine. The rare happy recollection was eons ago.

After breakfast, while entering a large greenspace, Michelle noticed the historic grandeur of Independence Hall.[111] There was also a long line of people waiting to view the Liberty Bell.[112] The two symbols of American freedom from tyranny offered no hope. Her own dream of freedom from Thanatos and Irene Shaw seemed unrealistic. No, improbable.

Ninety minutes later, Michelle gripped the steering wheel of the rental car while staring at her childhood home in South Philly. The late-nineteenth-century brick rowhouse[113] had recently been renovated. The dingy exterior had been cleaned but could not mask the ruinous history of the Ritchie family. Her heart pounded with dread. She felt nauseous.

Michelle mentally toured the interior. The musty living room. The cramped kitchen littered with dirty dishes and the lingering stench of booze and cigarettes. The rickety staircase leading to

Danny's bedroom and hers. Her mother dead on the floor. Her stepfather bleeding from a bashed skull and multiple stab wounds, her only justifiable murder. That horrible night was painfully vivid. So were the despicable acts she had been forced to commit since.

◆◆◆

Finding a place to park in the East Passyunk neighborhood was challenging. Cars were parked bumper-to-bumper in front of narrow brick trinity rowhouses originally built for the lower-middle class and increasingly home to frugal young professionals.

Michelle was hustling past a huge mural[114] featuring six painted images of recording artists from the 1950s and 1960s who were raised in South Philly. She stopped, stared and vaguely remembered her mother had attended the same high school as teen idols Frankie Avalon, Bobby Rydell and Fabian. A childhood flashback occurred of her being yelled at for using Mom's signed record albums as frisbees. Odd what the brain recalled and the memories it tried unsuccessfully to block.

Before crossing Ninth Street, the unmistakable aroma of fresh hoagie rolls, grilled strips of ribeye steak, sautéed onions and gooey Cheez Whiz whiffed into her nostrils. Judging from the broad shoulders and wavy black hair, he was already sitting at a red metal picnic table at Pat's King of Steaks.[115] She rushed up and threw her arms around him.

"I'm so glad you made it," she said with unbridled enthusiasm.

Ansel Meehan turned and, with sparkling eyes and a mischievous grin, said, "Of course I did. But don't flatter yourself by thinking I made the two-hour drive from Baltimore to see my little foster sister. I'm here for the original and world's best cheesesteak." Then he gave her an affectionate kiss on the cheek.

Chapter Forty-Six: Philadelphia, Pennsylvania

Photos 108–115

FORTY-SEVEN

Ansel wiped the final cheesesteak grease from his beard and mustache stubble — what he had called his carefully groomed ten o'clock shadow. His faded blue eyes locked on to Michelle. With a warm, nonjudgmental sincerity, he asked, "Why did you really invite me here?"

"Because you always loved Pat's," was her evasive answer.

"You know what I mean. When we saw each other — what was it, less than three weeks ago? — I thought we agreed it was too risky to get back together again."

"That was your conclusion, not mine. Besides, with me in Philly and you a short drive away, it seemed like a perfect opportunity to extend our Minneapolis reunion."

"It has been nice."

With a joking seriousness, Michelle asked, "What's this past tense bullshit? We're not done yet."

Ansel began a gentle protest. "Yeah, I should really be ..."

"No, you're not leaving. Take me someplace fun. That's what a good big brother would do."

With a bright smile of resignation, he said, "Well, okay. What did you have in mind?"

"Remember how Mrs. Miller often took us Three Amigos to the zoo? Let's go there."

They drove separately and rendezvoused at the front entrance. Michelle's single ground rule was they should enjoy the animals and each other with no heavy discussions.

That rule lasted about ten minutes until they were staring at the Caribbean flamingos.[116] Although she had lived with him for two years at the foster home, she knew little about Ansel other than he was a weapons and bomb expert assigned by Phonoi to high-profile assassinations. She had heard enough about that during their conversation in Minneapolis. She refused to perceive him as a killer. She wanted him to be a grown-up version of the Kevin she once knew and loved.

She asked, "So tell me, what's your life been like since the farm?"

Ansel stiffened, crossed his arms and said, "There's really not much to tell. I was initially rebellious. You know, partying, drinking too much and dabbling in drugs. I guess it was my way of coping." With growing discomfort, he admitted, "But then one day I really screwed up an assignment. And I mean big-time. I missed the target, accidently killed someone else, and almost got caught ... all because I was hungover. That was sobering." He smirked at his self-deprecating pun.

"And after that?"

"So after that I struggled for a while. Actually, for a long time. I felt worthless. Hell, I was worthless. Eventually I turned myself around. Since then, I've learned how to be callous to the job."

"Really? I wish I could reach that stage."

"Okay, maybe numb is a better word." He paused as if searching for something positive to say. "I do enjoy the plotting. I mean, I've always been good at planning every contingency. You know, like a high-stakes chess game." He scowled. "But I dread the implementation. And I always fear slipping back to my old ways after every assignment."

While Ansel admired the plains zebras,[117] she admired his physique as he leaned over the animal enclosure railing. Broad shoulders.

Muscular arms. Toned runner's legs. Cute butt. *God, this man is handsome.* She admonished her thoughts before shuffling up beside him. "So what are your goals?"

He looked perplexed. "Really? In this job? Can you have goals? I mean, other than not getting caught" – he lowered his voice – "or getting killed."

Michelle realized that was also the extent of her goals. How pathetic. "Are you dating anyone?"

"Nope. I've had my share of relationships. Nothing serious. In this job you can't have anything long term. That bothered me for years. But at this age, I guess I'm over it." After a quick laugh, he added, "So I got a black Lab instead."

"That's awesome. They're a wonderful breed. Any hobbies?"

"Good lord, Michelle. This is sounding like a first date. By the way, I'm a Leo, in case you forgot."

"Come on. I want to know how you handle the stress because it's eating me up."

"Okay. Well, I work out a lot. Oh, and I also carve wooden ships," he said with enthusiasm. "Famous ones. Like the *Mayflower*, the Columbus fleet, *Old Ironsides*, plus Viking, pirate and Egyptian vessels. They're about eight to twelve inches long. Very intricate."

"Really, with those big hands?"

"Yeah. It takes about nine months for each model. The tiny details keep my mind focused and away from work. It's great therapy. And when I'm done, I can stare at them with pride. Frankly, it's one of the few things that make me happy."

A mental diversion … was that what she needed?

Two giraffes[118] were necking and seemed amorous. A mother shuffled her two small children away before something happened that she didn't want to explain. Seeing the toddlers prompted her next question. "Do you think about your childhood much?"

Ansel shook his head. "No, I try not to. Too depressing."

Michelle quietly admitted, "I returned to my childhood home this morning."

Ansel studied her with a frown. "Really? You mean where your parents died? Why would you do that?"

"I don't know. Maybe a moth-to-a-flame kind of thing. It was awful." Casting her eyes downward, she added, "In fact, all I've had are terrible thoughts since returning to Philly."

While extending a comforting hand, he said, "I hope that doesn't include me."

"Of course not. You're wonderful."

That came out wrong. She sounded like a schoolgirl with a crush. Or maybe what she really wanted was a surrogate brother to substitute for Chris. Had she become that dependent? Was she incapable of being self-sufficient?

As they walked up to a pacing cheetah,[119] Ansel said, "Look at that magnificent animal. I remember how a trainer made us study that cat for two days … how it moves, hides, stalks and readies for a kill. They are incredibly patient and calculating. Then with a burst of speed – up to seventy miles an hour, if I remember – it attacks, cripples the prey with a single paw swipe, then goes for the throat."

"It sounds like you're envious of them."

"I am. I could never be that capable."

"Do you think they ever have regrets?" Michelle asked.

"You mean for killing? No way. They're designed for it."

"Like us?"

Ansel quickly rejected the comparison. "God no. Evolution created them, not Irene Shaw."

The sound of Irene's name made Michelle stiffen. "Do you resent her for that?"

"Of course," he said with pained bitterness. "Every hour of every day. But what's done is done, we are who we are, and we'll probably die doing it."

The stark reality had never been stated more pointedly. Her destiny was to die prematurely. But how soon?

With caution, Michelle said, "I've been thinking lately. I want to get out. You know, start a new life. Do you think that's possible?"

With a sigh of dismissal, Ansel said, "Highly unlikely."

"I agree, but then maybe not completely out. I remember you telling me one of your farm roommates washed out, so they made her a facilitator. Do you think that's possible for me?"

"You'd be good at it, there's no doubt about that." After a moment's consideration, he suggested, "Why don't you plant the seed with Irene tomorrow?"

"You say that like she's a rational human being. I doubt tomorrow is going to be a career-mentoring discussion. Has she ever called you back to the farm?"

"Once, when I screwed up that big assignment. It was a serious come-to-Jesus meeting. Then she gave me a second chance, but on a very, very short leash." Perhaps to rid himself of the unpleasant memories, he quickly switched gears. "Let me ask you this. Have you done anything wrong?"

"No, not really," Michelle said while trying to remember if she had violated any of Irene's sacred rules.

"You'd better be more convincing than that tomorrow."

She mustered up the inner fortitude to say with resolution, "I've done everything by the book. I always do."

"Great. Then you have nothing to worry about."

She didn't share his optimistic assessment. "But Chris is another story." She proceeded to tell him how Chris had gone rogue and purposefully failed to finish a commission by today's deadline.

After listening to Michelle's explanation, Ansel concluded, "Then Chris is the one who needs to worry. Do you think he'll show up?"

"Yes, he's on a flight now from San Francisco."

"So then talk to him tonight, or in the car tomorrow, and come up with a plausible game plan that'll appease Irene."

"That's not going to happen," Michelle said.

"Why not?"

"We're not allowed to travel together, so we agreed to meet at the farm."

"You mean he's stopped talking with you?" Ansel asked.

"Yes. I tried several times to get him back on track. But he's cut me off. I have no idea what he's been doing for the last week."

"Has he ever done anything like that before?"

"No, never," Michelle said firmly. "He's always been dependable. We're great partners."

"You're lucky. I've always had to work solo. At least you had a partner."

Michelle got irate. "Don't you dare use the past tense. He's still my partner. Most important, he's my brother."

"That's the spirit. Show that type of emotion tomorrow. And defend him at all costs."

"Do you think that'll work?" she asked.

"Sure. I don't know what else to tell you."

"You don't know? Or you don't want to say?"

Michelle was rattled when Ansel didn't say anything before wandering forward.

The premise of going to the zoo had been to have fun. The only oasis of enjoyment was in a swan boat[120] in an artificial lake. They had ridden the attraction several times as kids. Kevin and Danny always had one boat. She had to share another with Mrs. Miller. For the first time, Michelle got to help paddle too fast, bump into walls, chase floating ducks and act like a knucklehead. The laughter was refreshing. But the emotional cloud returned by the time they reached the zoo's parking lot.

Ansel reached his car first. He turned with a warm smile. "This has been great. Wonderful, in fact. I now agree we should do this again."

Michelle didn't respond. She rushed up, held him tight and felt herself tremble.

Without letting go, Ansel asked with concern, "What's wrong?"

"I'm terrified. I have this horrible feeling about tomorrow." Her voice trailed off.

"I'm sure you'll be fine."

She studied his face. "I can tell by looking at you that you're not sure at all."

"Maybe," Ansel mumbled. "But I don't know what I can do about it."

"Don't go." Her sudden desperation increased her anxiety.

Looking at his watch, he said, "I could stay another hour or ..."

"No. Stay with me tonight," she blurted out.

His eyes widened. He took a surprised step backward. "That's not a good idea, Michelle."

"Why not?" Her tone was emphatic.

"As I said last time, you'll always be my little foster sister."

"I don't mean sleep together."

"Then what is it?" Ansel asked.

"I'm petrified this might be my last night alive. I don't want to spend it alone."

Chapter Forty-Seven: Philadelphia, Pennsylvania

Photos 116–120

FORTY-EIGHT

Saturday

The panic attack felt life threatening. Pounding, erratic heartbeats echoed in her ears. Shallow staccato gasps were suffocating. Her face was hot, yet her core was chilled. Her skin tingled with dread. Fear assaulted every limb, constricted her chest and crippled Michelle's ability to drive closer to the farm.

She slammed on the brakes of the rental car, threw open the door and ran to escape the inner torture. The impending doom followed relentlessly. She squatted in a roadside ditch, clutched her knees and squeezed her eyes.

Deep breaths. Deeper. Lower the heart rate. Imagine a sunset. Relax your jaw. Unclench your fists. See a large orange globe glistening across ocean whitecaps. Watch as it hovers on the horizon. Beautiful. Soothing. Loosen the shoulders. Breathe the Dutch Country air. Clear the mind. Hear the birds, their peaceful singing. Now normal breathing. Slower. That's it. Slower. Regain control. You've got this. You're strong. You'll prevail.

Five minutes later, the terror had retreated and Michelle had recovered. She had learned techniques to manage anxiety on the farm. Ironically, her pending return had caused the most frightening panic attack since leaving sixteen years before.

Ansel's last words of the morning replayed in her memory. "Yes, the meeting with Irene will be ugly. But just tell her the truth and do what she says and everything will be fine. Trust me."

That was easy for her foster brother to say. He had survived Irene's wrath after making a mistake. But Chris had intentionally defied Irene. Michelle wanted to believe Ansel's prediction was right, but every instinct screamed she and Chris were about to die. That assumed her brother showed up so she wouldn't die alone.

Clip-clop. Clip-clop. Clip-clop.

Michelle looked up at an approaching horse-drawn buggy over-flowing with children. At the reins was a gentle Amish man with a scraggly black beard. He slowed the horse and said, "Gut daag. Wie bischt?"

"I'm doing fine," Michelle responded with a forced smile.

"Brascht hilf?"

"No, I don't need help, thank you."

"Al rite. Machts gut," he said while tipping the brim of his straw hat.

Michelle doubted she would have a good day despite his best wishes. She watched as the family resumed traveling down the road, then laughed at the sight of two boys wearing inline skates hanging on to the back of the buggy.[121] A young girl looked back and waved. Precious innocence. Michelle had forgotten how gracious the Amish people were and how rich their lives were without needless posses-sions. Their happiness and lack of stress were enviable.

With a sigh of controlled calm, Michelle got back into the car and drove the remaining three miles to the farm. According to the clock on the dashboard, she would arrive ten minutes early. She had been taught that being punctual was not good enough.

Gravel crackled beneath the car tires as Michelle pulled parallel to a large barn[122] and smaller horse stable. While stepping out, an unmistakable smell of cattle manure assailed her nose. The rusted blades of a windmill[123] made a familiar high-pitched creak while turning in the mild breeze. Memories of her tormented teens came flooding back. She had hoped to never return, yet was ready to face her fate.

A screen door opened and slammed shut. Standing on the porch of the farmhouse was a woman she wouldn't have recognized if not for the white bonnet, thick glasses and bland gray dress. Her former foster mother was frail with pasty wrinkled skin. Time had been cruel but her aged face was excited.

"Welcome," Mamm yelled out in a crackling voice, then cautiously navigated down a small flight of wooden steps.

At first indecisive, Michelle approached and accepted the woman's embrace. Unexpected emotions emerged. This was the only person other than Chris who had provided some comfort and compassion during the decade of silentcide training. Mamm's warmth was again providing the fortitude needed to endure the distress. Michelle leaned into the kiss on the cheek. The woman's elderly fingers patted her on the face.

"Let me look at you," Mamm said while holding Michelle's hands outright. "You look wonderful. So pretty and grown up, just the way I imagined. It's so good to have you back."

"Thank you," was all Michelle could think of saying.

The screen door slammed again. Leaning over the porch railing were two teenagers. No doubt they were the next generation of Irene's recruits.

The boy – maybe eighteen or nineteen – stood tall, strong and confident, wearing a white shirt, black trousers with suspenders and a hand defiantly on his hip. His black bowl haircut framed an apathetic expression.

The girl, maybe three or four years younger, seemed reserved, perhaps timid, yet enthralled. Her brown hair was mostly covered by a bonnet. The denim-colored dress hid her figure. Her cheeks were round, her eyes were bright, and her lips were tense. She fidgeted as if nervous or unaccustomed to outsiders. She was a reflection of Michelle at that age.

"Don't be rude," Mamm called out to them. "Come meet our guest."

When they arrived, the teens stood at attention, just as Michelle had been taught how to talk to elders. Mamm said, "This is Michelle Barton, the woman I was telling you about. She and her brother Chris lived here – what was it? – for about ten years?"

Michelle nodded and extended her hand. "Nice to meet you both." The boy's grip was strong. The girl's was limp and uncertain.

Mamm said to them, "Please introduce yourselves."

"I'm Jacob Conners," he said with a hint of arrogance.

The girl quietly said, "I'm Rachel Phillips."

Sensing the girl had not yet become hardened by silentcide training, Michelle leaned forward and asked, "Is Rachel your real name?"

Startled, the girl looked at Mamm then Jacob for guidance.

The boy commanded, "Don't tell her anything."

Michelle said with sympathetic compassion, "Rachel, regardless of what happens to you here, please don't forget who you really are. Hear me? That's the most important lesson you'll ever learn."

Rachel seemed to comprehend before lowering her eyes. Michelle prayed the girl would heed the advice. Self-worth was critical to surviving the self-loathing that lay ahead of her.

A car raced into the driveway before abruptly stopping. Chris emerged. His clothes were wrinkled. He seemed exhausted. The stance was tense and defensive. He surveyed the scene without acknowledging anyone, then motioned for Michelle to join him near the car.

"Is Irene here yet?" he asked anxiously.

Looking at her watch, she said, "Not yet, but probably soon."

"Listen," he said in a whisper, "I know what I did was wrong. Worse yet, I lied and deserted you. I'm sorry. Really sorry. So whatever happens, let me do the talking and I'll take the blame. Understand?"

Michelle was strengthened by his presence but hurt by the sketchy apology. If Chris were really sorry, he would've explained himself days ago. "No, I don't understand. Why'd you do it?"

Mamm called out with a scolding tone reminiscent of when they were children, "Chris, join us please."

He yelled back, "Be right there," then returned to his sister. Distress creased his face. "I can't explain now. But I will. I promise." He grimaced, then his expression softened. "Just remember one thing, Michelle. I love you."

His emotions were heartfelt. The sibling bond had been tested but was restored. They could argue later. Maybe she could forgive him. Maybe not. But now they needed to confront Irene together, just as they had partnered against every other adversity. They'd do it again and succeed. In a hushed voice, Michelle said, "And I love you too. We can do this."

With renewed confidence, Michelle and Chris began walking toward Mamm and the teens when a barn service door opened. A brute in his early forties emerged pushing a wheelchair. His black hair was short with misshapen bangs across a broad brow. The square face, flat nose, protruding chin and inset eyes portrayed cruelty.

Slumped in the wheelchair was a white-bearded man wearing a heavy coat and wool blanket despite the summer heat. The left side of his face drooped. His distorted mouth exposed yellowed teeth. Red and purple spider veins crisscrossed his cheeks and nose. The glassy eyes were unresponsive. The only movement was a twitching left arm, which he tried unsuccessfully to calm by clutching his hands. The senile man appeared near death.

Mamm began the introductions by pointing toward the menacing caregiver. "This is Wolfgang König. Meet Chris Davis and Michelle Barton." No one said a word. "And of course, you already know Lionel Jørgensen."

Michelle stared at the drooling man. There was no resemblance to the former chiseled Scandinavian trainer they previously abhorred.

In similar shocked disbelief, Chris asked, "You mean he's Preceptor?"

"No, I'm Preceptor," the bruiser said in a commanding voice.

"Of course you are," Chris said with disdain. "Congratulations, big guy." Turning to Mamm, he asked, "What the hell happened to him?"

"It was terrible," Mamm said with sadness. "About eight years ago, Preceptor inhaled a poison he was preparing and had a major seizure. A series of strokes followed. Now he can't walk or talk, remembers little and needs constant care."

Chris huffed, then blurted out sarcastically, "It couldn't happen to a nicer guy."

"Chris!" Michelle admonished him.

"What? The guy traumatized us for years and never showed an ounce of compassion. Oh wait, he did once in northern Italy. Let me return the favor." Chris bent down, stared within inches of his nemesis, and said, "Golly gee. I'm sorry you're a vegetable. But you deserve it for what you did to us."

Chris scoffed, Michelle was perturbed, Mamm was angry, the teens were talking, and the brute seemed poised to retaliate when everyone stopped at once. A polished black limousine approached the driveway. Irene Elizabeth Shaw was making her grand entrance.

Chapter Forty-Eight: Lancaster County, Pennsylvania

Photos 121–123

FORTY-NINE

When the front doors of the limo opened, two steroid-enhanced musclemen stepped out wearing black suits and carrying black SIG P229 pistols. The chauffeur maintained a threatening pose while his counterpart approached Chris, grabbed his collar, slammed him against the barn and frisked him for weapons. He then motioned for Michelle to spread-eagle against the wall.

"Watch your damn hands," Chris shouted to protect his sister.

The warning intensified the groping. When finished, the bodyguard pushed the gun barrel into Chris's temple and nodded toward the car. The driver opened the back door. One long, high-heeled leg emerged. He held her hand. After Irene exited, she pulled down the hem of a tight black skirt and stared.

Silver-white hair was meticulously coifed in a French bun. Her skin was taut and wrinkle-free. What surgeons hadn't fixed was covered by layers of makeup. Her protruding jawline was rigid, almost skeletal. A gaudy diamond necklace failed to conceal the protruding cords of her thin neck. The purple orchids on the white silk blouse appeared hand-painted. Irene's glare was more sinister than Chris remembered. She was the personification of evil.

"Oh my," Irene said while pushing an errant hair into place. "It's breezy. John, do me a favor and fetch my scarf, will you?" While she made a production of positioning and tying the scarf, everyone stood rigid during the display of power. Chris laughed to himself.

He hoped the fragrance of her Chanel No. 5 perfume didn't mask the stench of the surrounding cow shit.

Satisfied she had everyone's attention, Irene walked in silence toward the old Preceptor. She lifted his chin, studied his unresponsive face and held his quivering hand. "How are you doing, Lionel? Not good, I see." She looked up at Wolfgang behind the wheelchair and snapped, "Goddamn it. Get something to wipe off that drool! Now!" Then, with uncharacteristic tenderness, she kissed Preceptor on the forehead – a long, lingering kiss – and said with empathy, "Take care, my love. My heart aches for you."

For decades, Chris had suspected the two were lovers. The image gave him the creeps.

Irene's melancholy disappeared in an instant. She gave a cordial nod toward Mamm, forced a smile at the teens, ignored Michelle, and focused her wrath on Chris.

"Mr. Davis," she said with annoyance. "I had my doubts you'd join us today. From my understanding, you've been a very bad boy."

"I'm not ten anymore, Irene," Chris said in defiance. He deserved to be treated as a valued professional and not as a cowering orphan. "So stop the condescending attitude."

Initially startled by his bravado, she quickly resumed her air of supremacy. "That's Ms. Shaw to you."

"Just be glad I'm not calling you what I really want." He knew that insubordination might cross an unrecoverable line.

Unfazed, Irene looked at the man holding the gun and said, "Admonish Mr. Davis, will you, dear?"

The bodyguard gut-punched Chris. Michelle reached over to comfort her brother until the man turned the gun on her. She gave Chris a frightened and perplexed look.

"Don't interfere, Michelle," Irene warned. "He's fine. The two of us are just chatting. In fact, I have a marvelous idea." Irene faced Mamm. "Would you be a dear and take Michelle and the children inside for something to eat?"

"Yes, Ms. Shaw," Mamm said with a slight curtsey, then began leading the threesome toward the house. Chris heard her say to Michelle, "I have a big pot of vegetable soup on the stove. One of your all-time favorites. Remember how you used to help me harvest the garden?"

At the top of the stairs, Michelle exchanged a worried glance with Chris. He tried reassuring her by mouthing the words, "I'll be fine." As she passed through the screen door, he doubted he would ever see her again. At least she wouldn't have to watch him die.

To the bodyguard, Irene said, "I'm confident Mr. Davis will behave now. Please give us a bit of privacy." The man lowered his weapon, walked over to the wheelchair and maintained a stance of readiness. The chauffeur leaned against the limo with a similar vigilance.

In a belittling tone, she said to Chris, "Now then, it seems we've gotten off to a rocky start. Let's try again and be more cordial this time, shall we?"

Chris stood tall and silent, refusing to show his pain despite being winded from the blow. He also refused to show his distress. Irene respected strength and loathed weakness.

She lurched forward. Her expression turned venomous. "What the fuck is your problem?"

Without flinching, Chris responded, "Could you be a bit more specific?"

With a mocking chuckle, she said, "You're right. Your list of egregious actions is long. Perhaps we should discuss them one at a time. Let's start by telling me why the hell Anna Monteiro is still alive."

"Well, the initial plan was to swap her Midol tablet with one laced with carfentanil."

Irene nodded with approval. "That was a very clever idea. I've always been impressed with Michelle's ingenuity. Proceed."

"So we accomplished that and then had to wait for the results."

"And remind me, was that during the cruise? The one you booked under your own name and then never wore a disguise?"

Chris rebuked himself. Of course Irene would discover his breach of protocol. Maybe by admitting to the minor transgression, she'd believe he intended to be honest about everything. "Yes."

"And how did that plan work out?"

"It didn't."

In a sarcastic voice, she asked, "Pray tell, what happened next?"

"An innocent woman overdosed instead."

"I assume you're referring to the former Jessica Daly. I've seen photos of her. Seemed like a lovely gal." In an instant, Irene's tone transformed from saccharine sweet to bitter anger. "But that was your own damn fault! You were sloppy. And maybe, just maybe, I can understand why you might've felt bad. But then you had the audacity – no, the stupidity – to attend her funeral. What the hell were you thinking? There's no room in this business for remorse over collateral damage."

He became livid. "Jessica was more than just collateral damage. She was the mother of a four-year-old."

Matching his intensity, she shrieked, "So what? Get over it!" Then Irene displayed a smug look of satisfaction. "Besides, I'm sure your generous donation will help with little Billy's upbringing."

Chris was speechless. He had foolishly underestimated Irene. She was a consummate attorney who was meticulously leading him toward a guilty verdict. She already had answers to every question. During this adversarial trial, she was going to be the judge, jury and executioner while savoring every minute of it.

Irene continued the interrogation. "So after you screwed up plan A, tell me about plan B."

"Well, Michelle coated tampons with a bacteria that would cause toxic shock syndrome."

As if not wanting to miss a single chance to demonstrate her superiority, Irene said, "I believe the proper word is bacterium and its name is Staphylococcus aureus."

"Yeah, something like that. Anyway, the tricky part was getting close enough to make the exchange."

"So, of course, you immediately decided to sleep with her, right? And not only on the cruise, but also in Boston and again in San Francisco. I thought I fixed those distracting boy urges."

Chris imagined strangling her. But he knew after one aggressive step forward, he would be dead. To avoid the temptation, he locked his jaw and bored into her eyes with hatred.

After a conceited smirk, she resumed her accusatory arrogance. "So as of ten o'clock Eastern, Ms. Monteiro is still alive. And I sincerely doubt Michelle's chemistry is at fault. So either you couldn't make the simple exchange during several nights of passion, or you never tried. I'm guessing I know the answer, but I'd like to hear it from you."

"The latter," Chris quietly admitted.

"I'm sorry, dear. I didn't hear you."

With forceful contempt, he said, "I have no intention of killing Anna."

"Tsk, tsk, tsk. That's most unfortunate. You see, Thanatos has a reputation of always fulfilling our client obligations. And your job is to defend that reputation."

Chris said with false hope, "How about if I pay you twice the commission fee to spare Anna's life."

"That's not the way it works, Chris, and you know it."

"But the client is in no condition to care one way or the other," he claimed.

"Are you referring to George Henniker?"

"Yes, he's broke, a paraplegic and a scumbag."

Irene laughed. "All of our clients are scumbags, dear. That's not a justifiable cause for shooting the man."

"I heard he was shot, but I didn't do it." He immediately regretted the impulsive lie.

"Chris, Chris, Chris, you're fibbing now, aren't you? Perhaps I should have one of the boys wash your mouth out with soap. I've seen the police photo of Sully running from the scene in Little Italy. I must say it was very sloppy work. But you'll be happy to learn there's now no chance Henniker can identify you."

"What do you mean?" Chris asked.

"It seems late last night he tragically died in the hospital from complications."

"Great. Then the commission is nulled. Problem solved."

"You could at least show me a little gratitude for covering your incompetent ass."

"Thank you," he mouthed the empty appreciation.

"You're welcome. But unfortunately, the problem is not solved. You see, Henniker was not the client."

Chris knew she was lying. Or at least he thought he knew.

Irene continued, "Do you see the mess you caused while trying to identify a client? The Preceptor warned you countless times, but you never listened. You always thought you were the smartest guy in the room."

He shuffled with growing discomfort. He still couldn't detect if Irene was lying about the client's identity.

As if delivering a closing summation, Irene said, "So let's list the consequences of your unprofessional transgressions. You exposed yourself to the police, we have two innocent people dead, a target who is very much alive, and a pissed off client who graciously extended the deadline to next Friday after I offered him a thirty-percent discount. Now do you understand why I'm displeased?"

He said nothing in his defense. Why bother? She had declared him guilty before stepping out of the car. The silent standoff was agonizing. Irene prolonged the angst by adjusting her scarf. Chris sensed the end was near regardless of what he said next. He might as well die as a man of principle rather than a groveling coward. And perhaps by shouldering all the blame, Michelle would be spared.

Irene said, "I see the seriousness of your misguided actions has finally sunk in. So I'm going to ask you one final and very important question. Consider your answer carefully. Will you kill Ms. Monteiro by the end of next week?"

He answered softly, "I'm not sure I can."

"Can't or won't?"

Chris didn't answer.

She shook her head in disbelief. "Chris, I respect your convictions and tenacity. I really do. But I'm sure you understand why I can't tolerate insubordination. If I do it once, it's a slippery slope. So as much as I had hoped to resolve this amicably, it would appear I can't. And that's too bad because I always admired you."

When Irene snapped her fingers, the bodyguard and chauffeur raised their handguns, pointed them at Chris and advanced. Dying seemed certain.

FIFTY

T he chauffeur wedged the barrel of his SIG P229 into the bridge of Chris's nose. All Chris could see was the gun's black slide, the man's massive fist on the pistol grip, and an index finger poised over the trigger guard.

The bodyguard wrenched one of Chris's arms behind his back, then the other. Wolfgang produced a zip tie. After both wrists were secured, a powerful kick behind the legs dropped Chris to his knees. A handgun was jammed into his skull.

This was it. He was about to die execution style with one bullet to the head. Squeezing his eyes, Chris waited to take his last frightened breath. The chauffeur stepped aside so he wouldn't be splattered with blood.

Irene taunted Chris by saying, "Any last words?"

"Yes. You sure you don't want to offer me clemency?"

With a perplexed tilt of her head, she asked, "Why on earth would I do that?"

"Because despite everything I did wrong, I always turned in my daily reports on time."

She blinked, smiled and then cackled loudly, prompting the other men to laugh too. "I've always enjoyed your sophomoric sense of humor, Chris. I'll miss that. I really will." The joviality disappeared as she commanded the bodyguard, "Frank, please shoot on the count of three. One."

Chris saw the Preceptor's eyes widen as if saddened to see his former pupil die.

"Two."

Chris straightened his posture and peered at Irene in defiance. His only regret was her demonic face would be the last thing he'd ever see. He exhaled for the final time.

Irene did the unexpected. "You know what?" she said. "We're missing someone in this equation."

Chris panicked. "Leave Michelle out of this. Please! She's done nothing wrong."

Irene ignored the plea. She instructed Wolfgang to ring a large brass bell. Instinctively, nearby fenced cows stood up and started heading toward the barn. They obviously assumed it was feeding time. As the clanging continued, Mamm poked her head out of the screen door of the house.

While flapping her fingers – signaling Mamm to come out – Irene shouted, "Join us, please. And bring the children and Michelle."

Chris kept begging until he was kicked in the spine. Sprawled facedown across the dirt, he gasped when a shoe pressed into his neck. The chokehold was suffocating.

He heard but could not see Michelle's horrified reaction as she ran down the porch steps screaming his name. When the chauffeur hit her, she began to whimper. Chris squirmed. The shoe felt like an anvil. The sound of another zip tie tightening. The demand for Michelle to get on her knees and the ensuing shuffle until she obeyed. Then a dreadful quiet.

Using her grating, condescending tone, Irene said, "Hi, Michelle. With all of the excitement this morning, we haven't had the chance to talk. I hope you've been well."

Michelle said nothing but emitted a muted sniffle.

Irene continued, "My sincere apologies for this unpleasant situation. You've been excellent at your job. Frankly, remarkable. And you've always been the consummate rule follower. I thank you for your dedication."

Irene then gave a phony sigh of regret before saying, "But recently, you've failed to control your brother. And I'm afraid you may no longer be productive if you watch him die. So it's with my deepest apologies that I've invited you to endure the same fate."

With a powerful force from behind, Chris was lifted back into a kneeling position. The siblings made horrified eye contact. He said to his sister, "I'm sorry. I'm so, so sorry."

Michelle's nod was almost imperceptible.

Chris added, "I love you."

Struggling to control her emotions, Michelle managed to reply, "And I love you."

Irene couldn't resist one last insult. "Ah, isn't that lovely? So sweet." Then, with a horrid chill, she asked her henchmen, "Are you gentlemen good to go?"

"Yes, Ms. Shaw," they said in tandem while guns made contact with the back of the siblings' heads. They waited for her next instruction.

Agonizing seconds ticked by. Irene stood stiff and contemplative. She methodically peered at each person in the crowd – no doubt wallowing in her power and control – then abruptly declared, "Do you know what? This feels like a teaching moment to me." Looking at Wolfgang, she asked, "Do you think the children are ready?"

"Absolutely, Ms. Shaw."

"Excellent. Then you may proceed."

Wolfgang commanded the teens to approach the wheelchair. From the back saddlebag, he pulled out two Glock 17s and handed an oversized, semiautomatic pistol to each of them. The big gun barely fit into the girl's palm. The bodyguard and chauffeur stepped aside so the children could take their place.

"No, no, no," Irene scolded. "I want them to be in front so they can stare into their eyes before pulling the trigger."

The boy quickly complied. The girl was disabled with indecision and fear.

Irene insisted, "Come on now, Rachel. I know you can do this. Stand in front of Michelle like I asked or you will not enjoy the consequences."

Trembling, the girl finally moved, then closed her eyes while trying to control the shaking gun.

Of course, Irene had to pontificate. "This situation is most appropriate for your first kill. Kneeling before you is the best team I've ever had. But they defied me. So, as I've said before, if you always do exactly what I tell you, I'll take care of you. But if you don't, well, something unfortunate like this will happen. Excited about your big moment?" She didn't wait for their reply before screaming, "Fire!"

The boy's gun clicked but the girl's did not. Rachel had not pulled the trigger. Chris was stunned he was still alive.

"Congratulations, Jacob," Irene declared. "Excellent job!"

The boy's confusion converted to pride during Irene's praise, then turned to shame when she added, "Except for one minor point. You didn't check the chamber to see if the gun was loaded. A mistake like that could get you killed in the future. Understand?"

"Yes, Ms. Shaw," Jacob said apologetically.

Then she aimed her vengeance at Rachel. After yanking away the handgun, she slapped the girl and yelled, "You're a coward! A goddamn coward!" While handing the Glock back to Wolfgang, Irene said, "That girl needs a lot more work. And if she doesn't shape up soon, flush her out of the program. Hear me?"

"Of course, Ms. Shaw."

Irene stared down at Chris and Michelle. "I'm assuming today's meeting will leave a lasting impression. So here's what I want to happen. Do not, under any circumstances, talk to each other before returning to the Twin Cities. I want you both to think about this second chance. Then regroup before going back to Boston and killing

Monteiro by end of business Friday. If you follow these instructions perfectly, then all is forgiven. Understand?"

Michelle said, "Yes."

In a final act of defiance, Chris only nodded. After they were helped to their feet, the bodyguard used a switchblade to cut off the zip ties.

"Good." Irene then asked the chauffeur, "John, do you have that lovely parting gift for Chris?" As the man handed Chris his Thanatos-issued cell phone, she said, "One final bit of bad news. It seems Kathryn O'Donnell, aka your dogwalker, met an untimely demise."

Chris was appalled. "Why the hell did you do that? She wasn't a threat."

"On the contrary. Anyone smart enough to be a grad student at Harvard is smart enough to make an association between Sully and the George Henniker assailant."

"Did she go to the police?"

"No, but it never hurts to be careful, does it? Think about that the next time you're writing a daily report on a company laptop while the GPS on your Thanatos phone is gallivanting around the city." With a wink, she added, "But I do appreciate the timeliness of your daily reports."

Chris and Michelle embraced, happy to be alive, then quickly retreated to their rental cars before Irene could change her mind. Michelle drove off, but the limo was blocking Chris's exit. He considered honking the horn but didn't want to risk the ire of the chauffeur. He would have to wait.

Through the windshield, Chris watched as Irene affectionately stroked Lionel's cheek while he remained slumped and unresponsive in the wheelchair. Then she said something to Wolfgang. The new Preceptor nodded, removed an ammunition clip from his pocket and handed it to Jacob.

With ease, the teenager removed the empty magazine from the Glock 17, pulled back the slide, shoved in the new clip, then released the slide. He looked up at his trainer and Irene for approval before stepping back and, without hesitation, shot the old Preceptor in the back of the head.

It was the first time Chris saw any semblance of remorse on Irene's face. She seemed reflective, perhaps genuinely saddened.

FIFTY-ONE

O scillating trauma had shredded Michelle emotionally, physically and mentally for twenty-seven hours. Vomiting two miles from the farm. Pounding heart and frightening shakes during the ninety-minute drive to Philadelphia. Numb anger at Chris during the flight home to Minneapolis. Unable to eat until dizzy and faint. Unable to sleep, then nightmares and night sweats. Guilt mixed with blame, plus a toxic combination of self-doubt and omnipresent danger.

Her brain was locked in suffocating terror while relentlessly replaying her brush with death. First, the gun to her skull. Then Rachel's trembling finger on the trigger. Irene yelling, "Fire!" Over and over on an endless loop.

Michelle was a professional. Death was her business. Yet she had never felt so out of control. It was as if decades of suppressed dread had been violently unleashed and was consuming her with gloom. The hopelessness was paralyzing.

When Chris knocked on her car window, she jumped with fright behind the steering wheel. Then she swung open the door, leaped out and enveloped him with joy. They were alive and together again. Neither wanted to let go. The reunion was unbridled happiness and relief.

After a few minutes, he placed his company phone on her driver seat, motioned for her to do the same, pressed a finger to his lips and a hand around his ear. He was obviously concerned someone was watching or listening.

The siblings walked from the parking lot in silence, leaned over a balcony and watched Minnehaha Falls[124] cascading fifty-three feet over a limestone bluff. No one around them seemed suspicious. They took a trail down into a gorge until confident the roar of water rushing[125] toward the Mississippi River would cover their conversation from a distant listener.

Michelle confronted him. "Tell me what you talked about with Irene yesterday."

She listened in dumbstruck disbelief as Chris described Irene's frightening ability to know most of what he had done wrong since taking the cruise. His growing confession of recklessness and defiance was surreal. She winced each time another body was added to the count: Jessica's funeral, the shooting and death of Henniker, plus the needless killing of the Harvard student. When Chris finished, she took a stunned breath, then began pounding on his chest.

Her rampage was frenzied. He tolerated the outburst. He knew he deserved it. As the furor weakened, he gently held her wrists until she emotionally collapsed in his arms. The anger was slow to subside.

An elderly man approached. "Are you all right, miss?"

She whimpered, "Yes, I'm fine."

Chris added, "We just learned our mother died."

"I'm sorry for your loss," he said while studying Michelle's face as if searching for clues of abuse. After a moment, he shuffled away.

Michelle turned on her brother. "Another lie?"

"What?" Chris asked in confusion. "It was just a fast and easy way to make him go away."

"Is that why you've been lying to me? Because it was fast and easy and you hoped I'd go away?"

"I didn't lie to you," he said emphatically. "I just didn't tell you anything so you could have deniability with Irene. Don't you see? I was trying to protect you."

"And how did that work out? Your so-called protection almost got me killed. Hell, if I had known all the shit you did, I'd never have gone to the farm." With a fury that drew attention from those passing by, she yelled, "You betrayed me, Chris!"

After an icy stare, she stormed off. Her thoughts seethed with rage. He was no longer the brother she knew. He had been careless and reckless. No, foolish and stupid were better words. There was no justifiable rationale for his erratic actions. He had jeopardized everything – most importantly, their lives. But they were still in jeopardy as long as Anna was alive. There was only one way out of this. Anna had to die.

She heard Chris moving closer from behind. He seemed genuinely worried and remorseful when stepping in front of her. "I'm really sorry, Michelle."

"I don't want to hear it," she snapped. "Now you're going to listen to me for once."

He nodded.

After leading him off the trail and under a grove of trees for privacy, she looked both ways for possible eavesdroppers, then began the ultimatum. "You purposely fucked up – big-time. But we got a second chance and we're going to take it."

Chris stood motionless.

"So here's what's going to happen. Tomorrow morning, I'm going to have a sanctioned pharmacist lace birth control pills like Anna's prescription with ecstasy and carfentanil, the same mix that killed Jessica. Then tomorrow night we're going to fly to Boston and you're going to make the exchange. Then I'll personally watch her house until the coroner wheels her out in a body bag. Everyone will assume she took the same batch of bad drugs from the cruise. Case closed. Then we'll have our lives back. Do you understand?"

Chris was unexpectedly calm. "I understand what you're saying, but I won't help you kill her."

"Why not?" she asked with intense irritation. "Because you love her?"

"No, I barely know her. But if I was who she thinks I am, then maybe, just maybe, there'd be a chance I could love her and she could love me."

"But that's all based on lies. You can't possibly have a future with her."

"I know." He nodded with sad resignation. "And Anna agrees. She broke it off with me in San Francisco." Then he added with conviction, "But she still deserves a future. She's a good person."

"So suddenly her life is more important than ours?"

"There's more to it than that. Just hear me out." Chris proceeded to explain the financial death spiral of Longfellow BioSciences, the meeting between Liz Walker and Robert Nole, and how he subsequently blackmailed the big pharma president into buying the biotech company.

Michelle was aghast at his audacity and apparent motive. "Why would you do such an asinine thing? So Anna can keep her job?"

"No, to help Longfellow achieve their dream of curing cancer."

"Do you even know if it works?"

"Not really. All I know is Anna and Liz strongly believe in their platform – they're incredibly passionate – so I'm a believer too. Think about it, Michelle. Most of our lives have been dedicated to killing people. This was my one chance to help save thousands if not millions of lives."

"If that eases your conscience, fine. But that doesn't change our situation. Irene gave us explicit orders to kill Anna by Friday. When we do, everything will be okay again. So let's get this done and put Irene's threats behind us." With rising fervor, Michelle pleaded, "Please!"

With dreadful certainty, Chris said, "That won't solve anything. It'll just delay the inevitable. Someday she'll kill us anyway."

"Not if we prove our loyalty. You heard her say we're her best team."

Chris ignored her optimism. "Do you think the Preceptor was loyal and valuable?"

"Of course."

"Well, after you drove off, Irene had that Jacob kid put a bullet in his head."

"What? Seriously? Oh my god!" Michelle shrieked.

"Yeah, at first, I wasn't sure if I was supposed to see it happen. But the way Irene sneered at me before stepping into the limo made her message very clear. Believe me when I say no one is safe from that woman. When she's done with us, it's over. She could even kill us on a whim because she's having a bad day. There's only one way to escape this hell."

"You're not suggesting what I think you are?"

"Yes," he said flatly.

"No! That's a suicide mission!" Michelle yelled, then raced down the path until it ended at the river. She crossed a wooden footbridge,[126] sat on a boulder, covered her head and tried to think.

Is Chris wrong? Will Irene's threat end with Anna's last breath? Or is he right? Will Irene kill us anyway? And how soon?

The answers seemed obvious. Strangely, the realization gave her strength. She had lived in crippling fear for most of her life. Against all odds, she had managed the horror through denial and by believing obedience would prevent a worse fate. Since childhood, she had relinquished all hope for a normal life while taking solace in Chris. Then, the first time he seemed to abandon her, she panicked. That panic spiraled into a terrifying breakdown exacerbated at gunpoint.

But maybe dying wasn't what she feared most; that might be a relief. Her biggest fear was continuing in this life without having the courage to change it. This was her opportunity. Killing Irene was not about revenge. It was the only way to start anew.

The decision was liberating.

She sensed Chris standing beside her. She didn't acknowledge him. He waited for the longest time before softly asking, "Are you okay?"

"Yes."

"Are you sure?"

She turned to face him. "Chris, I still can't believe all of the stupid things you did, especially their impact on me. Someday I might forgive you. But trust me, it won't be soon. There's only one thing I thank you for."

"What's that?"

"You made me realize, if I want a better life, I've got to take charge and define it alone."

With an expression of sorrow and abandonment, he asked, "Where does that leave us?"

"Frankly, I don't know. But right now we have to do this together. After that, we'll see."

With hands in his pockets, slumped shoulders and downcast eyes, Chris seemed dejected, maybe heartbroken. Rarely had he looked so miserable.

"Look at me, Danny Ritchie," she began with tenderness. "You'll always be my big brother, I'll always love you, and I'll always appreciate what you've done for me. But it's time for my independence. I'm not entirely sure what that means, but I owe it to myself to find out. Can you understand?"

"Yes," he said with a weak smile.

Their new relationship was sealed with a long embrace.

They walked along the river's edge while plotting how to kill Irene. To Michelle, the conversation was invigorating as her mind developed creative scenarios. They bantered ideas back and forth as they always had. They were a professional team again, maybe for the last time.

After about an hour, Chris shook his head in resignation. "This isn't going to work. There's no way we can pull off a silentcide against Irene. She knows every trick. She'll smell any scheme from a mile away."

"Maybe we don't need to get much closer than that," Michelle cryptically said.

"What are you suggesting?"

With a hint of uncertainty, Michelle said, "A sniper rifle."

"Jesus. Sure, that's possible, but I doubt I'm capable enough."

"I know someone who is."

"Who?"

Michelle hesitated before saying, "Kevin."

"Our Kevin? From Philly? I thought he was dead."

"He's not." She asked Chris to keep quiet and listen before telling him about her meetings with Ansel in Minneapolis and Philadelphia. She explained everything except how he stayed with her the night before the farm. There was no reason to send Chris's mind down a distracting rabbit hole.

After finishing, it wasn't long before his reaction was clear. Chris was mad. Furious. "So you accused me of keeping you in the dark, but you've been doing the same damn thing."

"The difference is your secrets almost got us killed."

"How do you know this idea is any different?" Chris asked. "Do you trust him?"

"Yes, explicitly. He's our foster brother, for god's sake."

"Sure, but that was over twenty-five years ago. People change a lot in that time."

"Of course he's changed," Michelle concurred. "We all have. But he's had a crappy life thanks to Irene, he hates her for it and, most importantly, he wants out. Sound familiar? Plus, he's an expert sniper and planner. And wouldn't it be great to have the Three Amigos back together again?"

"If that reunion would be so great, then why did he tell you to be quiet about it?"

"Because he's already gotten his only second chance from Irene. He knows what'll happen if he's caught defying her again. In short, he considered it too risky."

"He's right about that. This all sounds too risky."

"Listen, I promised to call him back after our meeting at the farm.

Let me just talk to him and feel things out," Michelle suggested. "If it seems safe, I'll ask him to join us."

"No," Chris said emphatically. "Don't tell him anything about our plans. Just ask him to meet us in Boston tomorrow night. I want to look into his eyes first."

"I think you're being overly cautious."

"No, I'm just following the first lesson Irene taught me at the farm. She said never trust anyone, regardless of how well you think you know them. And frankly, I knew Kevin, but I've never met this Ansel Meehan guy."

Chapter Fifty-One: Minneapolis, Minnesota

Photos 124–126

FIFTY-TWO

Anna knocked on the glass door of Liz Walker's office with her foot, then pushed it open with her hip while carrying two cups of coffee and a bag from a pastry shop. Her boss and best friend appeared unusually exhausted for a Monday morning but seemed determined to hide it with a smile and a smart-alecky remark. "Are you bearing gifts again to suck up for all the time you've missed at work?"

Anna retorted, "If you're going to look a gift horse in the mouth, then you can watch me chow down on this entire bag of apple fritters."

"Oh my god, this is delicious," Liz said after the first bite. "I thank you from the bottom of my cellulite."

The quick exchange of laughter felt great, then dissipated. Liz asked with concern, "How did things go last week in San Francisco?"

With a shrug of her shoulders, Anna said, "As you can imagine, very difficult."

"I was really sorry to hear about the death of your friend," Liz said with compassion.

"I appreciate it. And thanks for sending flowers to her celebration of life. They were gorgeous."

They both sipped coffee to fill the void. It seemed obvious Liz didn't want to hear the depressing details of Jessica's death and funeral, nor did Anna want to relive them. She changed the subject. "So what's been happening around here?"

Liz unexpectantly cringed. "Do you want the good news or bad news first?"

"I could use some good news for a change."

"Okay, you became a millionaire while you were gone."

"What?" Anna said with excitement.

"Well, technically nine hundred seventy-nine thousand and change."

In disbelief, Anna asked, "How did that happen?"

"That's the worth of your shares from your first year when you took stock in lieu of a salary."

"But does that mean …?"

"Yes, a deal went through this weekend with Fármaco. They agreed to buy Longfellow for one hundred eighty-five million. The announcement will be made public this afternoon."

"That's fantastic!" Anna exclaimed. "Then why aren't you doing a happy dance?"

"Well, that's where the bad news comes in," Liz said with a sour expression. "The unspoken gentleman's agreement is to keep the company running for about six months. Then they'll kill it and bury the technology in protective patents."

"Why would they do that?"

"To prevent cannibalization of cancer drug sales."

Anna tilted her head. "I'm sorry, but I don't understand."

"Okay, let me explain it like this. Remember Kodak? They were in the film business, not the photo business, so they got displaced by digital photography. Well, Fármaco is in the oncology drug business, not the business of curing cancer. Our new approach threatens to change the entire industry from R&D, to distribution, marketing and training, to medical and patient treatment procedures. It could also jeopardize Fármaco's twelve billion in oncology drug sales. So bottom line – and that's all that's important to them – it's easier to kill our technology than to adapt to the change."

"But won't that change happen someday?"

"Sure, personalized medicine is the future for cancer. But well before that happens, Robert Nole and his Fármaco cronies will be rich and retired, so they won't care. And frankly, neither will Todd Milken."

Anna scowled. "What's our beloved CEO get out of this?"

"About eighteen million, plus a fat two-year consulting arrangement, which is bogus. He'll just cash in his chips and then go rape and pillage another biotech company in town."

"Oh god," Anna moaned while leaning back in the guest chair. "This is awful. So what happens to you?"

"Well, I was given three options. One, I can finish the clinical trials, and if I declare them a failure, I'll get a big bonus."

Anna was appalled. "You're not going to do that, are you?"

"Of course not. My second option is to run a new fifty-million-dollar-a-year foundation to address sexual harassment in America's workplace."

"What prompted that?" Anna asked in confusion.

Liz hesitated, as if holding something back, before answering, "I don't know, other than big drug companies love sponsoring philanthropic causes to prove they're good corporate citizens and really care about people."

"I'm detecting a hint of cynicism," Anna probed.

"Don't make me speculate on their real motivation for this foundation. But judging from what they're doing to Longfellow – trust me – I doubt this is coming from the goodness of their heart."

"Okay, and door number three?"

"I can quit now with my stock buyout and a big performance package."

Anna sat up with hope. "That makes the most sense, right?"

"No, not really," Liz answered with dismay. "My noncompete says if I resign from Longfellow or Fármaco, I can't work for another biotech, drug or medical company for five years."

"But you'll have millions. So enjoy the next five years and then start over."

"Anna, you know this industry. A lot will change in five years. By then, my knowledge will be outdated. Hell, I'll be a dinosaur. Besides, I don't do boredom well. So I'm considering running the foundation. It might be a stepping stone to a meaningful job at Fármaco. Want to join me?"

"I'd have to think about it. I'll let you know. But I'm guessing when the company closes, I'll probably take some time off and regroup."

"You're not going to have to wait that long." The statement was ominous.

"What do you mean?"

Liz nibbled her lower lip before answering. "The omnipotent brain trust declared your job redundant. So I'm sorry to say, I have to let you go ... today." As Liz handed over an envelope, she appeared to transform into the role of a dispassionate corporate officer. "This is a six-month severance check based on your full salary rate. And your million is tied up in a stock swap with Fármaco. But after a six-month restriction period, you can cash out if you want."

Anna held the envelope while staring at her boss in disbelief.

Liz continued. "And finally – and I know this abruptness is no way to treat a loyal friend – but I've been instructed to have you pack up and be out by lunchtime. At least I talked them out of having security usher you to the door."

Anna shook her head in stunned disgust, stood, then left without a word. She didn't trust herself to say anything appropriate. Maybe she could after cooling off for a few days. But if she talked now, she could inadvertently start burning bridges.

She knew none of this was Liz's fault. She was only the messenger. In fact, Liz was the real victim – her brainchild and dream had been killed. Their shared animosity was toward corporate management who placed personal gain above employees and the lives of cancer patients.

But those bastards were hiding in boardrooms in their expensive suits and would never hear their wrath or suffer any consequences for their actions. Longfellow was just another casualty of the silent biotech war in Cambridge and Boston.

Anna began collecting knickknacks from her office cubicle, then slumped over with her hands on the desk. Within a few days, everything that had kept her up at night had been resolved. Jessica was buried. Chris was gone. Sergeant O'Neill emailed saying George was dead. And the fate of Longfellow and her job were now certain.

But she was also a millionaire. That was a huge accomplishment, right? A success that might make her father finally proud of his only daughter.

Anna plopped down into the chair in despair. All she felt was emptiness.

FIFTY-THREE

After conspiring with Chris on Sunday afternoon, Michelle again had purpose, focus and renewed hope. For once, she could envision a better life. There was just one dangerous task in the way. Killing Irene was risky, but not taking the risk was untenable.

She spent much of the prior evening coordinating Boston flight and hotel arrangements with a Thanatos facilitator. She debriefed Ansel by phone and, without revealing their plot, convinced him to meet in Boston. She wrote a daily report explaining how she and Chris planned to finalize the commission against Anna Monteiro. That night, she had the best sleep in ages.

First thing in the morning, she met with the local sanctioned pharmacist, Dr. Yasin's middle-aged son. Despite his father's endorsement of Michelle, she had never been able to develop a personal or confidential rapport with the younger pharmacist. The transactions were always mechanical and professional.

This meeting with him was frustrating. He was too conscientious about everything. He debated the dose of carfentanil and said there wasn't space in the tiny contraceptive pills for measurable ecstasy. He explained the challenge of swapping the tainted pills with real ones inside the packaging's foil backing. He agreed one pill would do the trick but said the challenge was knowing how many the target had already swallowed of her one-month supply. The swapped package should contain the same amount.

The needless debate lasted over an hour. She tolerated it because Yasin's son would strictly follow protocol by reporting to Thanatos his considerations, final recommendation, reasoning and the actions he took. Two more hours slipped by before the work was finished. He did a masterful job creating a means of certain death that would never be used.

She drove back to her Minneapolis high-rise,[127] grumbled about the slowpoke driver in underground parking, tapped a foot impatiently during the elevator ride, was challenged to find her condo key at the bottom of her purse, then swung open the door.

Terror.

Sitting in a living room chair was a middle-aged woman – stringy black hair beneath a denim bucket hat, oversized sunglasses partially concealing a bloated face, and wearing a shapeless dull dress. A gun was in her lap.

Michelle lunged toward a pistol stored in the entryway cedar chest. Her fingers never reached the pull handle of the top drawer.

"Don't do that, Michelle," a male voice threatened.

"Ansel?"

"Yes. Sit down. We have a lot to talk about."

Fear pulsated through her. Death seemed probable. But maybe there was hope. If he planned to kill her, she would already be dead. Maybe this was an Irene follow-up warning. *Keep things cordial, be cooperative, and hear what he has to say.*

While taking a position on the couch in front of him, she said in the most relaxed voice she could muster, "Damn, you're a very ugly woman."

He chuckled. "I know, but witnesses never remember seeing me."

"Will you please take off that ridiculous costume, at least the mask and wig?"

He complied.

She considered making another joke about him screwing up their agreed rendezvous in Boston later that night. But her foster brother's expression was deadly serious. She might as well start the unpleasant conversation. "How did you get to Minneapolis so quickly after our phone call last night?"

"I've been here since Saturday," he flatly admitted. "After your meeting with Irene, she told me to fly to Minneapolis immediately and await further instructions."

"So while I was pouring my heart out about what happened at the farm, you were, what, two blocks away?"

"Less than that," Ansel said. "And after we hung up, I got a text message from Irene that simply read, 'Proceed.'"

Now his intent was undeniably clear. She would be dead in minutes if not seconds. While clutching a large couch pillow over her lap, she asked, "But why? Even if Irene was listening to our call, I didn't say anything she didn't already know, except for inviting you to Boston."

"I know, but the real problem was your meeting with Chris at Minnehaha Falls. That was damning."

Feigning innocence, she said, "But we didn't talk about anything other than how to kill our target."

With a scowl and a shake of his head, Ansel said, "That's not true, is it? I know exactly what you discussed because I monitored your conversation."

"But how could you? We kept watching for anyone suspicious."

"Obviously you didn't watch close enough. Hell, I even tried intervening by sending you a warning, but you ignored it."

"When did that happen?"

"I was the old man who stared you right in the face after asking if everything was all right. I was sure you'd recognize me."

Michelle bowed her head and, while pretending to recover from the trauma, casually slipped a hand in the pocket of her shorts concealed by the couch pillow. As a distraction, she wiped away a nonexistent tear while saying, "So you've been a sham all along?"

"Not entirely. It was great to see you. I really mean that." Then he lowered his voice. "But yes, Irene sent me to Minneapolis the first time to do recon on you both. Fortunately, you didn't say anything incriminating. So I assumed after Irene heard the recording, she'd conclude you were both still loyal and then relax. Obviously, she intensified the surveillance instead."

"So that's how she knew everything Chris did while in Boston, the cruise and San Francisco?"

"Yeah, that's my guess based on what you told me Irene knew at the farm meeting."

Michelle inched a finger along the edge of her phone, then pushed the button to lower the media volume almost to mute. "So then you deceived me again in Philadelphia?"

"Yeah, but Irene insisted that I go. Listen, in my defense, I kept trying to get away from you before you said something wrong. But you kept asking me to stay."

She became irate. "Don't blame me for your guilt. All you had to do was get in your goddamn car and drive off!"

"I know, I know. I felt like such a traitor, especially when our conversation got personal. So before reaching your hotel, I reported back to Irene that everything was fine with you. But there was no way to cover for the damaging stuff you said about Chris while we were at the zoo."

Michelle felt wretched. She had accused Chris of betraying her with his rogue actions. Yet her loose lips had sealed his fate. That guilt would follow her to the grave.

"Listen," Ansel said in an obvious attempt to console her, "don't feel bad about what you said in Philly. It didn't change Irene's plans. Her goal Saturday was to scare the hell out of you and then give you a second chance like she did to me a few years ago. But then you both blew it yesterday afternoon. There was no recovering from that."

While Ansel talked, Michelle never broke eye contact as she mentally pictured her cell phone screen, trying to remember the exact location of the phone call icon. Despite using it countless times a day, she wasn't sure where it was without seeing it.

His large hand dwarfed the grip as he raised a revolver. She recognized the model. The Ruger's short-barrel Alaskan was compact, yet the .44 magnum bullet could drop a charging grizzly bear. Remembering the mission of his Phonoi group made her shiver. Her violent death would definitely send a strong warning to Irene's other assassins.

She dared to ask, "Are you also assigned to Chris?"

Ansel didn't answer the question. Instead, he apologized. "Listen, Michelle, I didn't mean for any of this to happen. But I had no choice. Really. This is all part of Irene's sick way of testing my loyalty to her. And she made it very, very clear that if I disobeyed her orders or warned you, there was no such thing as giving me a third chance. God, I'm sorry." His apology seemed sincere.

Michelle was silent. Being killed had always been inevitable. She suddenly realized not knowing when it would happen was what had caused the greatest anxiety. Now that the time had come, an unexpected calm washed over her. She was ready.

"I can't do this," he said while lowering his weapon.

"Why not? It's just another kill."

"No, all of the others were faceless targets. You're different. I could never live with the memory of killing you."

Michelle saw her chance to talk Ansel out of pulling the trigger, then reconsidered. "Look, if you don't do this, Irene will have someone else do it. I'll always be looking over my shoulder. Then she'll turn her vengeance on you, and we both die. That's not worth it. Besides, I'd rather be killed by someone I love." Michelle pushed what she hoped was the speed dial for Chris's phone.

Ansel flinched. His face was twisted with indecision. He seemed ready to say something, but swallowed deeply instead. He hesitated, then raised the revolver and pointed it at Michelle. His hand quivered.

Chapter Fifty-Three: Minneapolis, Minnesota

Photo 127

FIFTY-FOUR

Since the meeting at Minnehaha Falls, Chris had been absorbed by the details of their final assassination mission. The outcome of trying to kill Irene was binary. Success meant freedom. Failure meant their death. He was confident he and Michelle would soon end Irene's tyranny. But they would only have one long-range shot. There was no room for error.

Late into Sunday night, and again on Monday morning, Chris studied Google Maps and live satellite feeds of Irene's downtown Philadelphia law office. He also searched travel routes to her isolated estate in Elkins Park. Six potential kill sites were identified. He would explore them later in the week.

He also tried researching Ansel Meehan. As expected, all of the information was bogus. The factoids had obviously been created to legitimize his persona and conceal his role as a violent killer. Chris did uncover one photo of his former foster brother. He stared into the man's handsome face and pale blue eyes. Could he be trusted? Their lives depended on it.

Chris pushed back from his study desk and stretched. He needed fresh air. Performing mindless tasks often generated his best thinking. After mowing the small front lawn of his modest Highland Park home,[128] he sat on the steps and tugged at his sweaty T-shirt in an attempt to cool off.

A sweeping smile crossed his lips as Rascal came running out from the house across the street. As always, the yellow Lab was boundless energy. Chris followed his routine of feeding the dog two biscuits, then encouraged his furry friend to find a tennis ball. When it was dropped into his palm a minute later, the felt was soggy.

"Hey there, stranger," his neighbor for the past decade yelled out as she stepped outside.

Nicole looked alluring in Daisy Dukes and a halter top. Her black hair was curled and she was wearing makeup. Most unusual. Perhaps the shy software programmer was bored, lonesome and fishing for a date. Whatever her motive, it was working.

They chatted in her yard about his recent travels until an alarm went off on her cell phone. She said, "Sorry, that's my timer for the oven. I'm making cookies for a church bake sale. Would you like a few? They're chocolate chip." How could he resist?

When Nicole returned, the paper plate was stacked with cookies and was warm on the bottom. They looked delicious. He was about to try one when his cell phone rang. As he reached into the pocket of his shorts, Rascal jumped up and knocked two cookies on the ground. Before Chris could react, the dog scooped them up and ran off.

Chris said with a laugh, "Don't blame me if you get a stomachache."

The caller ID on his company phone said Michelle. As he swiped Accept, he wondered why she wasn't calling on his Miami-purchased burner. They had agreed clandestine communication was essential. "Hello."

Michelle screamed, "Chris! Run! You're in danger!"

She was silenced by a gun blast. The roar echoed in his ears. Horror flooded his brain.

"Michelle! Michelle! Michelle!" he kept yelling.

A male voice calmly said, "I'm sorry, Danny. I really am." Then the phone disconnected. That bastard Ansel had killed his sister.

Looking up in stunned disbelief, Chris saw the dog rolling on the ground in agony. The Lab was wild-eyed, convulsing and foaming at the mouth. He turned toward Nicole just in time to see her swing a SIG P229 pistol from behind her back. The first shot whizzed by his head before he could react.

Chris zigged, zagged, rolled and dodged while trying to outrun the assault of 9mm bullets. A tree splintered. Chunks of lawn puffed to the left and right of him. Two divots in the asphalt erupted before rounds began penetrating the façade of his house. A picture window imploded. As he dashed through the front door, a splinter pierced his leg. Crippling pain with oozing blood assailed his calf.

He heard Nicole reloading while he twice pushed the Auxiliary button on the security keypad, then pressed 1 before lunging behind the couch. As her foot cautiously crossed the threshold – with two fists firmly gripping her outstretched weapon – her body disintegrated in a blast of fire, smoke and flying fragments. The explosion from the C-4 rang in his ears as he lifted his head to assess the damage.

The barrel of an AR-15 appeared through the broken picture window. Bullets sprayed across the living room. Lamps fractured. Picture frames crashed. Furniture shattered. The big-screen TV burst into pieces. An uneven row of dime-sized holes punched into walls, creating plumes of scattering plaster. The relentless thunder of thirty rounds from the semiautomatic rifle lasted only a few seconds. Then an eerie silence.

The pattern of gunfire suggested a rookie, not a seasoned pro. The attacker must be from Irene's B or C team. But even a single lucky bullet from the idiot's assault weapon could pulverize bones, liquefy organs and leave an orange-sized exit wound at three times the speed of sound. Chris heard the assailant extracting an ammunition magazine. There were three seconds or less to react safely.

Chris raced to the coffee table and grabbed the TV remote. As he ran into the kitchen, he pushed the Mute button twice followed by the number 2. He took cover at the end of the hallway and listened.

Footsteps crunched on debris at the massive hole that was the front door. The approach was more cautious while crossing the living room. Chris waited. The noises stopped except for the combatant's heavy breathing. Chris waited. The gun barrel emerged at the kitchen entry. A leery face followed and quickly retreated. Chris waited until the man stepped forward before pushing the number 2 again.

A bombardment of ball bearings, nails and razor blades ricocheted through the kitchen. The shrapnel mangled everything in its path. The man screamed while dropping to his knees. His wounds looked serious but not mortal. He struggled to his feet, lifted the AR-15 and stumbled forward.

Chris ducked into his bedroom and entered a code into the security keypad. A panel in the wainscoting popped open. He grabbed his Glock 19, checked the chamber, then silently opened the screen door leading to the backyard. As he left, he pushed 4 on the TV remote control. The command armed the explosives in the doorframe. Walking past the invisible sensor would detonate another bomb.

Chris scrambled across the lawn, took refuge along the garage, readied his handgun, and anticipated the blast. But the assassin had obviously learned from Nicole's mistake. Instead of going through the door, he used the rifle butt to smash a window. Then he sprayed about fifteen rounds to cover his entry into the yard.

As the assailant searched for his rival, Chris pushed button number 7. A full-sized shooting range target holding a gun popped out from behind an apple tree. While rapid fire pulverized the plastic dummy, Chris slowly squeezed the trigger of his Glock 19. The 9mm hollow-point bullet traveled at twelve hundred feet per second before entering the attacker's rib cage. The man blew backward and collapsed on the ground.

Hissing and sucking sounds – plus foaming pink blood – escaped from the misshapen wound in the assailant's chest as he struggled to breathe. His eyes fluttered with terror. He begged for mercy.

Chris walked over. He stared down with hatred and malice before saying, "I hope you enjoyed your visit to the Twin Cities." Then he put a single bullet into the face he recognized from Jessica's funeral and the Boston hotel lobby.

Chris readied for other enemies until hearing advancing police sirens. While wincing in pain, he limped through the door of a neighbor's garage he had rented for emergencies.

A hammer from the workbench was used to smash the company-issued cell phone. He dropped his wallet into a jar of acid. After tapping five numbers into the security keypad, he knelt down in front of an opened safe. The go-bag contained passports, IDs and credit cards of two off-the-books personas, including corresponding disguises. Additional weapons and ammunition were also inside. The bulk of the duffel contained two hundred fifty thousand dollars in cash.

He got behind the wheel of a 2000 Ford Explorer. The dark gray SUV was inconspicuous on Minnesota roads yet was retrofitted with a 450-horsepower engine in case of a high-speed pursuit, plus ballistic glass and armoring. Equally important, the counterfeit license plates, fake VIN number and lack of GPS made the vehicle untraceable.

The getaway car inched out of the garage and entered the alley. He peered around the corner at the cross street while his heart raced with adrenaline. Chris drove the speed limit along Shepard Road parallel to the Mississippi River, dutifully gave right of way to two patrol cars that screamed by, and proceeded toward downtown Saint Paul.[129]

Every nerve was misfiring. His brain was flooded with angst. He had to emotionally recover. He needed a sanctuary with enough wide-open space to detect an assailant's approach and also someplace with sufficient police presence to intervene in case of a large-scale attack. He drove onto the grounds of the state capitol,[130] parked and turned off the ignition.

After lowering his head on the steering wheel, he sobbed with overwhelming grief and remorse. Michelle was dead. His actions had killed his sister. Soon Thanatos would erase her electronic presence as if she had never existed. How quickly would he forget her voice, her face and her smile? The mourning and guilt would last forever.

An hour passed. The emotional pain was suffocating. Yet he had to move on and leave his Chris Davis persona behind. He questioned whether his new life would be tolerable.

Before backing out of the parking space, he thought of Anna. Surely someone from Thanatos or Phonoi would kill her next if they hadn't already. He had to save her. Although that goal had cascaded into ruinous results, he could not fail her now. The question was how?

He would never arrive in time by flying to Boston. If he called with the truth, she would go to the police. That would only delay her inevitable death while implicating him. Somehow, he had to lure her to safety without alarm.

He dialed her cell. A recorded message said the number was out of service. Of course it was; he had disabled her phone in San Francisco. While searching on Google for the Longfellow phone number, he saw the acquisition announcement. He realized helping the biotech survive by blackmailing Nole was the only good thing he had done in years.

So he was surprised when the receptionist said Anna had just been laid off. "Do you know how I can reach her?"

"Well, she just walked out the door. Why not call her cell in a few minutes."

"Her phone is disconnected and I must speak with her. It's important. Could you see if you can catch her before she drives off?"

"I'm sorry, sir, but I'm not supposed to leave the front desk."

"Please," Chris pleaded. "This is an emergency."

The music while on hold was insipid. The songs were interrupted with fifteen-second glowing explanations about Longfellow's achievements and their promising cure for cancer.

"Hello?" Anna answered with concerned confusion.

"Hi, this is Chris."

"Yeah, what's the emergency?"

"I'm sorry for the ruse. It was the only way to reach you because your cell phone is disconnected."

"Yeah, it went funky on me in San Francisco. Jeez, you scared me. Let me catch my breath." She paused for a few seconds before saying, "Okay, what's up?"

"I know we cut things off last week. And I promised myself I'd honor your request to sort things out by yourself. But you also said something about wanting to run away and start over. It got me to thinking. I want the same thing. So I quit my job today and am going to take some time off. Want to join me?"

"When?"

"Now," he said decisively. "Right now."

"Are you kidding me? That's kind of impulsive, don't you think?"

"Exactly. I've never been impulsive about anything, so it's the first step in my new life. I'm betting you've never been impulsive either. So let's give it a try."

"I don't know, Chris," she said with hesitation. "Let me think about it."

"What's to think about? The receptionist told me you were laid off today."

"Yeah, do you believe that?"

"No, and I'm really sorry because I know how much Longfellow's dream meant to you. But that means you're free of responsibilities. Nothing's holding you back. Let's run away together, at least for a couple of weeks."

He could almost hear her thinking before she asked, "Where did you have in mind?"

"I don't know, someplace where they serve endless bacon and wine while we act childish day and night."

Anna giggled before saying yes.

Chapter Fifty-Four: Saint Paul, Minnesota

Photos 128–130

FIFTY-FIVE

While Anna waited at Longfellow for his call back, Chris booked a hotel and purchased a plane ticket using a new personal credit card so the transactions couldn't be traced by Thanatos. The flight departure for later that afternoon gave Anna only enough time to return home, pack, and get to Logan Airport, where she could print a boarding ticket at a kiosk. He promised to meet her the next day. As he turned off his cell phone so she couldn't call back with second thoughts, he worried about her being ambushed at her brownstone.

He started the Ford Explorer containing his worldly possessions and began the arduous drive to Québec City, Canada. The twenty-two-hour trip was extended five hours by bathroom breaks, catnaps, and shopping for necessities such as clothes, luggage, a laptop and camera, plus snacks and lots of energy drinks. But the best stimulant to stay awake was hatred.

He brooded endlessly about Irene, from the day his parents died to her decade of brainwashing, plus sixteen years of omnipotent demands for silentcide in order to build her wealth and power. She had destroyed him and countless others. She was the essence of evil.

Several times – in moments of weakness and exhaustion – he considered trying to outrun Irene. But escaping her seemed improbable if not impossible. With renewed conviction, he repeatedly vowed to get revenge regardless of the cost. Irene Shaw must die.

He also worried about the ramifications of blowing up his neighbor and leaving a corpse in the backyard. There was no doubt a massive manhunt was underway. This one promised to be more ominous than Boston because he had left behind plenty of incriminating evidence and ways to track him down. The police would be relentless in their pursuit, especially if one of their own tripped off the back door's explosive.

Chris was thankful his years of training, preparedness and instincts had helped him survive and escape the onslaught. But now he was the hunted instead of the hunter. Would a purposeless life on the run be worth living? Or was he guaranteed a fate worse than death? Maybe he should have just eaten the damn cookie.

As city after city passed by, his shoulders and hands stiffened from clutching the steering wheel. Every muscle was still tense from the shootout. And the denial, remorse and mourning over Michelle deepened with every mile.

How many times had she warned him and begged him to comply? How many times had she asked if Anna's life was more important than hers? Every time, he hadn't listened. Most despicable was talking her into a plot against Irene. He blamed Ansel for pulling the trigger. He blamed himself for putting the gun to Michelle's head.

He had killed his sister. She was gone. Unforgivable.

✦✦✦

When Chris knocked on the door of their hotel room at Fairmont Le Château Frontenac,[131] Anna greeted him with a precious smile. She was gorgeous, and not because she was dressed up to enjoy their first night on the town. Her deep-brown eyes sparkled. Her lips were soft, warm and welcoming. Her affection was natural and unrestrained. For the first time in an eternity, he felt at peace.

"Oh my god," she said while stepping back, "you look like hell."

He managed a laugh. "I'm surprised I look that good."

She grabbed his rollaboard luggage, ushered him into the room and began pulling back the comforter and sheets. "I'm putting you to bed."

While struggling to act sensual, he asked, "You can't wait to start acting childish, right?"

"Are you kidding me? You're the child for driving nonstop. You need sleep."

"But that's not fair to you," he protested.

"I'm fine. You're not. So get some rest. We'll have plenty of time together."

He was asleep before she closed the curtains and turned off the lights.

Chris was the first to wake in the morning. He watched her sleeping inches away. Her short black hair lay comfortably on the pillow. Slow, rhythmic breathing. A radiant and serene expression. She stirred, opened an eye, gave him a kiss, said, "I missed you," then flipped into a spooning position. As he draped his arm around her, she snuggled closer before falling back asleep. This was perfect contentment.

When they awoke, however, reality returned with Anna's natural curiosity. "Why did you drive rather than fly? Is that new luggage and clothes? How did you bruise your stomach and hurt your leg?" The innocent questions and convoluted cover-ups seemed endless.

Most of the next two days were spent sightseeing around Old Québec City. While Chris took endless photographs, Anna used his cell phone to read descriptions from Encircle Photos travel guides. They ate lunches at outdoor cafés and dinners at charming restaurants, and he impressed her while ordering meals in French. They ran together, slept together and often held hands. Those times were good as long as they stayed in the present. But any time a topic arose about the past was troublesome.

He had to fabricate a story about what happened in Philadelphia that prompted his sudden resignation. Of course, a simple answer wouldn't suffice. Anna kept probing for information about his job, what he liked and disliked, and his aspirations for a future career.

Another time, Chris was livid but could only act appalled while she explained about the buyout of Longfellow and the secret plan to kill their life-saving technology. While voicing sympathy for Liz and Anna, he contemplated retribution against Robert Nole. When Anna disclosed she was a millionaire, he was genuinely excited and congratulatory, then surprised she wasn't happy. She explained becoming wealthy could never compensate for failing to realize the dream of curing cancer in memory of Jamie. In fact, it felt like blood money.

Most difficult were his relentless waves of guilt and mourning over Michelle. He tried hiding the crippling emotions, made several excuses for the moodiness, but Anna sensed something was seriously wrong. Fortunately, she didn't inquire too much into his moments of silent grieving.

It was exhausting trying to stay on safe topics. Equally exhausting was worrying if they were safe. Twice he suggested driving to Montreal or, better yet, taking a long road trip through New Brunswick, Prince Edward Island and Nova Scotia. His anxiety spiked each time she said, "No, let's just stay here and relax." He sensed danger at every corner.

The third night was sleepless. Chris realized they were clinging together to forget their old lives with a vague hope of starting new ones together. He could love her someday. He sensed the feelings were mutual. But he knew that someday would never happen.

Anna was deeply rooted in his past despite their short courtship, and his past was filled with inescapable lies. He had vowed to stop lying but wasn't ready to divulge the truth. When he did, the sanctuary of belonging would be shattered. He would be forced to start a new uncertain life alone and on the run. Worst of all, he couldn't protect her forever. Losing someone else he cared deeply about seemed unbearable. Anna was all he had left.

Twice the following day, while they were walking around the city, Chris tried mustering the courage to explain everything. Twice he failed by delaying the inevitable. He couldn't begin the conversation that would end everything between them.

Anna was reading aloud the description of La Citadelle de Québec[132] – a star-shaped fortress built by the British in 1850 – when ringing prompted her to look at the caller ID. She handed over his cell phone and said, "It's Michelle calling."

Instant bewilderment and angst. Chris struggled to conceal his alarm while saying, "Do you mind if I have a few minutes of privacy?"

"Of course," Anna said with a hint of suspicion. "How about if I meet you back at the hotel?"

She jogged off. He stared at the phone. Was this a Thanatos trap to learn his location? If so, they would have to escape immediately. But what if? He pushed Accept and listened.

"Is that you, Chris?" she asked.

"Michelle!" he exclaimed with tearful relief. "You're alive!"

"Yes, but we can only talk a few seconds."

"I thought you were dead."

"I know. I'm sorry about that. And for a while, I thought you were dead too. But now you're …?"

Chris interrupted. "No, now you're going to tell me exactly what happened."

With a breathless staccato, she said, "Ansel and I staged my death so we could escape Irene."

"Is he with you now?"

"Yes."

"Where are you?"

In exasperation, she said, "There's time later to explain everything."

He shouted, "No, that time is right now."

With greater intensity, Michelle screamed, "Stop talking, god-damn it! You're in danger again! So listen to me. Are you in Québec City with Anna?"

"How'd you know?"

"Ansel's former roommate from the farm is a facilitator. She was assigned to track Anna down and found a credit card transaction from when she checked into the hotel. She just called Ansel to warn us that the kill is scheduled for today."

"Holy shit! Where? When?"

"All I know is the code word *boardwalk*, whatever that means."

His stunned disbelief lasted a millisecond before disconnect-ing, then sprinting a hundred yards to a cliff overlooking the Saint Lawrence River. He entered Governors' Promenade.[133] The half-mile, elevated boardwalk was flanked by steep fortress walls[134] on one side and a 330-foot drop on the other. The narrow, fenced-in corridor was a perfect kill zone.

He leaped over vehicle-restraint barriers, dodged couples and families, raced along straightaways, navigated winding turns and flew down multiple staircases[135] with over three hundred steps. His legs ached. His lungs burned. He was desperate.

When the last steep staircase ended at another boardwalk, Chris gasped while studying the crowd. The quarter-mile-long Terrasse Dufferin[136] was glutted with tourists. Most were strolling. Others were viewing the river. A few were taking selfies. Children laughed and played. Anna was nowhere to be seen.

Over his shoulder, Chris heard the faint yet unmistakable sound of a cartridge being dropped and locked into the chamber of a rifle. All he could see among the thick trees was a camou-flaged elbow and one leg of a bipod. He pictured an expert killer peering into a high-powered scope with a finger lightly on the trigger.

Chris finally saw Anna. She was walking a hundred yards ahead. He yelled her name. No response. He sensed the sniper regulating his breathing and heart rate while waiting for a clean shot.

He kept yelling while expecting a bullet to shatter her body.

"Anna!" he screamed in desperation.

She turned, smiled and began to wave.

His final warning – "Run!" – was drowned out by the explosive sound of gunfire.

Chapter Fifty-Five: Québec City, Canada

Photos 131–136

SILENTCIDE 2

VENGEANCE

Kill or be killed while US senators die.

A SUSPENSE THRILLER

RICHARD EBERT

The thrilling sequel starts with explosive gunfire at Chris Davis and Anna Monteiro, a woman he was hired to kill yet now protects. A determined foursome then outruns bullets in Canada and the US while avenging the ruthless mastermind of an assassination network. One by one, US senators are mysteriously poisoned. When a Russian suicide drone hits Washington, DC, a political firestorm ignites during a presidential campaign. The final showdown against Irene Shaw is do or die after 28 years of oppression.

This action-driven sequel thunders across 21 cities and 4 countries.

Included are 140 online photos of scene locations.

Silentcide 2 photos on author website: www.RichardEbert.com

ONE

Monitoring Québec City, Canada

Friday

D eath was imminent. Watching would be divine.

Irene Shaw tingled with anticipation yet portrayed dispassionate elegance. Heaven forbid the hired help detect anything but her poised control over the pending termination of Chris Davis and Anna Monteiro. Their demise was long overdue yet rapidly approaching. The ambush promised to be splendid vengeance.

Irene's intense blue eyes focused on four large monitors suspended over an ornate marble fireplace. Each live video showed the view of a killer's bodycam or rifle-mounted camera. Two assassins had been stationed for over an hour at the north end of Terrasse Dufferin[1], a quarter-mile promenade overlooking the Saint Lawrence River. The third had been conducting surveillance of Old Québec City[2] from a high-rise until recently ordered to reposition in the south. The fourth showed a ham sandwich being eaten at Tourny Fountain while the targets toured the adjacent Parliament Building.[3]

The trap was almost ready. Irene detested waiting. Yet perfection required patience.

A handsome young manservant approached her, paused to be acknowledged, then delivered a third dirty martini in a frosted Baccarat crystal glass. "Thank you, dear," Irene said with a suggestive smile. She ogled Pierre's retreat from the Ops Room of her

Philadelphia mansion while fondly recalling their last tryst. Then she placed a Sicilian stuffed olive on her tongue, withdrew the ivory cocktail skewer with her perfect teeth, bit down, and savored the zesty burst of gin, bitterness and blue cheese. Life's simple pleasures were often the best. Excessive wealth paid for every other indulgence.

While placing the stemware on the Louis XV period end table, Irene's bejeweled fingers spasmed. She cursed the sign of weakness. Arthritic hands were among a growing list of physical imperfections that had been accelerating since her sixtieth birthday twelve years earlier. Managing or masking her body's degeneration was increasingly time consuming and expensive. Yet aging was just another formidable adversary to defeat. Irene was accustomed to winning.

In subservient silence, an elderly Vietnamese manicurist used an embroidered washcloth to pat dry the splash of martini before it seeped into the table's rosewood inlay. The woman then retrieved a fresh towel for the top of the portable cosmetic workstation, gingerly lowered Irene's hand again and resumed airbrushing her fingernails. The illegal immigrant was a gifted artisan, nonjudgmental and discreet.

Irene Shaw stole a glance at the full-length dressing mirror. A few tufts of silver-white hair needed to be ushered back into the French bun. She admired the taut pink skin stretched over high cheekbones. Her authoritative eyes were accented by layered mascara, long lashes and dark microbladed eyebrows. Yet her neck needed a nip and tuck. She must remember to ask her assistant to make an appointment with the cosmetic surgeon. He was always booked months ahead. The doctor's scalpel was sheer genius.

Irene's thoughts shifted to Chris Davis, her protégé for the last twenty-eight years. Since he was orphaned at ten years old, she had meticulously honed his skills for silentcide, the art of undetected killing. Along with his younger sister, Michelle, they had become an outstanding team, far exceeding initial expectations. They had rarely failed to execute a silentcide commission on time and without repercussions from police. Their near-flawless record was remarkable. Irene had envisioned the siblings becoming heirs to her murder enterprise … until recently.

For some reason and without warning, Chris Davis had become rebellious. A simple disobedience would have been distasteful yet manageable. A bold resistance against her authority could have been dealt with harshly and then forgiven.

Yet his increasing acts of defiance were much deeper, reprehensible and unpardonable. Chris had refused to kill his assigned target, Anna Monteiro, because he had become infatuated with her. The police were also investigating his rogue actions in three cities. The needless body count was now at five. Worst of all was the avenging conspiracy: he had plotted to kill Irene.

His audacity was outrageous. The consequences would be severe. Soon, Chris Davis would lie in a pool of blood. Simultaneously, Anna Monteiro would die on this last day of the extended deadline as promised to the client. Two birds, one stone, and marvelous retribution. Plus, the spectacular slayings would be a stern warning to potential malcontents in her network of assassins. You don't screw with Irene Shaw.

"Ms. Shaw," came a booming voice from the computer screen on the nearby Baroque writing desk. Jürgen van Oorschot was the middle-aged head of Phonoi, the group named after the Greek personification of violent murder. His square chin, thin lips, bulbous nose, and narrow menacing eyes beneath a black crewcut created a fierce appearance.

"Yes, dear," Irene acknowledged the ruthless man.

The former mercenary replied, "The targets have left the Parliament Building and are heading toward the promontory."[4]

A glance at the wall monitors confirmed the news. Camera four – from the man discreetly tracking the couple – showed them strolling on the lawn at Plains of Abraham Park. Camera three was a shaking view of Porte Saint-Louis[5] along the old city wall as a sniper hurried toward his newly assigned position. The noose was tightening.

Irene looked down at the Vietnamese woman. "I'm afraid we'll need to suspend this for now, dear."

"Yes, ma'am," the nail technician said while pushing aside the cosmetic station. She graciously lifted one of Irene's feet, causing the Garra rufa fish that had been feasting on dead skin cells to dart wildly within the ichthyotherapy tank. After Irene's second foot had been dried, the manicurist helped her into designer slippers, bowed, and humbly left the room. The closing door echoed off the mahogany walls, crown molding and coffered ceiling.

Irene retrieved the martini, plodded across the Persian rug, sat down in the Chippendale desk chair and adjusted her floral silk dress. She took a sip, relished the harsh warmth sliding down her throat, then took another. The emerging buzz blended perfectly with rising endorphins.

On monitor four, Chris and Anna appeared to be admiring the western wall of La Citadelle de Québec[6] – a British fort built after the War of 1812 – until they abruptly stopped walking. Anna handed Chris a cell phone, stared for a moment, then curiously hustled away. Was she pissed? Had the love birds been arguing?

Irene asked into the computer screen, "Are you seeing this, Jürgen?"

"Yes, Ms. Shaw," the commander of the assassination team replied into the boom mic on his headset.

"Where's she going?"

"On her present course, there is only one way she can go," he said with a reassuring voice, "and that's directly into the kill zone. The boys will be waiting for her."

Irene insisted, "They shouldn't fire a single shot until she is reunited with Chris. Understood?"

"Understood," he said with a nod.

Perhaps Jürgen understood, but did those idiots behind the triggers?

Irene intently watched Chris talking on the phone. He was animated, perhaps agitated, while pacing back and forth. His free hand alternated between waving wildly and rubbing his short blond hair. The conversation was obviously intense. Each ticking minute was putting greater separation between Chris and Anna.

Equally bad, the sniper on camera three was finally in position and getting camouflaged, but the unassembled rifle was still in the backpack. He was hideously slow.

A queasy feeling emerged in Irene's stomach. The mission was cracking, maybe crumbling. She sensed another failure, similar to Monday's assassination attempt on Chris at his house in Saint Paul that had cost Irene two people. Continued failure was unacceptable. "Where's Monteiro?" she demanded to know.

Jürgen calmly replied, "She's jogging along Governors' Promenade."

"Do you have eyes on her?"

"Yes, we have cameras along her path."

"That wasn't a rhetorical question, damn it. Show me."

The top two monitors switched to views of the half-mile boardwalk[7] suspended between the massive citadel walls and a 330-foot drop-off. The narrow walkway was filled with meandering tourists. Anna was nowhere to be seen.

"Where is she?" Irene asked with escalating agitation.

"She should be appearing on monitor two just about …" After a lengthy pause, Jürgen added, "Now."

Forty-one-year-old Anna Monteiro jogged by with an effortless stride. Her black pixie haircut, fresh delicate face, olive complexion and sturdy build were a disgusting display of youth. Irene resented how the entitled hussy had bewitched Chris and turned him into a traitor. Killing him meant the loss of an outstanding asset and the collapse of her succession plan. What a waste!

Irene's eyes narrowed to slits while staring at video feed four. Chris was still on the phone. Who the hell was he talking to?

The plan now seemed hopeless. To be successful, Chris and Anna needed to enter the trap together. Irene was ready to abort when Chris suddenly ended the call, pocketed the cell, and began running down Avenue du Cap-Diamant. Within fifteen seconds, he leaped onto a platform and disappeared down a ramp.

"Tell your man to follow him," Irene commanded.

"He is," Jürgen said as monitor four showed bouncing movement.

"Hell, I can go faster than that. Get his ass in gear."

Before the tracking assassin reached the entrance of Governors' Promenade, Chris was seen on monitor one dodging summer tourists as his pace on the elevated boardwalk intensified. His androgynous facial features were red with exertion and determination. A minute later, monitor two showed him sprinting along a straightway beneath the enormous base of the fort. The tracker was hopelessly behind as his labored breathing grew louder over the speakers of the Ops Room. The man would never catch the prey. And the sniper on camera three was still assembling his rifle. At this pace, he'd be unprepared for the first shot.

The incompetence outraged Irene. After gulping the rest of the martini, she hurdled the stemware toward the fireplace. The shattering glass startled the Afghan hound sleeping on the camelback leather couch.

"I'm sorry to have disturbed you, Brutus my dear," Irene said with a comforting tone.

The fifty-five-pound purebred shook his long silky coat and circled twice before plopping down to resume his nap.

Irene aimed her wrath at Jürgen. "Your men three and four are bungling amateurs. Complete dolts! They're totally unfit for the high standards of Phonoi. I want them dealt with after this mission is over. Got that?"

"Yes, Ms. Shaw."

"Are your other two men ready?"

"Yes, Ms. Shaw."

"For god's sake," she bristled, "stop saying 'Yes, Ms. Shaw' and show me what they're seeing."

"Yes, Ms. Shaw," Jürgen habitually replied, flinched at his mistake, then switched the video feeds on monitors one and two.

Camera one was a bird's-eye view of Terrasse Dufferin. The sniper was positioned within scaffolding along the main tower of Fairmont Le Château Frontenac, an iconic railway hotel and late nineteenth-century landmark. The entire 1400-foot length of the promenade was visible below him. Camera two was from a man on the ground at the Samuel de Champlain Monument.[8] He was pretending to watch a street performer while awaiting orders to advance to the flash point.

"Jürgen, give me a full zoom on camera one." Within a millisecond, she added, "Do it now." When his response was too slow, she took control.

She pushed the command button on the desktop, placed headphones on her coiffed hair, raised the mic to her scarlet lips, zoomed in on monitor one, and began issuing commands. "Number One, see that long staircase at the far end of the boardwalk? Anna Monteiro will be coming down any minute. Number Two, start moving now and be prepared to engage. Number Three, for god's sake, stop screwing around. Lock and load your damn weapon. Number Four, move your sorry ass. Acknowledge."

The word copy simultaneously boomed into her ears four times. The team knew who was now in charge and the penalty for disappointing her. They were no doubt hyped up.

"Brutus," Irene cooed to the Afghan hound. "Come to Mama." The aristocratic dog sprung off the couch, lumbered over, and placed his long snout on her lap. "Such a good boy," she said while stroking the flowing hair on his ears. The love of her life always calmed her agitated temperament. "Mama will take you for a nice long walk after this nasty business is done. I promise." The animal's chocolate-brown eyes sparkled with approval.

"Visual on target B," came the announcement from the sniper on top of the hotel.

Irene concentrated on monitor one. Anna had passed the landing of a very tall staircase and was coming down the last flight of forty stairs. She was moving quickly. Was she trying to escape Chris? Or was this simply an obnoxious display of her daily obsession for running?

Regardless, she was jeopardizing the ideal point of attack in the center of Terrasse Dufferin unless Chris caught up soon. It was also essential that all four guns be in position for the deadly crossfire. But Chris was off camera and only one killer was in range and ready.

The pending debacle was infuriating. Anger pulsated across her forehead.

Irene watched as the crowded boardwalk modified Anna Monteiro's pace, forcing her to weave among the throng of people. She was walking parallel to the second sniper, hidden in the brush behind a long wooden toboggan slide used during winter. Within thirty seconds, she appeared on his camera. Her back would soon become the perfect target for a .30-06 cartridge.

"Where the hell is Chris?" Irene bellowed at Jürgen while slamming her fist on the desk. With a startled whimper, the Afghan slinked away.

"Any second now, Ms. Shaw," was his totally unsatisfactory answer.

The delay was excruciating. Rapid heartbeats echoed in her eardrums as she clenched her jaw. The rage was blazing until the sniper atop the hotel reported, "I've got eyes on target A."

There, on monitor one, was Chris. He was bolting down the staircase, pushing people aside as he jumped down two stairs at a time.

The strategy was working. The mission was a go.

An intense calm swept over Irene. With composed authority,

she confirmed the assignments. "Number One, your target is A. That's Chris Davis. Number Three, your target is B. That's Anna Monteiro. Number Two, you'll verify they're dead and finish them off if needed." She didn't bother giving instructions to Number Four. It was doubtful the fat sloth would arrive before the carnage was over. "Are my assignments clear?"

In her headset she heard, "One, affirmative. Two, affirmative. Three, affirmative."

"Good. Now hold your fire. I repeat, do not fire until my command."

Chris leaped onto the boardwalk, sprinted for fifty feet, appeared winded, stopped, cocked his head, searched the crowd, then began yelling something in desperation. If he was calling out for Anna, she either couldn't hear or was ignoring him.

Time to execute.

"On three, gentlemen," Irene announced while staring at Chris and Anna on the monitors. "One. Two."

An instant before Irene said "Three," Chris doubled over with his hands on his knees as if gasping for breath from running. The bullet intended for him hit a teenager. Anna had suddenly turned around and was beginning to wave. The abrupt stop caused an elderly couple to bump into her. An old man spun violently from the velocity of a bullet before collapsing.

Chaos ensued. The crowd scattered. Screams of terror. Most people ran up a small hill lined with historic cannons. A few crouched or lay flat on the boardwalk. Some hid under benches. Anna plus two others took cover beneath a decorative cast-iron gazebo[9] overlooking the river.

Irene was inflamed by the incompetence. "Keep firing!"

Successive bullets slammed into the base of Anna's kiosk and ricocheted off a nearby ornamental fence. It was impossible to see if Anna had been hit.

Monitor one showed Chris climbing up the wooden slats of the toboggan slide[10] as chunks of debris exploded around him. He leaped into the foliage and disappeared. Immediately, the video feed of the sniper on the ground began gyrating. Sounds of a fight blasted in Irene's ears.

Then an eerie silence. Chris's furious face filled monitor three. "Hi there, Irene," he said with contempt. "Your time is coming soon, dear. Very, very soon."

Irene shrieked, "Number One, start firing into position three."

The hotel sniper said, "I don't have a visible target, Ms. Shaw."

"I don't give a damn. Empty your magazine. Now."

A series of bullets shattered trees, bushes and rocks as fast as the sniper could work the bolt, refocus and squeeze the trigger again. The sound was deafening.

Suddenly, his camera tumbled until coming to rest beneath a scaffolding platform. A splash of blood covered the lens. Now both snipers were down and presumed dead.

The bodycam of the killer from the north showed him racing down the boardwalk while approaching the kiosk. He had a two-handed grip on the company-issued SIG P229 pistol and was taking aim at Anna. As his index finger slipped into the trigger guard, he was blown backward. Chris had claimed another victim using the commandeered sniper rifle.

Irene was stunned by the debacle.

The last functioning video displayed the surveillance tracker reaching the bottom of the staircase. He was wheezing and coughing as he held out his weapon.

She shouted, "Number Four. Team is dead. You're alone. Chris Davis is on the hill behind the toboggan slide. He's armed. Anna Monteiro is in the next kiosk. Make this happen!"

A successful outcome seemed doubtful.

Irene leaned within inches of the desktop computer screen and berated Jürgen. "Your plan sucked. A real shitshow. We'll discuss this later."

Despite his attempt to remain stoic, Jürgen's battle-hardened face turned ashen. "Yes, Ms. Shaw."

Chapter One: Québec City, Canada

This action-driven sequel thunders across 21 cities and 4 countries.

Included are 140 online photos of scene locations.

Scan QR code to see entire Silentcide 2 photo gallery.

If you enjoyed *Silentcide*, then please ...

+ **Write a review** on Amazon, Goodreads or where you purchased the book. Favorable reviews are essential to authors.
+ **Tell your friends** and family so they can also enjoy the story.
+ **Buy the sequel**, *Silentcide 2: Vengeance*, to follow the clashes with Irene Shaw.

Thank you for allowing me to entertain your imagination.

ACKNOWLEDGMENTS

Writing and publishing a novel is a difficult journey if not encircled by people who graciously offer their support and encouragement. I want to acknowledge many of the people who helped *Silentcide* become a reality.

To my subject-matter experts, especially Brian Rank, Matthew L., Kathy Jonsrud, Bill and Sarah Armstrong, Tom Emmerich, Jackie Couette and Mike Hankee. Your willingness to share your expertise added immeasurable realism and credibility to my story.

To my editors Alyssa Matesic and Megan McKeever, plus my copy-editor Lisa Gilliam. You have made me a stronger writer.

To Kraig Larson for a decade of technology, design and marketing assistance with Encircle Photos and Encircle Books. Your skill, knowledge and creativity are invaluable.

To my loyal group of beta readers who always give their suggestions, corrections and kudos. I appreciate your feedback and inspiration.

To the countless tour guides and cab drivers who showed me their cities with pride and were patient during my endless photo stops. Thank you.

To the instructors who taught me how to write and the mentors who motivated me to pursue my passions. Your early guidance shaped and fostered my career.

To my parents, Bob and Trudy. My sister Kathy and I will be forever grateful for the wonderful lives you made possible for us.

To Bobby and Michelle, thank you for your continuous support of my creative projects. We are immensely proud of you both.

And last but most important, to Mary Beth. You are my first-line editor, critic and muse, my cheerleader, travel companion and counselor, plus an amazing mom, grandmother, wife and friend. I can't remember much about life before you, and can't imagine a life without you. Love you lots.

ABOUT RICHARD EBERT

Richard Ebert started as a photographer and cinematographer. Then he was president of two advertising agencies before becoming president of a consulting firm serving Fortune 500 companies in the US, Canada, Mexico and Chile. Since retiring, Richard has pursued three passions: writing, travel and photography. He lives in Saint Paul, Minnesota, with his wife and has two adult children plus two grandsons.

Contact the Author

Author website: RichardEbert.com
Travel guides website: EncirclePhotos.com
Author Facebook: Facebook.com/EncirclePhotos
Author email: Author@RichardEbert.com

Send an email to Richard for updates about new book releases.

Milton Keynes UK
Ingram Content Group UK Ltd.
UKHW010832230424
441593UK00017B/391/J